£1- oo

He was not an outsta... ... ...ty shape or form. Most people ...ge looking sort of person. He .... of medium build. Today he was dressed in slacks and wore his shirt over the top of his trousers. His blue parka jacket was well worn and remained unbuttoned showing his cream-coloured cotton shirt, which was buttoned all the way up, except for the top button. He walked with a light wooden cane although he did not appear walking impaired. His hair was slightly unkempt and was a mousy brown colour. His ethnicity was that of white Caucasian. This though said nothing about his nationality or even his background. To most he would appear to be a man, who had not done too well in his life. No one would assume that he owned a massive property or have the financial ability to buy and sell on the stock markets. That was fine as far as the man was concerned because it meant that he could walk through life with complete anonymity. He would never make eye contact with anyone, nor would he engage in conversation unless on the odd occasion that he was directly spoken to. Then he would normally say something like

"I don't know" or just shrug his shoulders and continue walking on. His life was as a speck of flotsam in the ocean, of those that walked through the streets of London, on their daily routine from point A, to point B.

It was true that he did not own a fine house, although that did not mean that he was homeless. He lived for the last year or so in Brompton Road, London. It had the postcode of SW3 1HY. This was in one of the most expensive areas of England's capitol city, Chelsea. Here was where millionaires lived and if you were an 18-year-old, then your parents would buy you a Porsche or perhaps even a Ferrari. Although those that were not quite millionaires, would probably just settle on a new Range Rover Evogue.

This though was not the life that he had. He did own a couple of cars, which he kept in long term car parks, that were scattered around the city. He would use these, on the rare occasions that he had to leave the city. Like the way, he dressed, his transport was decidedly average. The cars were both silver in colour and both were about 10 years old. The cars were a VW Passat and a Vauxhall Astra. Both cars were extremely popular in the UK and these would blend in perfectly when driven in and around the capitol. About one Year ago, he had acquired a short-range video scrambler, through a friend of a friend, the sort that don't ask questions. He could at any time of his choosing, literally scramble the feed from these cameras, that continually watched the streets of London. That said he would only use this device when he had selected his next target.

There was a time he had been a respected man. He had worked tirelessly for the UK's Government, on one project or another. He had been fundamental in the discovery of a new and successful treatment of some types of cancer, that was before they had taken his work away from him.

Before that time and just after he had left University, when his desire to help mankind had been all he craved. After qualifying as a Medical Doctor, he had taken a post with the voluntary organisation, Médecins Sans Frontière, or Doctors Without Borders as it was more commonly known, and he had chosen to work in the Philippines. It was here he had first come across the Vespa Luctuosa.

This insect had been responsible for hundreds of deaths over recent years in the Philippines. It was while working in a small rainforest medical centre, he had tried to save the life of a young girl. She had been brought in screaming and in excruciating pain. The local medical translator tried to explain just what the girl was feeling. He stated that she had been burned inside. Yet he, as a Doctor, could see no burn or even broken skin. The girl continued to thrash about and was beating at her skull with her fists. He had instructed the nurse, to tie the girl's arms and legs to the gurney with bandages to stop her beating and harming herself further.

The Doctor managed to get a drip into the young girl's arm, which gave her Paracetamol in liquid form. Still the child screamed. The Doctor injected some morphine into the catheter, and it did reduce the screaming for a few minutes, then once again she started howling and moaning. The translator informed him, 'the girl said her whole body was on fire'. Still she banged her head up and down as well as thrashing it from side to side. As a doctor, he could increase the amount of morphine, but as he did not know what was causing the girls terrible suffering, he was reticent in doing so. Suddenly the girl's body arched backwards and the was the sound of some of her ribs parting ways with the rest of the ribcage. Her Eyes rolled back in her young skull and she let out a final moan, before she simply died in her anguish and pain. For her it had not been an easy death. The young Doctor had seen people die before, but not like this. The child's parents were obviously distraught.

Between the interpreter and the Doctor, the girl's father said, 'that she had eaten apple and there had been, what he thought to be a wasp in it'. She had been stung and she thought the wasp had died, but then a lot of other wasps had chased her. The father had not seen any of this, so it was just second-hand information, which he had initially gleaned from his distraught daughter. As a young and newly qualified doctor, he was not able to perform a post-mortem and there were no others within a day's drive, who could. Consequently, he released the body back to her father and went about his normal medical duties.

Some weeks later however, he had been called to a small settlement, upriver from where the medical centre was located. The radio message which had been passed onto him, was that 'several people in a village had been stung by some form of bee' and they needed immediate medical help.

He had arrived at the village some two hours later and been directed towards some very basic housing made from wood and tarpaulin, though he could have found his way there from hundreds of yards away. It was the sound of a child in extreme pain and terror. There were women wailing as well, though theirs was because to the children's plight, rather than any physical pain on their part.

Upon entering the shack to which he had been directed towards. There were three children laid out on small webbing beds. Two had obviously succumbed, to whatever the third child was suffering with. The child was constantly clutching at his arms and legs, upon which they had some minor looking red blotches. There was almost no swelling around these areas. One of the men in the rooms said in broken English, that the children had been playing in the tall grass at the side of the village and had been chased by a swarm of bees or hornets, perhaps even wasps, but that the insects had come out of the ground. This man said that the children had then jumped into the river, the same river that the doctor had just arrived on, to get away from the insects. After the children, had come out of the water, the parents had taken them into this hut. Two of the children had died over an hour ago.

The farmer who owned the field of tall grass, pleaded with the young doctor to save the child. And to kill the pain that they were in. If it was an allergic reaction to a bee or wasp sting he too out a pre-loaded up a syringe with 0.5ml of 1:1000 epinephrine, in the hope of saving the child. After 15 minutes, it should have shown signs of working, but still the child was in agony. He looked on in sadness, knowing full well that this child would go the same as the others had done. Their small and young bodies, unable to fight of the painful venom of this insect.

Over the next year, the young doctor worked on a specific antivenom for this wasp, whenever he was not working on his normal duties, he worked on synthesising and developing his serum. Finally, he managed to get it to work at least in the laboratory and had planned to make it in such quantities to hand out to local medical centres and first responders. He knew his true calling to medicine now.

About three weeks later, he was once again called out to the same Philippine village. This time it was a toddler of a wealthy farmer. Yet again the child was in mortal agony and would die for sure. The doctor had in his medical bag, a small quantity of antivenom. Although it had not been tested on humans. He knew it worked on the rats that he had let the local wasp sting. However, he was unsure if it would work on any human, yet alone a child as small as this. It was also illegal, what he was planning on doing. The choice was losing the child or commit a theoretical crime. There was a risk it would harm the child further, but it was a better risk than doing nothing. He loaded a small quantity, about five times as much as he had previously used on the rats, and then prayed to God that it would work. The child screamed louder, as he inserted the needle into the most prominent cephalic vein in the child's left arm. Then he pushed gently on the hypodermic plunger and the clear liquid entered the toddler's bloodstream. There could only be two real outcomes to his actions. And he would have to wait for either.

After 30 minutes the child's screaming dulled down to a whimper and then a gentle sob. The doctor waited at the side of the cot with the parents looking on from the other side. Three hours later the toddler was breathing slow and steady. The mother was on her knees praying and saying, the doctor was a miracle worker, because no child as young as this, had ever survived a sting from this specific species of wasp from the Philippines. The father had offered to give the farm and all the wealth he had. He produced a bag filled with thousands of US Dollars. The young doctor refused the money and said that he was so happy, just to be able to save the child. They promised to keep in touch with each other. The Doctor and the man were destined to meet many years later.

A year or so after this incident the young Doctor had returned to England and went back to university, to do a degree in Entomology, with the emphasis on venomous insects. After three more years, he had completed his degree. Then it was back to medicine and an extra two years in immunology and Toxicology.

It was around this time that he had been approached by Medical Research Council based at Porton Down. They had offered him a laboratory and a complete research team. This was to help find cures for cancer as well as to provide antidotes to various toxins. Many of these substances did not have names just code letters and numbers. He had excelled and was then asked to look at more efficient ways, of harvesting venom from a multitude of animals and insects. He had been working on level five toxins which involved a quite a lot of security not just for the research, but because he was involved in the production of the various toxins and poisons for use at the other facility at CDE Porton, the military one.

He now had pretty much unlimited access, to any equipment he wanted, as well as to all species of venomous critter in the world. This research took him back to his early days in the Philippines. He had mentioned this to the council and asked if it would be possible, to have several Hornets and Wasps, to milk them of their venom. When asked which species, he wished he simply replied.

"All of them"

Act 2

One year into his research, he found that both the Asian Hornet and the European Social Wasp venom, was extremely useful in attacking and even destroying, certain cancerous cells. It was especially useful in the treatment of prostate cancer and bowel cancer, as well as cervical cancer. The active enzyme, which was effective against cancer cells, was just one part of what made up the venom. The venom first broke down the outer wall of the cell, before destroying the nucleus of that cell. It had been an accidental discovery as many cures have been.

Originally before working at CDE, the doctor had been researching as to why the Yellow Jacket sting, was so painful and in doing so, they had discovered an enzyme in the venom, which attacked the red blood cells in the same way. After following the blood stream and extending the pain, by leaching out into the nerve endings. It would then signal the damage up the central nervous system to the brain, with the message that part of the body where the insect had stung, was severely injured, hence it generated the pain to match the signal. Now they had a partial cure to cancer, this would be the discovery of the century.

Finally, he knew that all his work, would not have been in vain. Mankind would forever remember his discovery. In future years, he would be as famous, medically speaking, as Alexander Fleming, or Marie Curie. This was the holy grail of medicine. This discovery would be almost impossible to calculate the monetary value of. It was way beyond quintillions he knew that, but he would give it to the world for free. He could now set up his own Medical laboratory and choose the research that he wanted to do. His mind had begun to race, with all the other cures that he could offer mankind. Later the authorities would enquire, was this the specific point, where the doctor's sanity had left him.

When he had first tried to speak openly, they had reminded him, that he had signed the official secrets act. Then when he tried to take his research with him one day, they had pointed out that it was the MRC, that owned all the patents to anything that he had created. They owned the cure to cancer. The Medical Research Council, said that it could not just be launched into the world as a miracle cure, they first would have to run selective and deep testing, on one form of cancer at a time.

The following day when he arrived at the CDE Porton Down he found that his pass had been cancelled and that there were a pair of large gentlemen waiting for him. They bundled him into their Toyota RAV4 and drove him back to his home in Swindon. After first tying him to kitchen chair, they searched his house. They found and removed all his text and notebooks. His desk-top computer and even his mobile phone. Before leaving they beat him up and deliberately broke the gas pipe to his cooker, leaving him battered on the floor. He was destined to die a horrible death, in some supposed 'accident'.

Unbeknown to the men, who had done this to him and even unknown to the doctor himself. By sheer chance or perhaps bad luck. Another man had been in the house before they had arrived. A young man who made his living, by breaking into homes and robbing them of small valuable items. These possessions he would then sell on to unscrupulous second-hand shops, jewellers, and the like. All the young man had been able to snatch, before he heard the key turning in the door of the house, was the Doctors laptop and a few flash drives from a drawer. He had been in the process of searching the upstairs bedrooms when the doctor and his two escorts had entered.

The burglar barely made it under a bed in one of the rooms. Quickly he pulled the cover of the bed down until it touched the floor. One man had entered the room and had gone about emptying the drawers and wardrobes. Initially he had thought that these men, were from some criminal gang or another, then when he heard them beating the doctor up, he assumed that this must be a bad debt gone wrong and the two men had been sent to get the money back, one way or another.

He had waited under the bed too frightened to breathe or even move, until he heard the front door open and then close again. It was only then he slid out from hiding place, under the bed. He raced down the stairs and was going to go out the back door of the kitchen, so as not to be seen by the two men or anyone else that might be around the front of the house. As soon as he opened the kitchen door, he was almost choked by the unmistakable smell of gas. The next thing he noticed was the doctor lying bloody and beaten, on the floor of the kitchen. He was still alive and still tied to the overturned chair. Just then the doctor regained consciousness.

"Help me please" The doctor had said.

The burglar was just going to leave him to sort himself out when he changed his mind. It had become obvious to him also, that the men who left, intended to let the man on the floor die either by choking on gas or in some terrible explosion. He untied the doctor and was helping him out of the doorway when it happened.

There was an old toaster on the worktop, which they had some bread stuffed into its slots. The temperature settings along with the timer, had been turned up to maximum and switched on. Initially there was smoke from the top of the toaster and then a single small red ember of burnt bread, floated up into the gas filled kitchen, then a flame licked over the top of the electric toaster.   There was a whooshing noise followed by a sudden and thunderous explosion, this was followed almost instantaneously, by a sudden intake of oxygen filled air, to feed the flames. That completed the cycle of everything that was required, for the mammoth explosion, oxygen, flammable gas, and a spark. The windows and door at the back of the house, were blown out and at the same time the roof of the house, moved upwards a mere six inches before crashing back down, through the bedroom floors. The Doctor felt an enormous gust of superheated air, pass by him. The burglar had taken the brunt of the explosion and the resulting fireball on his back. This unknown and selfless act had protected the doctor from the worst of the explosion, as the rubble of his home fell all around him and rained down on top of his saviour. It was now only two or three seconds since he had been thrown clear of the doorway, before he could stand up and go to the assistance of his good Samaritan.

The man was dead that much was clear, even if he had been a surgeon rather than a doctor. A large chunk of brickwork, from the collapsing chimney breast of the building, formally known as his home, had landed on the Samaritans back and head. The burglar was far beyond any medical help.

Strangely the doctors Laptop, was still clasped in the thief's hand. The doctor took it, it was damaged, but perhaps its internal hard drive, was salvageable. Then he rummaged in the pockets of the burglar and came away with three USB Flash Drives, he put them in his own pockets. The doctor was not going to hang around for the Police or the Fire Brigade. As far as his ex-employers were concerned, they wanted him dead that much was sure, so he would now be dead. The doctor removed his father's white gold Rolex watch from his own wrist, and put it on the dead man's, the watch had been a gift when he first qualified as a doctor. After this he took out his wallet, slipping that, into the back pocket of the burglar. He even left the fifty-five pounds, he had just this morning, drawn from the bank, along with all his bank cards, and driving license.

With luck, due to the security clearance and ID still in his wallet. the local police would contact CDE and they would send their security people down, who having orchestrated the murder, would just formally identify the body. They in turn, would state that it was that of Dr James Pearson Research Scientist late of The Medical Research Council at Porton Down. They had stolen his research; they had stolen his cures and now they had his life. He would build a new life and then he would extract his revenge. First though he had to find a place to hide out and it could not be local.

Fortunately, Swindon, does not have the volume of cameras that London does. Being careful to avoid those he could and keeping his hat brim pulled down when he could not avoid them, the doctor made his way to the railway station and caught the first train to London. He knew of only one man, who he could trust with his life and with the secrets of what he was about to do.

Act 3

He made it to London with no problems and then made the phone call, to an old and trusted friend. He still had a few coins in his coat pocket. He inserted the cash into the telephone booth dialled the mobile number he had been given, when they had renewed their friendship again just a couple of years back.

Alejandro Del Rosario had been a wealthy farmer when they had first met. The young doctor had saved his sons life. The son was now 13 and his father a very wealthy man. The farmer had sold all his land, to the large Spanish Hotel

Conglomerate, Melia. They hotel giant, had chosen it simply because, his land had a beautiful white sand beach attached it. This was a prime location for their 5-star beach hotel. He he took the money and moved to the UK where he now lived in Chelsea.

The call was picked up after just three rings.

"Del Rosario residence, Ale speaking".

"It's me. You once said, if I ever needed anything just call you. Does that offer still stand? Also, before you answer, please do not use my name."

"The offer I made, will always stand for you my dearest of friends".

"Can you collect me from McDonald's on Praed Street."

"You are here in London? When would you like me to come?"

"Yes, that would be perfect, if you could please."

"I will be there in 15 to 20 minutes".

"Thanks" and the doctor hung up.

Life from now on, would be quite different. He would have to learn some new life saving skills. They would not be anything like the ones he had learned previous, but some of the knowledge he had amassed, would come in useful, especially for what he had in mind. He walked the short distance to McDonald's, all the time keeping his head down and his trilby pulled low down over his eyes. Even in the fast-food outlet he deliberately made sure his face could not be seen on camera. He took his coffee and sat with his back to the counter and a wall to his side. He had a good view of the road outside.

A bright yellow Humvee pulled up outside and tooted its horn twice. The doctor looked at it but due to privacy glass, he could not see who the driver was. They horn blew again and this time the passenger window wound down, Ale's hand waved, beckoning to the doctor. James stood up and walked directly out and into the passenger seat of the Humvee. Ale drove off as soon as the doctor was in, then he buzzed the window back up.

"Subtle Ale, real subtle! Was this the only colour they had when you bought it?"

"Is it too much? Do you think James?" Ale said with a smile, he then drove away and headed back into Chelsea, before continuing the conversation.

"It really is good to see you James, but I have to ask you, what kind of trouble are you in?"

"As always Ale good to see you also. As for the kind of trouble? I am not really sure, except that some people tried to kill me today and now hopefully they will think I am dead?"

"Why would they try to kill you and only think you are dead?"

"Because they accidentally killed another man, who they did not know was there and who really should not have been there."

"Wont they know when they see the body?"

"Not really, as there was not much of a body left to see."

"So how can I help you James?"

"Are you still involved in real estate?"

"Yes, I have several offices, in and around the Chelsea area".

"I will need somewhere to hide Ale".

"James, will you not stay with us? There is plenty of space in our house and it is very private."

"Let us talk about it tonight, after one of your fine meals. If that is OK with you Ale?"

"OK, let's get you there then" Ale answered.

He followed the road into the suburbs of Chelsea, until he came to a small driveway, which led to a set of very sturdy looking, solid wooden gates. They opened automatically as the car approached. Beyond the gates, there was a small gravel driveway, that went around a substantial botanical island and then under a large, covered entrance to the house. Ale parked the Humvee under this cover and led the way to the main double doors of the house. Inside was nothing like the farmhouse, which Ale had back in the Philippines. The parquetry flooring was stunning but only served as an introduction, to the gilded marble double stairway to the first floor. Ale led James into a room to the left of the splendorous stairs. Again, this room had double doors, that mirrored those at the front entrance. James noticed that there was a matching pair, to the other side of the impressive hallway. They entered the room, which Ale referred to as his 'Office' To James it more resembled a drawing room, of a gentlemen's club. He even had a Humidor section, at the far end, where looking at the selection of boxes, he had an assortment of cigars from around the world. An ornate fireplace took up almost a third of one wall, while the opposite wall was mostly glass. An immense desk made from what was either Brazilian Rosewood or something remarkably similar. It had a lustre that came with age and behind it sat a captain's chair, upholstered in green leather.

"Have a seat please James" Ale said, as he motioned to a pair of matching green leather winged chesterfield chairs that sat next to the fireplace and an onyx and marble covered coffee table.

"Drink James?"

James had not thought how close he had come to dying until, that very moment and the shock of everything hit him all at once. He held his head in his hands and started to cry.

"I am sorry Ale, I don't know what came over me, please forgive me."

"James do not be afraid to show your emotions, to your friends. I remember how I cried like a child when you saved my son. Please, let your emotions pour out and when you have finished, perhaps you would like a drink?"

After his sobbing, had subsided, James wiped the tears from his eyes and then put his glasses back on.

"Harewood?" Ale asked.

"Sorry?"

"James my friend, you know I have a passion for fine rums. Well a friend of a friend of mine came across a bottle of 'The Harewood Rum' which was bottled in Jamaica for the

Harewood estate here in England. Bottled from the cask in 1790. I would think it is probably ready for drinking by now?"

"Sounds Nice, but it also sounds awfully expensive."

"I think my accountants, said something about it being worth around £80,000 and something else about it would double in price in five years if I sold it. But then if I did that, I would not have had the pleasure of having drunk it or being able to share with my closest friend. We should have a Cigar, to relax with it as well. I remember you had a good taste for cigars." Ale said.

"I think you would need a least a Gurkha Royal Courtesan, to go with that. Mind you, I think they are harder to get than rocking horse shit" James replied.

"Your wish is my command James" Ale said

Then he walked down to the Humidor Room and returned with a pair of cigars in Gold tubes. He placed two crystal goblets on the coffee table and then uncorked the rum with a resounding pop. He sniffed the contents then with an approving smile, poured out a generous measure to each glass. After cutting the ends of the cigar he passed one to James, along with a cigar lighter. James puffed until the end was evenly lit and then dipped the other end into his Rum before sucking once more on the Cigar. Ale followed suit.

"You remembered James, A cigar soaked in rum, is a marriage made in heaven, so perhaps all is not bad in the world. We shall not speak of those things until we have finished our cigars and rum and then we shall see what can be done, about your predicament."

Act 4

James relayed the events of the day and then got down to the reason for wanting his friend's assistance.

"I need somewhere with space, that is far away from prying eyes and ears. Also, I am going to want it for some time Ale, it even may run into months, perhaps it could be years. I will also need some working capital, at least to begin with. I want to be able to set up a large laboratory, with a lot of equipment. I know that you somehow have managed to get on the good side, of some of London's more nefarious personalities. Some of whom may require medical assistance, from time to time. The kind of treatment that they can't easily get at hospitals or from their local GP."

"James what are you insinuating?" Ale said with a smile.

"I know that as a new immigrant, coming into this part of London and setting up numerous businesses. At some point, you would have to pay somebody off and that somebody, would be a crook. Probably involved in organised crime. That sort of person does not go to Accident and Emergency at your local hospital, to have his knife or gunshot wound patched up. What I am asking is just make it known that you have a pipeline to a Doctor, that does not make medical notes or contact the authorities. As I have said I will also need a base to operate from, preferably away from prying eyes."

"OK I can do that for you, and I do know of a building, that is away from people's eyes. it might need some work doing to it, to make it suitable for you. In fact, it is just down the road from here."

"When can I see it Ale?" James asked while sipping the last of his rum.

"Let us wait until tomorrow. Tonight, you will stay here."

The following morning after breakfast, Ale and James set off in Ale's, less conspicuous Range Rover. Ale was right, it was just 5 minutes down the road from his home. At first glance and from the outside, it looked to be a substantial three-story red brick, end of terrace, commercial building. Although it also looked a bit tired to the exterior. James pulled the hood up and over his head, on the grey sweatshirt, that Ale had given him to wear, after which they both got out of the car and walked to the front door of the building.

"Welcome to Brompton Tube Station. I had this on my books for a long time and finally sold it a year or so back to a Ukrainian oligarch for £30,000,000. He had all sorts of plans to make part of it a museum and shops and flats. But now it looks like he is planning to sell it on, as such I have the keys." Ale said as he opened the black painted personal door.

The inside of the building was cavernous, and the sound was hollow. There were stairs to the upper part of the building, but Ale took him to another section and removed a large plywood sheet revealing a gated entrance with a large brass padlock on. He unlocked it and gave the key to James. Ale took a torch out of his pocket and pulled the gate open. James followed and then they started to descent the steps which seemed to go on forever. When they finally reached the bottom, Ale went to a red electrical switch box and pushed the lever up. There was a clunk, and some dim lights came on.

"This is the disused Brompton Tube Station. Its dry and has electricity and very few people even know it is here, as it closed in 1934. During the second world war, the Ministry of Defence took it on and used it as number the 26, Anti-Aircraft Brigade for London. Then after the war, it had a variety uses, until the 1970. Then the building was finally closed, and the escalators were removed. There are two lifts though and I think they still work; I know a man who could give you a proper electrical feed from the railway line the passes by this station. That way the Electric company would not come looking to see who is using this station now."

James looked around the main corridor where they were standing. It was dirty but it had potential. The walls were covered with green and cream, ceramic glazed tiles. They would be easy enough to clean.

"The best parts are through here" Ale said, indicating that James, should follow him through a heavy steel door.

"This was the war room, during the second world war and then again for the University of London Air Squadron. As you can see it is a bit dusty and you may have a problem or two with rats, but it is a good size to set up your laboratory?"

"Ale it would be perfect, and you are sure no one comes down here? Not even tramps?"

"No tramps or neighbours and I am sure I can help you get rid of the rats. Follow me there are more rooms down off the main floor of this room" Ale said as they went down a steel staircase, to the floor of the actual war room.

There were half a dozen doors off from it. Two of the doors were half glazed and at one time or another, they would have had writing painted on them, but time had erased that. Both rooms were large offices one still had two large desks in. The other was full of old filing cabinets and chairs, along with other old office equipment. One of the other rooms, appeared to be a bunk house with a shower room and bank of toilets. The next room was empty, another room looked like it had been used as a kitchen and had sinks and stainless-steel tables. There were old gas boilers and a large stove, that looked to have been left there from the 1940's. The final room that they looked at must have been the commander's office. This really was a double sized room when compared to the other offices and it had been divided, making it into two smaller rooms. The first being an office area with another internal door, leading to the second interior room. Every room was filled with dust, old newspapers, and cobwebs, along with rat droppings.

"What do you think?" Ale asked while lighting a cigarette and offering one to James, who refused politely.

James could instantly see the see the potential. He knew he could do his work here, but he also knew, he could not complete the modifications and repair to the building on his own. He knew nothing about electricity or gas and water installation. He knew even less about structural engineering. Some of the equipment he would require, would have to come down on the lifts and they would first have to be made safe to work with. But if they could cross those bridges it would be perfect. No one would be able to see him working, better still there were no cameras in or around this building, apart from the ones that he would have installed.

"Perfect Ale but wont the building sell in the next year? I am afraid to say, I am at this point completely penniless".

"Do not worry about money and I will have it sorted to your specifications, also I will make sure that all the offers are refused, or I could buy it?"

"I think it would be better that it remains on the market and officially unused, that way no from Chelsea Council one will come snooping. I will accept your offer of some help in fixing it up, Just the parts of the building that I need. Do you think you could help with that?

"James if I gave you all the wealth that I have, my debt to you could never be repaid. You will stay at my home until the building is sorted to your undertaking. I will make sure that only men I trust to keep a secret will do the work for me. I have been thinking. Why do you need to help criminals from the underworld? If it is just about money I can and will help you with that."

"Ale, I want to make connections, because the things that I will be doing, I will want deflected away from me and onto others who deserve to be punished."

"OK James I will not press you further, let us go back up and start organising things."

They both climbed back up the steel stairs and then along the corridor, where Ale switched the electric lights off and the torch back on. Then they made their way back out, into the bright spring morning.

Act 5

The work took almost 9 months to complete Ale oversaw all modifications under the instructions from the James. Ale had put the word out that there was a doctor, who could fix injuries without asking questions. These consultations, he would do in the 'Victims' own home, or place of their choosing. Most were stab wounds or head wounds caused by being struck with something solid, like a wall or a baseball bat. Some though, were small calibre gunshot wounds. Some injuries he was called to, were beyond even his skills and the person would die, but they would die without pain. Payment for these services were to be in the form of favours owed. James had a little black book of names and the surgeries he had performed. Some of the bigger London gangs, were now coming to him on a regular basis, to treat one or more of their members. No one ever asked his name he was just referred to as 'The Doctor' and no one apart from Ale, would know what he was be doing down in the bowels of Brompton Road Tube Station.

True to his word Ale had fixed the 'War Room' and the surrounding rooms up to a high standard. New lighting and multiple electrical points had been installed along with a basic ventilation system that vented into the tube-ways. The kitchen was now equipped with a new gas cooker. Gas came from a series of LPG cylinders which were located up in the main lobby of the station and the gas pipped down. There were complete single and triple phase electrical circuits installed, with the power coming from, the adjoining tunnels of Knightsbridge Tube Station.

Ale had a new lift hoist installed in one of the two shafts. An air conditioning unit which took air from outside and then vented it back out into the disused tunnels. One of Ale's men had installed a cold-water feed from a water main so now he had Gas, Electric, Water and fresh clean air for his Laboratory. He had spacious and quality living quarters. Wastewater was piped direct into the main underground sewers.

Ale had bought the small tobacconists shop next door to the tube station and knocked a doorway through from it into the main foyer of Brompton Road Tube Station. This meant that James did not have to use the main entrance, where any late-night comings and goings, might start to look suspicious. The man that Ale had let the shop too, was told he could have a free lease providing he asked no questions and allowed James to come and go as he pleased. James had installed a complete CCTV system with cameras both on the outside and on the inside of the disused tube station. Every entrance way was covered, including from inside the tobacconists.

The next thing he had to do; was to order all the laboratory equipment he would require. it was first sent to one of Ale's other properties and then brought to into the station at night. Where it was left in the main foyer. James and Ale moved the equipment to the lift and then once down in the new laboratory installed it all. Finally, the time had come to set the wheels in motion, and for James to leave Ale's home.

Act 6

The first supply the doctor required was wasp venom and a lot of it. Strangely it was not as difficult as he had thought it would be. The Social Yellow Jacket wasp is not uncommon in London. James looked in every local newspaper he could find and searched Facebook, for pest control companies. These were the people who would be his supply chain of live wasps. Many initially offered dead wasps as they gassed the nests. Soon however, there were a dozen or so pest control companies, who would now just bag up live nests and then call a burner phone, so that one of Ale's men, could collect it in a van and then drop that bag off at Ale's home. Either Ale would deliver to James, or James would then drive to Ale's and enjoy a good cigar before collecting the wasp's nest and taking it to the lab, where he would place the bag of wasps into a large glass room. This room had a double door with a positive air entry system. for safety

After milking all the stinging wasps of their venom, James would burn the wasp's bodies and nests and then move on to the next bag. It took him a further 3 months to have accumulated almost 2 litres, of pure wasp venom. There were times when James himself, had been stung whilst collecting one of the bagged nests. The pain of the stings only gave him further impetus to continue his mission. He had made around 250ml of anti-venom, a loaded syringe of which, he always carried in a cigar case. This he kept in his pocket, just in the event of there being any accidents.

The British wasp was not as deadly as the Philippine species but the amount of yellow jacket venom, he would use, would balance this out. He had a plan, and he would need others to help in what he had to do. This is where those criminal contacts would come in. Ale had made sure that only those villains, who were connected to major criminal gangs, would get their personal Doctor. This way he was sure they would never talk to the authorities, for fear of being a snitch by their peers. If these men were caught, they would do the time and get their rewards, when they were released. For those that would have a longer jail term, then their families would be well looked after. The question now was, who would be first victim for retribution?

James and Ale had sat down in the 'Office' at Ale's home and discussed when, where and who, would be the first. Then where it would all end, if everything went to plan. Initially no one would know what was happening, but James was sure at some point, people would realise that they were being targeted. This is when things would become much more difficult, to bring to fruition.

"I don't know their names. All I know is they work as security guards for 'The Medical Research Council' at CDE Porton Down. I want to borrow some old cars, so that I can go down and not be noticed. I only want to use each car twice, while down there, do you think this is something that you can arrange?"

"Remember Mr Travis, you fixed his son up when he was stabbed. He owns a used car lot; you should call him."

"Thanks Ale I will do that. Thank you for all your hospitality now I must go seek my revenge and reclaim my work. I may not see you for some time, but I will check in on a regular basis. I really do not know how to repay you for your generosity and help."

"Before you go James let me give you a little something." Ale said and walked outside to the front of his home with James at his side."

There was a silver VW Passat. Sat next to Ale's bright yellow Humvee.

"The engine has been changed and the suspension tightened up. It was an unmarked police car, but they sell them off after 5 or 6 years of use. I had my mechanic take out the 2-litre turbo diesel and replace it with 5.8 litre twin turbo petrol engine from an Audi. He also replaced the standard gear box with a seven speed, short-shift sports box. New anti-roll bars and wider low-profile tyres. From the outside, it looks quite normal inside it is not. It has a full anti roll cage the two front seats have been replaced with full bucket type. The driver's seat has a full race cross harness seat belt. Oh, and I had my mechanic install a Dr Dre Sound System. Finally, if you open the glove box you will find a gift from one of our more felonious friends. There is a similar item is in a secret compartment on the driver's door. That can be opened by pressing the electric wing mirror control button, rapidly three times." Ale said as he held up a VW keyring which he gave to James. And then continued.

"Stay safe my friend".

The Doctor took the keys and climbed into the driver's seat of the Passat and then switched on the ignition. He buzzed down the privacy glass window and listened to the burble of the twin exhaust pipes and then the thunderous roar as he pushed down on the accelerator.

"Nice"

"By the way James I have fitted a sensor in the front so if you ever have to come in here fast the gates will automatically open for you."

With that, they said their farewells and the Doctor drove up the driveway and the gates opened then closed behind him, he drove left towards London proper.

Act 7

He was on his way to find a man called Dean, who The Doctor had fixed a broken arm for, as well as stitching a four-inch knife wound about 5 months previously. Dean was going to help in the abduction and of the first victim of revenge. The Doctor did not even know his name of his would-be abductee all he knew was what this man looked like. Dean as it happened, was the man who father owned the used car place, just on the edge of Knightsbridge.

James drove to the edge of Brompton Road. He put enough money in the parking meter to last for 12 hours and walked to the Tobacconists shop before making the call. He dialled the number from memory and let it ring. It rang for about a minute and then disconnected. James stood and waited, he knew that someone from that number would call back, even if it was just to see how the caller had managed to get hold of the number. Sure enough, his mobile phone vibrated in his parka pocket. He answered it.

"Yes."

"Who is this?"

"The Doctor. Who's That?"

"It's Mike, what ya want?" the voice said in a north London accent.

"Is Dean there?"

"Nah."

"Then tell him, I will call back in five minutes" The Doctor said and closed his egg-shaped mobile phone.

It was not a smart phone just a small older style cell phone. You could do text on it but using its one-inch LCD screen was hopeless, so he never bothered with text. Besides, it was a sure way to trace things back to you. James had learned many skills over the last year and most of those skills were not that an honest person would use. He always kept his calls short, never storing anyone's telephone number in the directory. And he would use a new SIM every call from now on. One of Ale's friends had obtained 500 SIM cards, which was given in payment for some minor surgery that The Doctor had performed. He kept himself in the shadows outside the shop and waited. Five minutes had passed when James opened the phone redialled and put it to his ear.

"It's Dean, you wanted me?"

"Yes, I need you and a car. Nothing flash, the more ordinary the better and bring some rope and some tape. Bring some gloves and a ski mask."

"I am not a complete fucking beginner ya know."

"See you at the tobacconists next to the old Brompton Road tube station, in 30 minutes." he closed the phone again and then he entered the shop. The man behind the counter moved over to let The Doctor through and then went back to his duties. James went through the door and into the station entrance. Using a small torch, he walked over to the elevator and entered. The doors opened two floors down in his laboratory. Quickly James grabbed what he needed including a jar filled with a couple of hundred or so live yellow jacket wasps. Then he checked that he had his syringe of anti-venom in the cigar case, which was in the inside pocket of his coat. In his other pocket was a syringe loaded up with more than enough venom to kill a large man. There would be no going back after this night. Taking the lift back up, he retraced his steps back to the door at the tobacconists. After checking the camera showed no one in the shop, except for the shopkeeper he went back through the door and out to the front to wait the arrival of Dean.

A dark red Ford Mondeo pulled up at the kerb and Dean was in the driver's seat.

"Get in" Dean shouted from the driver's window.

The Doctor did and then gave Dean the address he wanted him to go to. The car pulled off and they headed towards the M25 ring road and then to Wilshire. The journey took just over two hours and in another two it would be 7am. That is when the day staff would start to arrive. Neither Dean nor The Doctor had spoken apart from giving the destination. They drove in virtual silence apart from listening to the radio. They were parked in a lay-by about 100 yards from the main gate to CDE Porton Down and The Medical Research Council. First, they would have to identify the man he wanted and then make a note of his car and registration number. They would follow him that night, to find out where he lived and then The Doctor was planning to make his own house call.

At 7:05am a white Toyota RAV4 slowed down at the gate and the man produced his ID Card before being let through and into the complex. They now knew, which car to follow at the cease of work, so they left and found a quiet spot to grab a few hours' sleep. The Doctor asked Dean, to set the alarm on his Smart Phone. Which he did

"What are we doing here Doc?"

"Me I am getting a bit of revenge and you, well you are paying off a debt to me. By the end of today you and I will be even."

"Just the one Job then?"

"Only one job for you Dean"

"Are there more Doc?"

The doctor never answered. He just closed his eyes and went to sleep. At 4pm Dean's smart phone rang and woke them. Dean silenced the phone.

"What now Doc?"

"We drive back to Porton Down. Then we follow the big man home."

"And then?" for you not a lot you are here as muscle to hold him down, if needs be".

"And then?"

"Dean, its better if you don't know and I thought you, would know better than to ask so many questions."

"Just making conversation, was all." Dean replied sulkily.

They drove back in silence again and then they waited, as the cars and the staff came back out the facility. At 5:15 the White Toyota RAV4 came out through the gate. Now though, there was a problem. There were two people in the car. The other big man, who had beaten James up almost a year ago, was sat beside his friend. Dean pulled out and followed them keeping his Mondeo between 3 and 6 cars behind. They pulled into Swindon and into the car park, of a pub called The Manor on Cheney Manor Road. Dean pulled in behind them and parked several places up.

"Wait here I will be back in a minute" James said as he exited the car.

The Doctor's hair was a good length now and he no longer wore a suit. A change in style of glasses along with a good beard and moustache, even James did not recognise himself in the mirrored glass of the entrance way. Now there was little chance of either of the two men, recognising him. He just had to be sure, that the other man was also the same man, who had taken part in his beating and in the murder attempt on him, not to mention destroying his home. James walked up to the bar and ordered a drink.

"Pint of Larger and lime please"

The barman poured the pint and attempted to start a conversation.

"Not seen you in here before".

"No I am just passing through".

"Do you work down the road?" He asked referring to CDE/MRC Porton Down

"Just the pint please" James replied indicating that the conversation was dead.

"£3.40p Please" the barman said in a sultry tone.

James paid and moved over to the table, next to the one, where the two men had sat down with their drinks. He sat with his back to them. He recognised both their voices. It was them no doubt. Perhaps he could kill two birds with one stone, so to speak. It would mean a change in plan and Dean would have to be good at his job. Leaving his drink on the table, James made like he was going to the toilets instead he slipped out the front door of the pub and made his way back to Dean and the car.

"Let's go".

"Where?"

"Out of here turn left and wait about 50 yards down the road."

"What makes you think they will go that way?"

"Simple, it's rush hour and you don't want to be waiting, to cross over to the other side of the road especially when there is a roundabout in another thirty yards down this road. They will be gong this way. Watch for them, and then follow."

They waited, then almost half an hour later the RAV4 drove past, and over the roundabout. Dean pulled out and followed the Toyota. They seemed to be heading out of Swindon and into the countryside. A few minutes later they were on a single-track road.

"Did you bring the mask and baseball bat?"

"Yes"

"Where are they".

"On the back seat"

"Gloves?"

"In my pocket"

"Put them on now".

James put his gloves on and took out a black ski mask from inside his coat and put that on. Then he reached in behind to the rear seat and grabbed hold of the ski mask and bat. The ski mask he passed to Dean, who put it on. Now the bat was in James's lap and both men had ski masks on as well as black gloves.

"Dean can you actually force them off the road, without actually hitting them with your car."

"Does a Hen lay eggs? I used to drive for the Boss, back in the old days in London. That was back when the gangs would fight a turf war. On a road like this and without someone shooting at me, I can do that easy."

Dean sped up and drove awfully close to the rear of the other car before speeding past when they pulled over. When they were out of sight of the other car Dean turned the car around and started to drive back the way they had come. Soon he saw in the distance, the glow of the other car's lights, he increased the speed and drove in the middle of the road. James could see the bright headlights of the other car coming towards them.

"I bet they don't play chicken often" Dean said and then added.

"But you might want to buckle in tight, just in case" He said while tightening his own seat belt.

The Doctor followed suit. The lights grew closer at an alarming rate. The other car flashed its lights wildly. Still Dean gave up no road as he sped towards them. Their lights continued to flash and then they heard the horn, just before they were going to crash into the Mondeo. James braced for the impending accident that never came. Instead the white car, shot up the bank at the side of the road before losing control and rolling into a farmer's field. Dean slowed to a stop and then reversed down the quiet country lane, until he was level with where their car was.

James passed the baseball bat to Dean and then got out of the car. They walked to where the Toyota lay on its roof, with its wheels still spinning uselessly in the air. Both men were hanging upside down in their seats, still held in place by their seatbelts. The pair were disorientated, although neither appeared to be too severely injured.

The Doctor had taken his bag from the car as he exited. Not sure how much of this venom it would take to kill a man, he would now have to share the entire syringe between both men.

The driver of the RAV4, had a cut to his hand no doubt caused by the broken windscreen. Quickly the Doctor took out the syringe and injected half of it into a vein on the back of the drivers cut hand. Almost immediately, the driver became fully conscious and his screaming brought his partner, into the here and now. By sheer chance, there had been no need to use Dean as an enforcer. He was still handy to have there just in case.

"Why did you force us off the road? Are you mad?" The passenger said between his partners screaming.

"You don't recognise me do you" The Doctor said to the passenger.

Then he realised he was still wearing his ski mask, so he rolled it up into a watch cap.

"What about now?"

"No I don't know who you fucking are? But I know you are in a whole lot of trouble when I get out of here" he replied again over the screams of the driver.

"Imagine a young research doctor who used to work at CDE Porton, who one day was followed home and then beaten, before being left to die in a gas explosion".

"What? Who? You? You're dead."

"You made a really big mistake, you failed. There was someone else in my home that day and he helped me out but sadly he was the one, that died in that explosion." James replied and then injected the remains of the syringe into the man's jugular vein.

Instantly the passenger was screaming and clawing at his own neck, while the driver was having convulsions. Like the child in the Philippines his muscles were trying to break bones. The Doctor watched as the passenger bit down so hard that two of his front teeth snapped of cleanly at the gum and another shattered vertically. His sounds were now more of a guttural moaning almost feral and rising to a shriek. Dean looked on totally horrified. He could see the pain that both these men were now in.

"Dean! Get back to the car and keep a lookout I will be there in a minute."

After what he had just witnessed, with the two men dying in absolute agony, Dean was only too happy to get back in the car.

The men in the Toyota would die that was for sure. There was enough venom in their bodies and there would shortly be more. The Doctor reached into his bag and took out a glass vial with Adrenalin in. Using the same syringe as he had previously he loaded the syringe from the bottle. The Doctor new that at some point the bodies pain receptors of these two men, would kick in and switch the brain off at least temporarily and they would become unconscious. The Doctor wanted these me to suffer real pain, right up to the moment of their death. He injected both men who once again started to scream and arch their bodies. Now for the final part The Doctor reached into his bag and this time he took out a small bottle of Eucalyptus Oil and put some on his gloves before wiping his hands over his face and body. It was the one scent that Yellow Jackets hated. They would not go anywhere near it. He knew it worked as he had tested it in the laboratory.

Finally, The Doctor picked up the tall glass jar containing about 200 live wasps. He shook the jar vigorously in both hands to deliberately make the venomous insects more angry and ready to attack. Then he carefully placed it midway between the passenger and driver before removing the top and emptying the wasps into the upturned car.

The Doctor knew that when you are stung, or in this case where wasp venom is injected, then other wasps pick up on the pheromones that has been released into the air. They then attack further. The wasps did exactly that, they swarmed over the faces, of the two screaming men who lashed out wildly. The Doctor stepped back from the car, but not before he placed all his items back into the bag including the now empty wasp jar. The doctor moved further away but he could not help but taking a last look, at the painful dying moments of these two murderous men. He had felt sorrow and pity for the innocent children, who had died because of wasps. For the death of these men though, he felt nothing but satisfaction. The Doctor turned and walked back to where Dean was waiting by the car.

"Take me back please Dean. Your debt is cancelled".

Dean dropped The Doctor off at the tobacconists and drove off into the night, happy that he had to nothing more, than drive the crazy doctor around for a few hours. He had expected to beat someone to death but even he was horrified, by what The Doctor had done to the two men in the car. Their screams would have woken the dead. Even if he did not know, exactly what he had done to them, whatever it was, it was blood curdling. Still it was not his problem.

Act 8

The Yellow Jacket

The Doctor went in through the Tobacconists shop and through to Brompton Tube Station. He took the lift down the two stories to his laboratory. He had not expected to get both thugs together and he could have used one of them to tell him the name, of who it was that sent them, but no doubt one of the others would spill the beans. Scientists and bean counters are not exactly known for their fortitude when it comes to violence and pain.

He went to his office, which had once been an office for the Commanding Officer of the Anti-Aircraft Battery, and sat down at the large desk, before unlocking the top left-hand drawer. He took out his new laptop and the external hard drive which contained all the material recovered from his old computer. He had been able to recover 99% of the data from the damaged laptop and mostly it was just some pictures he had lost, so all his scientific data was still intact. To avoid another possible accident with his computer he now regularly backed up all his material to an encrypted server and on to to a second hard drive. Once bitten twice shy and all that.

Next to the laptop, was his little black book. He removed Deans page from it and the two thugs from CDE. He lit the pages and set them to burn to ash, in a large green glass ashtray on his desk. He watched until there was nothing left but ash. Then he picked the ashtray up and washed the ash down the sink. One of Ale's friends had told him, that people forget that you can still read things from burnt paper, unless it is powdered up and washed away. So now there was no trace, that he had anything to do with the deaths of the two thugs. The police would find the car and some dead wasps and perhaps a lot of live and still terribly angry wasps. They would find multiple stings on both men. Any autopsy would show that they both that both men suffered cardiac arrest, strangely after they both suffered numerous stings from Yellow Jacket Wasp. They would conclude the high concentration of adrenalin found in the bodies of the two men, would have been because of extreme pain caused by the wasp stings. The men's bodies would show cardiac arrest from a combination of stress caused by fear, along with wasp venom and massive dump from the adrenal gland dump. Presumably there had been some wasps in the car and that had caused the men to crash into the field. There would be no signs of any other vehicles involved no other skid marks. Nothing to say other than this was just one of those strange accidents.

The police would contact their wife's, if they had them and they would also contact their employers. CDE may give the police a hint, that they were working for some of the professors, who were working on a project using in some cases, rare and exotic wasps from around the world. Perhaps the men had stolen some of these and somehow, they had gotten loose in the car and that had caused the crash.

The next target would be lot simpler, at least in The Doctors head, it would be. He knew he had changed on a personal level, since the day they tried to kill him. The Doctor was now a cold-blooded murder. He also knew that he would change more from today. He had committed a double murder tonight and from that, things could only get worse for him and for his intended victims.

Swindon police got a call from a farmer, who had seen a car upside down in his field. It was not that uncommon in these parts, for teenagers to go out and steal cars, then joyride in them for a few hours before dumping them. The desk Sergeant said he would send a car to investigate.

The patrol car arrived on scene about ten minutes later. As soon as he saw the two men inside he went and checked on their state of health of the occupants. The patrol officer checked first on the driver, no pulse. He was doing the same thing on the passenger when something landed on the back of his hand. He went to brush it away thinking at this time of night it would be a moth. The moment his hand touched it, the Yellow Jacket wasp stung the officer three or four times in rapid succession.

"Fuck, Fuck, Fuck, you little Mother Fucker" His hand felt first like he had received an electric shock and then it felt like someone was pouring boiling water over it. The pain did not decrease, quite the contrary it became more intense. The officer walked back to his car swearing and holding onto the injured hand.

"Mike Alpha Charlie 326 to Base"

"Go ahead Mike Alpha Charlie 326".

"Yes, that car in the field. It is a double fatal. You best get the traffic boys down here".

"Any idea if there were other cars involved".

"Not that I can see, but if you ask me it is a bit strange this one, best get the duty CID boy down here as well. I will secure the scene Mick Alpha Charlie 326 out."

The constable went and sat in his patrol car which he now used to block the entrance to the farmer's field. He sat and waited for the traffic cops to arrive and presumably the wagon to take them to Swindon Mortuary. Strange thing was he had lived in this area since a child and had never heard of wasps at night. He thought that they needed the warmth of sunlight. Perhaps he was wrong on that. Jesus his hand throbbed something rotten, he knew if he complained about a little thing like a wasp sting, then he would come in for some serious ribbing, from his fellow officers. Still it was difficult to ignore.

About 20 minutes later, he could see several blue lights in the distance and hear the two-tone sirens. This was a little used road that much was for sure, as these were the first cars he had seen since he got there. He wondered if perhaps the driver of the upturned car, was lost and that they had also been driving too fast, then the driver lost control. Or perhaps the wasps, attacked the men before the accident. Christ his hand hurt. A Land Rover Discovery, adorned in day-glow white, blue, and yellow squares, stopped just in front of his car and a uniformed officer, in a Hi-vis jacket got out. The Constable got out of his car and greeted him.

They both walked across to the upturned RAV4 and shone their torches around whilst circumnavigating the wrecked car. The officer from the 4 by 4, got down on his haunches and shone his torch inside and played it over the two dead men.

"So, tell me, what do you think happened?" He asked the young constable.

"There is only one set of skid marks, so no other vehicles involved" Still his hand burned and throbbed.

"They don't look badly injured; I think we need to get SOCO down here and best contact CID".

"I have already contacted them, and they are on their way" The officer replied.

The Traffic officer noticed the young constable rubbing and scratching at his hand.

"Hurt your hand?"

"If I told you that you would think I was crazy" the young officer said and left it at that.

More lights appeared coming from both directions this time. A light blue BMW 3 series pulled up at the side of the Police 4 by 4. A man in civilian clothing got out. Showing his police ID, he approached the two uniformed officers.

"Inspector Hamilton CID. What makes you think a car wreck, is my responsibility. Or that it is even important enough, to take me away from Mrs Hamilton and a good TV box set?"

The constable who had been first on the scene, stepped forward to give him his report, when the traffic officer answered first.

"Something just not right about it, Sir. There were no other cars involved and insufficient injuries for them to be dead."

"Are you a doctor? Have you checked that they have not broken necks? Heart attacks. You are not qualified to make that statement constable; however strange things may look." The inspector replied in a sarcastic tone.

"There were wasps!" the young constable blurted out both sets of police eyes turned to him.

"Explain?" The inspector asked him.

"There were loads of wasps in the car when I got here, I even got stung a few times".

"Wasps? You sure they were wasps?"

"Sir, yes sir and there are a few dead ones inside the car if you look."

The inspector shone his torch inside the car this time he shone it down on the roof lining, sure enough there were several dead wasps there. The Inspector took a pen from his pocket and pulled aside the driver's jacket. Then he put his pen back and took a pair of blue neoprene gloves from his coat. After putting them on he reached inside the driver's pocket and removed a wallet then he opened it. Inside a plastic window was a level five security pass for CDE/MRC Proton Down.

"Christ! Get a 50-yard perimeter around this car! No one gets inside the perimeter until forensics, say that it's safe to do so." He said.

Both officers stood and looked at him.

"Now! The inspector barked and took out his mobile phone and made two quick calls, before going back to his own car. He took out a pack of cigarettes and walked over to the police Land Rover.

Within a few 15 minutes more police had arrived, and a tent had been placed over the upturned car, by men dressed in white body suits. The police helicopter was working a wide search pattern in case there was any sign of there being a wider spread of whatever it might be. Then a black Jaguar pulled up and a Chief Constable in full dress uniform got out and walked to the back of the police 4 by 4. The inspector who had been sat on the tailgate of the Land Rover stood up and stubbed out his smoke, as the uniformed officer approached.

The Chief Constable removed his hat and placed it under his arm, before taking out a pack of Rothman's cigarettes. He offered the inspector, and then took one himself. After lighting both cigarettes he spoke with the inspector.

"What have you got here then Jack? I just got told that we may have another major incident like the Skripal one." He said referring to the Novichok incident that they had in Salisbury a year ago.

On that occasion, there had been a man-made toxin, used to murder an ex-soviet spy and it was the Russians who had not only invented it, but they also used the nerve agent Novichok to do it. It had cost millions to clean up the city, and cost millions more in the cost of extra policing.

"Well Sir neither of the men seem to have sufficient injuries, that would have killed them and there is this Sir." The inspector said and he carefully opened the wallet he had been holding. There was a pass card for Arthur Morgan, and he had a level five Pass for CDE Porton Down.

"OK Jack let us not set another panic going, I will get in touch with CDE and let's get a high screen up here. After that I want you and the other officers who have been next to that car to go through a full decontamination. Got that?"

"Seriously Sir? I just bought this suit?"

"Better to be safe than sorry. I will get a van sent for you but all your clothes into bags and they get burned".

A major incident was declared, and the cover story was that there had been a gangland double murder. This story had been invented by the Chief Constable.

Within a further 20 minutes of the Chief Inspectors arrival, an unmarked police car arrived. Three men in suits got out and walked over to the police command post. They showed documents. Two minutes after that a large van arrived with all sorts of equipment and they set up their command post, complete with mobile decontamination unit. Jack and the other officers went through a thorough decontamination and shower before dressing in grey police sweat suits. These officers then left the scene and returned to Swindon police station.

The new arrivals suited up in yellow bio suits and walked to upturned car, then after just a couple of minutes, they headed back to the command post.

"Not Novichok"

"It's Not?" the Chief Inspector replied in relief.

"Nope and as far as we can determine, it is not a Biological, Chemical or nuclear weapon".

"You sure?"

"Well as sure as we can be. But unless it is something new, that none of us know about then yes I am fairly sure."

The three men went back to the unmarked car and drove back off, to wherever they had come from. The Chief Inspector took out a mobile phone from the inside pocket of his jacket and dialled a number and waited for it to be answered.

"Put me through to Inspector Hamilton" He said into the phone.

While he was waiting, he lit a cigarette. He had planned to give them up after the Novichok incident, but it seemed, just when things were getting easier, another spanner threw itself into the works of his life.

"Jack?..... Turns out you are safe.............Yes Sorry about that. I will see that you are recompensed for your clothes.............................Yes, I know bit of a cock up on my part...............Listen Jack, I think you are right to some degree. ....It's not a normal accident. These folks that came down from CDE, were far too quick to give us, the all-clear. Whilst it may not be a chemical or nerve agent. They knew what it was, even before they had done any tests. Find out what these two men were working on at that germ factory." He hung up the phone and told the SOCO team to wind everything down and to get the bodies removed to the morgue.

Act 9

Back down in The Doctors Laboratory, he had been working on synthesising a mist, containing the Yellow Jacket venom. It had worked well on the rats, that he had collected from the tube tunnels that ran by Brompton Station. Using a mist spray, would be much easier than carrying hypodermics and live wasps. He knew where to find his next victim, as he had taught the man everything that he knew. The man had been his research assistant. This man was obviously complicit in the theft of The Doctors work. He had not even raised the alarm or reported those, who now claimed the advances in Cancer cures, were their own work. This man lived in London and commuted daily. He would catch the train from Kings Cross to Swindon. However, he first had to catch the Tube from Hammersmith to Kings cross. That meant that his tube would go through Knightsbridge, which was right next to Brompton. The Doctor would have to wait now until Monday. That gave him two days to perfect his delivery system and the technique for doing so. The last thing he wanted to do was to hurt innocents.

The Doctor needed to look distinctly average in every way. He would have to blend in with the crowds of other commuters. He knew that there were cameras everywhere, however this would give him a chance to test out his video blocker. It was not really a video blocker per sé, rather it interfered with the signal, that went from the cameras to their hub. So, what would happen is that any time he was within 50 metres, of anything which had to ability to video, it would be a corrupted picture that recorded. Meaning, no matter what they tried to do to, any recording would always remain screwed up. There were video cameras, on buildings, cash points, road junctions, shops even on millions of mobile phones. People just loved to video anything in this day and age, accidents, beatings, and murders were all up there on YouTube. Tube trains had their security cameras too. He would board the train at Knightsbridge. And get off at Hyde Park, assuming he could get to his man fast.

5am on Monday morning he walked out from the tobacconists and the short distance to Knightsbridge. He was dressed like a mid-level manager. A suit shirt and tie, brown lace up shoes. He had changed his glasses to a slight tinted pair with round lenses, a style he hated. He had his shoulder length hair, slicked back into a ponytail and a trilby on his head. He carried a plain black raincoat over his left arm and a briefcase in his right, in his left hand he also carried a folded copy of this morning's Times Newspaper. Inside the newspaper was a rubber bellows taken from an old sphygmomanometer, that previously he had used to test blood pressure. Inside the rubber bulb was 10cc of Yellow Jacket Venom and 10cc of sterile water. There was a piece of surgical tubing attached to the bulb and then it was taped down to the edge of the newspaper. Fixed to that end was a diffuser nozzle that would cause the spray to come out as a fine omnidirectional mist. He bought a ticket from the machine and waited for the 6:10 to arrive. He was starting to sweat now and was not sure if it was fear or excitement or the fact that he was wearing a tie, or that he had cotton wool stuffed up both of his nostrils. He had not won a tie in over a year now.

The train pulled in and he made his way to the front of the people, who were also waiting to catch the tube to work. The man he was after was standing in the second carriage. He had to push his way through the crowd before the train came to a halt. The train stopped and some people got off. The Doctor forced his way onto the train, making sure he could get close to his intended victim. The tube doors closed with a hiss and The Doctor sidled up to his ex-assistant.

Unbelievably the assistant looked directly at The Doctor, without any sign of recognition. The doctor moved closer and placed his briefcase on the floor between his legs. Then as he made as if he was reaching for the grab handle, on the rail above him. The Doctor aimed the folded paper at the face of the assistant, then he waited for the train to exit the station. Now where the lights dimmed before coming back up again he took a breath through his mouth and held it. With his right hand, he reached over and squeezed hard on the outside of the newspaper and once more for luck, before reaching down for his briefcase and sitting down in the one empty seat near the door.

"What the Fuck" The Assistant said to no one and started to wipe his face with a handkerchief.

"Fuck..........arghhh .... help.......... please arghh.."

His body was starting to contort. People moved back from him as he fell to the floor of the carriage, coughing and choking. His eyeballs bulged forward. A woman screamed.

"Arggghhh"

The ex-assistant puked up his breakfast as the tube rattled on. The ex-assistant tried to get to his knees, while at the same time, coughing and choking and trying to call for help. Blood started to pour from his nostrils, even his tear ducts started to show pink foam like tears. His eyes became bloodshot. More people moved back in fear that the man might be contagious. No longer speaking the man's howls were almost inhuman. The total amount of time lapsed, since he had sprayed the venom onto his victim was less than 20 seconds. The Doctor breathed out and carefully breathed back in again. There was no joy in watching such a fast death, even though he was sure, the pain the ex-assistant was feeling now, was immeasurable. The Doctor wanted to kneel on the floor and whisper in his ex-assistant's ear. He wanted to tell him, why this was happening. He wanted to tell him, who it was, that had caused him to meet with such a gruesome end.

There was that final rasped breath followed by a gurgle and then the assistants twisted and cruelly contorted body, slumped face down in his own puke, on the dirty floor of the carriage. The tube train slid into Hyde Park. The doors opened and some passengers got out. Someone must have pulled the emergency cord, as the train stayed where it was. A few passengers like himself made their way to the escalators and up into the half-light of dawn. The Doctor took a taxi from the stand and told the driver to go to Gloucester Road Tube station. When they arrived, The Doctor paid £5 for a £4 fare and walked away into the morning and then switched off the anti-video gadget in his pocket.

He felt strangely elated, He had got away cleanly from a murder scene and no one would remember him. He knew if he were to use this same system again, then he would have to reduce the amount of venom. His next target though, would be more difficult but he would work that out over the coming days.

British Rail Transport Police were called to the scene and the main Piccadilly line was temporarily closed while the body was photographed and then removed. Witness statements were taken. Not one person, mentioned the long-haired man with the newspaper. The Police collected the CCTV hard drive, from the drivers cab on the train, and it would be examined at the police station. 30 minutes later the line was opened again. By which time The Doctor was back at his Laboratory.

Act 10

Inspector Jack Hamilton was busy reading through the Medical Examiners report. Both men appeared to have died from heart attacks, brought on by multiple Wasp stings. Specifically, the European Social Wasps. Yet the amount of venom in their bodies suggested that they must have crashed into a large wasp nest. Or had been carrying one in their car. That said no nest was found at the scene, even though there were plenty of dead wasps around and in the car. Sure, it was possible that there had been a nest in the car, and they had thrown it out near the crash site. The DI would have Uniforms Branch, look at the route, the car had been travelling. Something else, struck him as strange, was that not only did both men, work for the Medical Research Council at CDE, but both men had some serious criminal records. To the best of his knowledge all the people working within CDE Porton Down, had to pass a thorough security check and with records for violence along with theft, there is no way that these two men, should have passed that criteria. This was a line of enquiry he would follow up on. Perhaps their deaths had something to do with their past criminality. He was just about to send an enquiry to CDE, when a Detective Constable passed him a sheet of paper.

"What's this?" He asked the Detective.

"You wanted to know if there were any other incidents involving CDE Porton Down".

"Yes and? Save me reading the son, just give me the bare bones of it".

"There was an incident on the London tube, between Knightsbridge and Hyde Park Corner Stations. A man died in quite strange circumstances. But the main rub of it was, he works for the Medical Research Council at CDE Porton Down and carried a Level 5 pass. I did a bit of my own investigation before I brought this to you. Level 5 is…"

"Where they make all the nasty shit for our government".

"Yes sir"

"Right lad! Get me the Chief Constable on the blower and then get me someone in authority at CDE. Someone who deals with their Level 5. No forget that. Get me a marked car and meet me at the front. You and I are taking a trip down to these secret bastards, NOW!"

The Detective Constable took off at the run, while the Chief Inspector collected his notebook along with the files on the two men who had died in the supposed car crash. The phone on his desk rang.

"DI Hamilton"

"Hello Jack have you seen this thing that had happened in London this morning".

"Yes Sir, I have just been given the info, it seems that he worked in Level 5 at the same place at those other two. By the way Sir, those two in the car, they both had records, as long as your arm. Both have done time for violent offences, which include armed robbery and intimidation. Seems strange, that they managed to get a job at secret establishment."

"Jack tread lightly on this one. Do your job. And see what links you can come up with."

"I am just on my way over to CDE, to see if I can talk to one of their bosses. I will give you a full report when I get back".

"OK Jack just remember they have powerful bosses."

"I will Sir." He put the receiver down and signed out of the station.

The DC was behind the wheel, waiting in a marked Skoda Octavia at the foot of the police station's steps.

"Where are, we going Sir?"

"CDE and when we get near there, put the blues and twos on." Jack said referring to the blue flashing lights and the two-tone siren.

"Sir."

Jack Hamilton read the jackets on the two stiffs that he had in the morgue. There was no way people like this should ever have gained employment, by any government department, let alone a highly secret one. These two men had spent around one third of their lives behind bars. When he got back to the nick, he would get a warrant to search their homes. These were not the smart sort of criminals, their time incarcerated was proof of that. Hopefully, with luck, he would find some clues as to who employed them and why they needed this sort of muscle, around scientists and geeks.

About a quarter of a mile from the main entrance to CDE, the DC turned on the blue flashing lights and switched on the siren. Jack Hamilton wanted those in the administrative side of whatever they had at Porton, to know they were coming. He had always found that sirens and flashing lights, tend to intimidate those who have something to hide. They pulled up at the main gate and a toy-town security guard, dressed in black trousers and a white shirt, which bore the logo for Group Four Security or G4S for short, stepped out from his box with a clipboard.

"Can I help you?"

"No. Just point me to the administrative headquarters for The Medical Research Council."

"Do you have an appointment?"

"Listen son. I know you think you hold the power of God, in your pencil and clipboard but I hate to inform you, that you do not. In fact, I doubt he even knows you exist. So how about we make like you are a pretend copper. Then you do as I say and point us real coppers in the direction we need to be."

"I am sorry sir, but I can't let you in, without the correct pass, or an appointment with a specific person".

Jack Hamilton turned to the Detective sat next to him.

"Detective, do you have your hand cuffs on you?"

"Yes Sir?"

"Good then arrest this man on a charge of hindering a legal investigation into murder. No make that accessory to murder." then he turned to the wannabe cop and continued

"And I can promise you son, that when you have a charge like that over your head, you will not even have a job in a shopping mall. Now, what is it to be? You direct me to the person I need to see, or we arrest you and then we get to meet the administrative head of the Medical Research Council?"

"I am sorry they tell me what to do here, but I aint going to jail for no murder, I had nothing to do with. The building over there, then through the double doors and down to the end of the corridor that is the boss's offices are, in the administration section" the fake cop said.

"And?"

"What?"

"A visitor pass for my detective and me, and don't forget to sign our car in".

The G4S man copied the names and ranks down from their police warrant cards and then the car make and registration. Then he went back into his booth and came out with two visitor tags on lanyards. Finally, he lifted the barrier.

"Blues and twos son" Jack said to the detective.

They only had to drive about two hundred yards, but it was worth it. Heads appeared at almost every window of the building; they were going too.

"Park at the front door and leave the lights flashing. I want these people, to know that the police are here."

The constable did as he was told and then he exited the car. Then Jack Hamilton got out carrying a bunch of folders with him. They went up the three steps, into the offices of the Medical Research Council. There was another G4S man just inside the doorway, he checked the passes and wrote down the numbers that were on them.

"Which way to HR please?" Jack asked.

"Down to the end of the corridor and left. Then it is the second door on the right. May I ask who it is you are here to see?" The G4S man enquired.

"No" Jack replied and walked away.

As he was doing so, he noticed that the G4S man was on his radio, talking to someone but he ignored it. They walked to the end and then to a door with Human Resources emblazoned in gold letters on the half glass panel. He knocked and entered without being asked to do so. This was a technique he had used over the years. It does not give those inside any clue, as to who is coming in, nor does it give people, a chance to hide things or combine their stories.

"DI Hamilton and DC Burns, we are here investigating a possible double murder and perhaps a third murder this morning." He said holding up his warrant card. Before continuing.

"Who is in charge here?" Jack asked while looking around the room, that had three women and two men in it.

"I guess I am" A very smartly dressed woman in her mid-40's said.

"Good. Do you have an office where we can talk privately?"

"Yes, if you gentlemen would come this way please" she said and led them to a glass office at the side of the room.

She sat down behind a basic utilitarian desk and waved her hand towards two chairs at the side of her small office. Jack made a big show of reading one of the bundles of criminal reports on one of the men while the DC took out his notebook and a pen.

"Your name please? And position?"

"Jenny, sorry Mrs Jenny Mason and I am senior HR officer for The Medical Research Council.

The DC scribbled notes, while Jack continued to deliberately thumb through the pages of the file he held. He knew the woman would look, so he flicked the mug shots over and some crime scene pictures, of things that the man called

45

Arthur Morgan had been involved in. Jack listened as Jenny's breathing changed upon seeing some of the brutal crime scene pictures. Then Jack closed the file with a snap.

"We are investigating several murders and this man, who was employed here. Do you have the records of everyone who works here? Along with copies of their job applications and references?" Jack said as he slid a picture of Arthur Morgan over the desk to the woman.

"Yes, Inspector every person who works for the MRC, has to have proper checkable references. They are very thoroughly vetted."

"OK and you keep these records where?"

"Well we have all the hard copies, in one of our storerooms but everything is digitised and saved to computer these days".

"That's fantastic Jenny, may I call you Jenny?" Jack asked once again using another interrogation technique. Throw the person off balance by becoming their friend.

"Yes of course, would you care for a coffee while you wait?" she asked.

Jack really did not want a coffee, but it played into the friendship court, so he said that would be great. She buzzed an intercom, and a young man popped his head in, and she told him to bring a tray of coffee and three cups.

"This man, Arthur Morgan. I understand he was employed here on a level 5. I must tell you he is now dead, and we need to be able to find out why. Now if you could bring up his file and that of Steven Ward. Again, employed with Mr Morgan. If you could tell me, what exactly was the nature of their jobs?"

"I can do you a printout, of that. As far as I can see, they could go down to level 5 but were not actually involved in anything of a sensitive nature. Which is strange that they have such a high security rating."

"That would be amazing Jenny. It will help us a lot in being able to bring their murderer to justice. It is so nice to meet a public-spirited person like yourself Jenny. You are an absolute diamond." Jack said buttering up the HR Manager.

The printer next to her desk started to throw our sheets, with all the details of their employment. Jenny gathered them up and put them in a folder, which she passed over to Jack.

"Just a thought Jenny, I don't suppose you have heard about the tragic death of a young man who also works here and who died on his way into work here?"

"Yes, we all saw it on the news this morning, terrible he seemed like a nice man who had a great future ahead of him. Kevin Brown was his name."

"Can you look up where he worked?"

"Yes, just a moment please. More coffee?"

"No not just now Thank You Jenny, as we are a bit limited on time this morning, perhaps another time."

She clicked away on her computer keyboard.

"I can only let you have his job application and references as he was working in one of our secret laboratories. Will that be OK?"

"Yes Jenny, if it is not too much trouble".

She smiled and printed off the file, then passed it to Jack who put them inside the folder with the other documents. No sooner had he done that, when a tall and officious man barged into the room.

"Just who the bloody hell, do you men think you are? Coming in here and interrogating a member of my staff."

"I am Detective Inspector Hamilton of the Wilshire Police. We are here as a follow up, to two and possibly three suspected murders, all of whom were of your staff. And you might be sir?"

"I am the head of chair, for the Oversight Committee of MRC, which really means I am in charge. I really would prefer that you put any questions in writing and submit them through the correct channels."

"Surely you want to help us find out, who killed these men?"

"Were they murdered, and presumably you have some kind of proof to substantiate those allegations?"

"We are following various lines of enquiries, including, might it be possible that someone here, may have been responsible for their deaths."

"So, that would be a no then!" He snapped his fingers in the air and two G4S men appeared behind him.

"Escort these men, from this facility and ensure that they don't come back in, without the correct paperwork."

Jack got up from his chair and finished his coffee, before thanking Jenny for her time. Then he and the DC left the building followed by the two G4S pretend cops. As soon as they got in the car, Jack told the DC to lock all the doors. This left the real cops on the inside and the pretend cops on the outside, looking at each other.

"Drive really slow and make them walk behind" Jack said, and the DC complied.

Act 11

"Burns, I want every detail, of the guy that died on the tube this morning, as soon as we get back in the office" Jack said.

Then the DC drove out of the main gate for CDE, before turning off the flashing blue lights of the Skoda. Jack read all three personnel files, on the way back to Swindon Police Station. There were some interesting things to be read in the files of the two 'Security Specialists'. There was not much out of the ordinary about the scientist that had died on the London tube. There were also a lot of details about his work, that was missing. Jack would be making a bunch of calls as soon as they got back to the station. Three men dead, all from the same section of the MRC and no one seemed to have picked up on it, or they had and were deliberately ignoring it. They had been booted out of Porton Down, by some kind of head honcho. He really did not want any outsiders knowing, whatever it was they were involved in.

The DC signed the car back in and Jack went straight to his office. He had been there for about two minutes when his phone rang.

"DI Hamilton" He said as he picked up the receiver.

"Jack, I told you to go in gentle. Just what the hell did you do at Porton Down. I have had the Commissioner and the Head of MRC, not to mention the director of G4S, on the blower to me. What is more, they are all making formal complaints, about your behaviour. Some of them even want you kicked off the police force." Jack held the receiver away from his ear as the tongue lashing continued

"Did you listen to a word I said to you?" His boss demanded.

"Sir, I think you might want to see what I have found out before you send me to the firing squad. You know I am not a fly by night hero, and there is more to this, than just three dead employees of MRC. Besides when did Her Majesty's Police, cow-tail to an amateur crowd, like G4S?"

"My office now Jack! and your evidence better be as mind blowing, as you have made it out to be or both our butts are on the line".

Jack collected up all the paperwork that he had so far and stuck his head out of his office.

"DC Burns!" he shouted.

"Sir?"

"Have you got me anything on the tube thing yet?"

"Transport Police are just faxing it through now Guv.

"If you call me Guv once more, then you can kiss goodbye to your Sergeant's stripes. Just bring me the fax now!"

"Sorry Sir, Just Coming Sir" he said as he handed over three pages on the Tube Incident.

"Right, come on lad. The boss wants to see what we have, and you are my whipping boy today, if this goes wrong." Jack said and he led the way to the elevator and the Chiefs office.

Jack straightened his tie and knocked on the door and waited. Jack passed all the folders to his DC and whispered.

"Make like you know what I'm talking about! Got that?" Jack said and the DC nodded.

"Enter" The voice from inside the office called out.

Jack went in first with DC Burns at his heels.

"It had better be, better than good Jack. Or you and I, are about to be burned, by some exceedingly high up people. In fact, they are so high up, I get nose bleeds every time I visit them."

"Right Sir. The two men in the car. Both are career criminals, and both were employed by MRC as Security Consultants. The personnel records that we got from their HR people, show that they were theoretically vetted by the head of that department. They both had references given to them appear to have come by way of GCHQ. I have applied to get a search warrant for their homes, before any more evidence gets destroyed. They have fake employment records going back 10 years."

The Chief Inspector put his hand up indicating that Jack should stop.

"What makes you think the references from GCHQ are false?"

Jack put his hand out towards the DC who gave him Arthur Morgan's fat file.

"Because Morgan was doing a seven-year stretch, in Her Majesty's hotel Belmarsh, until just over a year ago," Again Jack put his hand towards the DC.

"The same applies to his buddy Steven Ward. Although the judge at their last trial, thought it best that these two villains be separated, so he had Ward spent his seven years stretch, in the Isle of Wight prison. Both spent most of their time locked up in solitary, until about six months before their release. Then both men were visited by someone from within GCHQ, unfortunately we have no name for that. On their release from prison, they were immediately employed by MRC at CDE. They worked with both level 4 and level 5 security clearance."

Once again, he out his hand out and the DC passed over the HR file, as well as the fax from London Transport Police

"This young man was a research assistant, working in the same lab as these two goons. It becomes even stranger Sir. It turns out that his boss, who was also working on the same project was killed in a suspicious explosion, at his home just about a year ago,. Now as far as I am concerned, one would be regrettable, two is perhaps a coincidence, three is suspicious, four there is a criminal cause and a massive cover up for all of this. I would bet my badge on it. I think it all has something to do with whatever is going on in the lab, specifically the one they all worked in. No let me rephrase that Sir I would bet your badge on it and you know how much I want your badge!"

The Chief looked at the papers before him and shuffled them about before looking Jack and the DC.

"OK I am convinced. Can you be a little subtler and step on a few less toes. I will run flack for you but bring me some results. Please make it sooner rather than later. That's all"

Having been dismissed Jack and the DC went back down to CID.

"Burns, set up an incident room. I want white boards, chalk boards, computers and whatever this 21st century police force uses these days. Then get me the constable who was first on the scene at the crash site. Next I want all the video footage, that we can get of the scientist, leaving his home right up until the moment he died on the tube. Then tell the duty officer. I want four wooden tops on my squad, and they need to wear civilian clothes. Along with two more for office work, so a total of six officers. Got all that?"

"Sir." The DC replied and went about his duties.

Act 12

The Doctor knew that at some point, people would join the dots and make the link to the research team. But there was no way, they could make the link to him. He had been officially dead for over a year now. The Doctor had no doubt that his colleagues, would have attended his funeral and drunk him well into the hereafter. They had stolen his life's work and claimed it as their own. They were all guilty, every member of that team even those that did nothing. They could have spoken up and told the world, that the honour belonged to him. He had made the link, in attacking cancer cells, by replicating the way the venom attacked the red blood cells of the body. The next man on his list was the Haematologist, who The Doctor himself, had brought this man into the team. That man still worked at the MRC, but he also worked at Guys and St Thomas Teaching Hospitals. This is where he would find Dr Bukhari. This was where someone would snatch him from.

Having tried out the aerosol delivery system as well as the direct injection The Doctor thought that he would try the 100% natural form, which meant that he would first have to capture Bukhari and then he would take things from there. Once again, he would call upon the services of one of the men in his little black book. The man in his book, had stabbed his own wife in an argument and rather than take her to a regular hospital, where questions would be asked and no doubt a report, made to the police. The man had heard from a friend of a friend about a Doctor who made house calls and kept no records.

A few phone calls later and The Doctor had appeared on his doorstep. The man's wife had been stitched up and sedated that was almost a year previously. Now though, this man was a member of the local council and next year, he hoped to be heading up the planning committee. To do that, he would have to remain squeaky clean and nothing from his past would be allowed to stop that. Previously he had been a gangster and a bully, but in a very insidious and silent way. He operated from behind the scenes and had others do his bidding. At times, that would call for the most extreme form of violence and a problem would be erased.

The Doctor made the call.

"Hello?"

"You know who this is?"

"Should I?"

"I repaired you wife."

There was a silence, and The Doctor could sense the change in attitude, of the man on the other end of the line.

"What do you want?"

"Some Assistance"

"I will send someone."

"No, it has to be you."

"Why?"

"Because it is your debt".

"I can't, as I don't do those things any-more, I am legit."

"Your debt! You pay! I am sure you would not want another of my debtors to come and pay you a little visit, say at your offices?"

"How dare you threaten me! I could have you wiped out."

"So, you are refusing to help me after I helped you?"

"That's right, I am sorry I can't?" The Councilman replied

"Just so you know. You refused and that was your choice."

The Doctor hung up the burner phone then removed the SIM card and snapped it, before throwing it in the bin. Then he inserted another SIM card and looked up his black book. He thumbed to the middle where he knew he would find a truly evil man. He had watched him kill another man just because he had insulted his girlfriend. This man was a Russian with a very shady and dark past. Now though he ran prostitution and white slavery. Girls from the East of Europe and from the newly released ex-Soviet states. These girls were promised jobs and security, they were smuggled into the country and their passports held by this Russian and his cohorts. Then they were sent to work in the sex trade in, London. The Doctor dialled the number he had been given.

"Da"

"Sergi?"

"Yes, who is this and how did you get this number?" He said in a heavy Slavic accent.

"I took two bullets out of you".

"Doctor?"

"I need the debt repaying".

"OK when?"

"I will come to you, same place as before?"

"Yes. When?"

"One hour"

The doctor removed the SIM and like the one before, broke it into two pieces then threw it away. He inserted a new one then he went to the back of his Laboratory and into the small, chilled room that had been installed. This had been early on, in the tube stations custom renovations. After unlocking and opening the door, he removed two large plastic bin bags and then closed the door and relocked it.

Exiting from the tobacconists The Doctor walked a half mile to a taxi rank. After getting in the back of a black cab, he gave the cabbie the address, which was a quarter of a mile away from where he really wanted to be. At the destination, he paid the cabbie and got out carrying his two heavy bin bags. He walked down the road and around the corner and then down an alley next to the Russian Night Club.

The Doctor pressed the button on the side door. He knew that Sergi, had a video camera over the door but that it only gave a live feed to the big doorman, who was sat at a desk just inside the side entrance. Sergi like to see who was coming but he did not want any records, of who was or had been, at his club. That would be like giving the police a full confession to his dealings.

The door opened and he was motioned inside. He taken by another large doorman, to Sergi's private office. On opening the door, The Doctor could see, there was an almost naked girl sat on the edge of his desk. Sergi had one hand on her upper thigh, the other hand, rested on the edge of his desk with a folded newspaper in front of it. The Doctor knew full well, that under the newspaper, lay a large handgun of some form.

"Doctor Welcome, have you become a bag man or are you homeless." Sergi said while taking his hand off the girl's thigh and pointing at the two large bin bags.

"Neither Sergi. These are the tools with which, I must get retribution with. How is your back these days?"

Sergi had been shot twice in the back by an Armenian gangster, this gangster who had been in competition to Sergi, had tried to take over Sergi's business. The Armenian had assumed, that the two 45cal slugs he had put in the back of the Russian, would do the trick and he had left Sergi for dead, in the very alleyway that The Doctor had just entered from. One of Sergi's men had known about The Doctor and had made the call. Some 20 minutes later there were two slugs lying in a stainless-steel dish and Sergi was getting stitched up.

The next day, whilst he may not have recovered fully from his wounds, Sergi and his men had gone to the Armenians club and killed every single member of his gang. They had collected all the bodies, then cut them up, after which they froze the bits. The body parts were shipped back to their families in Armenia. Attached to the pieces was a message, not to attempt form of revenge, upon penalty that all their families for four generations, would be wiped off the face of the earth. The Russian had been well known, long before the breakup of the Soviet Union. As such the Armenians knew this was no idle threat. It was also known that it was better to have Sergi owe you, then for you to owe him. As a debt to him, was a debt that you could never get out of.

"I need you collect two men for me and then I need you to lend me a room that we can seal up. Somewhere no one can see or hear anything."

"And tell me Doctor, do you require me to dispose of these bodies afterwards?"

"No"

"Ahhhh So it is a message you are sending out, Cossack style?"

"Yes. You could put it that way I suppose".

"But tell me Doctor, what is to stop me from just killing you and wiping out my debt that way?"

"Because Sergi, for you to operate, you have to be known to be a man of your word. If you were not, then people would not fear you as they do."

The Doctor knew that Sergi had a big opinion of himself and he loved the 'Godfather' lifestyle, that he had built up around himself. Sergi laughed a deep and resonant belly laugh then he stood up and came around and grabbed The Doctor in a bear hug practically lifting him off the ground.

"Of Course, I will help you. A Cossack always pays his debts, or he is not a Cossack. Now let us drink to this deal with good Cossack Vodka." he said letting go of The Doctor.

They sat down at an ornate coffee table and Sergi poured two shots. The Doctor knew that Cossacks were Ukrainian, but that it sounded better to Sergi to be known as the mad Russian Cossack. The Doctor had previously had a drink of Sergi's Cossack Vodka and knew it was 96% pure alcohol.

"How is it you English say it? Up the bottoms."

"That would be Bottoms Up" The Doctor corrected him.

"You have a strange language and strange ways. Please tell me who, when, and where do you want these men to be punished, I can do it for you at no extra charge. For it would be my duty as you are my friend."

"No Sergi. This will be my revenge, but I thank you. I will give you the names and addresses and I want you to collect them unharmed and take them to a suitable location and then I will call you and you can tell me where. I may want you to take them somewhere public afterwards If you could arrange for me to do that."

"My dear Doctor that might cost you a favour.....................Hahahaha I am only joking the is no charge for those services. Mezhdu pervoi i vtoroi, pererivchyk ne bolshoy."

"And that means?" The Doctor asked

"Doctor. It is an old Cossack saying, which roughly translated means 'Between first and second the gap is not so big'".

"You could be right." The Doctor said and then continued.

"Thank you for the drink Sergi, I need to leave these bags to warm up to room temperature in the rooms, in which the men will be taken. It would not be good for your health to open these bags there in a lot of pain within them."

With that The Doctor wrote the names and addresses, on a slip of paper and passed it to Sergi.

"I will call tomorrow." The Doctor said

He stood up, knocked back the Vodka and shook the Russians hand, before retracing his steps back to his Laboratory.

Act 13

Jack knew that to get anywhere with this investigation, he had to go back to the first death and that would be, Dr James Pearson. That had been around a year ago, and his death had been declared an accident by the Fire and Police investigations.

"DC Burns!"

"Sir?"

"I want the Medical Examiners report for the death of this Dr Pearson and find out which Officers attended the scene and get them to come and see me, as soon as you can. Preferably before I finish my coffee."

"Yes Sir" The DC replied and went off to perform his tasks.

Jack was starting to get worried, that this case would be taken out of his hands. He was sure this investigation, was the sort of case that every copper, wants to have his name on. If he was right, then he had a serial killer on his hands. He needed a proper profiler to work with him, but to do that, he would first have to prove to his boss, beyond a shadow of doubt, that they were dealing with a mass murderer.

Jack pinned a map to one of the walls it was a blown-up map of Swindon and then he put another map next to that showing the route that the Research Assistant had travelled on his way to his death. He marked a large X on CDE/MRC Porton Down, then an X on the address of Dr Pearson, followed by an X where the two men had been found. The pictures of the four dead men were pinned to another section of the board. Jack put thumb tacks in, where they lived and worked and where they died, then put cotton red thread between them. All roads led to CDE/MRC Porton Down. He was never going to get permission, to interview their research team, at least not without some help from above. Jack would also require the help of the British Transport Police and the Metropolitan Police. He needed to search all the dead men's homes. He was lost in thought when there was a knock on the door.

"You wanted to see me sir?"

"I might if I knew who you were and why you are at my door?"

"Sorry Sir I am PC White, DC Burns, asked me to come and see you I was the first officer at the fatal explosion of Dr Pearson's home."

"Do you have your notebook from then?"

"Yes Sir"

"Well?"

"Sir?"

"Well, what did you write down when you attended."

Christ, it was like pulling teeth Jack thought, but never said it for fear of exploding.

The Constable took out his notebook and nervously thumbed through it until he arrived at the right page. The read from his notes.

"I arrived on scene and could clearly see there had been some form of what I suspected to be a gas explosion. I first went around the remains of the building, shouting to see if there was anyone trapped inside. I got no reply, so I carefully entered at the front of the property, to check for any unconscious casualties, but found my way blocked by rubble. I then proceeded to the rear of the property, where I found one male, who was already deceased. After that I then enquired with the neighbours, as to the identity of the man. They told me that it was the home of Dr James Pearson. He was further identified by a friend and colleague, also the deceased had his wallet in his back pocket. The deceased also wore a Rolex Watch. This I removed and put in an evidence bag, along with his wallet. The watch bore the inscription 'To J Pearson well done, Love from Mum and Dad' I made the site secure and waited for the Fire Brigade and other units to arrive. I spoke with neighbours, who were able to tell me, that Dr James Pearson, lived alone at the property. I stayed on scene until relieved at the end of my shift. Upon return to the station, I handed the evidence bag, over to the duty Sergeant. I also made sure, that it was entered into the evidence log."

"Thank you, constable, if you could get me a copy of that. I will want it to be put on file".

The Constable turned and walked away towards the uniform section; it was just at that moment he heard the CID officer scream after him.

"White!!!!!! My Office Now!!!"

The uniformed officer rapidly made his way back to Jacks office.

"Sir?"

"You said he was identified at the scene by his friend? I don't suppose this friend gave you his name?"

The officer took his notebook back out and thumbed his way back through to the relevant pages.

"Yes Sir…… Ohh Sorry his name was Arthur Morgan."

"Thank you, Constable, that will be all for now. Keep yourself available, I might need you again."

DC Burns arrived just as the other police officer was leaving. He passed over a folder, containing the Medical

Examiners report, along with some rather gruesome glossy photographs. DC Burns then laid it down on his boss's desk. Jack looked up and said to him.

"I think we may have a serial killer on our patch, and I think, he doesn't like the folks at the MRC."

Then he opened the file that had been placed in front of him.

"How the hell could anyone, identify him visually when he looked like that?" Jack said as he turned the gruesome picture to his DC, before he continued.

"And you know who identified him?" Jack asked.

"No Sir"

"Of course, you do not, because I have only just been given that information myself, just two minutes before you gave me this file. It was none other than Arthur bloody Morgan. Did you get me my search warrant for Arthur Morgan's home?"

"No Sir, it would seem that it has something to do with the official secrets act. CDE and MRC are blocking our application."

"And the same would apply no doubt to Steven Wards home as well?" Jack asked.

"Yes sir."

"Are they by God? Right we will see about that. I am promoting you to Temporary Detective Sergeant for the course of this investigation. We will see how you fare from there and perhaps look at a more permanent position. Get over to administration and get your warrant card changed. Then take off for the day, but I want you here at 7am tomorrow morning. We have a lot to get through tomorrow."

"Thank you, Sir. I won't let you down." The newly promoted detective replied.

"I know you won't Burns, because if you do, then we will both be for the chop."

The following morning Jack held a war meeting in the incident room. And as soon as that was over, he made his way up to his bosses' door. He knocked and waited.

"Come".

Jack opened the door and entered. His boss was sat behind the desk and the tall officious guy from MRC was sat in one of the chairs drinking coffee. The hairs on the back of Jack's neck instantly stood up.

"I'm Sorry Sir I did not know you were busy; I can come back later."

"Ahhh Jack I am glad you are here, actually I was going to send for you. Come in and close the door please."

Jack did and stood waiting to see what sort of lashing, he was in for and he was not disappointed, at least it would give him some more information as to who this tall bloke was apart from being the administrative hammer for MRC.

"Jack I believe you two have met?"

"Sort of although I still don't know who he is? Sir."

"I am sorry Jack I thought you knew. Mr Jons is the Director of the Oversight Committee for the MRC."

"I see Sir, but I still don't know what that entails and how it fits in with our current and ongoing investigations."

Jons put his coffee on the table and stood up, before offering his hand to Jack and saying.

"I am sorry I did not properly introduce myself, to you the other day. Mike Jons and as your Chief Constable has said, I am part of the Oversight Committee".

"And what does your job with the big title entail Sir?"

"I solve problems and smooth the waters. Had I been made aware of the connection between the sad deaths of these men and the MRC I would of course have been more forthcoming."

"And can you?" Jack asked.

"Can I?"

"Be More forthcoming".

"Jack! That is enough, I will speak with you later. That will be all for now." His boss shouted at him.

"Yes Sir" Jack replied

Then left the room like a schoolboy who had just been told off by the headmaster. He went directly to the incident room and shouted for Burns.

"Sir"

"Find me everything you can on a Mike or Michael Jons apparently, he is Director of the MRC Oversight Committee at Porton. And when I say find me everything I mean right down to his shoe size and what he eats for breakfast."

The rest of the CID Officers, as well as the Uniformed Police who were dressed in civilian clothing were milling around and working on phones and computers.

"One of you lot go, and get me the constable, who was first on the scene of the double murder" Jack shouted a little harsher than he had intended. He needed some facts to put with his suspicions. He saw one uniformed officer.

"You what's your name?" Jack said pointing at a WPC.

"WPC Jean Short Sir"

"Right then get over to the legal eagle section and see if we can get an exhumation order, for Dr James Peterson, on the grounds of checking his Identity. It turns out that the visual ID came from an extremely questionable source. If they want details, tell them to bell me. Now girl, off you go!"

"Burns when you have set the wheels in motion for my first request, take one of the wooden tops and get yourself on down to London and go to London Transport Police Headquarters at Camden Road. Check all their video and then get over to the Metropolitan police and see what they have. After that get back here as fast as you can and give me the results. We are all going to be working double shifts on this one." Jack said.

Jack had not cleared it with the Chief Constable and going on this morning's meeting, he knew he would probably have a hard sell on this one.

Act 14

The Doctor knew that he had to get things moving along. Now, he had what he needed, and it was time to call Sergi.

"Hello"

"Doctor?"

"Yes. Did you manage to get me a secure room? And it is sound proofed?"

"I have got you something better, than just a room. I have got you a shipping container and yes Doctor, no noise will get out at all. I had my men install a plexi glass wall with a door in it, across the middle of the Container. I have left you some tools inside in case you may require them. Where would you like it and the men delivered too?"

The Doctor was originally going to take the two men's bodies to a building site behind the Royal Albert Hall, where they would be found the next morning, so a shipping container which he could have placed there at night, was even better.

"I want it delivered to the rear of the Royal Albert Hall, after 6pm and before 8pm, when everyone has gone home. They are doing some restoration work to the back of the building. Make sure you use a stolen truck to deliver it, so that it does not get tracked back to you."

"Doctor do not worry about that, the keys to the container, will be taped to the right-hand side."

"Thank you Sergi, your debt to me is cancelled".

"But we are still friends Doctor?"

"We are still friends Sergi, but it may be sometime before I see you again and I thank you for your assistance." With that The Doctor hung ended his call.

Once again removed the SIM card, broke it, and replaced it with a new one. His hatred for one of the men he was about to murder, had grown with every passing day. The Doctor had kept up to date, on what was new in medicine. He had read the articles, by his one-time friend and colleague, Dr Fahad Bukhari. This man was an average toxicologist and had lived on the coat tails of The Doctor, ever since project Yellow Jacket, had been started by the MRC. Now he was using The Doctors own writings, to have articles published in the British Medical Journal and in The Lancet. Other medical people were quoting his works and Fahad was being lavished with praise. There was even talk of a Nobel Peace Prize.

This was one of those things, that had worked like a maggot, in The Doctors brain, it was literally destroying his mental ability, to see things rationally. Perhaps though, it was the reverse of that The Doctor thought. This might really be the clarity, that he had sought throughout his life in research. Only time would tell, if he were to be seen, as an angel, whose work would save thousands of lives, or as a monster for taking a just a few.

The doctor put a new triple layer beekeeper suit into a holdall, he also made sure he had the anti-venom in his pocket. His bottle of eucalyptus oil just in case any of his wasps would escape prematurely. He had bought a kilo of cheap minced beef, this was not for eating, well not by him. This time he was going to video the whole thing, from the moment they were sat in their death chairs, to the second of their demise. So, a small digital video recorder, with a tripod stand. In with the other items was his video scrambler, which would be temporarily turned off, when he himself was filming and finally a torch. The Doctor closed his Bag and left the confines of his laboratory and exited the front of the tobacconists.

He walked the quarter mile back to the taxi rank and caught a cab, deliberately choosing to go in the opposite direction, of where he really wanted to be. Then when he arrived at the first destination, he walked across to the bus station, before catching a bus and going back towards, his destination. Then he took a taxi to Prince Consort Road. The Doctor waited until the taxi had left before walking back down the road to its end. He took a right turn at the junction and walked to the Royal Albert.

There were people going into the front of the building, as he went around to the rear. He found the container easily enough, as it was placed right across the main gates of the building site. It would be found, when the workmen arrived in the morning, perfect. The keys were as Sergi had said, they attached to the right-hand side with duct Tape.

The Doctor took the keys, unlocked, and opened the door, then switched on his torch, before closing the door behind himself. There were some work lamps attached to a large battery pack. The Doctor switched them on, and he had to shield his ayes at first, as the light was so bright. Soon though they became accustomed to the glare of the bright white LED lighting. There were two naked men, bound to chairs using duct tape, they also had duct tape gags over their mouths. Both men were separated by a plexi-glass wall, which had a door made from the same material, set into it. The doctor put down his bag and first removed his jacket. Next, he rubbed eucalyptus oil on the exposed parts of his own body, then he took out his Beekeeper suit and got into it. After that he brought out his video camera and checked it was ready to go, before setting it on its tripod stand.

The Doctor turned the first chair around in order that Dr Bukhari, could face the naked Councilman sat in the other chamber. He then placed one of the black bin bags in front of Bukhari. He looked at the naked doctor, just to see if there was any sign that Bukhari recognised him. There was nothing there except abject fear. Then he walked through the door and dragged the chair with the councilman right up to the glass facing Bukhari before he ripped the tape from the councilman's mouth. The Doctor became strangely excited by what he was about to do. Now he placed the other black bin bag in the lap of the councilman before walking back through to the first compartment of this shipping container.

Sergi's people had done a good job of insulating the inside of the container. There was a three-inch-thick layer of yellow insulating foam, sprayed to all the walls, floors and under the wooden slat flooring. Even to the inside of the container's large double doors. No sound would escape which is just as well because he knew there would be pleading and screaming, and it would last for several minutes this time and not for seconds. It was one of the reasons he wanted to video it because he would be sending the file with it on to his next victim. The Doctor set up the Video Camera on a lightweight Tripod stand, looking at the mini screen he made sure that the Councilman was in frame and in focus. Then he then removed Dr Bukhari's duct tape gag.

The excitement was building in him, his revenge on the councilman, for welching on his deal. The Doctor had fixed, what would have been a career ending incident, for the Councilman. This man had been a gangster, before his meteoric rise in local politics. He had blackmailed his way up the food-chain and those he could not blackmail, he terrorised out of the way. He was about to face something much more terrifying, than he could ever imagine. The Doctor had seen, how the European social wasp would attack other insects and animals, so much bigger than themselves. They would also take carrion. In his studies The Doctor had seen a swarm of wasps literally remove all the flesh from the body of a dead crow.

From his bag The Doctor took out the tray containing a kilo of fatty ground beef, he split it into two equal sized portions, leaving one half in the tray. Next, he walked back through to the rear section of the container. Then he proceeded to rub the fatty meat all over the Councilman's body, including his genital area and his face. Sergi had put brackets on the legs of the chairs and left a nail-gun hanging on a hook for The Doctor. Sergi had done this, so that The Doctor could fix the chairs wherever he wished them to be. The Doctor now nailed the councilman's chair to the floor. Then he went back through to the first section and repeated the process with the mince and nail-gun. The next thing he did was to superglue Dr Bukhari's, upper eyelids to the upper orbital area and the lower lids to an area just above the lower orbital area of the zygomatic arch above the cheekbone.

It was strange that neither man had said anything, so far, soon though, they soon would be pleading for their life's. He placed the beekeepers hood on his head, before setting the video running. He then went back into the Councilman's chamber and carefully undid the loose knot at the top of the black plastic bin bag. He held the neck of the bag closed in his gloved hand, before spinning, the now unknotted bag, over his head and throwing it in the rear corner of the room. The bag hit the rear wall and a large wasp's nest rolled out onto the floor. Quickly and before any wasps would be able to escape from the Councilman's compartment, The Doctor went out of the compartment and closed door behind him. Then he stood beside Dr Bukhari and watched, as the now extremely angry swarm of wasps made their way towards the Councilman.

Within seconds there were wasps landing on the Councilman, it was not until he started to move that he was first stung. The first sign of pain was the shaking of his head. Some wasps were just collecting scraps of meat, to take back to the nest. Other wasps though were now in full attack mode. There were wasps literally swarming over him now. Finally, he started to scream.

"Arggghhh Jesus arrgghhh. Doctor please Stop I will do it Arggghhh" The Councilman screamed and begged.

A single large wasp landed on his top lip before crawling up the Councilman's nose. He snorted, to eject the wasp. The wasp sensing a threat to its life, as the Councilman's nasal passages contracted around it. The was then arched its thorax up and pushed the rear of its abdomen down before thrusting its stinger, deep into the soft mucus tissue and released its first dose of ultra-painful venom. The horror in the eyes of its victim, was plain to see. The screaming became more animated and the councilman continued to shake his head. He attempt to push air through his nostrils. The result being, the wasp now unable to turn around, moved further up the nasal passage stinging several more times, before it reached the extremity of the nasal passage and into the rear of the nasal cavity where the airways reach the throat. The sudden intake of air, as the Councilman attempted to breathe, caused the insect to be drawn deep into his right lung. The wasp was now covered in all sorts of sticky mucus.

It had stung the man six times so far but still it had some venom left. One final long injection of venom from its stinger. The pain was immediate and excruciating. He could feel wasps eating the meat that covered his groin area. These other wasps now sensed the danger. This was due in main, to the pheromones that had been released by two wasps. The one that had been crushed under the left thigh, as the Councilman rocked back and forth in his fear. Also from the dying wasp in the right lung. They attacked in a true swarm and with a vengeance.

He was instantly stung on the side of his testicle sack and then on the circumcised glans of his penis. Never, had he ever felt pain like this. The next wasp would sting him on his eyelid and then directly into the soft tissue of the eyeball itself. His vision became blurred the moment he tried to block out the pain from one part of his body, even more would come from another. He opened his mouth to scream and two wasps flew in. He managed to blow one out without being stung, but in doing so he trapped the other wasp between his upper gum and cheek. It stung him three times, first on the bony side of his mandible by his teeth and then twice on the inside of his right cheek.

His body was on fire as he leaned his trembling body forward, to shake several wasps that were taking up residence in his hair. By doing this, several wasps, that had been crawling around and collecting some of the meat, that was on his back, fell to the seat of the chair. He could feel several crawling in the crack of his arse. Two angry critters made it all the way to his anus and then they attacked.

Soon his body would start to shut down, but not before he had been stung hundreds of times inside and outside of his body. His entire central nervous system was screaming out that his body was under a savage attack. Due to the amount of venom in his body, almost a third of his red blood cells were breaking down as the outer coating ruptured and then the nucleolus was exposed to the venom and it too ruptured. All this poisoned blood would be carried through the veins and arteries to the heart and then to the brain. The venom would continue its destruction on the body's internal motorways.

The pain was so intense, and it was continually growing in strength. Soon though he would not care. He would welcome death with open arms. He wished now that he had repaid his debt to The Doctor. A pink foam came from his mouth and nose. He had urinated over himself and that had further angered the wasps which had attacked his genitals. Bloody foam came from both tear-ducts. His eyelids were so swollen that he could no longer see. He felt a wasp enter his ear canal and then the pain subsided, and a blackness washed over him. Soon the wasps would become calm and just eat the meal, that was strapped to the chair.

Dr Bukhari having been unable to close his eyes, saw everything, that had happened to the man in the other room. Bukhari had worked on the Yellow Jacket Project. He already knew the pain of being stung by a European Social Wasp. It had happened to him several times previously, it was a risk he accepted. The last time he had been stung by a wasp, it had done so three times. The pain had lasted for 6 hours and it was still sore 24 hours later. He found that it was still uncomfortable 3 days later. Had he been able to, he would have closed his eyes to most of what had happened in front of him. He was a devout Muslim and was stoical about his death. Allah would take him into his bosom. But why did it have to be so painful. Why was this man who he did not know, doing this to him? The Doctor took the bag from in front of Bukhari and untied the knot. Then he started to bang it on Bukhari's naked body.

This time he would not throw the nest to the end of the room he would drop it right into the lap of the plagiarist, that was this sad and frightened scientist. The Doctor upended the black bag and the heavy paper nest fell neatly onto Bukhari's naked lap and thighs. Dr Bukhari screamed, even before a single was had stung him. His fear released adrenalin, into the air and mixed with the pheromone now caused an almost spontaneous and deadly attack. What followed was horrific to listen to and to watch.

"Allahum arjuk saeiduni ajealah yatawaqaf alan" he screamed.

From the little Arabic that The Doctor knew, he knew that Bukhari was asking God to help him and to make the pain stop. Allah though, had turned a deaf ear to him. This was Satan's territory and he ruled with a venom, that would inflict so much pain. The wasps for some reason swarmed over Bukhari's face, stinging everywhere especially his open eyes. Bukhari could not even describe the pain, not even to himself.

Dr Fahad Bukhari would die from a heart attack before he could reach the same level of pain as the Councilman had done. That said he had watched the Councilman die horrifically and he knew then what his fate would be. He had time to think about how painful his own death would become. It was that fear combined with the immense pain. That burned in his face and eyes which had brought on the fatal heart attack.

The Doctor would send out copies of his video, that would defeat any Hammer House of Horror Movie, for its horror and squeamishness. Copies would go to the police and the last Doctor on his list and then there would be two other people and that would include the administrative head of the oversight committee at CDE/MRC Porton Down.

After collecting all his items The Doctor switched off the lights and exited the container, closing the door behind himself. Then after he had walked some distance away he took off the beekeeper's suit and put that back into his bag. The Doctor walked off unseen into the night.

Act 15

DS Burns, who had only just got back from London, raced to DI Hamilton's office.

"Here you go Sir, I just got this faxed through. It is the exhumation order for Doctor James Pearson. The folks at GCHQ seem to have a friendly judge in their back pocket, as we still can't get the search warrant."

"Fuck fuck fuck" Jack said more to himself than to those around him. This caused them all to look up, fearing that his anger and frustration, might be directed at them.

Most of the uniformed officers, had gone off to the various crime scenes and Jack had been waiting for his boss, to come and give him a proper talking too. So far though, that had not happened.

"Sir, I have just had a thought and I don't know how you would feel about it" Burns said.

"Go on lad, spit it out. It can't make things any worse than they already are."

"Well Sir suppose, if there had been a break in, and it were called in as a 999-emergency call. Then CID might have to go out and investigate"

"Burns, I thought you had more about you than that. You know as well as I do, that is menial stuff and that, is what we have the wooden tops for" Jack said using the slang for uniformed branch.

"I know that Sir, but if it were to happen at a home of someone that we were to have a special interest in. Such as someone we were already investigating, it could have been a murder or even a suicide. We would have to follow that up. Right?"

"Short! Where the hell are you?" Jack shouted.

The WPC came running to Jacks office.

"Sir"

"What the bloody hell are you still doing in uniform?"

"You never asked me to be in civilian clothes sir" She replied.

"Do you have any other clothes with you at the station?" He asked knowing that many officers came to work in civilian clothes and then changed into uniform at the station.

"I do Sir. Do you wish me to change?" she answered?

"For God's sake! Does anyone around here this morning, have their brains switched on?" Jack almost screamed.

Most of the eyes in the room turned to the floor least they might meet with the Inspector's eyes.

"Yes please. WPC Short and can you do it quickly." Jack continued.

She returned several minutes later wearing a pair of faded Levi jeans which were threadbare at the knees. She wore a black AC/DC hooded sweatshirt, along with a pair of Reebok training shoes.

"OK Short! Take one of these morons with you, in an unmarked police car. The older the car the better and get down to Morgan's address. Then one of you, throw a rock through the window and the other on can run to a public phone box and put in a 999 call, about a break in. Got that?"

"Sir what happens if we get caught?"

"Don't get caught is all I will say. And take a handheld radio with you."

WPC and one of the other officers, hurried off from the incident room and down to the motor pool.

"Burns with me".

Jack took a marked police car from the garage and headed out towards the Arthur Morgan's address, which turned out to be nowhere near where he had died, so he would have been going out of his way to be somewhere else. Perhaps to meet with someone. Jack pulled his car over about three streets from the address and sat listening to the police radio.

They did not have to wait too long. The radio operator came on asking if there were any officers in the region of the address. The radio operator stated that there was a burglary in progress, with the burglar in the property. Leaving 30 seconds of free air, Jack had DS Burns respond.

"DI Hamilton and DS Burns we are just a few streets away; we will take it" Burns said into the radio.

Jack hoped that the window, which Short or the other constable had been broken, was either a door or downstairs window. He need not have worried. The officer who broke the door window, had also unlatched the door. Jack pulled his car up with a screech of tyres and the blues and twos going. That brought all the neighbours out to see what was going on. They would be able to attest that Jack had arrived because of the burglary.

Now he had a right, as a serving police officer, to enter the property without a search warrant. Making like they were being extra careful and vigilant, Jack and DS Burns approached the house telling the neighbours to move back, as they themselves proceeded inside the property with their extendable batons out. Jack used the tip of his shoe open the door, before going inside. Closing the door behind him, both he and Burns, put their extendable batons away. They would have to be quick in their search and they had no idea what they were looking for. Mobile Phones, Laptops, and letters along with any notes or scribbled down phone numbers. Wearing their neoprene gloves they instantly searched the downstairs lounge. Burns found a Mobile Phone and an extra SIM card next to it. Jack pocketed a small notebook that was on the kitchen table. Then he went upstairs and started to search the bedrooms the only thing he found was a couple of flash drives and a charger for a laptop. Burns found a slim external hard drive stuffed down the side of the sofa. Jack came back downstairs and was just about to go through the trash when there was the sound of outside of a car skidding to a halt. Quickly jack took off his blue neoprene gloves and stuffed them quickly into his pock and indicated to burns that he should do the same and hide any evidence he had found.

Burns had only just finished putting that evidence surreptitiously away, when the door burst open Mike Jons, who was accompanied by two other individuals.

"I thought we were on the understanding, that a search warrant was not to be issued because of security problems arising from where these men Morgan and Ward were working, on a sensitive project."

"Strange I don't remember that agreement, however we are not here searching the property as you can clearly see. I just remember that we were blocked from getting a search warrant by your office. Which is moot, as I said we are not here searching. There was a civilian report from a woman, stating that there was a break in in progress at this property. We were in the area and took the call, so we entered the building to try and make an arrest."

"And did you?"

"It looks like the burglar, made it away before we got here. Unfortunately, we were not able to make an arrest. May I enquire as to who you gentlemen are? As of now, this is an actual crime scene, and we will need to eliminate you from the enquiries." Jack said.

"These men are with MI5 and their specific prints and DNA are not required." Jons replied.

"That may be so, but this is still my crime scene, until I am told otherwise. So, I would like to see some form of ID, Gentlemen?"

The two men accompanying Jons, reached into their pockets and brought out identical leather wallets, which they flicked open in a well-practised manner. They were spooks and they were both armed with what looked like Heckler and Koch VP9 pistols in shoulder holsters.

"I assume you two have permits to carry concealed firearms?" Jack said.

Neither of them replied.

"As you have not found the criminal, who broke in here then I think it would be best if you were to leave." Jons said.

Jack was just about to arrest him, for obstruction of a police officer in the course of his duty, when another car screeched to a halt outside. Jack looked out and noticed it was the Chief Constable's black Jaguar. The Chief got out from the back and put his peaked cap on before walking up the path to the house.

"Jack I thought I told you there was no search warrant for this property?"

"You did sir, and we are not searching. We attended, to a report of an ongoing break in, and then these gentlemen arrived?

By the way, just how in the name of hell, did you guys know we were here? Are you listening in on police radio? You know that is also a crime as well?"

"Jack a word, outside, if you would please?" The Chief said

"Burns watch them and make sure they don't ruin my crime scene!"

"Yes Sir" DS Burns replied, although he did not fancy taking on the two heavy hitters from MI5, especially seeing as they were both packing guns.

The chief led the way outside and down to his car.

"Get in Jack" the chief said as he removed his hat and got in the opposite side.

Jack closed the door and looked at his boss who he had always respected. He was old school and had come up the hard way, through the ranks. The Chief told his driver to get out of the car. Then turned to DI Hamilton.

"Jack, I am getting some heavy pressure from the Commissioner, to remove you from the case. I am fighting your corner Jack. I do not like being told what to do by these suits, any more than you do. But they have political clout behind them. I know exactly what you did to get inside, you faked the break in."

Jack started to interrupt when the Chief held up his hand.

"Don't deny it Jack. I know because if I were in your shoes, it is exactly what I would do. You had me convinced at the double murder in the car, now with the list of dead, I am 100% sure we have a serial killer on our hands. However, the Commissioner is refusing to see it that way and your little stunt setting up a major incident room really put me on the spot. As far as I am concerned your major incident room is about a series of unsolved home invasions and rapes. If any of what you are really doing gets out, it will mean your pension and not to mention it will be my arse on the line too. Here is what I want you to do. Move your incident room out of the station and into an office block of someone else's investigation or something like that. Then work from there. As far as resources go, you have the team you have now. I need that deniability. There is nothing I can do to stop your exhumation, as it has already happened, and the ME has some information for you. Send a uniform to get it and do not let me see it. When you have solved everything, to a point where we can make some proper arrests, with a 100% chance of convictions. Then I will give you a full task force. Now get out of my car and take Burns and whatever evidence you have stolen from Morgan's home and stay out of my sight."

"Yes Sir" Jack opened the door and got out of the car.

The driver returned to his seat in the front of the Jaguar, which then drove off. Jack went and collected Burns and they too drove back to the station. He would wait for all the members of his team to return and then they would clear out this room and move across town to a commercial building where they would share a floor with a Serious Fraud Squad unit, who were investigating a major crimes ring that were scamming elderly people out of their pension funds. The head of the fraud squad, who was an old friend of Jacks, said, they could have four large rooms.

Act 16

Back at his Laboratory the Doctor was reviewing the Video that he had made of the two naked men, being stung to death. The quality of the video was fantastic. Now he would duplicate it. He needed one copy for the police, a copy for the MRC and one more for his next victim. There were to be three more victims, after that he would go back to his own research. He had all the data from the MRC. So, he had continued his work, in researching the effect of pure wasp venom as well as a synthesised version of it. What he needed to do now, was to break down the venom into is separate chemicals. The Doctor knew that the venom contained phospholipases, hyaluronidases, antigens including those of low a molecular weight. Peptides that included mastoparans, wasp kinins and chemotactic peptides. There were of course the bioactive molecules, such as histamine, serotonin, catecholamines, acetylcholine as well as tyramine.

He has written all of this on a large white board, even though he knew most of it by heart. He did it so he could visualise the entirety of his labours with more clarity. The components were an extremely complex mixture of powerful allergens and pharmacologically active compounds, they were primarily made up of proteins. The vespid venom contained three major proteins that acted as allergens and a wide variety of vasoactive amines and peptides.

The animal tests which he conducted on rats, had shown him that the antigen by itself was not a toxin, rather it was a member of a conserved family of proteins. These were normally found in eukaryotes, including those found in other naturally occurring substances such as yeasts. They had a joint sequence that identity with other proteins of diverse origin and tissues. Those were such as mammalian cystein-rich secretory proteins in salivary and reproductive organs. The secretory proteins of helminths produced during sexual maturation and human brain tumour proteins, reptile venom, pathogenesis-related proteins of plants and the fire ant venom.

It was this part, that The Doctor was trying to extract or even synthesise. He had managed to partially do this, when working at the MRC. He had already proved beyond any doubt, that the wasp venom could kill cancer cells, in some forms of cancer. They worked in the same way as it does with red blood cells. The specific part he needed to isolate and then reproduce in quantity, was called Polybia-MP-1. He could do this with the equipment that the MRC had at CDE. The mature antigen from yellow jacket and hornet have 201 and 205 amino acids respectively, with several highly-conserved regions. Almost all the sequence variations which are seen in Hymenoptera antigens, were found on the surface. The highly cross-reactive groups within the genera have a few changes. This was a science that few people, would ever know about and even fewer, would ever understand. But they would know about his work because of its ability to destroy cancer cells.

His work before at the MRC, had initially been to find out why the Wasp Venom attacked the pain receptors in the way that it did. However, during the process of solving that quandary, and its effect on the red corpuscles. Then how it had selectively destroyed them, whilst leaving other cells around it unaffected, was what had given him the lightbulb moment. If it could switch of one type of receptor on a specific cell, could it then be used to the same effect of another type of cell. He had looked at over a hundred different cells before he found another and that was in a mutated cell, in other words it was a cancerous cell.

The cell in question had come from a prostate cancer. The Doctor had then contacted the head of MRC and requested tissue samples of more types of cancer. His experiments were at that time, for the good of mankind. He found that the venom, worked on three types of brain cancer tumours. In some of the cells, the Venom, caused all the liquid element, to leak out. In others that it attached itself too, as a protein, to the outside of the cancer cell, the venom stopped the cell from growing or even replicating itself. This whilst not killing that form of cancer, it did stop it dead in its tracks, thus not allowing the patient's condition to deteriorate.

The research was his and he should be the one driving around, in the big flashy car, with a posh home to go back to every night. But it would not happen, at least not for him. The boss at MRC and the major shareholders at the drug companies, would live like kings, off his back. The more he thought about it, the more it plagued his mind.

If God could invent an insect, that that plagued mankind. There had to be a higher purpose for it, and this was it. He had that eureka moment, now all that was left to do was to remove the parts of the venom that were harmful and select the parts that cured. That may sound to the uninformed like a difficult task. To a toxicologist after mapping it proteins and enzymes it became a relatively easy process, but only if you had the key.

He had the one thing that those at the MRC had not got and that was the map. He had sketched it out, but he knew they would at some point bring in another who understood this work. He knew who that person would be. It had been his professor in Toxicology at university. He had been tempted by the massive difference between the pay for a university professor and that for a toxicologist, working for the military at CDE Porton Down. At this moment, he was working on Biological Weapons. Soon though he would take over the reins, of the work The Doctor had done so far at MRC.

The Doctor had worked out a new and more seditious way to deliver the Venom. It was this way he would go after his old professor. The Doctor felt nothing now about taking another life, this time though, he would send out a warning in the form of a copy of the video. There was no other person that The Doctor knew of who could unravel his work in a short time and this man, may already have the key. The professor had taught The Doctor how to create a virtual chemical key, in order to understand the proteins in poisons and venoms. Perhaps he would even remember the private discussion that he had with The Doctor, specifically about the protein and enzyme key. At that moment in time they had discussed this, it had just been theoretical. Now it existed.

The Doctor put the flash cards into their respective envelopes, after he had wiped his fingerprints from them. He had chosen self-seal envelopes, because he knew that people who licked the gum on an envelope, left behind a massive amount of tell-tale DNA. The same applied to stamps. After wiping the envelops with a cloth he. Went to the tobacconist and asked him to post it with the rest of his business mail.

The next day the letter arrived at CDE and went into the internal mail system for Operation Yellow Jacket, another went to Toxicology and finally one for the Swindon police force. All three would show that not only were the deaths of the others linked but that there would be more deaths to follow.

Act 17

Jack was sat in his new office, looking at a series of small boards he had put up. They were a smaller version of what they had in the new incident room. WPC Short had been over to the station and collected the mail for CID. what did not concern Inspector Hamilton, would be sent back over. To Swindon Police Station. She left the small bag of mail on desk of DS Burns, who was busy viewing the video footage they had got from the Transport Police in London.

"Thanks" He said in an absent-minded way and he moved the footage backwards and forwards.

He was filling up a legal pad with the notes he was making. He followed the research assistant, from street cameras near his home, all the way to the tube station. There was footage from the road junction next to his home and then again from the Lloyds Bank, as he passed by their cash machine. The next footage was from the front of the tube station, it caught him entering and then going through the turnstiles. The next footage was from the platform as he waited for the tube train to arrive. The final footage they had, showed him standing up, to give his seat to a pregnant woman. Then the train pulled into Knightsbridge and then the video was corrupted until 30 seconds after it pulled into the next station, which was Hyde Park. Following on from then, the video on the train was perfect. It clearly showed the man lying dead on the floor. Burns wound the film from the tube train backwards to the point just before where the video became corrupted, again and again. The corruption started just as a gentleman carrying a light tan briefcase entered the train. He wound the video back and moved it forward a single frame at a time.

Perhaps the man with the briefcase saw something as he entered. Burns looked through all the statements and no one had even noticed this man. He would let the technical people have a go at the video and see what they could pull from it. On a hunch, he called up the London Transport police and eventually got put through to the Duty Sergeant

"Hello, its DS Burns from Swindon here, one of your boys was good enough to pass on the video of the tube that came in with a strange fatality on it."

"Yes, that was me, how can I help you today?"

"Could you get a copy, of all the video from in and around the station. From when it pulled into Hyde Park, the footage I am looking for, is of those alighting and exiting the station. So, about a 15min window from the train to the street."

"How fast do you need it?"

"Like yesterday"

"I can have one of my lads run up a copy and put in on a hard drive and then he can bring it to you for about 3pm today".

"You are a star; I owe you big time" With that DS Burns hung up.

The next thing he did was to take the video, he had on a thumb drive. and sent it via the internal mail to it to the forensic digital sciences department. With specific instructions of what he would like them to do if they could possibly do it.

He was in the main office area when, a uniformed Constable came and put a report in his hand.

"My boss said, this is of more interest to you than us." He said as he laid the fax from the metropolitan police force, on Jacks desk.

Burns read it and almost choked on the coffee he was drinking at the time. He rushed over to Hamilton's office and entered without even knocking.

"Report just in this morning. Double murder at the back of the Royal Albert. Both men stung to death by wasps." Burns said as he passed the report over to his boss, who was already putting his jacket on.

"Get our team down there!"

"Which one's boss?"

"All of them and get a full forensic squad as well. Radio ahead and have the local police secure that crime scene."

Burns exited the office and called all the incident team together, paired them up and arranged for transport. Then he joined Hamilton down in the parking garage. They got in Hamilton's, 3 Series BMW and the Inspector put a magnetic blue light on the roof before racing out from the underground garage. They took off in convoy for London. Even though it was technically rush hour in London the cars moved out of the way as Jack and his team, drove through the streets like a mad man. He swerved quickly to avoid a taxi coming out of a side street.

"Who found the bodies?" Jack asked DS Burns.

Burns looked down at the file on his lap, and thumbed through the pages, before answering.

"Builders working on site. They arrived and it was right across their gateway."

"The bodies?"

"They were in a container, which had been placed there sometime during the night."

"Right get onto the folks at the Metropolitan CCTV section and get me all the footage from last night from the time the builders quit to the time they arrived this morning." Jack said and continued.

"Call it through, I want a cordon around the entire area before we get there and see if those builders have some sheeting we can put up to stop the public gawking. Then get me the incident commander at the scene. No cancel that. Get our chief inspector on your mobile phone NOW for Christ's sake".

"Yes Sir" Burns said and went about his tasks.

Two minutes later Burns put the Chief Inspector on the speaker of his mobile phone.

"Jack what is so bloody urgent that you call me before my breakfast?"

Jack gave him the basics and told his boss that he wanted the crime scene under his team, as they were already working the case. His boss hung up and then two minutes later Burns' mobile phone rang again and the Chief Inspectors voice came on the speaker.

"Jack, you have the crime scene The Met boys have secured the scene. And I will probably be there before you."

"Sir Thank you Sir" Jack said and indicated to Burns the call was over. The police convoy from Swindon sped down through the streets of London during rush hour. As soon as they arrived.

Jack went over to the uniformed officers who had their cars parked at the front of the container.

"DI Hamilton, who found the bodies?" He said showing his identity card.

"The foreman when he came to open up the yard".

"Where is he?"

"Hospital Sir, apparently when he opened the doors to the container, a swarm of wasps came out and he was stung a lot, the medics say he is in a pretty bad way."

"Right get over there and take a statement. I want to know everything that happened."

"But I was supposed to be off duty an hour ago, Sir. We have just finished a night shift!" The uniformed metropolitan police officer replied.

"Well put in for overtime and get over to the hospital. I will get you a relief as soon as I can" Jack responded.

The Constable got in his car and drove off.

As the door of the container lay partially open, Jack approached it with care, He stopped when he saw several wasps crawling over the front of the door.

"Burns!"

DS Burns walked quickly over to where his boss was standing, back at his BMW.

"Sir?"

"Get a pest control company down here pronto. And get a bloody screen up here. The last thing we need is for this to be all over Sky News or worse YouTube, before we have even written out reports."

"Sir, Yes Sir."

Jack went and sat in his car, while 4 workmen fixed up a screen made from scaffolding and a couple of tarpaulins. Almost 40 minutes later a 'Rentokil' van pulled in beside Jacks car. A young man got out wearing and a set of overalls bearing the company's logo on the back and his name on the front. Jack got out of his car.

"I am looking for a DI Hamilton" Said the man carrying a clipboard, who per his name tag was Tom Allison.

"Well you have found him Tom".

"I understand you have a wasp problem?"

"Yes, but this is also a crime scene and it's not going to be pretty for you. I have not seen it myself yet, but the reports state there are two naked and dead men inside that container, along with a bunch of very angry wasps. I hope you are not squeamish?"

"No problem I was in the Royal Marines in Afghanistan until a year ago, so there is not much that churns my gut anymore."

"I need these wasps gone but I don't want your chemicals contaminating my crime scene, I guess what I am asking you is, how can we go about this?"

"Where's the nearest fire station?"

"Why?"

"CO_2, we can freeze them to death."

"WPC Short! Get over here I have a job for you"!

"Sir?"

"Go with Tom here to the nearest Fire Station and get as many CO_2 fire extinguishers as you can and get back here pronto. Got that?"

"Yes Sir" with that she joined Tom in his van and left to get the Carbon Dioxide extinguishers.

More time wasted, before they could even enter the container. 40 minutes later a red Ford Transit van belonging to the London Fire Brigade, pulled in, with Tom and WPC Short behind them. She got out and went up to Jack.

"The Fire Brigade have 40 cylinders; they can let us use but they are staying here so they can get the empties back. They have accountants same as us Sir."

"Fine but I need to get this done quickly, so, if you could get on with."

Tom got into what looked like a Beekeepers outfit and grabbed a couple of fire extinguishers from the back of the Transit and then walked to the container with a Fireman behind carrying another two cylinders. Tom started on the outside and first covered the doors in a white frost of dry CO_2 Then as he opened the door wider several wasps flew out. Tom continued inside a short time later an empty carbon dioxide cylinder was thrown out the open door. The continual rasping sound of the carbon dioxide fire extinguisher being used. Tom appeared at the door and swapped his extinguisher with the fireman for two more the fireman went to the Transit van with the two spent cylinders and changed them for a pair of full ones. As it turned out he need not have bothered, because Tom came out the door and waved to Jack.

As Jack was walking to the container several police vans rolled up, one of which carried a forensic team the other carried their equipment. There way too many police vehicles here for Jack's liking. Lots of police equals lots of reporters, especially in London.

"DC Burns!" Jack shouted not realising that Burns was right behind him.

Burns walked silently into view.

"Jesus Burns! don't creep up on me like that unless you want me to have a heart attack. Get every uniform and marked car out of here and if there are any press floating around, just tell them it's an exercise which is now finished" Jack said!

Burns went off to carry out the DI's requests.

"You got a bee suit mate?" Tom asked Jack.

"Do I look like a Beekeeper, to you??"

"I have a spare on in my van, you had best tell those guys over there, that they will also need them" Tom said pointing to the forensic team who were donning white protective suits and blue overshoes.

"Short!" Jack called out and she came running.

Jack asked her to pass on Toms instructions to the forensics team, as he himself changed into Tom's spare bee suit.

"Thank you stay here for now." Jack said and walked up to the container.

All the workmen and uniformed police had been cleared from the scene. Jack entered the container with its two bodies. Initially as his eyes adjusted to the change in light, all he could see was the silhouette of Bukhari's back. Jack switched on his torch and shone it on the body. He could see that the man was completely naked and covered in stings and some form of fatty substance. As he walked in closer and around the body. He felt the crunch of dead insects under his boots. Then he brought his torch to the face of the dead doctor. Jack had seen murder victims before, but this was sordid beyond belief. It was at that point he turned his torch, to the second compartment and saw the swarm covering the Second body, those wasps were moving, and they were alive.

Act 18

After Tom, the pest control man, had inserted a tube into the second section of the container and dispatched all the wasps, by filling the entire section with CO_2. Jack could see the second compartment. The forensic boys were in and there was just too much work to do on location that they chose to seal it back up and bring in a low loader. The metropolitan police decided to let Jacks team take the lead. Jack wanted the container back on his patch and to have his forensic team sort things. The Metropolitan Commissioner was only too happy, as it would not be a drain on his resources. It had been agreed by those who had a much higher pay grade than Jack, that whilst there were two incidents in London the actual criminal, had something to do with the MRC at Porton Down and that was Jacks patch. The low loader was escorted back up to Wiltshire and placed in a sealed off section of the underground garage of Swindon police station. Even though the Commissioner had agreed that all these cases were now linked, he still would not give Jack all the resources he needed. The team he had, was all he was going to get.

Jack opened a letter that was addressed to the Senior CID Officer. Swindon Police. He turned the envelope over in his hands, feeling the flat flash card through the paper package. Taking a small penknife from his pocket and slit the envelope open, tipping the memory card onto his desk. Being careful to handle the plastic covered card, only by its edge. He inserted it into the laptop on his desk. There was a single file with an avi extension to it. After first running it through his virus checker, Jack moved the mouse pointer to the file and double clicked it. Some moments later the video player in his computer, started to play the file.

Jack watched the video for the full 30 minutes. His hands were shaking by the end of it. He copied the file to his computer and then carefully ejected the card, again holding it by the edge replaced it in the envelope. And then took an evidence envelope from his drawer, he signed and dated it in the text box, and then dropped the envelope containing the card, into the clear polythene bag before sealing it.

"Short!"

The young WPC came to his office door.

"Sir."

"Get this over to forensics and tell them, to get whatever they can from it, and I need it yesterday."

The young policewoman took the envelope and went about her duties. Jack called his boss to tell him about it. He knew it was not just a serial killer he was after now. This person committing these crimes, wanted his crimes to be known, by the police. So far there was no ID on either man. This was much different from all the other murders. This pair of murders were up close and personal. It would be impossible to tell just who it was wearing the beekeeper's outfit in the recording. The only thing that Jack now knew about this man, was that he was right-handed. He had swung the bag over the first man's head and dropped the nest on the second man using his right hand. No........that was not quite all he knew. When he thought about it, he knew a lot more than that and almost ran to the incident room.

"Gather round people" he said to the officers.

They left their desks, put down their phones and brought their notepads with them. Jack was a stickler for notes, and he would do these brainstorming sessions, from time to time. The smart people hurried, those that did not would find themselves directing traffic in the Outer Hebrides or something like that. Most of the team respected Jack. He was an old-school cop who got results. Even the criminals afforded him a modicum of respect. Jack turned the page on a gigantic notebook which was sat atop an easel stand and wrote.

'Who is the Waspman?' across the top then under it he wrote 'Someone involved with MRC/CDE Porton Down' followed by 'Right-Handed' 'Expert on Wasps' lives in 'Swindon or London' 'Doctor? Professor? Technician? Pest Controller?'

"Come on people work on it, anyone got any other clues or theories, even if now, you can't prove it?"

"Sir could it have something to do with the Russians? Like the Skripal thing? Asked one of the uniformed officers.

Jack wrote 'Foreign Agents' on the board even though he himself did not think so. It would give the impetus to the others.

"Our own agents? Like MI5 or MI6" again unlikely but he wrote it down

"Someone who was working on some project at MRC and got thrown off. Jealousy, it can be a hell of a driving factor" WPC Short said

"Good now we are getting somewhere" Jack replied and wrote it down.

It went on like that for about 30 minutes and jack had exhausted several sheets of paper.

"Where does he get all the wasps? and all the wasp venom? Surely that can't be an easy thing to do?" WPC Short said again.

"Fantastic point, run with that idea." Jack said to her.

Just at that point, a civilian administrator came in and passed a file to Jack. It had come from the forensics section, with information the video, also with it was a basic profile that someone had done for him. Jack thumbed through it while the other officer threw ideas across the metaphorical table.

"Right listen up. Per the profiler, our man is approximately five feet ten inches tall. Of athletic build and weighs in at around 185 pounds. He has intimate knowledge of Wasps. He is likely to be an educated person. He is probably Caucasian. His motive seems to be revenge or jealousy. I received a video of him killing the last two men. He enjoyed it. There is more than one single reason for him to be doing this and he wants those, who have in his mind wronged him, to know that he is out there and hunting them down. So far, he has used a different method each time. He is not doing this on his own, someone is helping him. Someone other than him, put that container there and before that, they soundproofed it. The dead men were abducted and put in the chamber before the wasps. You do not just go out and get a container. So, there was someone who has access to shipping containers, along with trucks and drivers. Get me the people, who are helping him, and then we will have our murderer" Jack said emphasising every statement.

"I have something boss. A positive. ID on both our John Doe's They are one Doctor Fahad Bukhari. Lives in Aylesbury, Senior Haematologist, and lecturer at Guys Hospital. Also, works on a project with the MRC. Looks like he is some sort of whizz kid. Has written several papers on The Social Yellow Jacket Wasp and Wasp venom. The people in the know stated that he has been nominated for a Nobel Peace Prize, also someone is going to want his body. The Other guy is a Councilman from London. Works on the planning department had something to do with the Docklands development committee. He is well off by all accounts. But I have another version of his life and its mostly criminal, although he was a bit of a Teflon character. Lots of charges and brought to court for extortion with violence, all the charges dropped after witnesses withdrew statements, or witnesses simply disappeared." Burns said.

"This councilman has a name?" Jack asked.

"Yes, Martin Colish Sir."

"Good work people let us see some more results. Because if we do not, this guy will kill again, that much is for sure."

There was no way the Police Commissioner could block his requests for search warrants now. Nor could he stop Jack from asking questions of the civilian staff at MRC. That said, Jack knew he would have to tread carefully around Mike Jons and his two MI5 associates. Jack was not entirely stupid, he knew that fighting the common cold, had truly little to do with the MRC or CDE.   Jack had only been a young officer when there was a legal case launched against CDE Porton Down, for the Murder of a young Airman who had been one of the 'Volunteers' in the testing of Blistering and Nerve Agents to further Britain's strength in Chemical and Biological warfare.

He also remembered the big fuss when some Islanders from the West coast of Scotland, had humped a load of contaminated soil outside CDE and outside the Houses of Parliament. The soil had come from the Island of Gruinard to the West of Scotland. CDE and the ARMY had conducted a test there in 1942 using a form of Anthrax Vollum 14578. The government were embarrassed into cleaning up the island. It took almost 50 years to make it safe for humans and animals again. As such Jack knew that the folks behind CDE and probably MRC were a bunch of sneaky murdering bastards themselves. The Irony of them being murdered one by one was not lost on him. Those that ran the secret establishment, would cover up their mistakes using whatever shady government branch they could.

Jack knocked on the Commissioners door.

"Enter."

Jack did and was not surprised to see The Chief Inspector there along with Jons and another man he had not seen before. The Commissioner waved him in.

"Detective Inspector Hamilton perfect, saves me sending someone to find you. Do come in. I believe you already know Mr Jons of the MRC."

"Yes, Sir we have met." Jack said without giving too much away about his feelings about the pen-pusher who worked for CDE or MRC of MI5 it did not really matter.

"Mr Jons here, has said that we can see the HR documents of all the civilians that work for the MRC, except for the scientists who are currently working of projects covered by the Official Secrets Act."

"I guess that leaves us with some of the typing pool and the coffee boy!" Jack said sarcastically before putting down his folder on the Commissioners desk complete with stills, from the video he had been sent.

"Sir we have a lunatic on our hands, who just happens to be a serial killer. When the press gets hold of this, it will make the Skripal incident seem like a bar fight, on a Saturday night. So far, in the space of a few days we have five dead. Which as far as I can see, is four men from some project called Operation Yellow Jacket! Added to that, there is one other a civilian who we cannot seem to link to anything to do with the others so far. Also, there was another death involving someone else from Operation Yellow Jacket, just over a year ago, bringing the total to six. I have a nagging at the back of my head that says this Doctor James Pearson was the key to all this. So it probably has something, to do with his death. I am just waiting for the results of the PM on his body which will probably show a load of this wasp Venom in his body too." Jack said.

"And if does not? What then inspector?" Jons asked.

"Then his death will probably have been the result of having a house dropped on his head I guess."

Jons seemed a little too cocky in everything he said. The other man seemed to be Mike Jons boss

"If that is all Inspector I will let you to get on with your investigation" The Commissioner said

"And I can run a major incident with a full team?" Jack asked.

"Well, I will have to read through this report thoroughly, before I come to any decision, but I will let you know as soon as I do. Until then carry on as you are doing now. That will be all and thank you." He replied to jack.

Jack stormed out of the room; this investigation was a joke it was as if no one wanted these murders solved. Fuck them. He would solve it, with or without resources. He slammed just about every door he went through, on his way to the front of the police station. Never had he seen the top brass, cow tail to this lot of cowboys up the road. Jack stood next to his BMW and lit a cigarette. He was still smoking it when the Chief Inspector came out.

"I am sorry Jack it's out of my hands. If it were up to me, I would close that shithole at Porton Down. Work with what you have Jack and if I can help you I will. But remember this, like you have your boss, I too have a boss and he is politically minded. Do what you can but please be careful, they might not care about their staff getting bumped off, but I do."

"Thanks Sir, who was the other guy in the boss's office?"

"I am Sorry Jack I don't know he was just introduced to as one of the associate partners for CDE Porton Down, so he probably has something to do with the manufacture of bioweapons or stuff like that. Hence I said be careful."

"I will Sir, thanks for the heads up." Jack replied.

He dropped the cigarette to the floor and crushed it out under foot. After getting in his car he pulled out of the police car park and drove out onto the main road. He had only gone about

200 yards when he pulled over, then reversed back up the road and parked on the opposite side of the road to the police car park entrance. He sat and waited. He did not have to wait long a Range Rover with Jons at the wheel came out and drove off. There was no one else in the car, so Jack waited. A few minutes later bright metallic orange, Tesla Roadster, with black alloy wheels came out of the car park. The unnamed man who was in the commissioner's office, was at the wheel. Jack waited until another car had pulled in behind the Tesla before he pulled out. It was better to have a car between him and this other man. His plan was to follow it to its destination. Being a Tesla Roadster, it was an all-electric car, so Jack assumed that it a had limited range. And a lot though, would depend on how it was driven. As soon as they got out onto the motorway the Tesla moved over to the fast lane. Jack did the same, as did the car between. At one point the Tesla shot ahead, but Jack need not have worried it was just its owner showing off his acceleration. All to soon the M4 motorway joined on to the M25 outer ring road for London and the traffic slowed down. Jack moved over to the middle lane and kept the bright orange sports car in sight. From the M25 they moved into central London and finally to Belgravia.

The man parked his car in a reserved slot outside the German embassy and then entered. He was not checked by security at the main door but went directly inside. Jack wondered if he were a diplomat, yet the car he was driving did not have diplomatic plates. After writing down the number plate Jack returned to Swindon. It was late and he needed to get home, but he had one more thing left to do tonight.

Act 19

The Doctor had also been following the Tesla and with his privacy glass windows on his VW Passat, the German billionaire would not be able to see him. When they had left the confines of single roads around Swindon and out on to the M4 the Doctor had teased the Tesla by deliberately pulling alongside and with its powerful engine, The Doctor had been able to goad the German into a sort of drag race. Even with his high-powered engine in the Passat, the best he could coax out of it was 180 miles an hour. The Tesla had an easy 250mph to hand. The Doctor had dropped back into the normal speed limit of the UK. He had also noticed the BMW as it had followed them both from Swindon. The Doctor correctly thought that it was someone other than himself was following the owner of the Tesla rather than someone following him. So, he had peeled off as soon as they came to the M25. He already knew the man who drove a flash car was, and now he knew where to find him.

Jack made his call to the Motorway Patrol Section, of Swindon Police. He spoke to an old friend and sometime drinking partner. They would often discuss other cases and provide assistance where possible.

"John. I have a car I want pulled and I want it done right. Do you have a pen handy?"

"OK?"

"It's a bright Metallic Orange Tesla Roadster, registration is Alpha Whisky one one one".

"Got it? When and where, do you want it tugged?"

"I am sure he will exceed the speed limit on the M4 just before he gets to the Turn Of for CDE. I need to know just exactly who he is and where he works. Can you do that?"

"How do you know he will speed?"

"I watched a VW Passat goad him last night and he bit. Can you do me this favour John?"

"We have an unmarked Subaru Impreza that we sometimes use. It has privacy glass and big rear wing. I suppose we could goad with that and then clock the Tesla then pull it over. With one of your BMW's"

"Perfect John I am sure there are not many of these bright orange Tesla's around in our neck of the woods. Also, I would like to keep this between us, and nothing recorded. Talk to you tomorrow."

Jack put the phone down and called the office to see if there was anything new. He had not expected there to be so when DC Burns answered the phone he was a little surprised.

"CID DS Burns".

"DI Hamilton. Anything new?"

"Yes, Sir we got the results of the autopsy on Dr Pearson and it makes no sense".

"How so?"

"Well there was no trace of wasp venom, but there is an anomaly."

"What sort of anomaly?"

"Well the body it's not that of Dr Pearson."

"I am on my way back in, DO NOT let anyone else see that report! Got that."

"Yes Sir" Burns said as the call was cut by Jack.

Jack had to call his wife; he always did when he had to work late. It was to stop her worrying.

"Jean I have to work late, leave my dinner in the microwave and I will heat it up when I get home." Jack said.

He had never discussed any murder investigation, he had worked on, not even the Skripal one, although that had rapidly evolved in real time on the TV, thanks to social media. Jean had worried that Jack might get poisoned accidentally, the same was as Detective Sergeant Nick Bailey had, when he was offering his assistance to one of the victims.

"OK Jack, I love you take care." she said and hung up.

Jack headed into the station and picked up Burns and the report before heading over to what effectively was the major incident room. There was still a few folks milling about in there but most of the lights had been turned down. Jack went to his new temporary office with Burns in tow.

"Right, give it to me again son. You are saying that the body we exhumed is not that of Pearson?"

"I am not saying that Sir. That is what the forensics are saying."

"So was there some kind of mix up at the morgue" Jack said knowing that it would not be the first time the wrong body had gone into the wrong coffin.

"Not quite Sir. They buried the body that they found at Doctor Pearson's home. It's just that it was not Pearson they found in the rubble".

"And they are basing that upon what son?"

"Doctor Pearson was called in at the start of the Skripal thing before they thought it was Novichok. The doctor was a toxicologist on our books, so to eliminate him from any crime scene, he gave is prints and a sample of his DNA."

"So, it beggars the question. who in the name of hell did they bury?"

"At this point sir, your guess is as good as mine".

"Right this stays between you and me, at least for now. But remember to book the report in the evidence log."

The Doctor, meanwhile, had parked his Passat in a grossly overpriced long stay car park in Chelsea. He collected the Astra from the same park and drove it to another park, near Knightsbridge. Then he walked to the bus stand and caught a bus to the other end of Brompton Road, before walking back to the Tube station.

By now Mike Jons will have received the letter sent to his home address. The police will also have their copy. They would now be looking either for him, or someone like him. It would be a game of cat and mouse. Two or three people left to pay for their sins. He still had a few people to offer him assistance as well.

He entered the underground home in the same way as he had exited through the tobacconist shop and down the elevator before going into his Laboratory. He switched on the lights.

There were two men standing there. The shorter of the men spoke with a heavy East European accent.

"I believe you are in my house?"

"No I don't think so. Though I think you may be lost. And how did you get in here?"

"Not so my friend, I still have the keys to the front door. I paid the British Government £30,000,000 for this property, Though I have to admit I do like what you have done with the old place. I was thinking about turning it into luxury Apartments and I was going to have a swimming pool and steam rooms down here. But I can see that it would make a perfect secret apartment, especially as you have now cleaned and fixed this part of the station. Tell me did you do this all by yourself and just move in and squat on my property. Or did Ale let you in. I think it was the latter. No matter we shall deal with him later. Now though, you must pay my rent. I think for a Luxury apartment in Chelsea, say £10,000 per month and I think you must have been here for over a year so I will be generous to you. £100,000 and we call it quits then I evict you. What is all this equipment that you have here?"

"I have been making drugs down here, what if I give you a cut?" The Doctor said and swept his hand to all the laboratory equipment.

"What drug is it that you make?" The Ukrainian asked

The Doctor had pitched it right. This man might be a billionaire, but he still wanted more. He probably made his money at the fall mother Russia.

"I don't have a name for it yet, but it is like speed only faster acting. Normally I would inject like Heroin, but the liquid can also be snorted. The thing about my new drug is it lasts for a long time rather than just being a 5-minute hit. Do you want to try some? For free?"

"Why would I need you to give me it when I can just take it and squash you like a bug."

"Because I am the only person making this, and it is essential that the right balance of chemicals are used, or it is useless." The Doctor said

To the blind side of the Ukrainian, he removed the syringe loaded with anti-venom from his pocket. He pretended to fill it from a bottle on his lab table and then offered it to the man. The Doctor was banking on the suspicion of the Ukrainian and his minder.

"The first shot of this is a real killer, it is amazing it takes you to places you have never been before" Jack said.

"I don't trust you. I do not even know you. How about first you inject yourself and then we will see?"

"Sure! I love this stuff."

Jack took off his coat and jacket and then rolled up his sleeve before putting a rubber tube around the upper arm. His lower arm showed what looked like track marks. What it really was, was where The Doctor had drawn his own blood, to test the venom on fresh oxygenated blood, consequently there were lots of needle marks.

Jack found a good Vein and depressed the plunger. He felt the burn of the anti-venom and he felt his heart racing. These were all-natural reaction to this life saving fluid. After 5 seconds Jack pretended, to be semi lucid but high on drugs. Still able to hold a conversation yet supposedly seeing things in front of him that were not there.

Jack picked up another syringe and load it with sterile water, although the bottle was not labelled apart from H20 35ml. He then injected himself and slowly he returned to normal.

"This stuff is the new and best sensation that blows Coke Crystal Meth and Heroin clean out the water. You should try some." The Doctor Said.

"I have to be somewhere later, but Victor likes to get high. Victor will try it and then he will tell me how good it is. If it is as you say, then perhaps we can be future business partners."

Amazingly Victor was only too happy to try. He took his coat which had a gun pocket sewn into the lining. The Doctor could see the butt of a revolver protruding, as he laid his coat on the bench before sitting down. He undid the cuff of his shirt revealing a lot of Cyrillic tattoos and a lot of what The Doctor presumed were prison tattoos. Victors roll his sleeve up revealing a lot of needle tracks, most of which were old, but a couple were new, showing that Victor was using again. The Doctor took a new syringe from a packet and fitted a new hypodermic needle to the end. Next, he drew up 2cc of pure venom.

"Ready" The Doctor said and first looked at Victor and then at the Billionaire. Then back down at Victor's arm, while keeping the butt of the pistol in his peripheral vision.

"Go for it" Victor said.

The Ukrainians eyes were locked on the syringe which was being inserted into the bodyguard's vein. The Doctor depressed the plunger all the way home and the big man's eyes went wide and wild. Still the oligarch looked at his protector's arm. Neither of the men noticed The Doctors hand, snake to the coat pocket and remove the pistol. It was an old-style pistol. The bodyguard was already dead, just he did not know it yet. The Doctor pulled the hammer back on the pistol. And pointed it at the Head of the rich Ukrainian. He did not think about what was going to happen. He just knew he had no choice. There was no safety on this pistol, presumably it had been modified so as there was no delay in its use. The gun exploded; the sound amplified by the tiled chamber that was his laboratory.

There was no real distance for the projectile to travel, as the oligarch moved forward, in a vain attempt to stop the Doctor. From less than one foot, at the same time the flash filled with tiny sparks of black powder burning up. The explosion pushed the lump of lead forward and it penetrated the flesh, on the outside of the oligarch's head. The bullet was busy punching its way through the frontal bone, just above the nasal cavity creating a star shaped hole in the flesh to the front of it. There would be lots of tiny powder burns around the entry wound. The membrane that held the brain together, was no match for a subsonic round fired at such a close range. He may or may not have seen the flash of flame, but no one would ever know. The bullet was slightly misshapen from striking the frontal bone, was now starting to tumble through the soft greyish white material, that controlled this ex-Russian's thoughts and movement. Even as it was being switched off, it would still try to protect itself, sending out messages to other redundant organs of the body. The bullet exited the back of the skull, tearing with it a large chunk of bone with parts of the hairy scalp with the boiled brain and blood. At this range the kinetic energy, caused the Ukrainians feet to leave the floor and moved him almost six feet backwards, where he collapsed on his back.

The Oligarch died a much faster and far less painful exit from this world, than his protector had. The pupils of Victors eyes which had become gigantic as the venom hit his bloodstream, were now so tiny it was almost impossible to see them. His back was trying to separate the individual vertebrae. Victor had put up with a lot of pain in his life. He had lost two toes when someone tried to get information out of him. They had used a rusty penknife to saw through bones. That had hurt they had pulled some of his teeth with mole-grips that had hurt more. He had lost one thumbnail and he thought nothing could equal that pain. He knew now that he had been seriously mistaken on that score, then he too died.

The Doctor looked at the two men lying dead on the floor of his Laboratory. A sudden horrible thought struck him. His friend Ale. Quickly he dialled the number from memory. It was not answered the worst thoughts struck him and then his phone vibrated.

"Who is this that wants me at such an hour?"

"Ale?"

"Doctor"

"Are you OK? Your family?"

"Yes, why do you ask? What is wrong?"

"I think you need to pay me a visit and very soon OK?"

"I will be with you in 10 minutes."

The Doctor hung up and removed the SIM card then broke it and inserted a new one. This had become as natural an act as flushing the toilet after you have used it. 11 minutes later Ale arrived with two big men behind him.

"You sounded like you were in trouble Doctor".

Ale said being deliberately careful not to use the Doctors real name in front of others. Then looked at the two bodies that now littered the laboratory floor.

"The owners came home and wanted to evict me, possibly permanently. I got the drop on him." The Doctor said

"I am sorry I did not know he was in the country, or I would have warned you. But you have also done me a favour my friend as now I can sell all of his properties."

"Won't someone come looking?"

"They might but only him and me, knew which properties he owned, as they were purchased using a lot of fake companies. Hence, they will find nothing. It is good you also took his brother out as well, now no one will miss him. I will take care of the bodies." Ale said and motioned to his hired help to sort that out. Before continuing.

"Stay with my family tonight. My son is home from boarding school."

"Thank you, Ale, I will."

Act 20

Mike Jons got home to his house at 7pm, it was not unusual for him to be that late, put simply it just came with the job. The last year had been worse though. There was now an added pressure to the job. It had been simple when he had worked over the road at CDE, initially he had seconded to the MRC, because one of the geek doctors over there had been working on the properties of Wasp Venom. The powers that be, at CDE Porton Down, had thought, there may have been some mileage in the possibility of a biological weapon, especially when the same Dr Pearson had discovered this enzyme in the venom, that broke down the walls of red corpuscles on a specific cellular level. That alone, would have been worth quite a lot of money, as naturally occurring biological weapon. Then this doctor had managed to get the enzymes to attach themselves to specific cancer cells. Now that made biological warfare a poor man's game, when compared to what could be made from a cancer cure.

Jons had contacted a friend of his in the pharmaceutical industry. He had shown an interest on the region of an initial purchase price of £50,000,000 with a further 10% in stock options. His friend wanted all the data and the copyright. This had been an opportunity far too good to miss.

Now some crazy bastard was wiping out the staff of Operation Yellow Jacket, which played right into his hands. So far, they had managed to get rid of the fool assistant and the Haematologist who had started to write papers, indicating that they were likely to be able to have a cure for cancer much sooner rather than later.

The two men that he had hired as assassins, had done their job efficiently but they had somehow ended up as victims of their own success. Still it had not been a total loss. He had spoken to GCHQ and they would clean up the mess that had been left behind. Mike Johns had already paid £100,000 to his contact there, to ensure that. Mike Jons had no idea who the other man in the container with Bukhari was, probably just someone who got in the way. Still it puzzled him, as to who the hell was behind all the deaths of the Yellow Jacket Team. He had only ordered the death of one man, the buffoon Pearson. He had acted like he was bloody Mother Theresa, wanting to give the cure to humanity.

Jons had spoken to him, even offered him his own laboratory with his choice of assistants and wealth beyond his dreams. He had been willing to accept the laboratory and the team but insisted that this cure, must be given to patients for free. Jons had likened it to offering diamonds and gold out for free to everyone, because it would on devalue pharmaceutical stock making them bankrupt. Jons had tried to convince Pearson that at first, they would have to charge but years down the line it would be almost free, just aspirin. So, there was only one choice open to Jons, steal the work and dispose of Pearson.

That worked fine on paper, trouble was there was one tiny bit of information missing from the equation. Jons had assured the main shareholder, in the German Pharmaceutical firm. That he would be able to crack it, from what Pearson had left behind, along with the notes of Professor Bukhari. All Jons had to do tomorrow was to officially shut down Operation Yellow Jacket. And then resign his position with the oversight committee. After that he would give the German all the data and collect his king's ransom and 10% in shares.

These shares were destined to go from just over £1 a share to probably something in the region of £5,000 a share, not forgetting of course his fifty million in diamonds and bearer bonds. He smiled to himself as he thought about his wealth, he would not just be a millionaire, but probably a billionaire within a short time.

After pouring a large glass of Glenlivet from a cut-glass decanter, Jons sat down in his favourite old leather armchair and looked at the pile of today's mail, that his cleaner had put on the side table. Most of the mail was junk but there were a couple that were not. One was an official letter from his ex-wife's divorce lawyer. That could wait there was no rush for that. The other was a plain white envelope, with a handwritten address. There was a London postmark franking to the front of the envelope.

The Doctor had whilst working at the MRC Porton, been working on various delivery methods to treat bowel cancer. He had looked at freeze drying the Toxin into a powder and then bottling it, before revitalising it with sterile water. Or even as a pill that was swallowed with staged release, that had worked on some forms of Bowel cancer. The only problem with that was people's digestion work at differing rates. In the end, though, he had an almost perfect way for the destruction of bowel cancer cells. It was at this point, that his job had been taken from him and they had attempted to kill him.

The Doctor had so far been unable to identify. Who it was, that seemed to be behind everything? Who was the person who really pulled everyone's strings? How did they have the power to control the MRC? As well as involve crooks like the two men, who had blown up his house? When he found that person, then he would have completed the cycle. The Doctor had followed a man from the MRC at Porton and then to the police station. From there, he had followed him into Belgravia. While they were on the motorway, the guy in the orange car had tried to lose him. Both cars at one point were travelling side by side at over 150mph, then the sports car had pulled away only to be slowed down by the M25 junction. The doctor had then dropped back and followed him, allowing other cars to come between them. It was at that point he noticed the 3 series BMW that also looked to be following whoever it was in the posh looking roadster. The Roadster had parked up opposite the German Embassy, the tall man in an expensive looking suit, got out, crossed the road, and went inside. The BMW slowly drove past before driving off. Was it some security team he had watching his back or was someone else interested in the man with the expensive car? The Doctor would call up the services of one of his ex-patients. This one could take some time.

Jons opened the envelope and emptied the memory card into his hand, before picking up his laptop case and taking out his computer. After powering it up, he inserted the flash card into the side slot of his laptop and clicked on the single avi file, then waited for it to open. He leaned back in his chair and he took a sip of his whisky.

The file played in windows media player and he turned the sound up. At first, he was not sure what he was looking and then he knew only too well. Although he still did not know who the man was, that was being tortured in the video. He continued to watch as the horrific scene played out. He felt the same terror that the man in the video looked to be feeling. The screaming became unbearable and Mike Jons, had to mute the sound. It took around 10 minutes for the man to die a horrible death. But why was the video sent to him.

Then the camera swung around to another man, strapped similarly to the first victim. Jons hit pause. He knew this man, it was Bukhari. Another member of his team murdered! This was the man he had built his hopes of unravelling Pearson's work.

Now he would have to find someone else. There was no way, he trusted that rich bastard to keep his deal, without having a backup plan for other possible clients. He hit play and brought the sound back up. Reaching over to his side table, he took hold of the tumbler of single malt whisky, before bringing it tremblingly to his lips, then taking a deep swig, almost emptying it of the amber liquid.

Act 21

Jack was looking at the board, in the main incident room. There was now a great big red question mark over the picture of Dr Pearson and the same with the blank head shape of John Doe. If Person did not die in the home explosion? Then where the hell was he. In almost 15 months no one had seen him, or even heard from him. His bank account had every penny that had been in it the day of his death, which they had included the £50, that had been in his wallet. His white gold, Rolex watch, was on the body at the scene and that alone had to be worth at least £10,000. His passport was found in the wreckage of his home and his driving license in his wallet. Even his BMW M4 was parked at the kerb, on the day of the explosion, this was now in the police pound. They had missed something, when the had sent in a forensic team. Jack picked up the phone and asked records to send a list of items recovered from Dr Pearson's home.

Burns came into the room.

"We have looked at the prints of the John Doe and it looks like the belong to a young toe-rag by the name of Robert 'Buddy' Friends. He was a part time burglar and full-time drug addict. When he was reported missing about 10 days later, everyone assumed that he had probably overdosed and had fallen in a ditch or something like that. No one thought, to cross refer the prints with CDE/MRC as they would have Pearson's on record in case of accident. We all made the fatal mistake, of accepting the word of a workmate, who we now know as the criminal, Morgan".

"Good work DC Burns, at least that answers one question but throws up a thousand more. Starting with where the hell is Dr Pearson? Had he gone the same way as all the others from the MRC and we just have not found the body yet?" Jack asked.

"That would not fit the pattern Sir."

"Not quite. All the other murders, which we have seen so far, have been highly visible. The person committing them, wants us to find the bodies. There is a message in these murders' son. The sooner we find the answer to that question, then the sooner we find our murderer and put an end to all of this." Jack replied.

They were interrupted by a knock on the door frame and one of the civilian employees of the station, was standing there with an internal manila envelope.

"Yes?" Jack asked.

"Records asked me to bring this up to you".

"Thank you" Jack said holding out his hand.

The woman stood looking at the board and suddenly felt a wave of nausea flood over her.

"Anything interesting in this?" Jack asked, referring to the envelope.

"I have only glanced at the list Sir and yes there was something, that stood out."

Jack looked at her and there was a pregnant pause and Jack realised she was not used to answering unasked non-rhetorical questions.

"And that would be?"

"Computers" She replied

"I never could do the Times Cryptic Crossword" Jack said with a sigh.

"Sorry Sir I meant that there were no computers. He was a scientist, right?" This question had been rhetorical and really did not require an answer, so it got none and she carried on.

"Most geeky people I know, have at least a laptop and a tablet PC plus a smart mobile phone".

"Yes, that would seem to be a logical conclusion." Jack answered this question, for fear of looking like a throwback to the analogue age.

"Well there were none. Not in the house or the car"

"Thank you." Jack said ending the conversation and pulled the three pages out of the envelope, as the woman left.

"How the bloody hell can a civilian typist have noticed that, when the police who worked the scene, not have detected something so blatant as that?"

DC Burns was just about to answer when a look from Jack told him not too.

"Burns find me the dildo of a police officer, who compiled this list and who it oversaw the investigation to the Dr Pearson's 'non-suspicious death'" Jack said while using his fingers to imply speech marks over the words 'nonsuspicious death'.

"Short! I want a complete list of friends and acquaintances of James Pearson from one year before his disappearance and find any old colleagues, who can give us some more information on what he was working on, since he first qualified as a doctor. Next get someone over to the MRC, now we can see their HR files, we might be able to find out, who the hell is next for the chop."

Jacks mind was now racing. Everything was back to front. If Dr James Person was still alive? Where the hell was he? Was he in hiding for fear of his life? Did he see this coming? Or was he perhaps dead and buried somewhere where he could not be found? Jack really needed more resources than he had. Just 12 officers were a joke, for a murder investigation of this level.

They had thousands of officers over the years investigating Myra Hindley and Ian Brady. They had only killed five, not that it diminished things. One murder was one too many in, his mind. Jesus when the Novichok incident happened the Commissioner had put half the force on the job not to mention the team for MI5 and MI6 along with the military. They had sent a top-level team from SIS and from the Foreign

Office and that was over one single death. What pressure was being put on the Commissioner NOT to fully investigate? Was he being controlled by one alphabet soup or another. Something sure as fuck was stinking in Denmark, as Shakespeare had said.

Jons sank back down into his chair, partly in shock and partly in fear. There were others working on Operation Yellow Jacket, but they were just technicians. After Dr Pearson and Dr Bukhari. The next victim could be him. How the hell could this person even get a list on the people working on the project? That information alone was classified as secret. There must be someone working either inside CDE or MRC. Perhaps the leak was from one of the security services? There was a lot of money to be made just for selling information like that. Jons wondered if his contact at GCHQ had sold him out to a higher bidder? That was possible, in fact now it all made perfect sense. Well fuck him, Jons would screw him over for trying to derail his plans. It might cost him a few thousand more than he had already paid him, but it would plug the hole.

Mike Jons picked up his mobile phone and scrolled through the contacts list before choosing the man's number. He listened to the ring tone.

"Hello"

"Do you know who this is?"

"Yes"

"We need to meet, as I have another little job for you."

"I thought we agreed that what I did for you was a one off."

"I know, but this is really important and will benefit both of us. You will be able to retire after this little job."

"What is it you want me to do?"

"Not over the phone, never know who is listening from your workplace".

"Where do you want to meet?"

"Stonehenge"

"Do you mean the stone circle?"

"There is a car park at the entranceway, there will be no one there at night, say two nights from now?"

"How much am I getting?"

"I told you more than enough to retire" Jons replied knowing the man's greed was almost as much as his own.

"Does that retirement have a figure?"

"How does 250K sound to you?"

"See you two nights from now." The man replied and then disconnected the call.

There was no way that he would be paying that much, he would though have to shell out at least another £10,000 for his plan to work.

Act 22

The Doctor, needed to have two men, followed at the same time. That was obviously impossible for him to do alone. Once again, he looked through his little black book. And found the person he was looking for. He dialled the number.

A woman's voice answered.

"What?"

"Do you know who this is?"

"Should I?"

"Perhaps I should call your husband, and share some intimate information?"

"What do you want?"

"I told you at the time, at some point I would require a favour, so do you know who this is?"

"Doctor?"

"One and the same."

"What do you need me to do?"

"I need you to occupy someone's time and steal their phone."

"I am not on the game anymore."

"You are this one last time. And I will send you the details" The Doctor said and hung up.   After sending her a text message, he removed the SIM broke it and inserted a new one. The Doctor had performed an abortion and cured the woman of a nasty case of syphilis. Originally, she had been in debt, through her gambling habit and had been working her way out of it. This was while her husband, who was a Major in the army was serving in Iraq. The gang she was in debt too, had put her in touch with The Doctor. He was not proud of the things he had done since they had tried unsuccessfully to murder him.

The Doctor knew that Jons, had gone through a messy divorce. Mike's wife had taken him to the cleaners. Mike Jons had been messing around with just about every female, who would have him. He had screwed one of the secretarial staff at the MRC and then unceremoniously dumped her, before going out with her best friend. They then had attempted to blackmail him; MI5 had become involved. The two women had been fired from their positions at MRC Porton Down. Jons would have been too, had he not been so necessary to CDE. The Women though, had then carried out their threats and had contacted Jons wife and given her irrefutable proof, by way of an identifying fact about Mr Mike Jons. He had a Prince Albert piercing.

Mrs Jons had immediately set the wheels in motion, for not just their separation but also to remove as much of Mike Jons wealth as was feasible. He had finally agreed that she could have their home in London as well as the small farm they had in the Chiltern Hundreds. She also took 50% of the money and the Bentley. Johns now had the small home that he rented in Swindon and the 4-year-old Range Rover. At the time, he had been seriously pissed off, but his wife was unaware of the £50,000,000 and the shares, which would be due to him. He would soon be an incredibly rich man. He would not be buying a house; he would be purchasing a tropical island.

The Doctor's female contact, followed Jons for a night, just to get an idea of where he would go in his free time. He liked to frequent a titty bar in Aylesbury. Fortunately for her, a lot of lesbians also frequented this night club, as such a single woman in this establishment did not raise suspicion.   The third day she made sure, that she was there at least 30 minutes before Jons. It appeared that the smoking ban introduced years earlier, were not adhered to in this venue. The woman made herself noticeable, wearing a skirt that was closer to a belt and a see-through blouse, that did little to hide the joys that lay below. In her previous life, when she had made her living in the sex trade, she knew just how to get a man like Jons. Flattery, men like him craved it, in the same way as a drug addict craves their hit.

He came in at 9:45pm and went to his usual table which coincidentally was just 2 tables removed from where she sat. The topless waitress came over deliberately flogging her sad and tired tits in his face. The waitress was well passed her sell by date, the cellulite in her thighs were like scars, caused by years of ping pong weight problems.

"The usual Sir? The waitress asked him.

Jons just nodded and took out a silver cigarette case, along with a matching lighter. He made a real show of using these two items, like in some way it made him better than those with the cardboard packet of cigarettes and a throw away clipper lighter. The woman continued to watch as drew deeply on the Dunhill before exhaling the smoke. He laid the lighter on top of the case and scanned the room. He was still scanning the room when his drink arrived. The woman had a practised eye and knew that he had seen her, even though he pretended that he had not. She also knew that he was still watching her, when she vainly attempted to attract the attention of one of the waitresses, that were sulkily walking the room. This was not a high-class joint, it was a place where sexually hard-up men and sometimes women, went to ogle or to pick up a sexual partner. The woman feigned frustration, at not being able to catch a waitress.

It worked as she knew it would, he said something to the ugly tart, that was taking way too long to get his drink, from the tray to the table. The waitress left and then walked to the bar, getting a drink, and then walking directly to the woman's table.

"From the gentleman over there. With his compliments." The waitress said as she laid the drink on the woman's table.

"What is it?"

"A double Gin and Tonic." She said and waited as if she would get a tip.

Sure, the woman could have given her a tip and it would have been. 'Get on home to your grandchildren'. The waitress left and the woman raised her glass to Jons, then sipped the drink. She should have gone on over to his table but did not want to make things so easy for him. She knew that she still had the body and the looks. Her husband was on military exercise in the USA, so would not be home for at least another two weeks so she had time. She stayed at her table while he had a few old slappers come and do lap dances for him. She waved to him and left. She would return in two days' time and sit at the same table as she had been when he bought her a drink.

This time the woman had been to the hairdressers and even bought a new white silky slip of a dress, no bra. She had great nipples and she knew all the tricks on how to make them rise, almost on command. They poked upright against the sheer fabric of the slip dress. She had decided that tonight he might get a little taster and wore no knickers. Even though she had done this, when she worked as a prostitute, she was out of the game now and the feeling of being unrestricted made her feel horny and wet below. This further increased the sensitivity to her nipples; it was like a self-charging phone. Tonight, the man came to her table.

"Do you mind if I sit with you?"

"Please yourself, it's a free world." she replied and moved over as he sat on the bench seat next to her.

He raised his hand and snapped his fingers. Something she had a pet hate against, but she let it slide for now. Another topless waitress came to the table wearing so much make up that the woman feared it would crack and crumble into their drinks when she brought them.

"Gin and tonic?" He enquired of the woman who was holding an empty glass, which had previously contained some expensive tap water.

"Why thank you sir" The woman replied in an overly and exaggerated manner.

"I have seen you in here quite a lot, and I have to enquire what is a beautiful woman doing in a place like this. Sorry if that seems a bit corny."

"My husband is away a lot, so I come and look at people. I find the people that visit this place are far more interesting than most places."

"Men or women?"

"I don't get you?"

"Which do you prefer to watch?"

"Oh, I don't mind. Some are sexy some are not so, but they are all interesting in their own way. Some of them even turn me on." she replied before flipping the question back to him.

"Me? I just got divorced and I come just to look. Its beasts 4 walls and a TV."

"Do you like the sexy ones?"

"I don't know. What is it that makes for a sexy one?" He replied as he lit a cigarette.

She stared into his eyes. She wanted to cause a reaction in the body's chemistry. All her comments were designed to create that throb, as if she had reached out and put her hand over his genitals. She could see she was having a success, as the cigarette trembled in his fingers.

"Well, let's see. Do you find me sexy?" she asked as she crossed her legs letting the silky material flow across her thighs.

She had wanted to remain in control but the excitement of going back to her old trade was making her wet. She sipped her drink and let a small amount spill down onto her white silky slip. The result being that her right nipple was now almost showing through the semi translucent gossamer thin material.

"Oh, my, I seemed to have spilled some" She said while reaching for a napkin.

Jons made like he was a gentleman, though nothing could have been further from the truth. He was a lounge lizard, and she knew it. It removed a white handkerchief from his outside breast pocket.

"Allow me" he said and reached over to dab on the wet spot.

"Mmmmm you would not be trying to turn me on now would you sir?" she asked.

"I might and I would have to tell you that you are a very sexy woman."

She brought her hand up and put it over his. Pressing it in a little harder to her now fully erect nipple.

"You know I am wet somewhere else and that will need moping if you are not careful."

She was telling the truth. Talk about getting enjoyment from your work. She removed his hand from her breast and took his handkerchief, before guiding his hand down below the table and in between her now open thighs. Her hips moved forward as she felt his fingers touch her wet lips and then slide just inside her warm and welcoming vagina. Then she removed his hand and reached over with her own hand and unzipped his fly under cover of the table, before taking his erect member and rubbing it until his breathing told her that any more would cause him to climax. She took her hand away and he looked so sad. Then he put himself away.

"I told you I was turned on by the people in this place" She said.

Then she stood up without even noticing the wet patch on the back of her slip dress.

"Will I see you again?" He asked.

"Perhaps I might come back and complete what we have started, you never know."

"Oh, but I don't even know your name." He said expecting her to give him it.

"That's right you don't. It makes it all the sexier don't you think? Like ships that pass in the night." she said and blew him a kiss before walking out.

He would see her again she knew that, and she might even fuck him. Or perhaps she might make him a little sex slave. The Doctor was pressing her for results. This would be one fun debt to pay off.

Act 23

It was now almost four days since a pair of 'Druids', as they liked to be called, had found the body in the middle of the stone circle. His head had been completely caved in with a rock. He must have been struck multiple times. Such was the damage it was almost impossible to recognise as a human head. Mike Jons had been going to ask a final favour from his contact at GCHQ, when he suddenly realised that this man was the only link that anyone could make between him and what was really going on with Operation Yellow Jacket.

They had initially met in the public car park at Stone Henge and then they had walked and talked. Jons had asked him for inside information on the very man he was planning to sell the Cancer Cure too. His contact had then asked for double what Mike Jons had talked about. Jons had suggested that they walk and talk far away from where they had parked, claiming it was possible that their cars could have been bugged or followed. It seemed a reasonable enough request, especially seeing as how it was a bright moonlit light It was not quite a full moon that would be tomorrow. They walked all the way down to the historic pagan stone circle.

"I want double the figure you talked about. £500,000 or I am not doing it".

"Seriously? I am not asking you to kill anyone. I just want a copy of the file, that you hold on him. Do not pretend that you don't have one. I know for a fact that you have files on every single multi-millionaire that ever sets foot in this country. Especially those that have links to one embassy or another. It is much simpler than last time, just copy the file onto a flash drive and bring it to me. For that one small task I am willing to pay you a quarter of a million pounds!"

He could have agreed to the 500K, but it was the insolence of this peon, who was little more than a pen pusher. There was no way he would let this man jack him. He would find another hard-up civil servant to provide him with the details he required. Fuck him!

"£250,000 and not one penny more" Jons had said.

The man had turned away from him and had started to walk away. It was then that he saw the neon glow from something held in the man's hand. It was either a mobile phone or some other digital recording device. The bastard was setting him up or just recording him, to blackmail him at some later day. He saw a brick sized rock on the ground and instantly he knew what he had to do.

He picked the brick up and slammed it as hard as he could, into the back of the man's head. That one blow was all it had taken to kill the man. He had not seen it coming. His life just went black. The mini digital record unit fell from the man's grasp even before his knees hit the earth below. Jons was in a fury with the man and kept pounding on the back of his head with the rock as he lay on the ground, until all that existed above the neck was just a wet and pulpy mass.

He picked up the recorder and searched the man's pockets, for his mobile phone and car keys. Both of which he put into his own pockets. Using the same rock, he smashed the digital recorder to pieces. Then he walked back up to the car park and used the keys he had taken, to unlock the man's car. As he was searching for it, he suddenly realised he had been covered in blood and other matter, he was now leaving bloody fingerprints and DNA all over this car. He had to get rid of anything that made a link to him. Jons drove the almost a mile away until he found a small side road that went in behind some trees. He parked up and set fire to the car, using his Dunhill lighter to start the fire. When it was well and truly alight Jons walked back to his own car. He drove home using as many side roads as he could and being careful to stick to the speed limit.

As soon as he was home, the first thing he did, was to remove all his clothing and put them temporarily into a large black bin bag. Then he showered and even wiped a mild solution of bleach over his hands and face. He scrubbed his fingernails in 50% bleach. Then wearing a pair of rubber gloves he went to his car and wiped the leather seats and removed the floor mats, adding them to the bag of bloody clothes. Then he power washed the car, inside his garage. He copied down all the numbers from the man's phone and then broke the SIM card before smashing the mobile phone to pieces with a hammer. Finally, he took the black bag with his clothes and the smashed phone along with the mats from the foot-well of his Range Rover, out to the back yard and put them into his garden burner. After pouring Bar-B-Q liquid over the bag he went to light it but could not find his Dunhill lighter so used matches instead. Now all the links to him were literally up in smoke.

Act 24

Jack called a meeting with all the officers, who had anything at all to do with the murders connected with Project Yellow Jacket. He looked at the memo that had just been passed to him by one of the civilian administration staff. Then excused himself from the meeting and passing control over to DS Burns. After driving over to the Swindon station, Jack went straight up to the Chief Inspectors office. He stormed past the Chiefs secretary and barged straight in on the chief. At this moment in time he was ready to tell the chief to shove this job up his arse.

"What's this shit all about then?" Jack demanded as he laid the memo down in front of his boss.

"Good Morning to you too Jack! If you think this was my idea, then you are wrong Jack. This came from the very top and I do mean the bloody top of the tree. As in from the Commissioner, who was given the instruction from the security services."

"I can't believe that any serving police officer would stop investigating the number of murders, that we have in connection to CDE/MRC Porton. You know as well as I do Sir.

All these murders are connected. I promised to obey the laws of this country and to fight crime without prejudice and to do so to the best of my abilities and you took the same oath Sir. This notice to stand down and to shred all documents pertaining to the investigation is an illegal order Sir." Jack said while pounding his fingers on the memo.

The Chief Inspector stood up so quickly that the chair he had been sat on flipped over backwards.

"How dare you tell me how to do my job Jack. I promised I would have your back and I still have it. Don't you think I know the Fucking Law! I know it is a fucking illegal order. Which is why I know, that you, will disobey the order. You have your people over with the fraud squad. I have had a private meeting with their chief inspector and supplied him with all the evidence that you have managed to get so for. He has agreed to second you and the rest of your team to consider the financial aspect of these crimes. When someone at government level steps in to stop an investigation, it can only be for one of two reasons. Money or someone from the crown, is involved in the crimes."

"There is a third reason boss and that would be both the first and second reason combined. So, who do I send my reports to?"

"You don't Jack you keep every bit of information, entirely within your team. I told you before when we can nail some bastard for all of this. Then and only then, do we go in mob handed. Now get the hell out of here before someone sees you. I want you to be invisible. By the way Jack are you and Burns firearms trained and up to date?"

"Yes Sir"

"Then go and draw a firearm. Any problems with the armoury have them contact me just in case I will slip them a memo. Now go before I change my mind and have you locked up, just to save my pension."

Jack left the Chief's office, a little less pissed off, than he had been when he saw the memo, telling him the investigation had been closed. Jack phoned DS Burns and told him to meet to up, at the firearms section. Both men drew out a Glock 17 pistol with full magazines and two spare clips, totalling 51 rounds each. To go with them they signed out what was euphemistically called a bullet proof vest. Both men were also issued with shoulder holsters as well as a belt clip, giving them the option to wear their weapons on the shoulder or hip. Jack also went to the motor pool and signed out an unmarked Skoda Octavia, DS Burns went for a Vauxhall Insignia, also as an unmarked car. Jack left his own BMW in the underground police car park. Both unmarked cars had a Lockbox, in the boot, to keep the firearms in. along with their tactical vests and spare munition. As far as Jack was concerned it was now game on.

Jack had been a good copper all his life he had never broken or bent the rules to get a prosecution. It would seem, the rules of policing, had been changed, by those much higher up the totem pole than him. The rulebook was well and truly out of the window. No reporting up the ladder and keep your records to your team only, that is what his boss had not just implied but had said to him.

The two officers returned to the undercover offices of the Serious Fraud Squad. Jack had always had good relations with his opposite number in the Fraud Unit. Detective Inspector Ron Irvin. He would have to share some of what he had been told by his boss to keep him on side, after all Ron was lending him 8 men along with offering his own services. Now at least he had a task force of 21 experienced officers.

Act 25

The Doctor sat in his car all night long. The Tesla had not moved, since the man had returned here for the second night in a row. He must have either some diplomatic status or was an incredibly important man in Germany. The Doctor knew how he would find out, who this man was. There was a vacant parking space next to the Tesla this morning. The Doctor reversed into the space and waited. 7:45am the smart dressed man came down the steps of the German Embassy in Belgravia. The

Doctor had used his Vauxhall Astra today, as he had played with the Tesla on the motorway in his Passat. The Doctor waited until the man was halfway across the road, to the expensive electric sports car. Then the Doctor started his own engine. The man unplugged his Tesla, from the charge point and was just putting the cable away, when The Doctor pulled out and 'accidentally' clipped the rear quarter of the bright orange sports car.

The Doctor stopped and got out, first looking at the damage to his own old Astra and then at the scrape to the paintwork on the new Tesla Roadster. The cost to repair would probably outweigh the cost of The Doctor's own car.

"I am so sorry, I thought I had more room than that. Of course, I accept all liability." The Doctor said

The German was obviously, seriously upset, there being a 2-year waiting list, to get one of these super-fast electric cars.

"Are you insured?" The Doctor asked

"Yes of course I bloody well am." The German replied indignantly and then continued.

"And what is more it is not my insurer who will be paying, for the damage you have caused. What were you thinking? There was lots of room, for you to get your car out."

"I am terribly sorry I have my insurance documents in the car." The Doctor replied

The Doctor knew full well that, the documents that came with this car, were as fake as his driving license and the car ownership details. The Doctor made a great show of going to his car to get the documents from the glove box. He had forgotten about one of Ale's presents that lay in there, fortunately for The Doctor the privacy glass in the windows, was quite dark so the German never saw the Semi-Automatic pistol, that lay inside the clove box. The Doctor quickly removed the insurance papers and closed the door to his car.

"I will need your name and address for my insurers please" The Doctor said

"Why would you need my details when it is your insurers who will be paying."

"I am afraid it's the law in this country that we both have to exchange details." The Doctor replied. He knew the German could not get his car out of its parking space as his Astra was parked across the back of it."

"Please move your car I am in a great hurry; we will forget about it." The German replied

"I am sorry I can't do that because I always follow the law. If you can't provide documents I shall have to call the police"

"Look here is my card it has my name and address on it. Your insurer can contact me there now please move your car." He said as he took a card from his wallet.

The Doctor took the card and looked at it.

Klaus Tribourne
Tribourne Pharmaceuticals
Buunder Stradt
Berlin
Deutschland

There were two numbers at the bottom one of which was a mobile and the other a landline. Below that was an email and a fax number. So now everything was starting to make sense. Jons had sold him out to this German. He must be incredibly rich and influential to warrant being accommodated at the Embassy. He would be the final link in the revenge. Jons though would be first. The Doctor knew that there was no way Jons could take a project from the MRC without help from above.

After driving away from Belgravia, The Doctor headed for the car park, that contained the VW Passat. From there, he made his way to Ale's home. The automatic gates opened to a sensor in the car and The Doctor drove through. The gates had closed by the time he had made the short drive, to the covered porch-way of his friends lavish home.

When Jack had returned to his team, he called them together, then shut the door of the incident room.

"Right let's get things sorted here. This is what is going to happen and if anyone does not like it they can quit now. But I warn you if you do quit and speak a word to anyone outside of this room, as to who and what we are investigating, then your careers will be over. Please understand that is not un empty promise. So, we are going to be working around the clock and that means you are going to be doing 12-hour shifts. You will not be paid overtime at this point, but I can also promise you this. If we catch the people behind all of this, then you will get it backdated. Now anyone want to quit?. No?.... Good. DI Ron Irvin has agreed to provide us with support, if he asks you to do something then do it no questions asked. We will always work in pairs, unless specifically instructed to do otherwise. Copy down everything we have on those boards and keep them in your folders, which when not in use you will lock away. Let us go back to the very beginning of this mess. DS Burns." Jack said as he passed it over to his subordinate.

"We think that it all started approximately 15 months ago, with the death of a young burglar, Robert Friends or Buddy to his associates. It looks like his death may have been accidental and that the real target, who everybody assumed was the body at the house, was one Doctor James Pearson. We believe he was initially part of a team at CDE/MRC Porton Down. We also believe he was working on a project by the name of Yellow Jacket. Stating the obvious we believe it was something to do with the European Social Wasp, though we don't know exactly what yet. There looks to have been a gap of around a year before the next victims. This was the pair of hired muscle, Arthur Morgan, and Steven Ward. Both these men were well known criminals with ties to the underworld of organised crime. Why they were employed by the government? Again, we still do not know. This pair were killed in a supposed car accident, although we now believe they were stung to death by wasps, in a deliberate act, either before or after the supposed accident. They like Doctor Pearson, had level five clearance, for the MRC labs. The next victim seems to have been one of Doctor Pearson's assistants. An undergraduate by the name of Kevin Brown. He died in extremely mysterious circumstances, while taking the tube, on his way into work. He too, worked on Operation or Project Yellow Jacket. Then we had the double murder down at the Royal Albert Hall. Both these men were killed by wasp stings again. Doctor Fahad Bukhari, he was a professor of Haematology and not only lectured, but he worked at Guys and St James's. For those of you who do not know the significance of them, they are both teaching hospitals. On top of this, he was also heavily involved in this Operation Yellow Jacket. The other man that was murdered was a Martin Colish. Like the first victim he seems to have no actual link, to any of the medical staff working at CDE/MRC or anything to do with Operation Yellow Jacket. We are assuming and until we can prove otherwise, that this Doctor Pearson is probably dead and buried somewhere out of sight. We are sure he was the first intended victim. So, the count is six possibly seven bodies."

"Sarge. What do the MRC say about so many of their staff getting wiped out? We know that the wasp thing they were all working on, has something to do with what is going on. But what exactly is Operation Yellow Jacket?" A Constable asked

"We visited the MRC when there were only three dead and they passed us their Human Resource files but not they did not tell us what was going on, or what the end game of their research is. Knowing what CDE/MRC Porton get up to, they are probably either looking to create a biological weapon of some form or a cure to something. It is possibly even a cure to something they have created. CDE does secret work for our government and for the greater part, most of what they do there is well above our pay grade. That though, does not mean, that you cannot investigate them within limitations. At some point, they will slip up and their lies will begin to unfold. For now, you will tail, who you are told to tail and covertly watch, all the people of have any links to those who have been murdered. You will be given a list of people, who are of concern to us. Please be aware that some of these individuals, may have MI5 or MI6 protection so be careful. Last thing I need is for one of you wooden-tops, getting your heads blown off as a would-be terrorist."

Act 26

A week later she was in the strip club come lap dance bar. Sat at the exact same table as she had been last time they had met. This time she would get the phone from him and possibly even his wallet full of cash. This mark was the easiest she had ever had. She was 100% sure he would be there tonight. She had worked his kind before. They were those that said, they would not sleep with a prostitute, but they always did. Posh guys like him, would wrap it by saying they were picking up the tab for a date or just buying a present, even saying they were just helping out. It all amounted to the same thing. They were paying for sex.

She ordered water on the rocks and waited. Two waters and two hours later he came in and sat down next to her, before ordering two large gin and tonics. She was wearing a leather skirt that had a zip fastener up the front and a skin-tight tee shirt, over her firm breasts. She could feel her nipples starting to harden, just with the thought of what she had in her mind.

"Hi how have you been since I last saw you?" He asked while they waited for their drinks to arrive.

"I've been in here a few times, looking for you?" She replied honestly.

"Really?"

"Yes honestly, I felt a connection last time I saw you."

Their drinks arrived and there was one of those pregnant pauses, where no one really knows what to say.

Jons felt that unmistakeable throb starting deep inside his loins. He wondered if they would fuck tonight. Or if they would just play with each other? He was not sure, how to playthings, she seemed to be able to take the lead. One of the dancers, came over to their table and started to gyrate in front of them. The dancer's hands moved up and down her thighs, before rubbing over the outside of the incredibly small thong that she was wearing, then moving on to the next table.

"What do you think?" The woman asked.

"About?"

"Her dancing?"

"It was OK I guess; I can't say I am an expert" Jons replied.

"Well I thought she was shit. It never turned me on."

"Oh" He replied and then instantly thought. What a fucking stupid answer

The woman looked at the dance floor where couples were dancing to the overly loud disco and then she knew how to catch this fish, hook line and sinker.

"Wanna dance?" She asked.

"Well I don't really dance. I have two left feet." Jons replied.

The woman pulled the zip on her skirt up, just to the point below her naked vagina, allowing him the fleeting glance of what might lay in store for him, before pulling the zip back down.

"Well OK if you insist" He said. With the simultaneous throb in his boxers

"Wait here, I will be right back." With that she quickly went over to the DJ's booth. She spoke with the man behind the decks and he nodded. She returned to their table and took his hand, guiding him towards the dance floor. Just as they got there 'Je t'aime moi non plus' started to play. He started to dance, about two feet from her. He was right, she thought to herself 'He could not dance'. She moved to him and put her arms around his neck and pushed her groin against his. It did not take long for him to become fully hard. Keeping one hand on his neck she reached between them and rubbed him through the material of his suit trousers. On the darkness of the dance floor she slipped her hand down the waistband of his trousers and inside his boxer shorts, before pulling the foreskin of his penis over the glans. She gave it a squeeze and then removed her hand. The song finished all too soon and they walked back from the dance floor. He kept behind her all the way back to their table, for fear that others would see the erection he was now sporting to the front of his trousers.

When they were seated once again, they finished their drinks and talked some more before she suddenly said.

"We should fuck!"

"When?"

"Well sooner rather than later, as it would be a real shame, not you use that hard on of yours. Have you ever fucked naked outside? Where you might get seen by someone?"

"No I don't think so, unless you count in a car when I was a teenager?" he replied.

This was not something his ex-wife would ever do. She had been a straight-laced person. When he thought about it, she had made him that way too.

"Come on drink up, lets blow this joint, and find somewhere to have fun. Do you have your car with you?"

"Yes, but we should take a taxi, as I have had a couple of drinks." He replied.

"Can't do what I am thinking of, in a taxi" She said as she unzipped her skirt completely revealing under the cover of the table her nakedness below.

She reached down and inserted two fingers and then withdrew them, before touching her fingertips to his lips. He opened his mouth slightly and let his tongue taste the sweetness. His penis throbbed automatically.

"OK! Yes, I have my car, it's in the car park." He replied and they left the club.

As soon as they were in his car, she unzipped her skirt completely before opening his trousers and pulling his penis from his pants. They were sat in the car park with their sex organs exposed.

"Let's go" she said.

"Where too?" he stammered.

"Just drive let's go to the countryside. I love fucking under the moonlight or even better in the rain" She said and directed him to go left at the junction. He started to put his member away.

"No leave it out" It is more fun that way.

Every now and then she leaned over and took his manhood into her mouth just to keep him engaged on the thought of a good fuck.

She had parked her own car almost ten miles down the road and got a taxi to the club. She knew how this night would end. She would have her pleasure and she would get what The Doctor Wanted. Nine miles from the club, she directed him to an empty lay-by. As soon as they were parked up she completely removed her skirt.

"You need to take your trousers off" she said to him.

Jons removed his shoes and socks before removing his trousers and underwear. He was excited beyond belief. This was a sexual high, that he had never experienced before.

"Now your jacket but keep your shirt on."

"Why keep my shirt on?"

"You will see" The woman said as she unbuttoned her flimsy blouse.

He did as she had instructed. She ran her hands up and down his thighs before cupping his balls in her hand and leaning over from her seat and guiding his penis into her mouth.

"Ohhhhh my God" He moaned as she moved her head up and down.

She knew from having worked previously as a hooker, just how close she could take him to climax and she did several times. She knew his balls would be aching so bad, they would be wanting to explode in their sack. She removed him from her mouth and licked the tiny amount of cum from the eye of his penis.

"Let's go somewhere else" She said.

"OK Where?"

"Further down the road."

He started to put his clothing back on and she stopped him.

"No! It's more fun naked, besides what people will see is a driver in his shirt sleeves." she said.

He did exactly as she had asked him to do. Driving out from the lay-by, he noticed she was fingering herself and thrusting into her hand. Christ, it was so hard to drive with her sat masturbating next to him. He realised he was only driving at 5 miles an hour, especially when a car came up behind them and honked their horn before overtaking and driving off into the distance. She was moaning and her whole hand, was almost buried inside her. Suddenly as he was driving she screamed and climaxed. He throbbed and a new drip of sex formed on the top of his penis.

"Over there, pull in over there. Next to the picnic table, park beside it." she commanded breathing heavily from her exertion.

When he was parked up, she opened her door and got out of the Range Rover. She left the door open and in interior light from the car spilled out on to her. She hitched herself up onto the wooden table and it felt cold and damp beneath her naked buttocks. Spreading her legs apart so he could see, she said.

"Lick me dry".

He went to slide over her seat and out of the passenger door and she stopped him saying.

"Out your door and walk around to me".

"But someone might see me naked in the headlights".

"They might and they might not. That is the excitement, of doing it in a semi-public place."

Again, he did as she asked, and no car passed. Next, he knelt on the gravel in front of he and buried his head between her thighs. He started to lick her wetness. She thrust into his face and he forced his tongue deeper and deeper inside she screamed again and grabbed the back of his head then she climaxed he felt it he tasted it. He did not even care about the gravel cutting his knees. She commanded him to take his place on the picnic table and took him in her mouth and then in her hand and brought him to the greatest climax of his life. Then she jumped naked into the passenger side of the Range Rover, locking the door behind. Then she slid naked except, for her unbuttoned blouse, over to the driver's seat, before locking that door as well.

Jons lay back on the table, covered in his own climax, unsure if this was just another of the woman's games. That was until she turned the ignition on and raced out from the lay-by. Unsure what to do now? Then he realised, that being found naked and covered in the biggest cum that he ever had, would look perverted to anyone who might come by. He moved to the other side of the table and crouched down. He could see that she had stopped his car about a quarter of a mile from him. He saw that the internal light had come on. What did she expect him to do? To walk down the road naked until he got there. Then what would she just race off again?

She had pulled up next to her own car and after putting her clothes back on, searched through the pocket of his jacket. First, she found his wallet, which she opened and took out the £250 that was inside, then she wiped the wallet down, using his silk handkerchief. From another pocket, she removed his mobile phone and then wiped her prints from around the inside of the car and from the door handles as well as the car keys which she placed on the driver's seat. She got out of the car and walked to her own car. And got in then drove off into the night.

Jons could see that his car was not moving and keeping behind the hedgerows as much as he could, he made his way along the road towards his Range Rover. At one point a car came along and he had no choice except to crouch down in a wet and muddy ditch. The car slowed and stopped by his car for a moment before it moved off into the distance Then he saw another set of lights moving away from his car. The realisation of what had just happened to him suddenly struck home. She had made a fool of him. The saying goes that there is no fool like an old fool, proved to be right on this occasion.

Finally, he got to his car and quickly got in the passenger door and pulled it closed behind him and the interior light went out. Thank God, he said out loud. Quickly as he could he dressed himself. It had been a lot easier to get naked in a car, than it was to get dressed. The car keys were in a parcel made from his handkerchief. He picked them up and slid behind the steering wheel.

A sudden thought hit him. Christ! His level five pass! If that fell into the wrong hands, he would be more fucked, than he was at this moment. He took the wallet from inside his jacket before flicking it open. The pass was where it should have been, behind the plastic window. Using his thumb, he opened the section of the wallet, where his money should have been, empty! Well he figured that would have happened.

Checking his other pocket, his iPhone was missing, no matter it was secured by his password and he had all his stuff backed up on a cloud server. He knew he had been fucked over by this bitch. Still, better that he was not caught fucking her in public. That would have cost him his job for sure. His contact in the European Parliament, would have dropped him that much was for sure and that would have killed, any deal he had with Klaus Tribourne. That man would have just bribed any replacement that MRC, would have for Jons.

Act 27

The woman drove all the way down to London and then called the number she had been given.

"Yes?"

"I have it where do you want to meet?"

"Meet me in Hyde Park station in two hours near the news stand" He said and hung up.

Then he completed his housekeeping breaking the SIM and throwing it away along with the single use burner phone. Two hours later he was standing by the news stand, when she appeared, the only problem was there were two uniformed officers behind her. She cannot have been so stupid, as to get caught then then to give him up. Like his friend Sergi, The

Doctor had let it become known, if you fail to pay your debts or cross The Doctor, then you would pay the ultimate price. By now those that owed The Doctor, knew what had happened to Mark Colish. The TV and Radio had said, he had been violently murdered with another man in London. Almost no details of how the murders were committed had been leaked to the press. This was Jacks effort, to stop any kind of false claims or even copycat murderers. Those who The Doctor had helped and were on the wrong side of the law, they knew just what had happened.

The Doctor turned away from her and walked to the opposite side of the tube passageway. She moved towards him and the two policemen carried on walking the other way.

"Don't worry so much Doctor, they were nothing to do with me, I am not that stupid".

"Good. Do you have what I asked for?"

She passed over the phone.

"We all square now Doc?"

"Yes, the debt if cancelled".

"You know if you ever get lonely? I can help with that, no charge".

"Thank you, but I think it would be best if you kept yourself for your husband. Bye"

The Doctor walked away from the woman and she walked back, the way she had come.

He dialled the number from memory.

"Sergi?"

"You know who this is?"

"Yes Of course"

"Hypothetically speaking. If I had an iPhone do you know of someone who could hack into it?"

"You know that even the FBI, have failed to crack Apples security code?

"I don't care about the FBI. I am asking you?"

"Can I call you back?"

"No I will call you, how long?"

"Give me one hour, OK?"

"OK" The Doctor Hung up.

After he had completed his cell phone housekeeping, he made his way back to Brompton Road. One hour later the Doctor put a new SIM card into his less than smart mobile phone and called Sergi again. After two rings, it was answered.

"Sergi?"

"No who is this?" A man with a Liverpool accent answered.

"He was expecting my call, tell him his Doctor is holding for him."

"He is a bit tied up at the moment" The man with the Liverpool accent who then hung up the phone.

Immediately the Doctor removed the SIM Card and snapped it in two before inserting a new one from his vast collection. Then he dialled his friend.

"Ale"

"Yes, my friend how can I help you?"

"Come to my home please" Then the Doctor hung up and discarded yet another of his SIM Cards. He was not even sure if his friend would be able to help him in this, but he had to try. If only because things could lead back to him. If they led to him, then there was a chance, that they might lead to Ale. That was something that he could never allow to happen. This new action might possibly mean, adding more people to the number of deaths, since he had first set out on his path of vengeance. He filled a small plastic bag with freeze dried and powdered wasp venom. It just looked like any other of tens of thousands of other white powders, including those used for recreational purposes. Then he waited for Ale to arrive.

"Hello, my friend" Ale shouted from the landing way above the laboratory.

The Doctor had seen him arrive in his big yellow Humvee, as he had driven past the station and then he had watched him walk in through the tobacconists and followed his travel on the security monitors, until he entered the Lab.

"Ale, I need your assistance to help a man like you, who has been of great use me. He is not a good man; in fact, he is probably one of the worst criminals in London."

"James I will ask no details; other than the ones you feel necessary for my help. What is it that you need?"

"I think, even though I am not sure, that I need men with guns." James replied.

"If you are in danger here James, I can protect you inside my home. I have a room under the garage. Just in case someone should come for my family. Without you I would no longer have a son as the Spanish would say "Mi casa es tu casa""

"I thank you, but it is not me that requires protection at this point. If I tell you who it is, and we do this thing to help him. He would be deeply in your debt. From what I have learned over the last year with London's subculture of crime. He would be a good friend to have."

"James does this man have a name?"

"Yes Ale. It is the Russian, called Sergi, do you know of him?"

"This is the man who runs the sex clubs and young girls?"

"Yes, that is him. I know under normal circumstances, you would never help a man that is as depraved as this, but he was in the process of helping me. If the person he was going to use says anything, then I fear I may be uncovered,"

"You are right James. I know this man and I do not want anything, to do with him but I can get you help. How many men and what sort of help do you require?"

"I don't know perhaps eight and with guns, can you help?"

"Can you give me some time?"

"From what I think, I do not think he has much time left available to him."

"Can you give me 10 minutes, if so I can help?" Ale replied.

The Doctor nodded and Ale made a call. Talking rapidly in English interspaced with Filipino.

"There will be two vans at the front of the tobacconist in five minutes. James be careful. Because I do not like what this man does, I will not come with you."

James thanked his friend before running up the steps to his lift, which would take him to street level and the rear of the tobacconist shop. The Doctor exited and few seconds later two silver Ford Transit vans pulled up. The side door of the first one opened and a man indicated he should travel with them. There were four armed men in the back and a driver in front,

"Where too?" the man asked with a Middle Eastern accent.

"The Cossack Club, do you know where that is?" The Doctor Replied

"Sergi's?"

"Yes."

The man then offered The Doctor a bullet proof vest along with an Uzi Sub Machine Gun, which was loaded with a long clip. The Doctor was also given two extra clips by the man. The Uzi had duct tape around the pistol grip. He was also give a black ski mask. All this happened in a matter of seconds. The Doctor slipped the vest over his head and the man sat next to him, closed the Velcro fastening on the side, before showing The Doctor where to store the spare magazine clips, in the vest pockets. The other men in this van were already dressed in their tactical vests and ski masks, they also wore gloves.

Both the vans sped through the streets of London. The Doctor knew that at some point both vans would be torched, to get rid of any incriminating evidence. The skills he had learned since they had kicked him out of Project Yellow Jacket, were not the skills that you would write on any résumé. He had learned how to kill using his work. He was now learning how to kill in a much more direct way. This was the way that London's criminal underground fixed problems. The Doctor knew what Sergi's men looked like and told the man in the van. He was in who in turn used a walkie talkie to tell the other van. They pulled up at the entrance to the alleyway. The way that they had parked nose to tail they blocked anyone being able to see beyond the vans. The man who seemed to be in charge produced a suppressor and fitted it to The Doctors gun before doing likewise to his own. Most of the men had guns though some seemed to have long machetes.

"Ready?" He asked The Doctor who just nodded.

Act 28

The Doctor, who previously would have shied away from crime and violence, was now leading a group of unknown gangsters into the Cossacks club. The fact that a Liverpudlian, had answered the direct line to Sergi and when asked to be put through, then he had then made joke about Sergi being tied up. The Doctor knew Sergi and when unavailable his assistants reply would have been for Sergi to call back. To which The Doctor would have said no. But that was not the way it had gone down. The Doctor might be overreacting and if he were, well then, he would apologise.

The camera over the side door to the Cossacks Club, was broken and lay on the floor, next to the trash cans. The Doctor remembered the last time he had been here, Sergi had a big guy sitting at a table just inside this doorway. He tried the door handle, it gave easily. On the plus side of things with the camera down, no one upstairs in the club, would be able to see the men outside. The Doctor carefully opened the door just enough to see inside, Sergi's doorman was laid at the bottom of the stairs. His blood was already congealing and turning black. The Doctor went in and felt for a pulse, there was none, and the body was already cold to the touch. Several of the armed men followed him into the entrance chamber.

He could hear muffled sounds, from upstairs, talking mixed with music. The Doctor climbed the stairs being cautious not to make a sound. There were now 9 men lined up in a snake fashion, on the stairs. The door at the top was open and ajar, The Doctor eased it open, enough to clearly see his friend Sergi, with his hands nailed, to the solid wooden top of the bar counter. There were four other men in the room, one behind the bar. Three sat at a table, with what looked like brown packages of drugs in front of them. Another man stepped into view, he seemed to be the one in charge. He walked over to and put a gun to the side of Sergi's head. The Doctor was not an expert on firearms, but it looked like some kind of revolver to him. The man who had kitted out The Doctor, moved him back from the doorway.

"How many and where are they?"

The Doctor told him what he had seen, then the man moved to the front and that made the doctor second in line. The leader signalled by a series of hand and finger motions, that three men, should go back down the stairs and go to the main doors of the club and come up that way. The leader of The Doctors group kept looking through the crack in the doorway. The Doctor wanted to rush in, but the leader held him back.

Then the others must have come up unchallenged and had given a signal of some form to the leader because he rushed through the door and instantly shot the man holding a gun to Sergi's head The Doctor was second man in and went to point his gun at the table where three men sat. There was a sudden tug to his right shoulder, that sent his Uzi spinning out of his hand and flying to the floor. The Doctor flew backwards and struck the door frame and then the floor. The sudden pain and the realization that he had been shot, came as a surprise. That surprise was superseded by a sudden bolt of pain that travelled all the way down his arm. Then came a searing heat like he had been burned. The Doctor knew that was his body sensing the sudden damage. Two men jumped in through the doorway and positioned themselves in front of The Doctor as a human shield. There were two short bursts of suppressed automatic machine gun fire and all three men at the table died in the blink of an eye.

The first man who had been shot was laid up against the front wood panelling of the bar. The man behind the bar had his hands in the air. Two of the team, that brought The Doctor, then went to the aid of Sergi. They managed to free his hands from the counter. Sergi had not seen The Doctor get shot, as he was facing the other way when The Doctor had entered, consequently he was completely unaware of who had come to his assistance. Nor did he even know at this point, that The Doctor was the man who was down on the floor wounded. Even when he turned inwards to face the room he was still unaware, because of the two gunmen who were shielding The Doctor.

"First I must thank you men even if I do not know who you are, or why you are here. I owe you all. And when Sergi owes you, he pays his bill. I am guessing you are not police because you shot and killed these men, except for him." Sergi said, whilst pointing at the one live intruder and then he continued.

"So please tell me who you are and how did you know I required a little assistance?"

The two men who had been covering The Doctor, helped him to sit up against the wall. They then parted so that Sergi could see him. The Doctor used his left arm to remove his black ski mask.

"Doctor? What are you doing here?"

"I called earlier and a man with a Liverpool accent answered the phone. When I asked to talk to you, he said you were tied up and said you would call back. You know I only use a SIM card once. So, you would not know which number to call back on. Also, I know you only employ fellow Cossacks in your affairs."

"Da you are a smart man I think, but where are my manners Doctor. You are wounded?"

"Yes, I am afraid so and I don't think I can fix this myself."

"I have a friend Doctor; she is a Vet, and she looks after my dogs and horses. She will ask no questions. Besides before you came along she used to treat my men when they were wounded. But I should tell you she is one ugly woman. I think before she was a vet, that she was a tank driver in the Ukraine army." Sergi said as he walked to where The Doctor was on the floor.

"Tell me Doctor? These men? They are your men?"

"No Sergi. They are from a friend of a friend. What about your hands Sergi?" The Doctor asked looking at the holes through both of Sergi's palms.

"It is just a minor scratch and will heal with Vodka. I think your friends should go now; I will look after you. The less people here the better I think." Sergi said.

"What about him?" The Doctor asked

"Him? Oh, he will be my good friend".

"Really?"

"Yes, I think so, because he wants to live so he will talk."

The Doctor nodded to the leader of the men that Ale had arranged for him and then he passed the Uzi that had fallen from his grip, back to the leader. Then he and his men left, leaving just a lot of dead men and one very terrified prisoner, who they had tied up before they left.

"I am sorry about your doorman, they killed him I think before they managed to get to you" The Doctor said.

"It is sad yes he was a good man, first now though I have to make a phone call to remove the bodies and then I will take you to my vet, yes?"

"OK I do not think I am in danger of dying, but if you could make it sooner than later. Some of their team, had to come in through the front doors and they may have been seen by the public. It would not be a good time to have an inspection of you premises."

Sergi helped Doctor into a chair and then made a call. Five minutes later six fellow Russians appeared with rolls of carpet. They laid each dead man down and rolled them up before carrying them down the stairs into the back of a large van that had reversed down the alley way. They took the dead doorman and carried his body with some respect. Then they proceeded to clean up most of the blood. A short while later another smaller van came and removed Sergi's prisoner. Finally, Sergi helped the Doctor down the rear stairs and locked up before helping The Doctor into a black BMW X5 with full privacy glass.

"Where to boss" The driver asked in what sounded like a Polish accent.

"To my stables and don't break any laws on the way there."

"I am sorry for bleeding over your white leather" The Doctor said

"Do not worry it will be reported stolen tomorrow and found burned out later in the day." Sergi said and then continued.

"Once again Doctor I owe you my life. It seems to me that you are collecting favours with me".

"As you said before, it is better to have Sergi owe you, than for you to owe Sergi" The Doctor said and closed his eyes.

He tried to block the burn that seemed to swell with every bump or turn in the road. He must have passed out from the pain, because the next thing he knew, was when he was in a soft king sized four poster bed with crisp white linen sheets. A woman was sat at the bedside taking his vitals and there were drips going into each arm. The Doctor tried foolishly to sit up and blacked out almost immediately. The next time he came too, Sergi was sat in a chair next to his bed.

"Ahhhhhh it seems you are not quite dead then." Sergi said.

"Where am I?"

"Safe, that is all that matters for now".

"I need to make a phone call and I need a clean SIM to do it with, please Sergi it is really urgent."

"Wait I will go and get one."

Sergi returned a few moments later with a cheap burner and a new SIM. The Doctor dialled Ale's number from memory.

"Hello, you know who this is?"

"Yes. Are you alright I heard you had some damage?"

"Yes, it is true there was some minimal damage, I am being looked after by a friend like you. My friend and I, thank you for your help in this matter, I will be in touch with you soon."

"OK. That is good. Talk soon my friend" Ale said and hung up.

As soon as he had finished he removed the SIM and then broke the burner phone into two pieces.

"You have learned a lot over the last year Doctor. Keep this up and you will live some time yet." Sergi said pointing to the now broken phone.

Just then the young woman, who had been sat beside his bed, when he woken the first time, now came back into the room.

"Ahhhhhh your doctor is here; Doctor meet my animal Doctor. I will leave you to her tender care for now and will check in on you later." Sergi said and left the room.

"Doctor what is in the drips?"

"Saline and Dextrose, as I did not know your blood group. There is only muscle damage the bullet went clean through and managed to miss all the bony areas. You were damn lucky, you lost a lot of blood, as it hit a large vein but fortunate none of your arteries. I have cleaned and stitched you up. I used a wide spectrum antibiotic just in case. You should get as much rest as you can and allow the fluids do their job. It will help you build your strength back up. I will return in the morning to check on your health." With that the Dr left the room.

Sergi returned and closed the door behind him before pulling his chair next to The Doctor's bed. The Doctor noticed that Sergi's hands were now bandaged,

"Do they hurt much?"

"No, my friend, not so much I think as your shoulder. Did your parents fail to teach you, lie on the floor when the bullets are flying?"

"Very funny Sergi. When I was a child, growing up we did not have bullets flying around our neighbourhood. I would not normally ask, but what happened at your club?"

"It was a slight misunderstanding, about who can sell drugs in my clubs. They wished to move in on my business and when I did not agree, they then decided that they would steal my business. They would have succeeded had it not been for your actions?"

"What of the men who died, can you dispose of them safely?"

"I will not dispose of them Doctor. I will send them back as a message." Sergi replied.

The doctor knew what that would probably involve in some butchering skills? So, he did not press further on that aspect. However, there was one man left alive, who had seen everything that had transpired in Sergi's club.

"And the man who saw my face? The one who surrendered" The Doctor asked, realising that his was the only face of the gang who had rescued Sergi, that the man had seen.

"He will be a useful man. Because he will want to tell me lots of things, that I now need to know. Do not worry, he will not be telling anyone about you. Now once again I am in your debt."

"I did not do it for that reason Sergi. I did it because when I needed help, you were there for me."

"Doctor we should stay here for a while, because someone called the police after seeing men entering my club with guns. Whilst the police might not find any bodies, they might find some bullet holes as I did not have time to sort that. It is a good thing that we left when we did. So, I will get my alibi sorted and I will come back and see you later." Sergi said as he stood up.

"Now eat your food." with that he left The Doctor alone in the room.

Act 29

"Sir I have just had a report from London about some form of a gang fight in a Russian club."

"And just what has that got to do with our case?" Jack asked of his DS.

"Well sir they found quite a lot of blood and bullet holes" Burns said and then continued.

"The Met Serious Crime Squad, sent off the blood to forensics and it came back with a hit on one of our suspects."

"OK give it to me." Jack said now slightly more interested.

"Dr James Pearson."

"Say that again?"

"Pearson Sir, there was quite a lot of his blood there".

Jack stood up and put his Jacket on and started to leave their incident room, in the office block.

"Well what in the hell are you waiting for let's get going?"

"Where to Sir"

"Your bloody Russian Club come on Burns get a bloody move on. We can call the Met on our way down there. Bring his file with you." Jack said as he left the office.

The Metropolitan Police after telephoning Sergi, sent a car to collect him. Sergi in turn had phoned his lawyer, who arrived at Sergi's house before the police. On the advice of his Lawyer Sergi had removed the bandages from his hands and stuck plasters over the holes before putting on a pair of leather gloves. He had then dressed as if he had just been out for a ride on one of his horses. When the police arrived, they told him that they had a search warrant for his club and that he and his lawyer should accompany him back down to London.

Upon arrival at his club there were two squad cars and a police van already there waiting. Sergi passed the front door key you the detective who unlocked the door and they all went up to the club. Sergi and his lawyer went behind the bar and both men had a drink, letting the officers get on with their job. It was just minutes before they found bullet holes. And then blood. At that point, the Metropolitan police removed Sergi and his Lawyer back out to the squad car and called for a full forensic team. Sergi and his Lawyer were taken to Scotland Yard Police station and placed in an interview room. They had only been there about twenty minutes before two plain clothes officers came in with a thick bundle and sat down at the table.

"Well well Sergi. It has been some time since we last saw each other, I believe the last time was when there was a turf war going on between the Russians and the Armenians." The taller of the two officers said.

"I seem to remember my client being totally exonerated, from all charges pertaining to that incident." Sergi's Lawyer replied and then said.

"Unless you have any new evidence to do with that, I can see no reason for you to question him on it. As that could amount to harassment."

"It was not a question, only an observation and your client was only exonerated as all the witnesses withdrew their statements." The officer replied.

"Again, my client had nothing to do with it as he was Grouse Shooting in Scotland at the time of that incident."

"Sergi, where were you this afternoon, specifically at 3pm" The officer asked.

Sergi and his Lawyer whispered together.

"I was at home."

"Can anyone other than your family attest to that."

"My vet came and had to destroy one of my horses, which had broken a leg. They will be able to confirm that" Sergi replied, knowing full well that as soon as he had got home he would require an alibi and as such he had immediately arranged one with his vet.

"Check that out" the tall officer said to his subordinate.

The officer left the room and returned ten minutes later and whispered in the ear of the taller one before sitting back down at the table.

"There looks to have been some kind of gun fight at your club. I don't suppose you would know anything about that?"

"My client knows nothing of what has happened at his club and had already provided you with his alibi."

"I am told that there is always one of your people at the club, and we have video of a brewery delivery at mid-day. Hence, we would like the name of that employee."

"My client would have to check his roster".

"We found a lot of blood near the back exit; can you explain that."

Sergi and his lawyer whispered again.

"My client was at his farm so has no knowledge of this".

Sergi completely denied everything, and with a rock-solid Alibi there was little the police could do. This is the way the questioning went on for about an hour before they were let go. Sergi and his lawyer headed back to the farm. Unbeknown to him the police had collected blood samples for DNA comparison. This did not worry Sergi as he had never given a DNA sample and he was sure that the blood of those men who had been killed, would lead to the gang members in Liverpool. Their associates would of course deny any knowledge of their activities. Especially as Sergi had arranged for their body parts to be delivered back to their families. The real problem was The Doctor. Sergi assumed incorrectly, that The Doctor did not have his DNA on file. However, his DNA had been collected during the Skripal incident and was on record at CDE/MRC. Sergi never even thought that the blood spilled at his club would be of interest to The Doctor. Normally the Doctor asked no questions, he just went with the flow. Besides the Doctor would be safe at Sergi's home. The only people who knew he was there, were the Vet and Sergi's family. None of his staff, knew who the guest in the granny flat was, and they have been barred from entering it. They were also smart enough to know never to ask any questions about Sergi's personal life.

Jack and DS Burns arrived at Scotland Yard and as soon as they had shown their credentials they were taken to the

Organised Crime Unit. Jack was shown into the Chief Inspectors office. They sat and waited for the senior officer to arrive. Some 15 minutes later the door opened and a man in a business suit entered.

"Hello to you I am Chief Inspector Randall of the Organised crimes unit. I understand that you have an interest in one of our crime scenes."

"Yes Sir, I am Detective Inspector Jack Hamilton, and this is DS Burns. We are both from Swindon and are currently investigating the possibility of a serial killer with multiple sites including two sites her in London. That would be the Royal Albert and the Tube station murders."

"I thought the tube station was a heart attack of some form?"

"That is the story we put out to stop the nutters calling and claiming to be the serial killer. The same applies to the Albert. These murders are linked, to the murders in Swindon. We initially thought that there was another victim at least until one of your officers flagged up the DNA records of Doctor James Pearson, earlier today. We really need to talk to Dr Pearson."

"Is he your murder?"

"Let's say the jury is out on that, there is nothing in his past to suggest that he is, however he is definitely a person of maximum interest to us."

"Surely if there are three murders in London it would be the Met Murder Squad leading the investigation."

"That would normally be true sir but as the first three murders were committed in Swindon means he is technically our serial killer. For political reasons, which I still cannot figure out my boss has been basically told to back off and as such we do not have an official serious incident team. I have been working with your Murder Squad and with British Transport Police. We moved all the bodies to Swindon Mortuary in order that they can compare their findings. What I can share with you, is that apart from two of the victims, who turned out to be unsavoury characters. The rest of them worked at CDE/MRC Porton Down. Further to that, we know they were all working on something called Project Yellow Jacket. Again, we can't be sure because CDE likes to keep secrets. What we do think, and this is quantified by what our ME, on examination of all but one of the bodies, is that somehow, they were all killed by wasp venom, although they were not necessarily stung. Dr James Pearson was head of this project." Jack said as he passed the thick folder on his investigations over to the Chief Inspector.

The CI took his time reading the report and thumbing through the pictures.

"Let us say for a moment that I believe to Inspector. Surely if your boss has been told to stop this investigation, that would be because of CDE being secret and all that?"

"Partly Sir, though I believe it has more to do with financial corruption, much higher up the proverbial totem pole Sir. Possibly even as high as the houses of parliament. I have had our fraud squad talk with your fraud squad and they are comparing records for now. But I cannot in all conscience, let a serial killer go un-investigated. You have seen what I have so far Sir and if Doctor James Pearson, has links to Organised Crime as well as having links to CDE/MRC, then that is even more of a worry. I believe that we should pool our resources to anyone connected to London organised crimes, you get the bust on. For now, though, I am only interested in our serial killer and Doctor James Pearson."

"I can live with that and I am quite happy to share information directly with you, so long as you give us everything you turn up. I will also create a small team to help you. But I can only let you have 8 officers and limited overtime please. I am guessing you want to visit our crime scene?"

"If we could please Sir and if you could give me some background on the people involved with it."

"I will have a file made up ready to give to you as soon as you get back from this club."

Jack stood up and shook hands with the CI who had arranged for one of his officers to take Jack and Burns to the crime scene.

Act 30

Jack walked the crime scene as if it were his own. He had noticed some blood in the rear doorway and noticed the broken video camera. It seemed strange to him that those upstairs had not heard the commotion coming from the rear doorway. Perhaps a knife had been used there. In the main room of the upstairs club there were spent shell casing all over the floor with yellow plastic numbers next to them the same applied to the bullet holes in the front of the bar and in the wall. It looked like almost 100 rounds had been used. Surely in the daytime this club would have been pretty much empty, as such the number of rounds used was serious overkill. It also told Jack that automatic firearms had been used.

In movies and TV cop shows, all the crooks have machine pistols, however in real life they are not that easy to lay your hands on in the UK. Once again it told Jack something. This was not your common crook. This was top end organized criminals, no bodies left behind just some blood and a lot of shell casings and bullet holes. Jack was willing to bet his pension, that there were less bullets in the wall and bar than there were shell casings on the floor. Ergo, a lot of bullets had landed in the bodies that were no longer there.

The spread of shell casings showed a double entry, which would fall in line with the civilian report, of men with guns entering the club from the front, and the blood down at the back entry and at the top of the rear stairwell.

"Where was the blood of Doctor Pearson found?" Jack asked.

"Over here by the doorway" A detective from Scotland yard, replied. Pointing to the rear stairwell entranceway.

"Now the question remains was he coming in? or trying to escape? Judging by the amount of blood over here, I would guess that he was either killed or was gravely wounded and fell here." Jack said.

"It looks that way, you might find this a bit more interesting, it looks like someone was nailed to the bar" The detective motioned him over and pointed to the bar top.

"And then killed?" Jack said pointing to the pool of blood at the front of the bar.

"Then if you look at that table that has been knocked over there are some more bullet holes in it, also the carpet is pretty soaked in blood and I would say at least a gallon. So, it probable that there were multiple victims here. I would say from the looks of things, we have one by the door at least. One at the bar, perhaps two. If I had to guess, two or three at the table. Then not forgetting perhaps one more at the rear door. So possibly 6 or 7 victims. Just over a year back, we had a similar issue at an Armenian owned club. Lots of blood and no bodies, again over kill as far as bullets were concerned. There was some talk, but no proof that the owner of this club, was involved in that incident. Perhaps this is a bit of payback, except my boss interviewed the owner of this club and he has an airtight alibi and was almost 50 miles away the whole afternoon."

"Do you think this was an Armenian hit? That missed its intended target?" Jack asked.

"Who knows, we have a lot of trouble between Russian, Ukrainian, Polish, Romanian you name it. Every gangster from Eastern Europe seems to have set up shop in London. They are all into drugs, prostitution, and muscle. Problem is they will not rat each other out. I would say that about 1/3 of our missing person's reports, are probably these people. So, every now and then we get called out to a room full of blood and bullets, but no bodies. They do not take their wounded to hospital either. There was talk of some surgeon, who worked freelance and would remove bullets from all sides of the divide or stitch up knife wounds and the like. The story I heard was that he works for free if you can believe that. If you ask me, it is probably some East European doctor that failed the NHS exams. It's that or else he is a drunk or drug addicted surgeon and has been struck of, could even be a vet." The Detective replied

DS Burns went back down to the back door, looked at the broken camera and then at the door, which had not been forced. Then at the CCTV monitor that was smashed on the floor next to the overturned table. He made a quick sketch of the area, before he walked back up the stairs and noticed something that no one else seemed to have,

"Sir" He called out.

Jack and the other Detective came across to the doorway where DS Burns was standing.

"What you got for me son?"

"Well sir I have a bullet hole out here on the landing that has not been tagged yet. Which means there was gunfire coming to this area as well as from it."

"Well done lad make a note of it and tell me what you think?"

"Well what I can say with certainty, is that the men in the room were armed as were those who came up the back stairs. It looks like they totalled the camera before they came in and then ran up the stairs before there was a gun battle inside the club."

"Or?" Jack asked him.

"Or someone else came into the club first, and then the Russians attacked them?"

"The point is Burns that we do not actually KNOW anything for now, all we have is a load of blood and bullet holes. Except for Doctor James Pearson, we don't know who was wounded or even killed." Jack said then turned to the officer from the Met and asked.

"Detective when did this mysterious freelance surgeon appear on the scene?"

"I don't have the answer to that sir, but I can check. Do you think it is this Doctor Pearson and maybe he was patching someone up and got caught up in a gangland feud?"

"As I said to DS Burns lad. We deal in facts. Although thoughts can lead us to them, so keep an open mind to everything, including that little green men might have done it and it was an alien abduction. The point being, until we can prove it, then it never happened."

Jack walked across to the bar where the two holes were in the top. They were small holes and uneven depth, so unlikely to have been a nail-gun. Someone had been nailed to the surface, but it had been done in the old school, Kray's sort of way.

"Do we have any overlooking cameras, from other businesses or street cams?" Jack asked the Detective.

"We are still canvassing the area. As far as street cams go, they all point the wrong bloody way or have been vandalised.

Act 31

The man and woman had been out for an early morning walk when they discovered what they had thought to be the body of a decapitated man and had instantly called the police. Upon arrival, a tent had been set up over the body and a murder investigation begun. DS Brownlee from Salisbury Police oversaw the initial investigation. That would all rapidly change when the wallet was found, and his GCHQ pass was checked out. At that point, the investigation was taken over by SIS, that being the Secret Intelligence Services. They in turn passed it over to MI5 who after a cursory investigation passed it over to the Special Investigation Branch. That was another section of the military police services.

Doug Brownlee was seriously pissed off at having his crime scene stolen by three other units, decided that he would throw out the name of the victim to other police forces just in case they had anything that could give him the edge on the government forces. It landed on the desk of Swindon CID. The young DC there just happened to remember something about two dead crooks, that had worked as security consultants at CDE/MRC Porton Down. They had somehow managed to get a false CV provided to them by someone at GCHQ. He went and checked. The same man was the signatory on the CV's of the two security consultants. There being a note on file to contact D.I. Jack Hamilton if anything turned up regarding his investigation. Being a diligent officer he emailed it to Jack.

A couple of hours later Jack checked his mail, and almost choked on the coffee he was drinking. He immediately contacted Swindon and asked for the name of the original investigating officer and then he contacted him by phone.

"Doug I understand you have a headless stiff out by your stone circle?"

"Hi Jack, yes mate I did have the investigation for about 30 minutes before the spooks took it from me."

"You got a name for this stiff?"

"Yes, Simon Powell. He was some kind of administrative clerk at GCHQ. There is something about that story that does not wash, as he had a top security with red seal. I know that they do not hand them out with the tea and biscuits. I had a friend who worked there told me that to get that he would have to be up at management level, possibly even on the international side of things".

"I suppose my next question should be. What was he doing up at Stonehenge? What can you tell me about the murder scene?"

"Well Jack, when we got the call, they said that it was a decapitated body and I suppose to the untrained eye it did look like it. A lot of blood and no head. However, what it was, was a head that had been beaten literally to a pulp. Whoever committed the crime must have been in one hell of a rage as there was no piece of skull any bigger than an inch. Most of his teeth were smashed making dental records useless. The rock used to do this was about the size of a house brick. So, what is your interest in this guy?"

"If I tell you, you have to promise me to keep it to yourself?"

"I think we both know that rule applies to both of us Jack."

"Right I am investigation multiple murders, which I think is being committed by a serial killer. Most of the victims have links to a project being run at CDE/MRC Porton Down. This guy Powell, he provided the CV's for a couple of real crooks who were working there. The CV's were fake as both the men he did them for, were doing 7 year stretched for 10 of the years he covered. So now I am thinking this is, yet another murder linked to my investigations. I am down in London at the moment, following up on what looks at first perception, to be some kind of gangland. turf war. Except for the fact, that blood found at the scene belongs to a Doctor Pearson. He also worked at CDE/MRC until just over a year ago, when he was supposedly killed in an accidental explosion. Now his blood turns up fresh in a Russian night club".

"Jesus Jack when you get a case you get the full deck".

"The other strange thing is, most of the murders so far, have been committed using wasp venom."

"Could you have two serial murderers working the same story?"

"I was beginning to think along those lines. Or there are some who seem to have been caught in the crossfire. If I find out more I will keep you in the frame. Thanks for your help so far."

Jack put the phone down and held his head in his hands. It was time to have another chat with that prick Jons at MRC. There had to be a link between him and this bloke Powell. It was starting to look like everyone and anyone who had anything to do with project Yellow Jacket.

"Burns!"

"Sir?"

"Get Mr Jons in for a formal interview under caution".

"You want me to arrest him?"

"No I want you to take him to fucking dinner! Just get that prick in here under any pretence you can think of. Take Short with you."

"Sir" Burns replied and went to get WPC Short.

The telephone on Jacks desk rang and he picked it up. He was still in a foul mood with not being able to run his investigation the way he wanted.

"What?!?" Jack shouted down the handset.

"Chief Inspector Randall here. Get me Inspector Hamilton"

"Sorry Sir this is DI Hamilton".

"Jack I just wanted to give you a heads-up. It looks like MI5, are going to be looking into your investigation. Apparently, you have been asking questions and upsetting the apple cart. You are a good man Jack, but this is becoming a political hot potato. Someone knocking of scientists working at the bug farm was one thing, but now they are killing folks at GCHQ. And a little bird tells me that MI5 seem to think the Russians are involved in this. Some folks at the Foreign Office think that Russian FSB are using the Russian Mafia here in the UK, to do their dirty work. What do you think about that Idea?"

"Quite honestly Sir. I think they have their heads up their own asses. That or they are trying to deflect our line of investigation. I still think we have a serial killer and that some people have been caught in the crossfire. The Murder at Stonehenge was personal the amount of violence was due to something deep rooted. If it were just a Russian hit they would have just killed him. This murder was up close, with a lot of uncontrolled anger. If MI5 think it's the Russians, then they are going after the wrong people."

"Who do you think are the right people Jack?"

"Honestly, I don't know, other than this Doctor Pearson is somehow mixed up in it."

"OK Jack run your operation silently and try not to step on too many toes".

"I will try."

"OK Jack if you need any more resources give me a call." Chief Inspector Randall said and ended the call.

Act 32

The Doctor woke and sat up in bed, He was surprised to see Sergi, still sat in the same lounge chair, that he had been last night.

"Good Morning Doctor, how are you feeling?" Sergi asked.

"Like I have been shot" The Doctor replied and noticed that the drips that had been in his arms were now gone and his arm was in a sling.

"Have you been there all night Sergi?"

"Not quite" Sergi Laughed and then continued

"You have slept for two whole days my friend. The Vet she gave you some Ketamine for the pain and perhaps a little extra to help you sleep."

"That would explain the dry mouth that I have. And, my hunger."

"There are some clean clothes in the bathroom along with a wash kit. Get yourself sorted and then join us for breakfast. Its downstairs turn left and the third door on the right. I will have the chef fix you something hot." Sergi said and got up from his chair and then left the room."

After Showering the Doctor decided to trim his beard so it was not quite so unruly, he could do nothing about his long hair for now but would get it styled in the near future. The Doctor dressed in the clothes all of which were brand new with the tags on and they were all expensive designer wear. Then went down to join Sergi. In the room was a woman about the same age as Sergi and a teenage girl both the girl and the woman were stunningly beautiful.

"Come on in Doctor, we are just having breakfast. Please join us."

The Doctor went and sat opposite Sergi and next to the teenage girl. A woman entered the room and Sergi said something to her, a few moments later a full English breakfast appeared in front of The Doctor along with a steaming cup of black coffee, laid next to it were a small jug of cream and a bowl of brown sugar.

"Allow me to introduce you to my wife Annika and my daughter Anastasia. They are my most precious possessions." Sergi said.

The Doctor found it strange that anyone should refer to family members as 'possessions' but smiled and said good morning to them. The Doctor also thanked them for putting him up in their beautiful home. Not being sure as to how much of his business life Sergi shared with his family, The Doctor kept the conversation about the weather and admiration for their home and stables.

When he had finished his breakfast Sergi asked The Doctor, to come and view his stables and horses. The Doctor correctly guessed that it was so they could talk freely away from any ears in the house be they family or members of his staff.

"Doctor as you know I have friends everywhere. I hear that the police have been asking questions about a Doctor who died over a year ago, and yet they seem to think that man is still alive. You know I am not normally someone to pry into the affairs of others, except where they may impact on mine. So, I must ask you because they found some of your blood at my club. Are you The Doctor they are looking for?"

"Will it be a problem for you?"

"Not if I know. Are you this Doctor Pearson?"

"Yes, Sergi I am."

"I owe you my life once again Doctor, so I will protect yours. Do you need a place to stay? If you do, you can stay at my home."

"Thank you Sergi, but for now I have a very safe place to live and operate from. What else have you heard from your friend in the police?"

"They say you are a serial killer."

"I would not define it as that Sergi. Let us say, when you had trouble with the Armenians who tried to steal your business, this would have cost you dearly. Then you fought back and got rid of the problem. I had a good life almost a year and a half ago, then some people came along and stole that from me. Then they used my work, to make money for themselves. They did try to kill me; however, they made a mistake, and it was an innocent man they killed. Well not entirely innocent he was stealing from me when my house fell on his head. The point being was it should have been me that the house fell on. Because there was not a lot of the man's body left whole, I let the world think I was dead. For a year, I have been planning my revenge and yes, I have killed some men, but I have not killed any innocent men."

"My friend at the police, also said something about a murder at Stonehenge, and he said there is a link to the other murders. Was this you?"

"No Sergi it was not me and I know nothing about it".

"Then someone else has put themselves into your affairs I think. Are you sure you do not wish to stay here?"

"No thank you Sergi. You said they found some of my blood at your club they will be coming back to see you I would suspect."

As if on cue two police cars and a police van pulled into the long driveway, to Sergi's home.

"Quick Doctor go and hide in the stables; I will see what they want." Sergi said as he started to walk to his home, The Doctor turned and walked to the stables.

Jack had a search warrant for not just Sergi's Club but also for all the Russians properties. The Organised Crime section of Scotland Yard had no trouble in obtaining their warrants going on what they had initially found at the Cossack Club. Even to a flunky police officer it was obvious that more than one person, had been shot and killed at the club. Over one hundred shell casings and three different calibres, not to mention an estimated 2 gallons of various blood groups. Even though the owner of the club had an airtight alibi. The police felt that there was a good chance they would find either illegal drugs or firearms, possibly both. Jack got out of the car he and Burns were in, then they both walked to the main door of Sergi's home and pressed the doorbell. Sergi appeared at the side of the house, with his mobile phone to his ear. He was already talking with his lawyer. After asking him who he was Jack issued him with the search warrant. Then he entered the property with several uniformed officers behind.

The Doctor made it to the stables and then realised that he was grossly over dressed to be a stable hand to went through the stable and out the back of the property grabbing a Wax jacket off a coat hook on the way through. Using the stable block as cover he made his way to the trees beyond. Before hitch hiking a lift with a truck back down to London. As soon as he got to Brompton Road he would call Sergi to make sure he was all right.

Sergi, never kept anything even remotely illegal at his home. His home was separate from his life, as a club owner and seller of sex to the depraved of London. The cops knew what he did, and it was one reason that he had kept out of the drug business. He could say that he did not know the age of the women who worked as dancers, as they all had the correct paperwork, albeit counterfeit. But drugs were a different thing. There were London gangs of every nationality pushing Crack, Heroine, Coke, and you name it whatever the latest version of some designer high was. No one died getting their rocks off. Drugs were a mugs game. Dangerous too, there were kids with guns selling on street corners and by kids he knew some were as young as 12. What was worse they had guns but at 12 years old they did not have the sense, to know when and more importantly when not to shoot. They all thought they were as hard as nails and they were unstable. So Sergi peddled sex and the odd bit of stolen gold. That did not mean that Sergi was soft though. He had and used guns on many occasions, but he did not leave them lying around for the police to find.

He knew they would want to see his firearms license and they would want to look inside his gun cabinet. Sergi had a farm and owned several shotguns as well as a triple two semi-automatic rifle. He also owned one pistol which was used to dispatch any horse that could not be saved. The only other rifle he owned as a Mannlicher 30-06, which he used to shoot the red deer that wandered onto his land from time to time. He held certificates for all these weapons and the firearms were securely stored separate from all the ammunition. These weapons Sergi would never use for any of his illegal's activities, for that he had a friend who was like him a fellow Cossack. The guns from him would be used and then returned until they were required again.

Jacks boys searched the house and then moved onto the outbuilding and the stables they questioned the stable boy and the two jockeys' that were training horses. Their practised replies sorry I do not know and yes there was a horse destroyed here a couple of days ago, the horse had broken a leg and the vet had come and put it down. Sergi had been there all the time, or so they had said. Jack instincts told him it was all bullshit and lies, but as he always told his young detectives knowing and proving are poles apart. At the end of the search and three hours later Jack and his officers left empty handed.

Jack was not sure what he had expected to find there, perhaps a lead for Doctor Pearson, there was nothing. It made no sense why a previously reputable research doctor would end up in a scene from gunfight at the OK Corral in the Russians club. Jack knew that at least up until a couple of days ago, that Doctor James Pearson had been alive. Was it possible that Pearson and the underworld surgeon were the same person. True when Pearson had supposedly died the Surgeon had come into being. But why would a respectable Doctor choose to live with the lowlife of London's gangs. Was Pearson hiding from someone who had something to do with Project Yellow Jacket. That sort of made sense. If he was, then there could not be many people left to choose from at the MRC. His mind was going around in circles as DS Burns drove back to their Office Block in Swindon.

Act 33

The Doctor arrived back at Brompton underground station and called Sergi.

"Hello?" Sergi said as he answered his phone.

"Did the police find anything?"

"No but they asked a lot of questions about my vet. I think they were confused between the Vet and you. They seemed to think that the two were just one person. I had my lawyer come down and then the police left after they had searched the house and all the other buildings. I thought they would find you."

"It's good that they think I am the vet because that takes the heat off me. I saw the police as they started to search some buildings close to your home, so I went out the back and up to the tree line and then I managed to get a ride back to London. Did you manage to get the list of contacts and messages from the phone I gave you?"

"The man I gave it too said yes. He said he can email it to you. Do you have access to one?"

"Yes, I have an encrypted on at Proton Email, I will send it to you and if you could forward all the data to that.?"

"OK Doctor. We will chat soon." Sergi said and hung up.

The Doctor removed the SIM and then destroyed it before inserting a new on onto his mobile phone. After logging into his Proton account, he emailed Sergi and awaited the reply. The Doctor barely had time to make himself a coffee before the reply pinged in.

There were a list of names and numbers as well as several pictures. Scanning the names The Doctor noticed that not all were actual names of people but rather things like 'GCHQ' 'Porton' 'German' 'Home' and 'Help!' The Doctor of course could only hypothesise, as to who or what they referred. Presumably, GCHQ would have to with either security or listening as that is what they did in the doughnut shaped building near Cheltenham. First, he would try the 'Home' number to see who answered. This time The Doctor was going to use an untraceable internet phone service. He entered the number which had a UK signature, not that meant anything these days of being able to use any country of the world to call from using the internet as your phone. The ringtone though gave the unmistakeable UK double purr, ringtone. It was picked up after three rings.

"Mr Jons residence how can I help you?" A woman's voice answered.

The voice did not sound young nor old so possible an assistant, or perhaps domestic staff.

The Doctor was going to hang up but thought better of it. He knew who Mike Jons was and knew that the man had an over inflated ego especially when it came to fine Scotch Whisky.

"Hello this is the Dalmore Distillery." The Doctor said in his best Highland accent and then continued.

"Mr Jons ordered and paid for two bottles of our 40YO, however he paid cash at one of our Whisky Fairs this summer. Obviously, we had to wait until the actual cask was 40 years old before we could bottle it. Now that it has we are ready to send it out. Unfortunately, somehow his address seems to have been left off the order. At £6736 a bottle we would hate for it to get lost or sent to the wrong address. Could you please let us know the address you would like us to courier this consignment too?"

"Oh Right, yes of course" The woman said and instantly gave out his home address, which The Doctor wrote down. After thanking the woman for her assistance, he hung up.

The Doctor switched on his Virtual Private network as well as his secure firewall before entering the number next the name GCHQ. Like before it rang with a double purr and quickly answered.

"Simon Powell's Office. How may I help you." a male voice said?

The Doctor had absolutely no knowledge as to who the hell Simon Powell was. He would have to be incredibly careful when asking questions, especially with GCHQ was the digital spy network for the UK's various intelligence services.

"May I speak with Mr Powell please" The doctor asked.

"Can I ask, what it is you wish to speak to him about as perhaps I can assist?"

The Doctor presumed that the person on the phone was some form of personal assistant.

"Sorry no. It is a personal matter. I am his doctor and I wanted to pass him the results of his recent medical tests."

"Ohh, I see. Well I had better let you know doctor. Our Mr Powell met with a serious accident the day before yesterday. I am afraid he is no longer with us."

"When you say, he is no longer with you, is he in hospital or what?"

"I am sorry, Doctor. He is dead. Can I ask your name please and the practice.......?" The PA replied.

The Doctor had already hung up. He knew that his call will no doubt raised some flags at GCHG and would raise some more as he had just hung the call up. They would however be unable to track his continually morphing IP address. So, the friend of Jons was called Simon Powell, who had died just two days ago, from an accident? The Doctor knew it was any accident that he had orchestrated, so perhaps it was a genuine accident, unless there was another player in the game that he did not know about. Time to call 'Germany'.

The call like the previous two rang in the UK tone. The Doctor knew even before it was answered that it would be the German Embassy in Belgravia, London.

"You are through to the switchboard for the German Embassy how may I direct your call?"

The Doctor hung up. Now for the next number that did not have a proper name attached to it. Having worked on both the military and civilian research centres. The Doctor dialled the Porton number.

"DSTL what extension do you require?"

The Doctor was aware of the various names that Porton had over the years this one was the Defence Science and Technology Laboratories. This name was rarely used by those that worked there. Mainly because the number always diverted you to an office in the Ministry of Defence.

"I have Mr Johns on the line." The Doctor said.

There was a click followed by several second of silence then a man's voice.

"Permanent Secretary's Office."

The Doctor once again hung up the Permanent Secretary to the Ministry of Defence was just a position name not an actual person whoever was in the job was effectively in charge of defence expenditure. With a budget of £50-60 billion to spend on a yearly basis. They would choose which project or purchase he wished to put before the expenditure committee. They rarely turned down anything that they were asked to rubber stamp. In short it was the proverbial leprechauns pot of gold. The Permanent Secretary also held the power to use a slush fund if needs be. Money that could be diverted to the Security Services if required. That left one number for The Doctor to call.

Help! Same ringtone so again based in the UK.

"Yes?" The one-word question that would imply you should know the next question if you were calling.

"Help?" The Doctor replied. Hoping this would be the correct response.

"One Moment" then another voice

"Who where and when?"

The Doctor did not have the response to that, so he ended the call, without ever having gained any more clues.

The Doctor started to read all the messages and sent emails. He was surprised that Jons had not deleted them, some were very incriminating to Jons but none of them had real names or positions attached to them. Whoever they were being sent to were far more security conscious than Mr Mike Jons. What it did tell The Doctor even if he could not put names to the individuals, was that they all in some way worked for one Government or another. There were ones to the pharmaceutical company in Germany and one which although they did not say so directly, were the various security forces of the UK. One that stood out most was the one to the World Health Organisation. It was offering Anti Venoms as well as some cancer treatments, these were to be in the form of field tests. These were to be paid for by the WHO and all the funds were to go to Tribourne Pharmaceuticals. The was another Email which acknowledged a payment from TP to MJ. Presumably from Tribourne to Mike Jons. It just stated as agreed 50+10%. That could be any amount really but as a paper trail it was incriminating.

First on the list now was to find out, what the man Simon Powell did for a living and how that worked with Mike Jons. The Doctor started googling every Simon Powell that were listed within the UK. Then he narrowed it down to those who lived in the Cheltenham area. That narrowed it down from 9,000+ to 28. from there it was a question of looking at Facebook accounts. There were all sorts of condolence messages from his friends on the page. It turned out that the police were being very tight lipped about how he died. There was a rumour that he had been murdered in some kind of Druid sacrifice. The Doctor doubted that. There was a 'Go-Fund' page set up for donations to the family and an address if anyone wished to send flowers to his family.

The Doctor would lose no sleep over the death of this man. He had in some way been complicit in his attempted murder. That though did not mean that he would get a guilt free funeral. The doctor would pay his home a visit and leave a calling card.

Act 34

Jack had been puzzling over the various murders and he had made the link to Doctor Pearson, although he had no idea if the doctor, would still look like the 8inch by 10inch photograph on his whiteboard.

GCHQ were now being surprisingly helpful about their dead employee. Apparently, he worked normally on the international desk, for visiting dignitaries. Prior to that he had worked on checking the CV's of the civilian employees of CDE/MRC Porton Down. Jack called DS Burns to his office.

"Yes Sir?"

"Bring me the files Arthur Morgan and Steven Ward and while you are at it send WPC Short up here."

"Sir" Burns said and set about finding Short, before looking for the two files for his boss.

WPC Short was the first to arrive.

"You wanted me Sir?"

"Yes Short, get on over to Swindon and take a copy of Doctor Pearson's mug shot, get the police artist to age him and add facial hair, or even no hair at all. I want to know, any possible look, that our elusive Doctor, could have now. I want the whole works, including if he had plastic surgery what he might look like. Then get back here a soon as you have some results" Jack said.

"Yes Sir" she said and left.

DS Burns came back with the two folders in his hands. He passed them over to his boss.

Jack looked first at Morgan's and then at wards, before placing them both together. He motioned Burns around to his side and then asked.

"What do you see?"

"They both have CV's from GCHQ".

"And?"

"Well we know that they are wrong because they were both in jail, for the period they cover".

"Come on lad! Look at them carefully, then think before you answer."

"They were both accredited by the same person Sir?"

"Burns, your eyes are younger than mine what is the name of that signature?"

Burns looked hard and squinted.

"Spowell?"

"Not quite son, but close. That is S Powell also known as Simon Powell. Our dead stiff from Stonehenge and GCHQ. Get a car we are off to Porton Down."

DI Hamilton and DS Burns arrived at the main gate to the MRC at Porton Down. The same security guard was there, as had been there, the first time Jack had cause to visit. He came out of his hut with a pen and clipboard in his hand.

"Do you have an appointment?" he asked when Burns buzzed down his window.

"No but if you call through to Mr Jons, he will see us, as it is of the utmost importance. Also, tell him he may be in mortal danger." Jack said while leaning over Burns to talk to the G4S man.

Jack and Burns waited while the man called through to Jons office. He came back out with a pair of red visitor tags. The man was in the process of telling them how to get there when he remembered they had been there before. He lifted the barrier and Burns drove through, then he parked in one of the vacant slots. Jack got out first and Burns followed carrying the two folders.

"Who are you here to see?" the G4S man at the door asked.

"Above your pay-grade and on a need-to-know basis and you don't need to know, we know the way" Jack said walking past.

At the HR door, he knocked and entered. A dumpy lady of about 50 approached and asked if she could help. Jack said they were expected by Mr Jons. They were told to take a seat and wait. After 20 minutes, Jack was pissed off being made to wait so long. He stopped the woman and asked her how much longer they would have to wait.

"I am sorry. Did someone not let you know Mr Jons left ten minutes ago?"

"You sure?"

"Yes, I saw him drive away".

165

Jack wanted to swear but rarely did so in front of women, so he bottled it until they were outside the administration building.

"The sneaky bastard, I will have his posh, fucking shiny arse, sat in a police cell before this night is through".

As soon as they were in the car, Jack called in and asked for the Home address of Mike Jons before entering it into the satellite navigation system.

"Right Burns blues and twos and get there before that slippery bastard does. I don't care how many traffic laws you must break to do it. Jons is now a serious person on interest into all these fucking murders." Jack said.

Burns really did drive like a bat out of hell. Fortunately for them, there was also a fire engine on its way down the road, it was also running on blues and twos. The traffic was moving over to let them through. They arrived at Jons house and there was no car on the driveway. Jack had burns park around the corner and then they waited. Five minutes later a Range Rover pulled up on to the drive and Jons got out with an aluminium briefcase, then entered the property. Jack and Burns, walked quickly to the door and Jack motioned for Burns to go to the back door before he pressed the front doorbell. Inside the house the doorbells chimed out like Big Ben. As Jack had thought, Jons had attempted to make a run for it out the rear kitchen doorway. He heard Burns shout at Jons, before the house lights came back on and Jons opened the front door.

"Inspector what a surprise"

"I doubt that Mr Jons. if that were the case why were you trying to run out the back?"

"I was not running Inspector, I just remembered that I needed some tools from my shed. It was your Sergeant who seems to have thought I was running."

"And would that also apply to the way you left MRC at Porton Down, where you managed to keep us waiting while you ran away?"

"A mere misunderstanding"

"But you knew we were waiting to see you?"

"Yes, but I forgot to tell my secretary to cancel your appointment".

"As you wish Mr Jons. In that case, you will not mind answering a few questions for us now?"

"Of course, not Inspector."

"Shall we go then Sir" Jack asked him.

"Can't you ask them here?"

"We could I suppose, but as you have tried to run away from us twice this afternoon already I would prefer that we conduct this at one of our offices."

"I want my Lawyer."

"Of course, you do Sir, you can call him from our offices".

"What are you arresting me for?"

"I am not arresting you for anything Sir. Let's just say you are helping us with our enquiries".

"What if I don't want to come with you?"

"Then I would probably have to arrest you for any number of offences. I am sure you realise it is better that we do this in a nice way."

Jons did not say anything more, rather he picked up his coat and briefcase. Burns opened the rear door of the car for Jons to get in and then closed it behind him before he and Jack got back in the front and drove in silence to the offices that they shared with the Fraud Squad.

"This is not a police station?" Jons said as they pulled into the underground car park.

"It is Sir, just not as public as our other stations. We share these offices with another police unit. It's the unfortunate ramifications of financial cutbacks."

Mike Jons could see that there were many uniformed as well as what he presumes were CID officers. The rooms were sectioned off into smaller offices. Jack led them into his office rather than the incident room. It would be up to Jons if he wanted to call his lawyer, of if he would be more helpful to Jack. The only thing Jack wanted, was to catch the serial killer.

Jons on the other hand thought that Inspector Hamilton, had lifted him for the murder of Simon Powell. Jack did not caution Mike Jons but did ask him if he wanted a lawyer. After being told, he was not actually being arrested, Jons then decided, he would offer his help to Jack.

"Coffee? Tea, Water?" Jack asked as they sat down in his fairly barren office.

"Black coffee please, If you could." Jons replied.

It would seem he had calmed down somewhat, on the drive back to the office block. Jack could feel that Mike Jons was beginning to relax. He nodded to Burns who left and returned minutes later with three mugs full of black coffee. Jack pretended to peruse the files of Morgan and Ward, what he was really doing was thinking of a way to throw a curve ball to mike Jons.

"What would you like me to call you? Mike Michael? Mr Jons?"

"Mike is fine."

"Do you remember the two Security Consultants, that you employed at the MRC?" Jack asked, while looking down at the folders before raising his eyes to look directly into Jons's.

"I am assuming, you are referring to the two men, who died in that terrible road accident".

"I am referring, to the two men who were murdered, in what was made, to look like an accident. They were both working on a something called Project Yellow Jacket?"

"I was not aware that their deaths had been ruled as murders. Obviously, they were only security officers. They had nothing do directly, with any of our projects. Also, you must understand that I cannot discuss any projects, which lie within the remit of either CDE or MRC. Those are all covered by the official secrets act." Mike Jons replied

"Let's talk about the two men, shall we then Mike?"

"I don't see as how I can help you, as apart from knowing they were security, I never worked with them, or had any dealings with either man."

"But you did know who they were?"

"I knew them only by sight and that they worked security for one of our projects."

Jack looked back down at the folder in from of him. Then made like he was reading from some piece of information.

"That would be Project Yellow Jacket" Again Jack looked directly into Jons eyes.

"I am sure, if you say that is the exact project, then it probably is."

"Let us assume that then shall we. So, who would these men have reported to?"

"In what respect Inspector?"

"Well, say in respect of a security issue?"

"Then I would imagine they would have contacted the oversight committee".

"When I first met you Mr Jons" Jack said, deliberately using a formal title before continuing.

"You said you oversaw that committee?"

"I think you will find what I said was I was head of chair of the oversight committee." Jons corrected Jack

"So, the question then is, would either of these men have reported to you, if there were any security issues?"

"That's a very broad-brush Inspector".

"Mike, suppose I narrow it down, say there was a leak of information regarding one of the more secret projects to an outside interest".

"Then yes, they would report to me via the committee."

"And did they ever?"

"As I said earlier some of the projects are covered by the Official Secrets Act."

"I am not asking you, what they would have said. I am just asking if at any point, they did come to you with any concerns. What this would tell me, would be, if you knew who these men were by sight, as well as by name and occupation." Jack said his frustration getting the better of him.

"For arguments sake let's say I did. Does that help you Inspector?"

"Let's say for now it does." replied with equal terseness and then continued his questioning.

"Who exactly employed these men? By that, I mean did they reply to an advert, in the Newspapers? Or through the job centre?"

"Again, I am not sure what you are getting at?"

"It's a simple enough question Mr Jons. Did they reply for an advert for 'Tough Guys' wanted for secret government projects? I looked them up Mike and both these men are career criminals. They would have been hard pushed, to gain employment as night club bouncers let alone level five security, in one of the most secret establishments the UK has." Jack said.

"These men would had been vetted by MI5 and GCHQ a long time before they were employed by Porton Down. As such someone else would have initially employed them."

"Yes, I remember you saying that they had been vetted by GCHQ. I will come back to that later if I can." Jack said and held his hand out to Burns in a practised manner.

DC Burns passed another folder over. Jack watched as Mike Jons fidgeted with his necktie. Jack's line of questioning was starting to get to Jons. He had to keep it going at least until Jons asked for his lawyer, as he would get nothing out of the MRC Chair, when he got himself lawyered up.

"Doctor James Pearson"

"What about Him?"

"Did you know him well?"

"I first met him, when he was working at CDE and then again when he moved over to the MRC side of things."

"What was he like?"

"In what respect?" Jons asked.

"Well was he good at his job? Did he get on well with his co-workers?"

"He did an adequate job I suppose, or we would not have employed him. I think he got on reasonably well with the others on the project."

"Did he have any problems with anyone on his team?"

"Not that I was made aware of?"

"Without giving out secret information Mr Jons, what part did he play, on this Project Yellow Jacket?"

"I believe he was one of our team leaders".

"I have read his file. He was a highly-qualified Doctor. He also had degrees in Toxicology and Immunology. With a specific interest in venomous insects."

"I would expect if you read the personal files, of most of our Doctors you would find that they are all highly qualified." Mike Jons replied

"That is a fair point Sir. Which would bring me on to Kevin Brown. Another member of the same team I believe?"

"The young man who had a heart attack on the train?"

"So, you know of him then?"

"In passing I think he was an undergraduate working as an assistant".

"On project, Yellow Jacket?"

"If you say so Inspector. Where are you going, with this line of questioning?" Jons said irritably.

"Well, that would be four members, of one small team. They all died in questionable circumstances."

"A car accident, a gas explosion and a heart attack?" Jons said while leaning back on his chair and looking at the ceiling in almost disbelief.

"Yes, going back to the gas explosion. There were some issues in that death. There were laptop chargers and no laptops. Don't you think that strange"?

"Inspector I deal with science I leave the criminology up to experts like you. Also, I don't see what laptop chargers have to do with Doctor Pearson's death".

That sarcastic comment ruffled Jacks feathers but he let it slide. He was trying to get information.

"Professor Fahad Bukhari, another member of your team who was found murdered in London. I would think by now, you as a man of your astute learning, would have realised that someone is out to get anyone, who has anything to do with this Project Yellow Jacket?"

"And?"

"Are you not worried for your own safety?"

"Should I be Inspector?"

"Let's Go back to Burke and Hare?"

"Sorry who?"

"Morgan and Ward"

"I thought I had answered your questions on that one."

"As Head of Chair, would you not be the person of would look at the references?"

"Yes, and as I told you previously Inspector Hamilton, they had CV's checked out by MI5 and GCHQ."

"They did indeed Mr Jons. Both were vetted by a Simon Powell of GCHQ."

"So, what about this Powell person?" Jons asked not quite so cockily as he had previously been in his replies.

"He turned up headless at Stonehenge."

"I can't say I ever met the fellow. He would just be a name at the bottom of a page. Besides, I read in the newspapers that this was some kind of Druid sacrifice."

"Yes. That was a story we put out when we started to join up the dots. I believe that we have a serial killer on our hands and for some reason, they are targeting your people at the MRC and specifically those involved in Project Yellow Jacket. Some others have been collateral damage, in these murders as well."

Jons seemed to relax. Which was exactly the way he felt. He had alibis, for all the murders because for all bar one, he had never committed. All apart from that fool Powell's. This as far as he was concerned, meant the police, were not looking at him, as a suspect in these murders. He thought to himself, they really are, trying to catch a serial killer. If they managed to catch that person, then he could sleep safer in his bed at night. To be quite honest with himself. Seeing his colleges getting knocked off, one by one, was scaring the hell out of him.

Inspector Hamilton knew in his heart of hearts that Jons and the German, were mixed up in these deaths somehow. Jack still had an ace up his sleeve. He was now 100% sure that Doctor James Pearson was alive, well he had been until three days ago, Time to let Jons know, how most of the yellow jacket team, had died.

"Project Yellow Jacket?"

"What about it, Inspector?"

"It has something to do with wasps and or their venom. There has been wasp venom, used in most of the murders. Sometimes directly, other times intravenously and in the case of Kevin Brown, he inhaled the venom. Now that makes it Murder. The two security men, they were both injected with the venom, as well as being stung by live yellow jacket wasps. That was done in some lame attempt, to make it look like a tragic accident. Doctor Bukhari was literally stung to death by thousands of wasps. That happened to him while he was tied naked to a chair and had also been covered in mince for some reason. Do you still think it has nothing to do with project yellow jacket?"

"Well obviously, I can't go into details other than yes Project Yellow Jacket has to with wasp venom."

"Who else do you think might be in danger from this serial killer?"

"I take it you mean apart from myself?"

"Do you feel in danger?"

Jons who had not given it that much thought until now, suddenly realised he would be next on the list. Mike Jons though, really did not have any idea, who it was hunting down and killing members of the Project Yellow Jacket team. Could it have something to do with that dolt Pearson? Had he shared his work with others. No, he would not have done that, in fact he had deliberately held back the enzyme key, which was making things a little difficult now. That though did not matter. Tribourne said his team could crack that little bit of science. Jack broke into Jons's train of thoughts.

"No inspector I don't think so, I am what I believe you would call a pen pusher or a bean counter."

"I thank you for your time Mr Jons, I will have DS Burns drive you back home." Jack said and walked out of the room.

After Burns and Jons had left, Jack went down to the garage and lit a cigarette. He was now sure that Jons, had the evil twins deliberately employed as his personal muscle. Jack was also convinced, that the accident, at Dr James Pearson's, was no accident. He was positive that somehow the Security Consultants were behind it. They had staged an explosion. They had also stolen computers which they no doubt gave to Jons. Was Jons behind the deaths of all the other members? Powell's death was way too coincidental to be a real coincidence. What the hell did the gang warfare in London. have to do, with all of this? Where and how did the rich German fit in. The linchpin in this, was Pearson. If he was alive still, where was he hiding? Or more importantly, who was he hiding from?

Act 35

The Doctor was sat at the oversized desk in his office checking some of the results of his more recent tests on cancer cells, when a thought struck him, who had killed Powell. The man from GCHQ was to be his next intended target. The Doctor had managed to figure out who the inside man was between the messages that Jons had deleted. People like Jons are not computer geeks, they forget to do basic housekeeping, like empty the deleted files folder.

All that had been in the deleted files, Sergi's man, had sent to The Doctor. Hence the Doctor had the cryptic messages that had gone between them. They almost looked like messages from some old spy novel.

'Meet at your favourite spot'.

'Bring the book'.

'I have some more paper for you'.

'I need more incentive'.

The messages were cryptic, but their content was easy enough to unravel.

Favourite Spot = Public House

Bring the Book = Files

I have some more Paper for you = Money

I need more incentive = I want more money

And so, they continued. There would be no doubt about it if these had been on their official phones they would have quickly been caught by the very organisation that Powell worked for. It had been his idea for them to use an extra phone and they chose to use iPhones, a good choice, given Apple's refusal, to give out encrypted data on calls and messages. But high-tech equipment in low tech hands was a recipe for disaster. The other person sending and receiving messages was the German. Who's codename on Jons's phone was Germany. The codes used by Jons were childish. It was a wonder he had not already been caught and burned. But there was someone in-between. That person it would appear to be the Permanent Secretary. He was, no doubt either paying the German or taking a big kickback from the German. Soon it would be time to find out more about him. But first a calling card to Powell's home, then to Jons

The Doctor carefully put a complete wasp's nest into a cardboard box before wrapping it in brown paper. He printed off a label and had the tobacconist, take it to the post office, after instructing him on the use of the video scrambler, had him take it to the main post office in Kensington. This meant that the package could not be traced back. It was unlikely that anyone in the home of Mr Powell would die, but there would be several painful stings. Perhaps the police would make the link between Powell and the MRC. The Doctor had no idea that Powell was the man who had provided the necessary paperwork to get the two thugs employed at Porton Down.

The Doctor had previously intended to use his freeze-dried version of the venom on his last victim. Now though he had recently completed work, on enhancing the venom by mixing it with both Honeybees and Hornet venom. He found when he combined and tested it on the rats, it the result was the same damage to the cell walls, but it seemed to trigger all the rats pain receptors at the same time. The Doctor had tried to imagine just what the result of that would be on a human body. He had no real way of knowing, the accuracy of his research without a human test subject. Obviously, he could not test it on himself so he would seek out a volunteer. Given recent events he knew just the man to provide him with a test subject.

The Doctor dialled the number. It rang just twice before being answered.

"Sergi?"

"Da?"

"Do you know who this is?"

"How could I forget. How are you my good friend? How is your shoulder?"

"I am good and feeling better. Sergi I must ask you for a favour that would be beneficial both of us. Do you still have the weasel, that you caught in your town house?" The doctor asked cryptically, hoping that Sergi would get what he meant about the Liverpudlian, who was the lone survivor, from the gang had been that had attempted to take over Sergi's turf with drugs.

"What? Ohhhhh Yes, I get you, that is not such a straightforward question or answer my friend. Technically yes, the pest, is still alive but I do not know how long for. Why do you ask?"

"I can't say over the phone, but it would help us both, if you could nurse the poor beast back to reasonable health, say for about 2 days' time?"

"This is important for you?"

"Yes, in the long term, it could greatly assist me."

"Then for you my friend, I shall have my vet try to bring the vermin back to health, well as much as they can in just two days." Sergi replied.

"Can you bring him to my home? If I give you directions? You are one of the few people I trust with that knowledge. It must be just you and the weasel."

"This might be difficult, but I will see what can be done. Am I to assume that only one will be leaving?"

"That remains to be seen. Thank you my friend I will call you in two days' time." The Doctor said and ended the call, as always he removed the SIM card and destroyed it.

Mike Jons was feeling good about the police interview. He waited until DS Burns had turned around and driven off. He laughed out loud as he turned the key in his front door, after entering he tossed his keys into the dish on the hallstand and hung up his coat. After switching on his TV, he sat down in his favourite chain and poured himself a large whisky from the decanter on the side table. There was a small stack of mail, that the cleaner had placed there. Mike Jons thumbed through it to see if there were any more handwritten envelopes. There were none in fact today's mail was completely made up of advertising and junk mail. He dropped the entire bundle into the wicker waste basket next to his chair.

After taking a small swig from his lead crystal glass, he looked at the notes that his cleaner had left for him. There had been a call from his wife's solicitor wanting to know if Mike had returned the documents they had sent to him. Then there had been a call from some distillery called Dalmore saying that they were sending out some special reserve whisky 40YO, that apparently, he had paid for. Jons knew this must be a mistake but if they thought he had paid then more fool them. If they sent it then he would drink it. He switched on the TV to catch the news, before microwaving his TV Dinner.

Jack knew in his heart of hearts that Jons had something to do with all the deaths even if he could not prove it. Jons had provided airtight alibis for all the murders, but that did not mean that he had not orchestrated them. Jack's intuition had never got it wrong; he knew Jons was a murderer. He would nail him.

WPC Short returned with a computer USB flash drive. She knocked on DI Hamilton's door.

Jack looked up and motioned for her to come in.

"How'd you get on with the police artist?" Jack asked.

"He made up several e-fit pictures Sir. He added beards and hair lengths of all sorts and is still working on the picture of what he might look after surgery Sir. That will take longer as it's a lot more speculative." She replied and gave him the flash drive.

"Good work Short, get yourself off home you have had a long day."

WPC Short left and Jack was once again alone in his office. He plugged the flash drive into his computer and selected the folder, which he opened. There were, around a dozen small images in it. Jack selected then all and clicked print.

DS Burns arrived back and reported into his boss. Jack told him to go home then he switched off the lights in his office, then he too headed off home to Mrs Hamilton. Jack had promised his wife that he would be taking early retirement. He had been offered it due to the downsizing of the police force in general, but more specifically the Swindon police where two inspectors had been offered the chance to take a full pension early retirement, which would save Jack a further five years of work. To be fair Jack had enjoyed most of his time serving in the police and probably could make the jump, to the desk job of Chief Inspector sometime soon. Jack though was a hands-on sort of officer. He liked going to crime scenes and figuring out the who, why and wherefores rather than working out the cost of policing and hammering the overtime. The police were being squeezed to the point where lesser crimes like a burglary most often were not investigated fully. That was not the way things should operate. He would see this case through to the end, then he and Mrs Hamilton, would first take a proper holiday together and then probably buy a pub, to while away his retirement.

Act 36

Jons now realised especially after his interview with the police and after seeing the video, showing the murder of Doctor Fahad Bukhari. He decided that he should seek protection from the security services. This would mean that he would have to hand over the flash card and they would investigate, hopefully better than that clot of an inspector, who was so stupid that he thought the serial killer had killed Simon Powell.

The following morning Jons made the call to MI5 and gave them his version of how things had gone down. They in turn told him to stay in his office and await the arrival of a personal security team to arrive. That would include a driver with a bullet proof Range Rover as well as armed bodyguard. In a way, this made Jons feel more important and it sure as hell made him fell a lot safer. That said he would have to be careful about what he let them see or hear, especially when dealing with the German.

All these thoughts were running through his head while he waited. Those fools that had killed Pearson, they had taken the computers and tablets but left all the bloody power supplies. No wonder they had spent so much time in prison. Powell had arranged them after Jons had contacted him about stealing James Pearson's work. Powell said, they would do as they were told and ask no questions. Powell though had never said how he knew these men. Jons wondered if they would trace the two security guys through Powell and back to him. Surely Powell would have enough sense to hide any links between either them or himself.

The time had come for him to make all the moves that he would require to finish this and simply disappear to some country, that had no extradition with the UK, the same would apply to any NATO country. First though he needed to get a new phone and then he would have to download everything from his cloud account. He had been extra careful, when he had done the deal with Klaus, through a friend of a friend, they had created an online bank account with a Swiss bank in Lucerne. It had been opened ready to receive his £50,000,000. In just five days this would be all over.

He was deep in thought when the phone on his desk rang.

"Hello?"

"Sir there are some people here from MI5 to see you" His secretary said.

"Send them in please" He said and put the receiver back down on its base unit.

Four men in smart business suits came in and lined up in front of his desk.

"I am Captain Phipps, and these are my men, Sergeant Mills, Sergeant Gorman and Lance Corporal Ravid. We have all bee seconded from the SAS to MI5 as your personal protection detail. We are to work in two shifts of twelve hours. Then we will be relieved in four days. We have been quickly briefed by MI5 and apparently, you are under a death threat? We have two armoured Range Rovers should we require them. All my men are armed. Do you have any immediate instructions Sir?"

"Thank you Captain I will only require you and your men when I am out of the office. I have not been directly threatened, however most of my team have died in strange circumstances."

"Would you like a bullet proof vest to wear under your shirt Sir? We do have some new ones, that are quite thin, and they can still stop everything except for a High Velocity round".

"Once again, I thank you for your concern, but that will not be necessary. Close protection when out of the office will suffice." Jons replied.

"If that is all Sir I shall have my men wait in your outer office. They will drive you to and from any appointments so you will not require your own vehicle."

Mike Jons had not thought about that, he would have to find some way to dump them when the time was right for him to run.

"That will be fine. If your men wish anything just ask my secretary." Jons said as he stood up and indicated that they should now leave his office, which they did.

The Doctor had given a lot of thought about how to kill Mike Jons. Preferably he would die publicly and in excruciating pain. The delivery system though would have to be something new compared to all the others, as no doubt Jons would be wary, also that copper was on the case now and he seemed to be following up the links. Was it possible to get more than one of the men, who were responsible for the theft of his work at the same time? Again, these were the thoughts of James Pearson who was descending into a mild form of madness, or so he himself diagnosed. The more he thought about that characteristic, the more he convinced himself that it was more likely to be a higher form of Asperger's, which had made him smarter than most of those around him. Let's face it, he had made the link to cure cancer. It was something that almost every research doctor had been looking at for hundreds of years. He would give it to the world for free. Then to be hailed the saviour of mankind.

The lightbulb moment came to him, in just the same way that he had discovered how to kill cancer cells. He would need money; he would need a lot of it, and he would need a prestigious venue. Perhaps he could get Jons and whoever it was in the British government, who was obviously aiding and abetting him. He called Ale who said he could arrange a venue in Kensington. Next, he called Sergi and asked if he could let him have £50,000 which he wanted bank transferred to an account that Ale had set up for him over a year ago. He would make the plans for two days from now. Ale had arranged for the invited to be made on expensive card and embossed in bold gold print.

It was to be a dinner and presentation ceremony, The Doctor knew that Mike Jons, liked nothing better than to be praised and given one award or another. The venue was to be the prestigious Belmond Cadogan Hotel on Sloane Street, in the heart of Chelsea. At almost £700 a room for one night, and a full dinner booked for as many research scientists and pharmaceuticals as he could quickly invite to a dinner to celebrate the amazing work being carried out by Mike Jons and to posthumously award Professor Fahad Bukhari for a lifetime service. Jons could not resist this offer.

The Doctor knew that it had probably cost Ale and Sergi quite a lot of cash as well as favours in setting up the presentation conference. He would repay their generosity several times over in the future. The Doctor would effectively be on home ground in Chelsea, making it a lot easier to get to the men he wanted.

The following day, the official invite to the ceremony arrived at MRC for Mike Jons. Upon opening it he was intrigued and a little puzzled especially due to the short notice, that said the list of official guests were far too important to say no too. If he declined now people would want to know why. He tapped the card with his fingers as he thought about it. It would be good to go out on a high. He looked further at the names and saw the Permanent Secretary was one of the honoured guests as was Klaus Tribourne. He almost laughed out loud at the incredulity of it. These were the very people who were making him an extraordinarily rich man. There was a telephone number at the bottom of the card that he was to call to accept the invitation.

"Hello. How can I help you?" The Doctor said as he answered yet another of his burner phones.

"I am calling with regards to the invitation for the presentation tomorrow night."

"That is fine you are through to the organising secretary. Could you tell me your name please?" The Doctor asked in the manner that a genuine personal secretary would do.

"Sorry I should have said. This is Mike Jons of the Medical Research Council at Porton Down." Jons said. He was sure he knew the voice on the other end of the phone; however, he decided not to ask in case he made a fool of himself to a stranger.

"Thank you Mr Jons. Will you be bringing a plus one?" The Doctor asked

"No I am afraid there will just be me" Jons answered

"Very good Mr Jons we will see you tomorrow at the Belmond drinks in the bar before a private dinner, after which will come the presentation." Then the Doctor hung up.

This was repeated several times before The Doctor had selected all those he wished to be present. The Doctor was starting to have a battle with himself, between revenge and being able to have his work recognised. If he was not careful then the Inspector in charge of the murder cases might catch up with him. Which was why he had also sent out an invite to him. It arrived at the Swindon Station that morning, but it did not get to Jack until the afternoon, when WPC Short brought over that day's mail. DS Burns sorted through the mail and set aside five letters for his superior.

Jack was just looking at his laptop and the various incarnations that the police artist had come up with as well as the pictures that had been computer generated, by working on some algorithm or another. It had aged him and then worked out what he might look like if he had elected for plastic surgery, although the finished picture was not yet available. Jack looked up from the computer as Burns handed him his letters.

One letter took his eye almost immediately, it was a quality envelop made from bonded paper. Using a penknife that he always had in his pocket. It was one of those Swiss Army knives with all the little tools built into it. He opened the knife and slid its blade across the top of the envelope. He tipped the card out onto his desk and sat there looking at it for a few moments, before he turned it around, with the tip of the knife, so that it faced him.

It was a very posh invite, to a posthumous presentation to one of the murdered men who had worked at MRC Porton.

"Burns Get back in here at the double and bring me an evidence bag while you are at it."

DS Burns did as he was told, then looked at his boss before asking the obvious.

"What's the problem boss?"

"Someone wants me to go to a posh hotel in London to see a presentation given posthumously to one of our murder victims." Jack said.

"Why would these medical types want a copper there?"

"That son is the right question." Jack said as he took hold of the card by its edges and dropped it in the clear plastic evidence bag.

He sealed it up and then dialled the number at the bottom of the invitation.

"Hello. How may I help you" The Doctor said?

"This is Detective Inspector Hamilton; I have just received an invitation to a medical award ceremony?"

"Yes, Inspector I have you on my list of guests. Will you be coming?"

"I am not sure; can you tell me why I have been invited?"

"Just one moment please." The Doctor said.

What he was really doing was trying to think of a realistic answer to this question.

"Ahh yes Inspector, the award is to Professor Bukhari and as you were the senior policeman on his murder case, his colleagues thought that you should be there. I believe also that his family have requested this. Will you be attending this event?"

"I will try my best to be there."

"Will you be bringing a plus one?" The Doctor asked

"Yes, I think I will, would it be all right if I brought Mrs Hamilton" Jack said thinking he could make great night out in London with the misses.

"That is fantastic, I shall put you and Mrs Hamilton down. There are pre-dinner drinks in the open bar and then a private meal in one of our function rooms followed by the presentation. Overnight accommodation is also provided in one of our select rooms. The venue as I am sure you can see from the invite, is in Chelsea. We have an underground private car park. If you require any further instructions on how to get to the Hotel please ask. We are only too happy to help our guests." The Doctor said.

"No that will be fine thank you" Jack said and then hung up.

"Take this to the lab right now and don't let it out of your sight. I want to know whose dabs are on it, then bring it back here. Now off you go lad."

"Who's are you expecting to find on it?"

"Burns do you see a crystal ball on my desk. No? So why are you still standing here do some police work and then you can tell me who sent it."

Burns took the evidence bag containing the invite, then he grabbed his coat and headed out of the offices they shared with the fraud unit.

A similar phone call had come from Klaus Tribourne and the Permanent Secretary. The Doctor had dealt with them all in pretty much the same manner. The only person who had asked questions, was the copper. The Doctor knew he was playing to the others sense of pride they all longed to be at this sort of event. It showed that they moved in the right circles.

A lot of people had died since they first stole his research.

Act 37

The envelope had too many dabs on it to be of any use. No doubt five or six postmen and the same number of coppers. The invite though was much more revealing it had none, absolutely zero, nada, squat, zip Not even a smudge or any trace of DNA except for a trace of Jack's, where he had touched its edge. That told a big story, the person who sent it did not want themselves identified. Had Doctor Pearson survived the gun battle at the Cossack Club? Was this a way of telling the world who was behind the murders of those on Operation Yellow Jacket.

Jack had accepted the invite. Mrs Hamilton was all dressed up and ready to go, she was wearing a smart trouser suit and would change into an evening dress once they were at the hotel. Jack like his wife was wearing a suit that he had bought seven years previous and it still fitted. He had only worn it twice once for their silver wedding anniversary and once to receive a Queens Commendation for his work on the Skripal case. Then he had an Evening suit which he had bought a year or so back on a whim. So at least he would not have to buy one of them. Jack had also packed his Heckler & Koch VP9. They would take his BMW, hopefully they would not look that out of place.

The hotel had been pre-booked and paid from an account that was now closed and gone. The same applied to the gifts that had been purchased. The fake awards, were just that. They actually meant nothing, but they looked right. The open bar, like everything else had been paid for along with a handsome bonus for the hotel staff.

Jack had not only taken his wife, but he had taken along DS Burns and WPC Short. They were going to listen in as Jack would be wearing a wire. Jack had not requested permission to do so, as he was not planning on using it for evidential reasons, more like just to give him an insight later.

Mike Jons had been driven down by the Lance Corporal with the Captain riding shotgun. At some point, he would have to ask them to stand down. Probably before the pre-dinner drinks. No doubt they would stay in the hotel car Park or across the road from the main hotel entrance.

The Permanent Secretary would of course come with his wife and his driver who was also another close protection officer. He would probably not stop the night, as he lived just down the road from the hotel where the event was being held.

The Doctor had arranged with Ale, to have several of his influential friends and their respective partners. Sergi had also provided several of his own allies and their spouses. The result being that there were around 50 people for the event. One of Ale's friends was a photographer, and another worked for the Times newspaper. Everything was set for what looked to be a genuine and prestigious event honouring the hard work of the late Professor Bukhari. The Doctor made sure that the special gifts he had ordered were hand delivered to the front desk of the Belmond Cadogan.

Ale's wife had trimmed The Doctors hair and pulled and slicked it back into a ponytail. A quick spray tan and the final touch a pair of light grey contact lenses over The Doctors dark brown eyes. This gave The Doctor an almost Middle Eastern look rather than his White British ethnicity. Black shoes white shirt with a maroon waistcoat over. He was to be one of the two bar waiters that were brought in for this event. The other was a real barman from the hotel, he was there just in case someone asked for a drink that The Doctor did not know how to mix.

The first to arrive at the hotel was Inspector Jack Hamilton and his wife, with DS Burns and WPC parked on the Double Yellow lines opposite the hotel. Jack would only wire himself for sound when he and his misses were ready to go down from their room. First though they checked in at the front desk, then a bellboy took their overnight bags and asked them to follow him to the lift and then to their room. The suite that they had allotted to Jack and his wife was room 118, apparently, this was ironical as this was the room where Oscar Wilde was arrested. The bellboy was at great pains to lay the overnight bags on the Ottoman at the foot of the bed. He showed them to the luxurious bathroom and where to get their towels also which number to get an outside line from the hotel. Finally, he gave them a floor plan and asked if they would require anything special that was not already in the mini bar. Jack knew that he would have to tip the bellboy in order that he would get a better service from him later. Mrs Hamilton almost choked when Jack took a £20 note from his pocket and pressed it into the hand of the young man. Jack watched from his window at the front of the hotel, as the other guests arrived. Jons had come in a black

Range Rover and it had left after dropping Jons of then it parked up opposite the hotel garage entranceway.

Most of the guests for this event would not be staying the night they would however be in the bar and at the dinner before they all attended the main event. Mike Jons had managed to persuade his two, armed guards to stay in the Range Rover, on the agreement that he wear a mini transceiver in his ear. He was told that if anyone asked about it, that he was hard of hearing in that ear, although he doubted anyone would see it. Once again, he turned down the offer of a Kevlar vest. His room was one of the three suites at the very top of the hotel and were absolute luxury, even for those that were used to it. Per the blurb on his room it had most famously been used to temporarily house members of the Qatar royal family. It looked like it too with its sitting room, bedroom, marble bathroom and even a small kitchen. There was a bar, not a mini bar but a real bar to the side of the lounge area.

The Suite next to him, was now just being used as a changing room for the Permanent Secretary. The room two doors down, had been allotted to Klaus Tribourne, he was used to this level of comfort, being a genuine billionaire. He had in fact stayed at this hotel twice before, although that was about five years previous. Nonetheless he was welcomed back as if he had only been there yesterday. When he got to his room there was even a bottle of his favourite tipple A special La Poire Williams from Miclo, presented in the traditional fashion with a pear in the bottle.

Once they had changed and Jack had switched his hidden microphone on, he and Mrs Hamilton left their room and took the elevator down to the ground floor. They walked arm in arm dressed pretty much as the other guests were. They found an empty table around the middle of the room.

"What would you like to drink?" Jack asked his wife.

"Oh, I don't know Jack surprise me" She replied and Jack rather than waiting until one of the bars waiting staff, came to his table, walked up to the counter.

A half cast long haired barman with a ponytail came to take Jack's order.

"Yes Sir, what can I get you tonight?" He asked.

"Can I have a Havana Club, with soda and a Shamrock Cocktail please" Jack said.

Jack watched as the barman went about his order, first making the Havana Club with soda water in a tall glass. He continued to watch as the barman made the cocktail for Mrs Hamilton. First, he poured a measure of Jameson's Irish Whisky followed by an equal measure of Martini extra dry Vermouth. Then he added a splash of Green Chartreuse Liqueur and the same amount of Gifford Peppermint pastille Cremé De Menthé. Then into the shaker he added a scoop of ice before bringing the cocktail shaker up to his shoulder and shaking it vigorously. He removed the cap and poured it into a tall, stemmed cocktail glass.

"There you go Sir; can I get you anything else?" The barman asked as he slid both drinks towards Jack.

"No thank that will be all. Thank you." Jack said and walked back to his wife. With a drink in each hand. His wife looked stunning in her Ball Gown. She did not seem to have aged as much as Jack had done over their many years if marriage. He sat down next to her and took a sip of his Havana Club. He thought it strange that the barman had not asked him if he wished it over ice, then again Jack had not asked for it that way. Perhaps the rule here was give the customer exactly what they ask for.

"I don't know how you can drink that toxic looking stuff" Jack said jovially to her.

"You should try this before you say that Jack. This is a real woman's drink and would knock most men flat on their backs." She replied in an equally mirthful manner.

"I am sure my dear I saw how many shots the barman put in it. So, I will take your word for it. I must remain sober tonight. Remember you can enjoy yourself as much as you like but I am here on official business, so this will be my one and only drink." Jack said as he blew his wife a kiss.

"You know the barman did not get my drink quite right."

"Oh, was there not enough alcohol in it?"

"No Jack nothing so important as that, just he forgot to dress it".

"It needs clothing?" He teased.

"Sort of, it should have had a fresh mint leaf on top."

"Perhaps he is a trainee barman, I will let him know for the next one."

Jack watched the door as Mike Jons entered. He was dressed like all the men in a black evening suit, although his was probably made by Hugo Boss or some other designer company. He went to the bar and got a drink before sitting down with his back to Jack. A few minutes later the German came in with a stunningly beautiful woman on his arm, there was another couple with them who Jack did not recognise. They like Jons, wore designer outfits. The Two couples got their drinks and joined Mike Jons, who stood up and greeted them all like old friends. Jack spoke quietly into the microphone, which was disguised as a small lapel Remembrance Day poppy, badge. He gave a running commentary when he could, to DS Burns.

The bar was now full of guests and no doubt some dignitaries. The background chatter rose as it does in a full bar. A photographer was walking the room and taking pictures of couples, while another man was making notes. They arrived at Jack's table.

"Would you and the lady care to have a picture taken?"

"Would you darling?" Jack asked his wife.

"Why not?"

They stood up and linked their arms around each other's backs before looking directly at the camera. They were three rapid flashes and even though Jack was partially blinded by the light from the camera, he noticed that the barman was looking over at them as he was wiping a glass in his hands.

"Thank you" The cameraman said and then asked their names and address, to send copies of the pictures to at no cost. The man with him wrote down the information.

Jack watched the cameraman as he worked the room he seemed to be selective of the people in the bar. Jack also watched the barman at the same time. He could not be sure, but it was almost like the barman was directing the photographer with his eyes.

A man dressed in a black jacket with tails came in and announced that dinner was about to be served in the private dining hall. The bar emptied of guest and they flowed behind the maître d'hôtel into the large and airy room. Jack and his wife waited until the very last moment before following the others. There were place names on the tables which were formed into a U shape, with the top table being reserved for the main guests. Jack and his wife were seated almost at the end of one of the wings. In a way, Jack felt decidedly uncomfortable at events like this, it was nothing to do with etiquette, more that he did not like mixing at events where most of the people were strangers to him. Jack was sure that the meal they were eating probably cost £250 per person. To be fair to the chef, the food was worth that kind of price tag. The Wagyu beef fillet steak, even though it looked miniscule in comparison to the plater that it was served upon. The meat surrounded by tiny green leaves and four thrice cooked chips that were stacked two on two sat upon a small puddle of sauce. The steak was so tender and juicy that Jack could have eaten it with the desert spoon. Jack declined to have the red wine that was offered with the meal. Nor did he have the white wine with desert, he intended to not only be legally sober so settled for iced water.

Act 38

The Doctor had got into the hotel as Agency staff after the regular barman called in sick as he had suffered a case of food poisoning. Well that is to say, he had £500 shoved into his hand and told to call in sick or his next call would be to his wife from the hospital. One of Sergi's men had made that threat clear. The Doctor collected the boxes from the front desk in the reception and took them first to the back of the bar and then after he had switched them with two of his own he brought them in and took them to the middle of the top table handing them to the Master of Ceremonies before the speeches began.

It started with all the accolades that were about the life and works of Professor Fahad Bukhari and how he had risen through the ranks of medicine, to not only teach at Guys and Saint Thomas's Hospital but had worked tirelessly to find a cure for Cancer. They said how he had come so close to it before his untimely murder. He had left behind a grieving wife and three children two of whom were now Doctors and following in their father's footsteps, for the good of all mankind.

When asked to give his own eulogy to Bukhari, Mike Jons stood up and cleared his throat.

"I had the greatest of pleasure to meet with Fahad when I was transferred from CDE to MRC at Porton Down. He worked tirelessly with my team, looking for cures to several forms of cancer. Without his help, we would not have managed to get as far as we have at present." Jons said looking down at the notes he had in his hands.

The Doctor listened as Jons gave his praise with a slant towards 'The Team' whilst not exactly saying it, he intimated that he had also put a lot of his own work into it. There was no mention of Dr James Pearson in his extolment of the professor. Jons finished by saying.

"I will see to it personally that this work will be brought to fruition by a team I will set up specifically to find a cure for cancer and we will always have the work of Fahad to help us."

Jons finished and looked around the room and got what he expected, rapturous applause, from an audience, most of whom he did not recognise. He sat down and looked around and was surprised to see, sat on the end of one of the wings, Detective Inspector Hamilton. It irked him somewhat mostly because things were starting to unravel, someone was out to get him. Perhaps some relative of Dr Pearson. Who would have invited a policeman to this award ceremony?

The next speaker was the Right Honourable Sir Peter Wilson, the man behind the office of the Permanent Secretary. He alluded to the continuing work of the laboratory working hand in hand with our European partners within the pharmaceutical community.

It was then left for Klaus Tribourne, who promised that he would give his financial backing to support the continuing work including all and any clinical trials, of their science. Adding that whilst Professor Bukhari had not yet found the golden bullet, he would always be remembered for 'input' into what could be the defining moment in medicine. As such they were posthumously giving the award of the Breakthrough Prize. The ball like, award was given to Mrs Bukhari, who took it with tears, and she thanked everyone for their kind words.

The Master of Ceremonies then called for silence and said that there were two further awards, they were by way of a thank you from all of those who had worked alongside them on many of 'unnamed' projects. The MC then called first Peter Wilson and then Mike Jons up to receive both a scroll of gratitude and a boxed bottle of the expensive Macallan 25-year Sherry Cask Scotch Whisky. Both men were loudly applauded. Then everyone retired to the bar including Jack and his wife. When they got to the bar Jack went up and ordered Shamrock for Mrs Hamilton and India Tonic with Ice and Lemon for himself. The same barman served him and when he brought the drinks Jack said.

"I think you forgot the mint leaf for the Shamrock mate?"

"I am sorry Sir I am just an agency worker and I don't normally do cocktails and I don't know where they keep the fresh mint. I can get someone else to do it Sir if you like?"

"No that will be all right thank you." Jack said and took the drinks back to the table.

"No mint?" asked Mrs Hamilton.

"The Barman is an agency worker and says he does not know where they keep it."

"Oh well never mind. Let's drink up and shall we test out that big fluffy mattress?" She replied.

Jack mumbled a "yes" as he knew that Burns would still be listening inn, the sooner he took the mike off the happier he would be. The guests started to leave, and Jacks mobile phone vibrated in his pocket.

"Yes?"

"Its DS Burns here Sir."

"I already know that Burns your name comes up on my phone. So, tell me something. I don't already know?"

"Well Sir the Permanent Secretary has gone off with his driver. There is also a Range Rover parked with two men in it and I think they have been here all night."

"What makes you think there is something to worry about them and what makes you think they have been here all night?"

"Well Sir I walked past their car about two hours ago, and I swear I saw the passenger checking out the other cars and guests. Then I sent WPC Short for a walk past them about 15 minutes ago. She walked past them and around the block so they would not see her come back here, and she said there were at least a dozen cigarette butts on the ground next to their car."

"Good work Burns, and did you run the plate?"

"Yes Sir, but there is nothing on it".

"You mean it not wanted for anything?"

"No Sir it's not, nor is it a fake plate. Just it has not been registered to a person or company. It is no longer an available number. What do you make of that?"

"Run the plate again and see what comes up, also run it against the car make and model. Do you have your camera in the car?"

"Yes Sir"

"How far away can you see things with it?"

"At 200 yards, I can get a full face close up".

"And how far away is the car now?"

"About 120 yards Sir."

"Tight take a photo of the driver's window, near the wing mirror. There should be a number etched on the glass it is the same as the chassis number. Take a picture of that and then run that through the database. When you have done that call me back as I am taking the mike off now. Got that?"

"Sir yes Sir." Burns answered and hung up.

Jack and Mrs Hamilton had just got in their room when Jacks phone rang again.

"Yes?"

"I got the VIN Sir." Burns voice crackled in the earpiece.

"In English for God's sake Burns?"

"Sorry Sir the Vehicle Identification Number."

"And could you get to the point?"

"It's the same as the Chassis Number Sir Just they call it a VIN these days Sir".

"Get on with it please!" Jack said as he unbuttoned his Jacket and took it off.

"It belongs to the Government Sir".

"That's a big brush son, care to narrow it down?"

"I am trying Sir, but I keep getting information restricted, what do you want me to do?"

"Right you're a policeman simply go and ask them who they are? and what they are doing loitering? Then if they don't play ball call it in and have them arrested." with that Jack ended the call.

Something about the barman bothered him, it was like he knew the guy, but he was not sure how. Mrs Hamilton was in the bathroom removing her makeup as she did every night before they turned in and jack was sat on the edge of the bed, He picked up the folder on the supposed James Pearson murder and was thumbing through it. That is why he thought the Barman looked so familiar, he sort of looked a bit like Pearson, except the Barman looked more Arabic than English, Pearson had brown eyes and Jack remembered that the barman had almost steel grey eyes. If they had been the same ethnicity they could have been related. His mind was rolling over the possibility of a distant relation when he looked at the printout at the back of the folder that WPC Short had got from the Police Artist. They were in monochrome and the photocopy made them look darker than normal. One of the pictures showed Pearson with his hair swept back Italian style. The man in the picture did not seem to have a ponytail but from the front neither did the barman.

"Fucking Hell!" jack said out loud just as his wife came out from the bathroom. She had not been there to remove her make up, but to touch it up and to put on a red and black silk basque with matching nickers. She was also wearing black stockings held up with a garter belt, her feet were still inside the red high heeled shoes she had been wearing with the dark rose coloured ball gown. She was stunning.

"Jack just because you like the look you should not use such vulgar language; you know I don't like it."

Life could be cruel at times and this was one of those times.

"I am sorry darling I was not swearing at you I was at my own stupidity. I love you so much, I really do and if you could hold the thought that you have at the moment, as I have to do some police work just now." Jack said.

He felt like a louse. Looking at his wife he could see the disappointment on her eyes. If this case were not so important, he would have said screw them, he would be there in an hour, but it was the most important case of his career. Jack opened his phone and called Burns. It rang and rang with no response. Next, he called WPC Short, she answered after just one ring.

"WPC Short speaking"

"Put Burns on".

"I can't Sir" She said recognising the DI's voice.

"Why the hell not?"

"He is not here Sir".

"The black Range Rover? Is it still there?"

"No Sir.

"Short, there is a lock-box in the boot of the car. Open it there will be a firearm and a tactical vest. Put them on and meet me in the lobby now." Jack said and hung up.

He did not even know if Short was firearms trained.

Mrs Hamilton had overheard Jacks side of the conversation, pulled her robe closed, more out of resignation that the romantic night was off, than from the embarrassment factor. Normally she would have said nothing about Jacks work.

"Jack what's going on?"

"Oh, just the usual thing, bad timing police work dear".

"You don't normally carry a gun!"

"It's just a precaution dear, as Burns is not answering his phone. It is probably nothing more than a dead battery which is why I have asked WPC Short to meet me in the lobby. I will be as quick as I can. I love you darling." Jack replied.

Now Mrs Hamilton was more worried than before, but she said nothing as she watched her husband, first check his firearm, and then take a tactical vest from his overnight bag. Jack put it on and connected the anti-theft lanyard of the pistol to his vest, then he left the room, closing the door behind him.

Act 39

Burns had gone up to the Range Rover and using the direct approach, he tapped on the driver's window, which was then wound down.

"Can I ask you what you are doing here?"

"No" The driver had said and started to wind his window back up.

DS Burns put his hand on the top of the glass and stopped it. He was reaching into his inside jacket pocket, to pull out his warrant card, when his lights went out. The other man who had earlier been in the passenger seat had got out unseen by burns as he was approaching the Range Rover, so that he could relieve himself behind a bush at the back of their car. He had seen Burns walk up to the car and the man had nipped round behind him. He saw DS Burns put his hand on the window and then reach inside his jacket. The passenger had assumed that this was some form of attack and had drawn his own firearm and used the butt of it to strike the officer on the back of the head. The he grabbed him as he collapsed backwards into his arms. Then quickly he dragged the unconscious policeman around the back of their Range Rover then bundled him into the back seat before he joined his partner in the front and they drove off at speed.

Jack did not bother waiting for the elevator, he ran as fast as he could and raced down the stairs taking three at a time. When he reached the bottom of the main staircase WPC Short was just coming through the front door, much to the anger of the doorman who had attempted to stop her and was now laid in a heap on the floor at the front of the hotel's glass door. Jack smiled inwardly at Short's ability to handle herself. No doubt tomorrow there would be a complaint of some sort, on the Commissioners leather topped desk.

Jack raced to the front desk with Short on his heels. The receptionist who had seen Short take down the Doorman, barely braking her stride as she did so, now stood open mouthed and frozen with the telephone receiver in his hand.

"I need to see the manager" Jack said to the man behind the desktop.

The Young man just stood there in his frozen pose, with his mouth a-gawk staring at jack and the WPC.

"Now!" Jack practically screamed at him. It was enough to get the young man's brain cells moving.

He replaced the receiver and pressed two numbers and spoke quietly but rapidly into the mouthpiece. He replaced the phone on its base unit.

"He will be with..........." was as far as he got as the doors behind him burst open.

"What in the name of hell do you think you are doing coming into this hotel with firearms. Some of our guests are members of the Royal family."

"Are there any of the Royal Family in tonight?" Jack asked.

"Well no, but……"

"So, it is NO. Now there was presentation here tonight, right?"

"I will have to check" the manager said.

"It was a rhetorical question; I was at it. I just wanted to know if you knew about it?"

"Yes why?"

"The Bar Staff?"

"What about them?"

"Who were they?"

"They were staff of the hotel."

"All of them?"

"Yes, I believe so".

"I want to see their names and addresses right now".

"You can't just barge in here and make demands like that, that is confidential information."

"I can have 100 coppers here in 2 minutes knocking on the doors of all your guests and see who they are sleeping, or you can wise up and give me the information I require now." Jack said.

"You had better come through to my office." The manager said and lifted the gated counter to allow them to pass and follow him to his office.

As soon as they were in, Jack asked to see who the bar staff for the presentation party were. The Manager looked on his computer and then went to a filing cabinet and removed three folders which he passed over. Jack looked at them and the photos that were on the front page of each.

"Only 2 of these people were there tonight and a third man who you have not given me a file for." Jack said.

"Really? Just one moment" The manager said and spoke rapidly to someone on the other end.

Moments later there was a light knock at the door and a stoutly built man entered. He was one of the barmen, that had been serving both in the main bar and in the dining room.

"This is Miles, he is the head barman he oversees the staff for private functions" The manager said. Indicating to Miles.

"You had a barman on duty to night, Asian with a ponytail?"

"Yes, he was an agency member as John called in sick."

"So, you have a name and address for this man?"

"His name is Rashid Kann, I don't have his address as we just call up the agency and then send whatever staff we require."

"Call them now." Jack said to the manager before continuing.

"I need his address as a matter of urgency".

The manager made the call and initially he seemed to be given the run-around. Finally, though he had an answer. Which he relayed to Jack.

"I am sorry to say that there seems to have been some confusion. We did request an agency barman and he was sent over to us, however as he got to our car park he was told that he was no longer required and paid a £50 bonus for his time." The manager said.

Jack looked at both the head barman and the manager and they both said that they had not paid anyone off. So, when the man called Rashid came in and said he was agency. It was taken on face value. The man had left about 30 minutes ago, at the end of his shift.

"Do you have Video footage of the bar areas?" Jack asked.

"Absolutely not we have standards of privacy to maintain the only cameras are in the garage area and behind the scenes such as kitchen and stock rooms. There may be some footage of this man behind the public areas." The manager said.

"Check your videos and if he is on any of them I want copies as soon as you can, thank you." jack said and left the Office.

Since Jack had originally spoken to WPC Short and learned that the Range Rover was gone it had only been five minutes. Jack walked briskly out of the office and through the lobby to the front of the hotel. He looked to the area where the Range Rover had originally been parked, it was of course gone, but it had been just outside the parking entrance for the hotel and there was a camera over the doorway.

"Have a look around and see if you can find Burns and when you do send him to me I will be back in the Managers office, and Short Be careful" Jack said, he had a bad feeling about thinks now.

Jack returned to the office and asked specifically to see the camera over the garage entrance. He sat down at the computer and moved the video forward a minute at a time. Then he stopped it. The video showed Burns following the instructions that jack had given him. The video only showed the bottom half of the Range Rover and Burns became a pair of legs as he reached the car then there was another pair of legs behind his. What followed was obvious to Jack. Burns had been attacked from behind and then dragged into the car before it drove off at speed. Jack immediately called WPC Short and told her to return to the front lobby where he would meet her. After he hung up he went to the manager's office.

"Pass key and room number for Mr Mike Jons? and don't give me any crap about confidentiality, his men have just taken one of my officers!" Jack shouted at the manager.

The manager quickly clicked his mouse and gave jack the room number but said he it was hotel policy that Only the manager could use a pass key while the guests were in their rooms. Jack let him lead the way when they were on the floor of Jons Suite jack drew his firearm. Jack took the pass key from the Manager and slipped it into the electronic lock and the unit flashed from red to green. Jack gave the key card back to the Manager and motioned that he should move out of the way.

"Your firearms trained?" He asked Short.

"Yes Sir"

"Then get ready. Take your lead from me and do exactly as I tell you OK?"

"Yes Sir" she replied again before un-holstering her semi-automatic firearm.

This was her first time to be in the field with a live fire situation and there was a mixture of emotions from the thrill and excitement to fear and uncertainty. No amount of training really teaches you how to feel the first time. Jack carefully pressed the handle down and put his toe gently against the bottom of the door. Then he too took out his firearm. He counted down on his fingers and mouthed the words one, two, three.

Jack raced into the room and shouted.

"Armed Police stay where you are and don't move".

WPC Short followed in and switched on the light. Jack raced through from the lounge to the sleeping area.

Mike Jons had been sat on the edge of his bed. He had just uncorked the bottle of expensive whisky and poured a good measure into a crystal glass. He brought the glass up and sniffed the aromas given off by the amber fluid held within. The glass almost made it to his lips when, they burst into his room and spoiled that moment.

He sat there and waited. Jack did a quick search of the rooms to make sure that there were no other people hiding. Then he holstered his gun and told Short to do the same. The manager came into the room to see what was happening and Short pushed him out and closed the door.

"Where's my man?" Jack said while facing Jons who put the Glass down on the bedside cabinet.

"Inspector have you completely lost your mind? Why the hell would I know, where you have mislaid one of your officers?" Jons retorted.

Jack was in no mood to play games with a creep like Jons who was so far up his own arse, it was amazing he ever saw light. Jack lashed out and struck the glass with the palm of his hand and swept it and the awfully expensive contents all the way to the other side of the room where it exploded against the wall in a spectacular shower of crystal cubes and amber droplets of Scotch whisky.

"Don't fuck with me! Your men took my officer from the front of the hotel and drove off. So, I am going to ask you one last time. Where have they taken him?"

"I really don't know what you are talking about Inspector. Why would my men take your officer?"

"Then you had better find out now or I will arrest you on assisting in the abduction of a Police Officer in the execution of his duties. Trust me if you are in any way involved in that I will see you get the maximum sentence." Jack said.

"Can I make a call to them?" Jons asked and then realised that he was just in his dressing gown and underpants.

"May I get dressed first?" he asked.

"Make the phone call first! I am sure that WPC Short has seen men in their underpants before, so just make the damn call" Jack said.

It was never supposed to happen like this, the guy that had come to the car had been a bloody copper. Lance Corporal Ravid had thought that the man had been reaching for a gun. Not an unrealistic thought, especially given the info that they had received about their protection mission. Most of the Yellow Jacket team, have been wiped out, by someone yet unidentified. As a close protection unit, they were always on the ball even when their charge was not about. The protection unit always had their heads on swivels. The LC had just been having a piss in a bush, when in the advertising billboard glass, he had seen the reflection of a man approaching their car. He had stuffed his pecker away in double quick time and using the blind side of the Range Rover with its privacy glass, he had snuck around the rear just in time to see the bloke who had one hand on the top of the window, reach inside his jacket with the other. The Lance Corporal had leapt from his position drawing his own gun at the same time. He cold cocked the man, catching him before he hit the ground. They did the only thing they could do given the circumstances. Loaded him into their vehicle and high tailed it out of the way.

Sergeant Mills had done his tree, he had immediately called it in to the Captain, who had then instructed him to find out who the guy was, but to do it somewhere safe. The captain would go back to the hotel with the other Range Rover and take over from Mills. They drove until they found an abandoned industrial estate. Driving the car into a disused factory. Both soldiers got out of the car and dragged the now semi-conscious Detective Sergeant out of the car before thoroughly patting him down. They took his phone and wallet.

"He's Clean" the Lance Corporal said to his superior.

"So, who the hell is he?"

Ravid could feel the blood draining from his own face as he opened the wallet and looked at the warrant card inside.

"Ohhhhh Fuck Sarge"

"What is it?"

"I think your man has just found out that I am a Detective Sergeant, and you two jokers are in real deep shit" Burns said as he started to come around. His head hurt like fuck and he reached behind to where it was most painful, and his hand came away covered in blood."

"What do we do now?" Ravid asked.

"We clean things up" The Sergeant replied as he drew his firearm.

"Are you mad he's a copper".

Just then the Lance Corporals phone rang.

"Sir yes Sir OK" He said as he answered it and then passed it over to the Sergeant.

"Yes, he is here, and safe and sound, just a small mistake and we are on our way back now." The Sergeant said and then closed the phone and passed it back to his subordinate. Then he put his firearm away.

"In the car now!" He said to both the Lance Corporal and DS Burns.

When they were back in the car and driving away from the factory and on their way back to the hotel, Burns realised just how close things had been.

"You little prick Ravid your stunt will see us guarding toilets for the rest of our years. You can say goodbye to any stripes both yours and mine. The boss is fucking livid." Sergeant Mills said. There was nothing more said until they were back at the hotel.

Jack was waiting at the front with the now suitably dressed Jons, along with the Captain of the Close Protection Unit. It was agreed that no charges would be placed, and that the CPU would work with Jacks team and share any information that they came across. After calling Mrs Hamilton, Jack took WPC Short and DS Burns up to his room, where his wife was now dressed in a pair of jeans and sweatshirt. She made Burns sit down on a chair and cleaned up the wound on the back of his head. Like most head wounds they bleed profusely, there was a small nick of about half an inch and it would not require stitches. Mrs Hamilton stopped the flow of blood by applying a small pressure bandage which she expertly wrapped around DC Burns head. In a previous time before she had met Jack, she had been an accident and emergency nurse. Jack had wanted Burns to go and get checked over, but he refused to go saying he was OK.

"He was here tonight; I can't believe it I spoke to him twice and I should have known something was wrong. It was Mrs Hamilton who noticed that the cocktail barman, did not know his drinks as well as he should have, in a posh place like this."

"Who was here Sir" WPC Short asked

"Sorry, I could have said that a bit better. Dr Pearson seems to have come back from the dead, to make a guest appearance as a barman. He must have been wearing coloured contacts and now sporting a ponytail, along with a beard. He has also changed his skin tone, no doubt with one of those spray tans." Jack replied.

Act 40

The policeman had recognised him, and he had known he was not a real cocktail barman, but that is google for you, not all the cocktails are made in the same way. As soon as the policeman had asked for the Shamrock he was screwed. However, it had taken most of the night before the cop had started to look at him with suspicion. The Doctor could almost feel the handcuffs being slapped onto his wrists. In a way, it gave him a strange form of excitement, it was becoming a game between two great chess players, or so The Doctor thought to himself. He could lay a trail of clues for the Inspector to follow. He had fled the event that he had organised before its conclusion. He had wanted to see the outcome, but that would have to wait for another day. As he had slipped out a side door of the hotel, reserved for the low-end staff like he was, at least for tonight.

He had seen a man who he thought was a police officer approach a black Range Rover, that was parked opposite the hotel entrance. He could not hear what was said but he saw a man come from behind some bushes and knock the policeman unconscious, before bundling him into their car and driving off. Presumably, there were other forces at play, that he was unaware of at this time, but he would find out by tomorrow.

The Doctor made his way back to his underground home and removed the contact lenses, before showering and getting rid of the brown staining to his body, it took a lot of scrubbing, but eventually he managed it. After he had showered and dried, he contacted his friend Ale.

Driving the VW Passat, he drove up to the gates of Ale's luxurious home. The gates opened as the sensors picked up on the chip located in the front bumper of The Doctors 10-year-old car. He drove towards the house and the gates automatically closed behind him.

Ale had the house maid, make up the guest's room and told the Chef there would be one extra for dinner, then Ale took The Doctor through to his office space. After pouring a large Rum for them both and bringing two cigars to where The Doctor was sat. Ale waited until The Doctor had lit his cigar and then sat down opposite him.

"My dear friend James what brings you to my home tonight, not that you are unwelcome here at any time?"

The Doctor puffed on his cigar and savoured the aroma before taking a sip of the fine Cuban rum. Then he answered the question, at least partially.

"The police, I think are on to me and I suspect that they also know our mutual Russian friend is involved in my affairs. I know that my work is almost finished and that I may be out of touch with you for some time. When I go, I will not be in contact with you, until my revenge on the people who have cheated me is done. Tonight, two of those who wronged me should have died. I need your help in finding out who these other men are. They seem to be protecting one of the men who wronged me. I wondered if you had any friends within the Metropolitan Police Force."

"I do have friends there, that I can call upon. If you could give me the details I will contact them tonight." Ale said as he too puffed away on his cigar making the ash on the end glow red.

The Doctor passed a slip of paper to his friend.

"What do the police know about your involvement with the Russian?"

"I was at his home when the police raided it. I managed to get away from the property before I was discovered by them. I invited the police officer to a function in London, the officer did not initially recognise me, but I could see the officer looking at me whenever my back was turned to him."

"But they did not arrest you James?"

"I slipped out of the staff entrance just before the end of the function. I am sure he would have arrested me if I had been there when it ended. I think the tube station is still safe. I want your help to get me out of the country."

"Getting out is easy but a lot depends on where it is you wish to go?"

"I want to go to Germany".

"When do you wish to go James?"

"Perhaps tomorrow or the day after. I will need documents as well. Of course, I will pay you for these. Normally I would have asked the Russian, but because the police are looking at him and his club."

"James I can help with all that you ask, but it will take at least two days to get the documents and to arrange travel for you. You can stay here for as long as it takes."

"Thank you, Ale, but I think after tonight I will return to the tube station as I need to get some things to take with me." The Doctor replied. The rest of the time was spent in small talk and the enjoyment of the cigar and fine rum."

Jack and Mrs Hamilton made their way back to Swindon with WPC Short and DS Burns following behind. After dropping Mrs Hamilton at home, he made his way to their temporary offices. He had been sat at his desk for just five minutes when his phone rang. It was the Chief Inspector.

"DI Hamilton my office now and bring Burns and Short with you" then the line went dead.

"Burns, Short with me now! Our boss wants us, and he did not sound happy. Either of you know what this is all about?" Jack asked and they both shook their heads as they followed him down to the car park.

Burns signed out an unmarked Skoda Octavia and got in the driver's seat with Jack beside him WPC Short got in the back. The journey was made in silence as jack tried to think what had upset his boss. They arrived at Swindon Police station as soon as they parked up they went to the Chiefs office and waited outside while the boss's secretary let the Chief Inspector know about the three officers waiting outside. The door opened and the Chief stood there looking decidedly unhappy.

"You three get in here now!"

Jack went in first followed by Burns and then WPC Short. Jack went to sit down in the chair opposite his boss.

"Did I tell you to sit Jack? I am still your boss, although I do not know for how much longer. Why am I hearing that you went in mob handed to one of the most elite hotels in London? One used by our own Royal Family and other dignitaries. I am told that you burst through the main doors with firearms drawn."

Jack went to answer but before he could the chief had continued.

"Then I hear that you allow one of your officers to interfere in a Close Protection operation causing them to remove themselves from their charge. Next I hear that your officer is attacked and kidnapped" Again Jack started to reply and once again his boss shut him down.

"So, while you were there, one of the guests who was also there, now turns up dead in his home." The chief Inspector stopped.

"The reason I asked WPC Short to come in armed to the hotel as we had just discovered that DS Burns had been attacked and kidnapped whilst conducting his duties in a lawful manner and on my direct instructions. It turned out the CPU were for a person, with whom we also have a special interest. In conjunction with my current investigation into several suspicious murders. Neither Burns or Short did anything other than follow my direct orders." Jack said.

"I told you at the start Jack to be careful how you conducted your investigation and not to step on any toes. I had a call from the Commissioner this morning, who had just received a call from the Prime Minister's office. It seems that Sir Peter Wilson, was found dead this morning by his wife. His wife said he came home and opened a bottle of whisky that he had been given at the ceremony last night. He had said he would just have one small glass and then he would join her. She had gone up and fallen asleep waiting for him. The Metropolitan Police have said they are working with you. So, the long and short, no pun intended to you WPC Short, is that you better get down there and find out how he died, my money says it was not natural. It seems people around your investigation, all die in mysterious circumstances. Against my better judgement, Jack I am sending you three back down to London, and Jack don't screw this up".

Jack left Swindon driving his own car and Burns drove an unmarked car with Short riding shotgun, quite literally as Jack had made her sign out her own firearm.

Act 41

Jack arrived at the address he had been given to find that there were numerous police cars along with an ambulance. Mixed in with that lot were obviously members of the various security services. It was such a melee that it was difficult to see who was in charge. Jack walked to the cordon and showed his ID card to the Constable who was taking details of all those entering the area. DS Burns and WPC Short followed their boss through, after signing in at the edge of the cordon. Another man at the door stopped Jack.

"Just where do you think you are going mate?"

"Two things, one, you have not told me who you are and two, I am not your mate. I am however Detective Inspector Hamilton and you are?"

"Sorry Sir I am Sergeant Bob Norwell of the Close Protection Squad."

"In that case Sergeant, I outrank you and it would appear, that you have not done a good job in protecting Sir Peter. So, if you would move aside or get someone who outranks me to speak too."

"Sorry Sir Yes Sir" he said and spoke quietly into his radio. Jack could not hear the reply as it came via the Sergeant's earpiece.

"My boss will be with you in a moment Sir" he said to Jack.

A few seconds later a man in a stripped business suit came and showed his ID card.

"I am Brigadier General Sir Robert Peterson; I am the current head of SIS. The Close Protection Units come under my jurisdiction. As such we have control of the incident." He said as he offered his hand to Jack.

Jack shook his hand using his right, while he inspected the Identity card in his left. He returned the card which Sir Robert closed and returned to his inside pocket.

"Nice to meet you Sir, however we are currently investigating several murders, of personnel who had been working on a secret project at MRC Porton Down. I believe that Sir Peter was in some way connected with that project. In fact, I was at a presentation dinner with him last night. As such he is part of our ongoing investigation. My boss has told me that the PM is aware of our investigation. So, if it is alright with you Sir? I would like to continue that and see the body and the murder scene."

"Yes, Detective I have been informed of your investigation, do you have any suspects yet?"

"It's Inspector or Detective Inspector if you prefer. At present, I do not wish to reveal that. That is because it may hamper our work. I don't suppose that you have a suspect in this murder?" Jack replied.

"Inspector you keep referring to this as a murder, what are you basing that on?"

"On the fact that every single member of the Project Yellow Jacket team that has died so far, has been murdered." Jack replied.

Sir Robert seemed to be mulling things over in his mind before he spoke.

"I tell you what Inspector, why don't we share the investigation, and we work on the theory that this, is as you say a murder scene. We have resources that we can offer you and in return you could share, whatever information you can with us.

You and your team will though, have to sign the extended version of the Official Secrets Act before we can share."

"OK Sir Robert but what about this murder here can we at least look at it?"

"Yes, Inspector I can work with that, but I will need one of my people to be with you at all times to make sure you don't accidentally see anything above your pay grade."

Jack thanked him, even though he really did not want one of these spooks looking over their shoulder all the time. He would share just what he wanted; he would not share his theories at this point as he was not even sure he believed what he was thinking. The head of SIS led the way through the hallway and into lounge area of the house. A man who Jack presumed to be Sir Peter was slumped in a leather wing chair. The man's grey pallor said everything that needed to be said about his state of health. There were men dressed in white coveralls milling around the body and the room. Jack and his team were offered forensic suits and gloves, which they donned before entering as did Sir Robert.

Sir Robert entered the room first and waved his hand, everyone that had been in the room, left apart from the body slumped in the chair.

"His wife found him that way when she came down this morning. She felt for a pulse and not finding one, she knew from the coldness of the body that he had been dead for some time, so she called for an ambulance. His driver who is part of the CPU, called it in to us as a matter of course. Our team arrived about an hour later and we have been working the scene since. The Metropolitan boys let us handle our own stuff, but as you already seem to have a vested interest in Project Yellow Jacket. In about five minutes Bob Norwell will have some papers for you to sign and then we can talk about that and other things. For now, though I would be happy for you to look at the scene and tell me your thoughts, on the whys and how's of Sir Peters death."

"Thank You. Has anyone moved the body at all?" Jack asked while standing behind the winged armchair.

"Not that I am aware of Inspector" The head man of spooks answered.

"He was given that bottle, last night at the function" Jack said as he pointed at the now opened bottle of Scotch, with his pen.

"Both he and Mr Mike Jons, were give a bottle of that stuff along with some kind of certificate for their ongoing services to medicine. Looks like your Sir Peter, never got a chance to have more than a few sips of it." Jack said looking at both the bottle and the glass.

Then he moved around to the front of the chair where the body of Sir Peter was. The moment he saw the face and even with his limited medical knowledge, he knew that somehow this had something to do with Yellow Jacket wasps. There was pink foam around the eyes and nostrils as well as a dribble at the side of the man's mouth.

"I don't suppose that anyone found any wasps around the body?"

"No inspector. So far, we have found none. I have read your reports on the previous murders surrounding other personnel who were affiliated to the MRC at Porton Down. As such it was one of the first things I asked my team to look for. And whilst we have not yet held the post-mortem, we have found no stings or hypodermic marks. The lack of nasal bleeding also tells me that it is not the same as Kevin Brown. His post-mortem would suggest that Mr Brown died from inhaling a potent version of wasp venom."

"You have read my files? Some of which I have not yet shared with my boss. So how did you come by them?"

"Inspector I am the head of all the security forces in the UK and that also includes anti-terror, organised crime and anything else that may or may not affect the security of our country. I know because of your involvement in the Novichok incident, that you are aware of what it is that we do at CDE

Porton Down, this also includes the medical side at MRC. Simply because of the things that the scientists produce there and that also means the things they find cures for as well. Bearing in mind, as I am sure you already know, we not only look for cures to known diseases, but we sometime have to be ready for the ones we don't yet know about."

If by that, you mean you used Dr Pearson to find a way to weaponize Wasp Venom, and he in turn worked out how to use it as a cure for other things. Then I already worked that part out for myself." Jack replied.

Just then Bob Norwell arrived with three clipboards that had forms attached that were marked Official Secrets Act Extended Version. These he passed out to jack and his team. Jack who had previously signed the standard version when the Skripal incident had gone down, quickly read the first page before flipping it over and reading the rest of it. He signed and dated his copy and nodded to Burns and Short, who then signed theirs. Norwell collect the boards and forms and left the room, leaving just his boss, Jack, and his team along with the stiff.

"Right Inspector some of the stuff you have correctly guessed, so I will now fill in some blanks for you. Dr Pearson is a certified genius. While he was working on creating anti venoms he discovered how the venom really works by destroying the outer membrane of the red blood cells. This then became of interest to the military side of CDE Porton Down. Dr Pearson then found a way to make it do the same to all the other cells in the body. The result being is that we had a weapon that could effectively turn the body to mush. It was a weapon that would have a shelf life and was not contagious like a bacterium or a virus would be. So technically it did not breach the NPT, that is the non-proliferation treaty of 1972 as it is a naturally occurring toxin but technically not a fabricated neurotoxin. Once he had discovered that, then it was just down to our boys to work out the best delivery system. Dr Pearson was not too keen to work on that, so he requested a move to the medical research section. We agreed to that, as we could keep an eye on him and follow his work. I had Mike Jons report back to me on everything he was doing. About 2 years ago, Dr Pearson first claimed to have found a cure to cancer. This of course would be the find of the century, so I had Mike Jons keep an even closer watch and make sure that if he really had discovered the proverbial golden bullet that it was not stolen from him. I allowed a huge amount of resources to be diverted to him, in order that we would manage to get it to work. Also, that our country and our National Health System would be the first to benefit from the discovery, before it was shared with the greater world at large for minimal cost. Rather than some big American medical company who would give it only to those who could afford it. I promised Doctor Pearson, that all people, no matter who they were, would get equal access to his treatments. Unfortunately, Doctor Pearson seems to have died, before he could get his key code to his work. So, at present we have a Weapon that he created, well that the wasps created, and he made more deadly. But we do not have the cure for cancer. From now, whatever you know, you cannot write down or record in any way shape or form. If you divulge any of what I have told you, then I promise you, that you will not see the light of day for the rest of your lives. Inspector that is not an empty threat. We do have places around the world not unlike Guantanamo Bay." Sir Robert said

"I knew most of what you had told me, and I would rather you had not told me the rest because it now makes it really difficult for me to catch my murderer."

"How So?"

"We did not know that SIS, whoever you are, were behind the financing and distribution of any of Doctor Pearson's work, to be quite honest with you I thought that it might be that slippery chap from Germany".

"Inspector if you are referring to Klaus Tribourne? It is my understanding that he is one of our main investors. He is in charge of a large European Pharmaceutical company that supports our National Health service. I realise that there are some drugs that his company supplies to the NHS, that due to their investment into research, that they have costs which his company require to recover. After all they are not a charity. You think that Mr Tribourne has something to do with the deaths of all the scientists?"

"I think that Mr Tribourne needs to be looked at as a possible suspect until proven otherwise. So, tell me Brigadier what is SIS's real interest in all of this, also who in the hell are SIS apart from a bunch of spooks, no insult intended?"

"Very well Inspector I will put a couple of my men onto watching Mr Tribourne. As to who SIS are, well that is really a tricky one. Imagine that we are sort of like an umbrella cover, for all our security services. They in some way, all work for my office."

"So, you oversee the security of the likes of Mr Tribourne and his team at MRC?"

"Not quite Inspector. We oversee the security of this country and that means that we keep a watchful eye on our scientists and especially the security of the work that they are engaged in. All the science at CDE and MRC belongs to the Crown, ergo it belongs entirely to the British Government and it is then up to the Government to decide what to do with it."

"Was Sir Peter involved in that process?"

"He would have been involved to some extent. What is it you are getting at?"

"He was the permanent secretary, right?"

"That is correct, hence he had our CPU driver. I still don't understand your line of questioning."

"Well I am not all that sure on what exactly what he was being honoured for at last night's function nor am I entirely sure of his role in parliament. Perhaps you could fill me in a bit on that? Then I could work out some reason for him to be murdered."

"Was he murdered? What makes you so sure of that when you have not even seen the body, apart from a quick glimpse that is?"

"You mean apart from being linked to Project Yellow Jacket?"

"Very well inspector if it would help you? Sir Peters role was not really that of a secretary, well not in the common meaning of the word. A permanent secretary is the most senior civil servant in a department. Each supports the government minister at the head of the department, who is accountable to Parliament for the department's actions and performance. The permanent secretary is the accounting officer for their department, reporting to Parliament. They are responsible for the day-to-day running of the department, including the budget. In short 'The Permanent Secretary for our government effectively holds the purse strings of the nation. Through his office, he would effectively decide if we buy missiles or potatoes and where we should buy them from. Whilst all the various departments have a permanent secretary, they would forward their requests for expenditure to the Chancellor who would then forward it to the Permanent Secretary for his stamp of approval."

"So, he would have approved the funding for the research at the MRC?"

"In a way, I suppose, the heads of departments, would have made a request and then it would have been down to Sir Peter. You think that there was something amiss in this".

"I have always found that money is a great incentive to wrongdoing. It is one of the biggest motives for murder. Would it be possible for your office to consider that, the reason I ask is I am 100% sure that if I asked then my own request probably would not get past the Police Commissioner."

"Again, I will see what my office can do on that score. Now shall we?" The head of SIS said whilst sweeping his hand towards the body slumped in the chair."

Jack walked around to the front of the chair and motioned to DS Burns and WPC Short that they should come and join him.

"First impressions Burns?"

"Well Sir we have seen other victims with the same pink discharge from their eyes and nostrils."

"Short?"

"It looks like as we were initially informed that Sir Peter sat down to have a whisky before he tuned in for the night."

"Anything more from either of you?" Jack asked and got no reply, so continued on his own.

"At first glance you are both correct but also It would appear to be the first drink from the bottle as the lead seal is next to the glass. It also does not appear to be any forced entry, nor does it look like there has been a struggle, So Burns you are the Detective Sergeant would you extrapolate from that?"

"Initial assessment sir would be that he was poisoned. Possibly in the glass itself but more likely in the whisky that he drunk."

"Anything to add to that Short?" Jack asked.

WPC Short moved in to have a closer look at the top of the bottle and then the cork stopper.

"Has this side table with the bottle and glass been photographed yet? She asked.

"I believe so" The man from SIS replied.

WPC Short moved in and was just about to pick up the stopper when Jack shouted at her to stop. Which she did.

"Has this place been checked for toxins? With special emphasis on wasp venom and its derivatives" Jack asked the Brigadier General

"Not that I am aware of Inspector, nor has it been dusted for prints and no one with the exception of Sir Peters wife."

"Burns do you still have the Camera you were using the other night?" Jack asked.

"Yes Sir" he replied.

"Well?" Jack nearly shouted at him, before continuing in a more level tone.

"Jesus Burns don't make me spell it out for you. Because if I do I might have to give your promotion to Short."

"I'll just go fetch it from the car Sir." Burns said and headed out the door removing his overshoes before exiting the front door and into the street.

"Just what do you expect to find that the other photographer has not already captured?" Sir Robert asked.

"Hopefully, nothing just it pays to check" Jack replied as burns came back into the room with beads of sweat on his forehead.

He placed the camera case on the floor and opened it. Inside there was a camera and an array of lenses.

"What pictures do you wish Sir?" Burns asked his boss.

"Everything on the table and do you have a Macro lens in that big box?"

"Yes Sir" Burns said as he disconnected the standard lens and inserted the stubby looking lens.

"Right take pictures of the cork and the lead seal and some of the label, I want to make sure that it came from the distillery and not some back street still." After that have the forensic boys come in and bag the table and everything that is on it, then have a hazmat team bag the body and send it to out lab if that is OK with you Sir Robert".

The spook nodded and left the room. Jack made sketches of where everything was, a sort of map that he could later refer too.

Act 42

The Doctor had been watching the BBC news when the announcement came from a solemn looking Prime Minister that 'Sir Peter Wilson had died suddenly at his home which he shared with his wife. As with any sudden and unexpected death, there would of course be a post-mortem to establish cause of death.' He went on to say that the press should allow the family to grieve in private. There though should have been two announcements. Mike Jones should have been listed, at least on the local news. Perhaps he had not been discovered yet.

The four bottles of Scotch that Ale had got for The Doctor had been expensive and the fake scrolls looked the part.

Ale had got the whisky and given two of them to The Doctor who had in turn taken them and switched them with the ones that had been delivered to the hotel. He had been extremely careful in handling them and ensuring the seals were unbroken and untampered with. He had wiped both bottles down before placing them on the tray for the top table. They would not find his fingerprints or even his DNA on either bottle.

If Jons were still alive, then he would have to try again. After that it would just be that bastard from Germany. He would have to ask his friend Ale to postpone the trip that had been arranged. The Doctor drove out from Ale's palatial home and the gates closed behind him. Leaving the car in a long stay car park he caught a bus to Chelsea and then walked to Brompton Road and entered the underground tube station via the tobacconists. After messaging Ale to ask him to cancel whatever escape plans he had managed to put in place for him, The Doctor then contacted Sergi.

The phone was picked up on the second ring.

"What?"

"I am sorry to put on you, but I require another favour, it is just information I need".

"Ahh My good friend, how are you? How are your wife and children?" The Cossack replied.

Sergi knew that The Doctor had no wife or children, so that must mean either that the telephone was being monitored or that there was someone in the room with him, probably the police, The Doctor thought.

"They are all well my good friend. They stayed behind in Jamaica, unfortunately I had to come home on business. I was wondering if you knew anything about any property for sale in Chelsea?" The Doctor replied. He was trying to get the Russian to come to his home so that he could have a private and secure conversation.

"I believe that I saw a commercial property that might suit you, although it will require some updating. There is a single sitting tenant, who has a lifetime lease, they only occupy a small corner of the extensive property. It is close to the underground so getting around central London would be easy. I am a bit busy at the moment, but I will try and get some time to come to your offices and see you tomorrow. I hope that is OK By for now." Sergi Replied and hung up.

The Doctor immediately hung up and performed his now routine mobile phone housekeeping. The fact that Sergi said he would be there tomorrow probably meant he was under the eyes and ears of one authority or another. The Doctor would bet it was the police. They had found his blood at the Cossack Club and would now be sure that he was still alive. It would not take that Police Inspector from Swindon long, to make the links between the murders of the MRC personnel, Sergi's Club, and the Swanky Hotel, where the function had been.

The Doctor was sure that if the police were following Sergi? Then his Russian friend would manage to lose them with ease, that said The Doctor would be extra conscientious when meeting up with the Russian Cossack.

Jack had decided to attend the port mortem of Sir Peter to get answers to the questions that his boss would want. Jack arrived at 10am accompanied by DS Burns. He had not expected to see the head of SIS there as they had told him he could continue to spearhead the current investigation. Sir Robert was on his own and greeted Jack and Burns. A man in hospital scrubs joined them.

"Shall we?" The man said whilst sweeping his hand towards a double door.

Jack, Burns and Sir Robert followed the man in green scrubs into the room. There was a single post-mortem table in the centre of the room and there was a body laid upon it which was covered in a green sheet. There was another man standing next to the table with a clipboard making notes. After switching on am overhead microphone he first man introduced himself.

"I am Professor Greenwood I am the forensic pathologist for Wiltshire, I shall be conducting the post-mortem toady on body of Sir Peter Wilson. With me today is my assistant John

Grey forensic technician and if you gentlemen would state your names for the record."

"I am Detective Inspector Jack Hamilton, and I am accompanied by Detective Sergeant David Burns."

"Brigadier General Sir Robert Peterson" Sir Robert stated without giving the title of his position within the security services.

The professor flexed his gloved fingers as his assistant removed the sheet covering the body on the table. Then the professor pulled the microphone down, so it was closer mouth.

"The body is that of a white male aged 56 years old. He is five feet eleven inches tall and weighs 13 stone and 7 pounds. Outward signs show no trauma to the front of the body. There is some discharge to both nostrils I am taking a swab for analysis" He said and then took the swabs which were placed inside tubes and passed over to his assistant, who labelled them and wrote something down on his clipboard. The professor continued to check the body. Then with the help of his assistant they rolled the body over and continued to talk. The assistant photographed the body as the professor worked.

"The rear of the body shows significant lividity, specifically around the lower limbs and more so around the Gluteus Maximus, again there looks to be no signs of trauma." The professor said while they rolled the body back over. Before continuing.

"Having taken the temperature of the body at his home this morning I have estimated the time of death to be approximately 11pm last night. Rigor has set into most of the body. I am taking swabs from the fingernails which appear clean and well-manicured." He repeated the process that he had done with the nostrils.

"There are no puncture marks that I can find" He then went on to draw up some blood which he decanted into three smaller vials.

"Full blood work up on these please John." The professor said as he passed them over to his assistant.

"Can you also check for wasp venom please?" Jack said.

"I can't see any sting marks but as you wish Inspector" The professor replied.

"I am now going to check the Heart, Lungs and digestive system." he said as he made a large Y shaped incision.

Jack had been to many post-mortem's in his long career so was not at all squeamish when it came to chopping up a body. Jack looked over at Burns to make sure he was OK, then turned to look back at the body on the table the Professor pealed the top section of the Y apart and then used what looked to be a pair of pruning shears to cut through the rib cage. After cutting away the tubing around the lungs he removed them and placed them on a large stainless-steel dish which was sat on the mobile table next to him alongside his other medical instruments. He picked up the dish to a stainless-steel sink area. He sliced open one lung and then the other taking samples from both which he placed into some tube and gave to his assistant. He repeated the process with the heart.

"There is significant evidence of a SCD and for the police that is a Sudden Cardiac Death however the causation of that Cardiac Arrest is a different matter. I can find very little fatty deposits also the veins and arteries look to be healthy. That said the heart appears to show some form of myocardial infraction brought on possibly by a trauma, on the other hand it could be anaphylactic shock. I am now going to look at the lungs again." He said as he took another sample direct from the inside of the lungs. He placed that on a slide and moved it under his electron microscope. After looking through the eye pieces, the Professor switched on a large computer screen.

"If you look closely at this tissue sample from the Alveoli, those are the little air sacks in the lungs. Their function is to expel the Carbon Dioxide from the body and to then oxygenate the blood. Now if you look at the edge of this balloon shaped Aveolar Sac you can see the small capillaries that surround it. Now look at it under greater magnification. As you can see it shows some mild leaching of blood. If this body had lived longer than a few moments after whatever it was that caused his demise then he would probably have suffered a pneumonia type of death where his lungs would have filled with fluid, probably his own blood. That though did not happen. I am going to check the Larynx next" He said as he moved back to the body and then continued to speak.

"On closer inspection of the Larynx I can see significant oedema although it is not completely closed he would have had trouble in breathing, again there is a mild leaching from the capillaries. Let's have a look further up while we are checking the airways," Then he made an incision across the hairline and literally peal the face down and over the skull to the area of the chin.

He swabbed the nasal cavity and put that into vial which he sealed and gave to his assistant.

"There is evidence of slight bleeding in the airways although this would not have cause death in itself. However, looking at the Heart and lungs it is safe to say that he suffered a sudden biological shock to the body which would have resulted in his death. As I can find no puncture marks I must assume that he either inhaled some substance that was toxic to him, or that he ingested something. I am now going to check the contents of the stomach." He said and reached back into the abdominal cavity before disconnecting the stomach. He brought that out and placed it in a container that his assistant was hold and then he carried it over to the sink area. On opening he sniffed the air.

"This man definitely had a whisky shortly before his death as there is the unmistakable smell of it in the stomach contents. There are remnants of a substantial meal taken about 4 hours prior to his death. I will take samples from here as well and we will get that tested in the lab. Strange like the lungs there is some minor bleeding from the stomach lining, again could be caused by a toxin but we will not know that until we get the results back from the lab. Right let's have a look at his brain. John, can you pass me the cranium saw." He said and John passed what looked like a battery-operated reciprocating saw.

The Professor proceeded to cut completely around the skull. He put the saw down and picked up what looked like a hammer and chisel, after a couple of taps he placed them down next to his saw and carefully took the top of the skull off. He inspected the organ and then looked at it with a magnifying glass before he removed the brain completely. Once again, he placed it in a bowl and after weighing it as he had done with all the other body parts, he cut a small slice from the rear of the organ and placed that on a slide before looking down the eyepiece of the microscope.

"Well that again raises more questions than it answers. I have never seen a body that has so many signs of allergic reaction that could not possible have happened in such a short space of time. Normally when someone goes into anaphylactic shock from a poison or external source then it will show in the heart and lungs and possible in the larynx but not in the brain. Well not if it was a sudden death rather than a slow exposure. If it were a drawn-out poisonous influence, then it might manage make its way to the brain. I am going to test the liver tissue and see what we find there" He said as he repeated the process that he had done with the heart, lungs and brain.

"Once again on close inspection minor capillary bleeding. I suspect that I shall find the same in the spleen and other organs, including the eyes which appear slightly bloodshot as if he had been suffocated. I can tell you with absolute certainty, that this man was poisoned, or that he had some kind of massive allergenic reaction, which had a rapid onset. I will only know the substance once we get the samples back from the laboratory. Though we do have one of the best places in the world for that here in Swindon. We could send the samples to CDE Porton down and they should be able to tell me in minutes, just what the substance was."

"Personally, I would not trust them to tell me the time of day" Jack said.

"What about if I were with you, and we both were in the lab, as they conducted the tests?" The man from SIS interjected.

"I could live with that, but I would want to maintain the chain of evidence myself. Professor would you be able to give me whatever samples you require testing, in sealed containers?"

"Yes, I could certainly do that for you Inspector. So long as you sign for every sample you take from here. Sir Robert and myself will also sign over the seals?"

It was agreed and all the samples were put inside another large container to keep the specimens cool and a lead seal was also put through the hinged lid. Jack and his team first went back to the Swindon police station before going to their offices that they shared with the fraud squad in the office block. Whilst Jack trusted his own team he was beginning to lose trust in any other organisation that had anything to do with the MRC or come to that any of the security forces. He had the chain of command of the evidence and he was going to literally keep it with himself, until tomorrow.

Jack switched on his computer and looked at the emails in his in-box. There were several from the Metropolitan force telling him they were following up on some leads. Then there was one for the Forensic Team. They had tested the contents of the bottle and they had found it to contain just whiskey, however there were some trace elements of something that they had not yet identified. The scientist that had written to him stated that the substance was of such a low level as it could not have brought about the death of Sir Peter. Jack thought to himself as he read it 'If they did not know what the substance was. how could they be sure that it was not enough to cause harm? The technician who had looked at the bottle stated that, the bottle did not appear to have been tampered with. Again, Jack wondered how they could say that, as they had not been present when the bottle was opened. Then he thought, surely someone like Sir Peter would have noticed if there had been something amiss with the seals when he had opened it. Jack was still thinking about it when WPC Short came in. She had a sharp brain and would make a great detective. Jack called her into his office and decided to get her views on the reports he had been sent.

"Take a look at these will you Short, and then tell me what I am missing?" He said as he swung his laptop around for her to see the emails.

She leaned on his desk and quickly read all the emails from the Forensic staff. Then she read them again and turned the laptop around to face her boss again.

"What is it you want to know sir?"

"I want to know what I am missing. I know even without the scientific tests, that Sir peter was murdered using some version of wasp venom. I am also sure that it is the trace element in the whisky. So, what am I not seeing?"

"What about Mike Jons?"

"I don't like the man, but I don't think he is our murderer. He is still alive as I got an email from him this morning, asking me not to harass his office staff."

"Well he also won a bottle of the same whisky Sir, could we not check his bottle? And see if it has been tampered with."

"Short you're a bloody genius. Call him up and tell him we think the whisky has been poisoned. Then get us a car and a couple of forensic people and go and get the bottle, assuming he is still alive, and he answers his phone. If you get no answer get a full team and get over there pronto"

Act 43

Jons was still alive and was just about to sit down and watch the news when his telephone rang. He did so hate it when someone interrupted his special time. That moment at the end of the day when he relaxed with a good whisky and unwound. He had decided to have a drink from the bottle they had given him at the presentation. It still stood unopened next to his chair a cut crystal glass beside it ready to accept the amber fluid.

"Yes?" He said a bit more tersely than he had meant too.

He listened and then looked over at the bottle with its seal still intact. Just prior to the telephone call he had looked the

227

bottle with longing and desire as if it were a beautiful woman. Now though it might as well have been a pariah of some form. The call ended and he went over to the drinks cabinet and reached for the first bottle there and poured a large measure into a tumbler, before just knocking it back. He sat down and waited for the police to arrive. He still had people from the CPS looking after him and they were sat in their Range Rover outside of his home.

Short arrived outside Jons home in a marked police car but she was still stopped by the Close Protection Officers and they checked with Jons before letting here and the two forensics technicians into his home. Jons showed them into his lounge and indicated with his hand that the bottle next to his chair was the offending item. One of the technicians went over and photographed it from every conceivable angle before the other bagged the bottle before sealing the bag. Short thanked him for his time and they left as promptly as they had arrived. Jons was still shaking as he watched their taillights disappear. If as they said it was poisoned, he had been moments away from drinking it. That was too close for comfort.

The two forensic technicians after having booked the bottle into the evidence log, then immediately went to their laboratory. The first thing they did was to dust the bottle for fingerprints, when they had don that they then concentrated their many years of experience at the top of the bottle and the unbroken seal. They shone every spectrum of light on it and even X-rayed the bottle top. Next, they carefully examined the rest of the bottle looking to see if perhaps something had been injected through the cork at the top and then the hard wax outer then resealed. They could see nothing to point that was what had happened. They looked at the bottom of the bottle. Then they carefully steamed the label from the front of the bottle looking to see if the bottle had been cut in half, they almost missed it and it was only when they shone a UV lamp on it that they saw the tiny bright yellow dot. Invisible to the naked eye through the normal spectrum of light it showed up like a drop of blood on a white cloth. The black light indicated a difference between the material of the Green Glass bottle and something else. Carefully they took a tiny having of the other substance and put it into their spectrometer. It only took minutes to give them a reading and then they had to check that against all hundreds of thousands of results in the digital catalogue. They wrote down their results and then they drilled their own hole through the top of the cork before removing a sample of the whisky which they then checked. As soon as they had results they called through to Jacks offices and passed on the information to WPC Short.

When the Doctor had got the bottles, he had carefully removed the Labels in the same way as the forensic techs had, then placed the bottles on their sides and drilled a pinhead sized hole using a hobby craft drill with a diamond drill bit, then injected a fatal amount of venom before sealing the hole with green candle wax and reattaching the original label. He had made a great job of it and it was only because the forensic techs followed the Sherlock Holmes Rule. If you have exhausted all other possibilities, then whatever is left is the answer.

Jack knew that he had his man, he knew it was Doctor James Pearson. So far though he could not figure out why he was out there killing off scientists and what did it all have to do with the Russian mob. He had several problems the first being before he could charge Pearson he would have to convince his paymasters that Pearson was still very much here in the land of the living. Then after that he would have to find the elusive doctor. That would be no small task. The chief would buy his theory, but he doubted whether the Commissioner would go for it. Ever since the Skripal incident the finances of the Swindon police force have been stretched very thinly. Jack wanted that slimy bastard Jons to answer some real questions. Like why they had fired Pearson in the first place. Doctor Pearson looked to have more clinical and academic papers than anyone else down at CDE or MRC. Pearson must be getting help from someone. Doctor Pearson's blood tied him to the Cossack club, where from the look of things something like the shoot-out at the OK

Corral had taken place in its upstairs room. Jack could not question the Russian without getting a warrant to have him arrested. The Cossack had an alibi for every occasion, if Jack so much as ask him a question without the Russian having a lawyer present, then it would mean Jacks pension. The Same applied to the German Billionaire he was lawyered up tighter than a duck's arse and seemed to be under the protection of Her Majesty's security services. Somehow Jons and the German were also deeply mixed up in all this. Jack had never had a case like this where the body count seemed to rise in a daily basis. The original death albeit not actually that of Doctor Pearson had taken place on his turf, then the next two were the so-called security consultants, after that things seemed to have moved to London.

"Short. Get DS. Burns and get into my office" Jack called out.

While he was waiting, Jack made a couple of calls and scribbled down some notes on a legal pad, before tearing the page out and folded it before he put it in his inside pocket. Then he picked up the phone and called his wife and asked her to pack him a case with three days' worth of clothing and his wash kit. DS Burns and WPC Short arrived in his office.

"You wanted me sir?" Burns asked.

"Yes, can you two go and grab enough clothing for 3 or four days and get back here as soon as you can?"

"But I have a dinner booked for tomorrow with my girlfriend Sir" Burns said

Jack just looked up from his desk with scorn.

"I'll cancel then" Burns said a bit harsher than he meant too and immediately wished he had just said nothing.

"Burns would you prefer I give your stripes to WPC Short? I am sure she would appreciate the accelerated promotion?"

"No Sir Sorry Sir, I will go get my clothes." He replied.

"Do the pair of you still have your firearms logged out?" Jack asked, even though he already knew that they both did. He only asked to ensure that they brought them and their tactical vests with them.

"Yes Sir," They responded in unison.

Jack made a motion with his hand letting them know the conversation was over and they both left his office. After they had gone, he made another call to his boss and got permission for him and some of his team to have some down time from their investigation, at least this is what it would say on their time sheets. They had earned 3 days paid holidays as extra to their annual entitlement.   Around an hour later Jack, Burns and Short were all tucked up inside Jacks BMW and were heading down to London. Jack had also arranged for them all to stay at the Federation Hotel and Conference Centre on the outskirts of London close to the M25. This would give them quick access to any London address. Also, as serving Police officer they would be able to claim back the expenses at the end of the investigation. Jack could give a hoot about making a claim for himself. This investigation was far more important to him than trying to get the cost of a few nights back. He would not though, see any of his officers be out of pocket when trying to catch criminals, no matter who or where they were.

After they had all checked into the Hotel, Jack arranged for them to meet up in the lounge where he had a tray of coffee waiting for them.

"I am going to level with you about what I think is really going on. Now it could take some time, which is why there is coffee here for the pair of you. Do not interrupt me or spoil my flow as I go through thing. If you have any questions or further input, please wait until I am finished. Got that?" He said and they both nodded their heads.

"All right here goes. I think that this Doctor Pearson really did crack the cancer treatment thing. That alone, would be worth billions worldwide probably even trillions. So, this is where greedy people start to make things happen. Perhaps Doctor Pearson wanted to go public with it, or maybe he just wanted to give it away to every country. Either way it would give a real motive for first his dismissal from the Yellow Jacket Project. I think that the two goons that Mr Mike Jons had employed at the MRC were the ones who had tried to murder Doctor Pearson, and somehow or other they botched it and ended up killing this young lad, who was in the wrong place at the wrong time. I then think that Doctor Pearson made himself disappear for a year. It would seem to me that he was the only one that had all the answers to the supposed Cancer Cure. So, when the goons tried to kill him they took his laptop and mobile phone. We only found chargers in the wreckage. Jons and his team were still trying to finish Pearson's work. When enough time had passed, Pearson changed the way he looked and probably changed his name. He then went after the Goons and killed them outside Swindon, using some of his wasp venom. Then he went after the junior assistant and murdered him on the Tube Train. Once again, he used some form of his wasp venom. Next, he went after Professor Bukhari and this councilman, although I still cannot fathom why he was murdered at the same time as Bukhari. Next, he goes after Peter Wilson and Mike Jons at the same time. That was at the Belmond Cadogan Hotel. Once again, he used wasp venom this time he managed to get it into the Whisky bottles that these two were awarded at the function. You were abducted by mistake Burns. The Close Protection Squad thought that you were a threat to Sir Peter and as such took you out of the mix. The real man they should have been looking at was the barman with the beard and ponytail. I was much to slow in identifying him myself or we would already have him in custody. No matter because we are going to put our combined brains to use in hunting down the elusive Doctor Pearson. The reason that Jons is still alive is pure luck. I have had the fraud squad take a good look at Simon Powell an also Mike Jons finances. It would seem, that Mike Jons is quite a wealthy man. He invests in a lot of property which he seems to buy and sell on a regular basis through a shell company. By doing things this was he has managed to hide most of his wealth from his actual bank account. There was a transaction that might be the one that tripped him up though. Apparently, Simon Powell was a co-owner of one of the properties that recently sold, and he received rather a large lump sum payment which he then transferred to an account in the Cayman Islands. Remember that it was Powell that did the security clearance for the two security consultants. So, I do not believe in coincidences. Powell and Jons are deeply mixed up in all of this. Then we come to Sir Peter. He is the man who effectively writes the checks for the British Government. He also carries a lot of weight when it comes to inviting companies to bid for contracts and supply of goods to this country. The man that links Sir peter and Mike Jons is Klaus Tribourne. He owns a multibillion pharmaceutical company in Germany. He is the man who stands to gain the most by having a new medical advancement. If his is the only company allowed to produce some new cancer cure. Then he effectively has the monopoly on who lives and who dies from cancer. That would be worth untold sums. If I am right Doctor Pearson did find a cure for cancer and it has something to do with this Yellow Jacket Project. His work was stolen from him and he is out for revenge. Which really leaves us with two people who are actively involved in this discovery, that he still wants to kill. Jons and Tribourne. I do not believe that any of the victims have been innocent, not even the councilman. He was in some way, mixed up with the good Doctor Pearson. Now there were some gang related incidents in London and at one such scene, we found Doctor Pearson blood along with his DNA. That was at the Cossack Club. The club is owned by a rich Ukrainian, who seems to have fingers in all sorts of dirty pies. There is a bit of a folk tale going around some of the less than honest residents of London. This folklore says that there is a surgeon, who will patch up any wounds, that perhaps a hospital might have to report to the police. I suspect that this is not just a fairy tale. I believe that this mystery man, is in fact our Doctor Pearson. So, we need to squeeze some people and see if we can't find our elusive pimpernel." Jack sat back in his chair and lifted his cup and awaited the barrage of questions that he thought would come at him, all he got for his troubles was confirmation.

Act 44

Sergi arrived at the tobacconist's entrance to The Doctors underground home. The Doctor range through to the Tobacconist so that he could let Sergi in. Then he waited while Sergi made his way down into the sub-terrarium home. After going through the routine of welcoming him they sat down and shared a jug of freshly made coffee.

"Were you followed?" The Doctor asked his Cossack friend.

"Initially yes but I managed to lose them on the M25 and then I switched cars with a friend at a service station so when they finally locate my car they will follow it up to Inverness. Then I parked on the outskirts of Chelsea before catching a bus to the underground and then doubling back before coming here. Do you think they are on to you my friend?"

"In a word, yes I think this Policeman called Jack Hamilton is putting together all the pieces of the puzzle. I think he is getting close especially by looking at my friends."

"I can have him removed from the scene if you like Doctor?"

"If by that you mean killed or kidnapped, then my answer to that is a definitive no Sergi. This policeman is completely innocent, so does not deserve anything bad to happen to him or his family. He is just doing the job he is supposed to do." The Doctor replied

"So how is it I can help you then Doctor? I am sure you did not bring me here for a cup of coffee, even if it is a genuinely nice blend." The Cossack said

"I missed one of the targets I set out to get. I think that the police managed to figure out that I had tampered with the bottles and they warned Mr Jons before he would drink any of the whisky. There are only two people left for me to take my retribution on Mr Mike Jons and the German Herr Klaus Tribourne. I was going to travel abroad and catch up with Herr

Tribourne in Germany by I fear that my face or at least drawings of what I look like with and without my beard. So, I intend to change my plans. I want you to snatch him for me."

"Is that all I thought you were going to ask something difficult of me" Sergi responded.

"It will not be as easy as you think my friend. He now not only has some of his own people guarding him, but he also has a team from the UK's Close Protection Officers. They are members of the elite Special Air Service. It will be a difficult thing for you to do." The Doctor responded.

"Doctor you forget I am a Cossack, and a lot of my wealth came from, how should I put this? Abduction rich Russians in Moscow and extorting their wealth. Most of these men were ex KGB or previously held position of power in the Politburo. These men employed mercenaries that were mostly made up of men from the Spetsnaz, they are special forces which is used by numerous Russian-speaking post-Soviet states. Historically, they used to be part of the special operations units controlled by the main military intelligence service GRU. They are not fussy who they kill when protecting their charges. So, unlike other protection squads they will use overkill. My men are more loyal to me than money so they will fight because they respect me. All I need from you, is to find out for me where he will be at a given time. Then we will follow him and capture him with no loss of innocent lives. There is one thing though, it will be expensive. I think that we have an even score sheet so this will be a big favour that you ask of me."

"How much will this cost?" The Doctor enquired of his friend while refilling their coffee cups.

The Cossack sat and thought things through for a moment or two before answering.

"This will cost £500,000. That is because the men who will do this for me must spend some time away from their families, as you know going into hiding can be an expensive thing to do." Sergi said.

"How soon do you need the money?"

"No hurry I know you are good for it".

"Thank you Sergi I appreciate that."

"And the other man, this Mr Jons?

"I have someone else in mid to help me with that one. He will be a lot easier to trap because he craves wealth."

"When a man without money thinks only of money then he is as you westerners would most likely say 'is blinded by greed'. So where do you wish me to deliver the German too?"

"To here of course. And If you could leave someone with him if I am not here at the time. Then I would appreciate that." The Doctor replied.

They finished their coffee and then the Cossack left, and the Doctor made another call before performing his normal cell phone housekeeping.

Ale greeted The Doctor and they booth been onto the office area of the hour. Alé closed the door behind then and they both sat down in the pair of wing chairs that were positioned either side of the ornate coffee table.

"What is of such great importance that you felt the need to come and see me directly, not that I don't welcome your company my friend?" Alé said as he pulled his chair closer to the table in order that they could speak quietly.

"I need your help once more in my mission to avenge myself and it is not something that I can do on my own. I will need your help in kidnapping and bringing a man to the tube station. Then after that I think I will have to disappear for some time." The Doctor replied.

"Who is this man that you want me to get for you?"

"He is a German National. When he is at his home or offices then it will be impossible for anyone to get close because of the people he has guarding him. They are professionals from the SAS and, he has a couple of his own men who are probably members of the German Special Forces they call them the Deutsche Kammando Spezialkkrafte or the GSG9 unit of the KSK. They are well trained and well-armed. The Germans Guard his apartment, which is part of the German Embassy and the SAS guard him wherever he goes in the UK. He drives his own sports car, but an SAS unit always follows him in a Range Rover. So, as you can see it is not going to be an easy take-down."

"When do you want, this doing James?"

"I am afraid it has to be done in the next couple of days. The UK police have managed to connect the dots and I think they are looking for me right now."

"James I know people who will do this job, but it would be expensive even for me. I will use my own men and do this for you."

"Alé you cannot, you have a family. Please just fond me the men and I will tell them what to do."

"James, you forget I only have a family because of you. Let me do this one last thing for you, then perhaps we are even." The Filipino said

The Doctor started to say something but Alé held his hand up to show that his mind was made up.

"All I need to know James is where he travels between and a rough time the rest I will sort. Like you James I have built up a book of favours in my community and my men are fiercely loyal to me. Most of my men were farmworkers for me back in the Philippines, from before I met you. I have always shared my good fortunes with my friends and families. Because of that my men have come to respect me. Besides, I have no intentions of seeing letting any of them come to harm. You say he drives a sports car between places?"

"Yes, he travels between London and Swindon most days."

"In that case, there will not be a problem all we have to do is put some distance between him and the men from the SAS after that it will be simple. Let us have a drink and we will work it out."

After several drinks and much discussion Alé had a plane formulated and said he would only require six of his men and they would not even require arming. It would just require 4

HGV Articulated trucks. And a single lane closure at one of the slip roads on the M25 ring road. The plan was audacious and brilliant at the same time and it was so brazen that it just might work without any harm befalling anyone.

The Cossack's take-down was like a blunt force trauma. There was absolutely no finesse to it all. Mike Jons left his home with one member of the SAS driving a range rover in the follow vehicle, the other man was stationed permanently outside his home, both men worked 12 hour shifts before being relieved by another pair. There in was the mistake it was a sublime take-down and would have been worthy of the SAS themselves. Jons had just left the housing estate where he lived and was about to take the narrow country lane towards the main road. There was a tractor in front of them and a van came up behind. The tractor stopped and Jons stopped. The van close that was behind Jons's Range Rover, stopped. The tractor driver climbed down from his cab and appeared to be examining the engine. When he stood up though, it was a shock not only to Jons but to the SAS Soldier. He should have been more attentive to the and the fact that the van had come to close to the rear of the Range Rover, meaning he could not escape the trap. The Tractor driver then appeared with a RPG on his shoulder, the SAS Man looked to the rear view and now saw the same vision from behind. There was nothing to be done If he used his HK Machine pistol there was no way they could escape one let alone two RPG's. He switched of the engine and raised his hands and indicated to Jons to do the same. Jons was first shocked and then seriously pissed off at his protection office.

"For God's sake man do something! You are supposed to protect me, use your gun and shoot them!"

The SAS man glared at Jons before speaking.

"It would be like taking a knife to a gun fight. The bullet proof glass in this vehicle will stop bullets but not rocket propelled grenades. Just stay calm and for now do as they say, and we might get to walk away from this. If they just wanted to kill us they would have fired their grenades by now. They will probably be here to kidnap you. My advice is go quietly and we will rescue you after. You are a rich man, and they are probably just after some quick money."

"That's it? You are a fucking coward!"

"My job is to keep you alive. If I fire then they will just blow us to hell and back, that is not being a coward it is protection."

The man at the front motioned that the driver should wind his window down and then he shouted at them.

"You in the car, if you wish to live, throw out your guns and do not be shy I know you are SAS."

The soldier looked once again at the rear view and saw that there were now two men behind one seemed to be carrying an evil looking 30mm rail gun. More than capable of shredding the bullet proof glass on its own never mind the RPG's the soldier wound the window down a slowly showed he was holding his own gun by the barrel and then dropped it out of the window.

"And your back up piece and do it slow" The man said in heavily accented English.

The soldier complied.

"Passenger get of the car" The Slavic voice said.

"What should I do?" Jons asked of his driver?

"I would say if you want to live then you should do as they say".

"Fuck you" Jons replied and opened his door another man appeared from behind the van and walked up and collected the guns that had been dropped out of the window. Then he took the RPG from his cohort. The man who had previously been hold the RPG to the rear of Jons car now came up and placed a black bag over Mike Jons head and then used a set of cable tied to handcuff Jons's hands behind the back. Next, he grabbed him by the shoulders and pushed him toward the rear of the van. The man who was holding onto the rail gun came up to the open passenger door and tossed in a pair of steel handcuffs to the driver.

"Throw the car keys out and then open your door and handcuff yourself to either side of the window. If you do as you are told no one will harm you but be quick as we do not have all day."

The protection officer did as he was instructed. Only then did the tractor driver put the RPG down. Then he walked to the car and made sure that the handcuffs were correctly on and tightened them a bit more. Quickly he patted down the soldier and took his mobile phone and smashed it to pieces beneath his boot. Then he picked up the Sig Sauer 9mm that the soldier had dropped out of the window. He cocked it and looked at the SAS Man. At first the close protection officer thought he was going to be shot. The man fired a single shot into each tyre and a further two into the radiator, totally disabling the car. After that, all the men got in the van which reversed down the road and turned around at the entrance to a field before driving out of sight.

Around the same time, Klaus Tribourne was on the M25 London Ring Road in his Tesla, with his close protection officers following in a Range Rover. As usual there were road works. It was one of the things that Klaus hated about England there were always roadworks on the busiest motorway in the country. The slow lane and hard shoulder were both blocked off and this was causing tailbacks. What was worse still there were three HGV trucks in front of him all belonging to the same firm. Klaus flashed the lights on his sportster to get the trucks to let him through. One of the trucks moved over and that meant he could overtake, this he did. Now there were two more that he need to make move. He flashed his lights again, the second truck moved over that two truck were nosed to tail and the third was to the inside. Klaus was just in the process of overtaking when the truck pulled in front of him making him the filling in an HGV sandwich. With the third to his driver's side and his close protection squad were just behind the truck that was immediately behind him. It took just seconds for the manoeuvre to come to fruition the truck in front of Tribourne suddenly and without any warning, slammed on its brakes. Klaus braked hard and he knew it was way too late. He was going to smash into the rear of the trailer and die, that was a given. In the blink of an eye or so it seemed a ramp shot out from the truck and his Tesla shot up and inside the rear of the curtained trailer. Then things went black. Klaus switched his lights on and was amazed to see he had not crashed but had stopped three quarter way down the 40ft trailer. He felt the truck sway as it made the turn for a slip road. The other two truck continued in convoy and then the tail one moved over to let the Range Rover pass. Both men inside it, vainly looking for the bright orange sports car but it was long gone.

Act 45

Jack was resting on top of the bed in his room, reading from a folder that he had made up before he left Swindon. He was thinking about ringing through to the head of the Close protection unit when the telephone on the bedside cabinet started to ring. Jack had given the hotel number to his wife just in case she needed something or if she just wanted to talk. Jack picked up the receiver thoroughly expecting to hear Mrs Hamilton.

"Hello?"

"Detective Inspector Hamilton?" A female voice that was not Mrs Hamilton, enquired.

"Speaking."

"Hold the line please Sir, I am just transferring a call to you." The woman said. This was followed by a couple of seconds of silence and then a click as an outside line connected.

"D.I. Hamilton?"

"Yes?" Jack answered.

"Brigadier General Sir Robert Peterson. I think we have a shared problem."

"How did you know I was here?"

"Because Detective Inspector I am paid to know these things. Let me get straight to the point. We lost Mr Mike Jons and Herr Klaus Tribourne."

241

"I would say losing one is bordering on careless but losing both is quite embarrassing for you Brigadier".

"When you are finished scoring points Detective. From what I understand you also have quite an investment in these two men as they are linked to the series of murders that you are currently investigating. Both men were taken within 30 minutes of each other. I would rather not discuss this over the phone. Have you had your breakfast yet?"

"I was just going to get my team and go and get something to eat when you called."

"Good then I shall be there in 15 minutes, I shall see you then." The Brigadier said and then the line went dead.

Jack went and collected Burns and Short from their rooms. He quickly briefed then whilst going down in the elevator. After entering the dining room jack ordered a pot of coffee while they waited for the man from SIS. They did not have to wait long for the Brigadier General to arrive. Jack stood up and greeted him and then introduced the other officers before sitting back down. A waiter approached the table and Jack was about to wave him off when the Brigadier, placed an order for three full English, without even checking with the others. As soon as the waiter left Peterson pour a black coffee and started the conversation.

"As you know my officers were the close protection squad for both Tribourne and Jons. Around 7:30 this morning both men were abducted whilst on their way to the MRC at Proton down. Jons was taken whilst driving on a country lane and Tribourne was taken whilst on the M25. As you can imagine this is of great embarrassment to my office." He said as he took a sip of his steaming black coffee, before continuing.

"Jons was taken in what can only be described as a professional abduction. They knew the route that Jons would take and they used military tactics to take him. At least 3 men were involved, and they had RPG's and heavy machine guns. Whilst there was no loss of life, our man was left with no option to stand down. He was found handcuffed to the door of his vehicle. The take-down of Herr Tribourne was even more amazing as it was done without even stopping either his car or the following close protection team in their car. We are still not entirely sure as to what exactly happened. What we do know is that they used three articulated lorries to carry out his kidnap. He was taken at 60 miles an hour. Personally, I have never heard of such a thing, even so I have to assume that this was a professional kidnapping." Peterson stopped and drank some more coffee.

The breakfasts arrived and nothing was said until the waiter had left the table.

"Have you received any ransom demands?" Jack asked him.

"No nothing, not a peep."

"I don't think this is a kidnapping per sé, I think as I told you before this is all about Doctor Pearson. I think these men have been taken to be murdered. You say that they were both taken professionally? Who do you think has the ability to pull off such a thing?"

"Quite honestly if we were still at war with the IRA then I would have said them. If it were for diamonds or cash, then we would be looking at organised crime."

"We have been following links with the Cossack club in London do you think this could be the Russian Mafia?"

"It could be I suppose they are well known to take wealthy individuals but Jons is not that wealthy."

"Are you sure that the same people took both men?" Jack asked.

"I don't believe in coincidences Inspector and I would find it difficult to believe that two separate groups just happen to have chosen two men who not only know each other but are involved in the same industry. Also, both attacks were within 30 minutes of each other. Tell me Inspector who do you think are behind these kidnaps?"

"I think that the Russians are in some way involved in everything that has been going on with the murders of the people from the MRC. Whilst I do not know what other group are involved I think that the elusive Doctor Pearson is the reason that it is all happening." Jack responded.

"You say that Tribourne was taken on the M25? Why don't you look at all the cameras? There are more cameras on the M25 than any other road in the UK" Short asked him.

"We did immediately we found out that Herr Tribourne had vanished. The video showed him overtaking a lorry and then his car is no longer there. We are trying to track down the trucks and their drivers at the moment. So far though we have drawn a blank. We cannot even find the company who's trucks they were. In fact, we have come up with zip."

"Have you looked at anyone who has hired three trucks over the last couple of days?" Burns asked.

Jack smiled to himself. He had a great team. They asked the questions that others never thought of. They had investigative minds.

"No I am sorry to say we have not done that yet. If I give you an office to work from and a support team would you help us investigate this?"

"Let's put it this way. If you give us an office and manpower, along with the access to your spy toys. We will continue to investigate our murders and if we find anything at all that is of use to your investigations then we will share that with you."

"Inspector this is not a negotiation."

"No? The way I see it you have manpower, and we have investigative minds. My team have already found two avenues of enquiries that you have so far not looked at and all before we have eaten our breakfast. I would say it sounds very much like a trade-off."

"Very well Inspector I will have transport sent for you in 30 minutes."

With that the Brigadier General stood up and removed a £50 note which he placed next to his uneaten breakfast and left.

Burns and Short looked at Jack for their instructions.

"What?" He asked them.

"What do you want us to do?" Burns asked.

"Eat your breakfast of course, the Government has just paid for it." Jack said tucking into a Lincolnshire sausage.

Immediately after breakfast they went to their rooms and collected their tactical vests and firearms. The transport was waiting for them as soon as they arrived back in the lobby of the Hotel.

"If you would come with me please." a man dressed in a smart suit said, while showing an identity card that stated he was in MI5.

Less than 10 minutes later they arrived at a building in Vauxhall Cross. The driver took a slip road to an underground car park. He parked next to the stainless-steel doors of a lift that had a CCTV camera over it. There was an alpha numeric keypad to the right of the doors. The driver entered a code and the doors opened. There was a security officer there wearing a tactical vest and carrying a HK mp5 machine gun.

The driver indicated they should all enter the lift. He looked up at a camera in the lift and the doors closed. They went up several floors and the lift opened into a large open office space. Again, the driver showed them the way to a reception desk. They were asked to sign in and then they were told to leave their guns at the front desk. Each firearm was signed in using the serial number and the name of the person that it belonged to. Next, they were led to an office that stated on the door that this was the Officer in Charge of SIS. They entered and sat down on the seats that were in the room. Less than two minutes later the Brigadier General entered and closed the door behind him.

"Right I hope you all enjoyed your breakfast but now we have to get on to of this investigation as quickly as we can. The people at those desks out there are now part of your team they will be working for you in any way you see fit. They are all members of one security branch or another. Most are field operatives, but some are what you would call as technical staff. They can access anything you wish. Computers, cameras, and any written document, so long as it pertains to this investigation. I have been given full access to the cameras on the M25 along with all the entry and exit roads, including all the service stations. Hopefully, we will have tracked all the trucks that were involved in the snatch of Mr Tribourne. We are also looking at any London gangs that have access to heavy weapons. I have authorised a cash budget for your team so that if we have to pay informants then we can do so without having to fill in requests that only slow investigations down. How do you want to do this are you going to split into three teams or all work together?"

"I think it is better is we split into three with DS Burns working on the Mike Jons abduction and I will work on Tribourne. I assume that you have already contacted the German Embassy. WPC will collate information received from the two team and as such she will be in charge administratively if that of acceptable?" Jack replied.

"I agree apart from putting WPC in charge of my staff who are much more experienced at this kind of thing."   "Yet it was Short who told you to check all the cameras and to consider companies who hire out HGV trucks. WPC Short has my full support and she see things that others have missed. It is a deal breaker for me. Also, this is not a normal kidnapping. These men have been taken to be murdered and the last time I checked; murder was the responsibility of the police force. If this were international terrorism, then it would be your game. You are only involved because your men were supposed to protect these two victims and you want them back, to save your team further embarrassment."

"It is not the way I would have put this inspector and I really don't see the need for a dick measuring contest between us, and apologies to WPC Short for my language." Peterson said,   "That's OK sir I have seen small dicks before" Short said and immediately regretted it as Jack shut her down with a glare that would have cut through steel. Burns only just managed to stifle a snigger and turn his head away, so that Jack would not see his smirk.

"Very well Inspector WPC short can run the office and collation of information and evidence. However, if it turns out to be anything at all to do with the official secrets act or terrorism in any form then one of my team will take the lead. If that is it inspector? Then we can get started."

Jack agreed and they set about building the teams. Burns briefed his team on the Cossack club and its owner who lived the life of luxury, in the countryside. They liaised with WPC Short to set up surveillance, that included a phone tap along with watching the Russians home and club. They accessed his official bank accounts and those of his employees. Listening devices were set up in and around the club and a tracker was put on as many of the Russians cars and those of his staff. Jack had Short get four of her team to go over every second of video working forwards and backward of the motorway abduction. She had two of her team contacting every haulage firm and truck leasing companies within the London and Swindon areas. For now, Jack could do little until Short could point him in some direction so he asked that his team go through facial recognition software after adding the E-fit picture of Doctor Pearson. Jack looked at the office working away in front of him and was jealous. His police force should have been like this but as always it came down to finances. Obviously, the secret services were better financed than the police force.

It was about an hour later that WPC Short knocked on the door of the office that had been given to Jack.

Act 46

"Boss I got a hit for the Van that was used in the snatch of Mike Jones. It was stolen in London during the night. Strangely it was caught on camera. The house opposite where it was stolen from managed to catch two men stealing it at 2am this morning. I backtracked the video from there and found a car that they had used to get there. From the registration of that car we found its owner. He is an immigrant from the Philippines and works as a cleaner for a firm in Chelsea. I have printed out the address for you." WPC Short said as she handed over the sheet of printed paper. Jack took it and left the office.

"Right you lot, get your arses into gear and let's go pay this man a visit. I assume that like us you are all armed if not then do so in the next two minutes. Short arrange the transport for us and the kit for a heavy knock." Jack said referring to the door breaker often referred to as 'The Enforcer' a heavy steel battering ram with two handles, used to literally force a door open and smash the locks and hinges. It is not a subtle instrument, but it gets the job done. When they arrived in the garage there were two vans each with six men in and a 5 litre V8 Range Rover, all the vehicles were painted gloss black. The Range rover was fitted with blue flashing lights that were hidden behind the front grill. These were already flashing when Jack got in the passenger seat. As soon as he put his seat belt on the driver gunned the Range Rover and it shot up the ramp from the underground parking garage, the pair of Ford Transit vans followed suit. Like the Range Rover they were also fitted with blue lights behind the grills. The Driver of Jacks car obviously knew London well as he raced through the streets and roads heading towards Chelsea. Their first stop would be to the address of the man who owned the car that had been used in the theft of the van that morning. There were times on the way to the address that Jack though they would die in a horrible accident, especially as they were only running on flashing lights, this was because they did not wish to warn anyone that they were on the way. Soon enough though they arrived at the road where the house was located.

There was nothing special about the house it was a standard Victorian 2 up 2 down style terraced property. Jack put on the radio pack and inserted his earpiece. Slowly they drove past the house and then parked up three doors down, with the vans either side of Jacks car. The men from the first van would be breaching the property the men from the second van would be securing the property from the rear. As soon as everyone was in place Jack gave the order to enter the property.

Just like it is in the movies after the 'Go Go Go' command is given the door is smashed and the officers rush in shouting 'Armed police' 'On the ground' 'Show me your hands' One of the entry team shouted out 'Secure' and Jack entered. The team at the front had destroyed the wooden front door. The team at the read had come in through the unlocked back door. There were four people face down on the floor of the living room.

"Anyone else in the property?" Jack asked the first of the four people.

"Hindi ako marunong mag-english" The man said.

Jack tried with the other three people and got the same response.

"Anyone know what language that is?"

"I think its Filipino" said one of the team.

"Can you speak it?" Jack asked.

"Sorry sir I just know the odd word or two but not enough to hold a conversation." The MI5 man replied.

"Then get me someone who can and make it fast." Jack responded. The MI5 man got on his mobile phone and spoke rapidly, then he ended the call."

"The metropolitan police are send a car with an interpreter; they are five minutes away sir." The man said.

"Right apart from one at the front and one at the back search this place and see what you can find. I am looking for passports and employment records or anything that shows who they are where they work and any other documents including photographs. Someone should check the attic in case there is anyone hiding in there, while you are at it count the number of beds in here. After making sure all the occupants were secured with cable ties Jack helped them to sit on the well-worn sofa and chairs. Jack have visited places like this before normally full of illegal immigrants as such he expected that they would find three or four beds to a room. That is exactly what they found. They also found Passports for Filipinos, Chinese, Indian and Korean. Going on the number of passports there were up to 16 people living in this house. The bedrooms had been divided into sections using blankets that were hung up. The lounge had seating for perhaps 8 people at a time. In the corner of the room was an old 36" CRT style TV set. It was connected to some form of satellite box and a DVD player. The kitchen has a single large fridge freezer that was packed with food each item had a label on it presumably stating who it belonged to. These were written in a multitude of languages and all written by different hands. The MI5 officers handed over all the documentation that they had recovered from the various rooms. Jack thumbed through them and sorted them out into nationalities. He found the passports for the four that were currently restrained. There were two men and two women. He found employment details that simply stated the hours worked and the amount that they had been paid, Jack was sure that it was well below the national minimum wage.

Act 47

The Translator arrived in a marked police car driven by a uniformed officer. Keen to get on with finding information jack ushered the translator into the living room. Then he separated the men from the women and moved one man into the kitchen where he indicated the translator should follow him to.

"I want you to ask, where he works and where he has been since midnight last night."

"Ikaw ay nagtatrabaho para sa?" The translator asked.

"Mas malinis ako para sa Cleanworld" The man said although Jack already knew as much from the wage slip. He just wanted to know if the man would tell him the truth. The translator related the answer to Jack and then asked his next question. To which the man had a lot more to say.

"He says his shift started at 11pm last night and finished at 7am this morning. He was cleaning in three restaurants in

Central London. He also said that the other three people were with him as they work together in a team." The translator said.

"Ask him who owns the old Audi A4 that is registered to this address" Jack said.

"Sino ang nagmamay-ari ng matandang Audi A4 na nakarehistro sa address na ito?"

"Hindi ko alam ang tungkol sa kotse"

"He said that he does not know about the car."

"Tell him if he does not tell me I will have him, and his family deported within the hour. Make sure he knows it is not an idle threat." Jack said to the translator.

Jack listened to the conversation and noticed the change in body language of the man.

"He said if he tells you then he must have protection as they will kill him."

"Who will kill him?"

"Sino ang papatay sa iyo?"

The man seemed to shrink before answering the translator.

"Kailangan ko ng proteksyon"

Jack looked at the translator and then at the man, the back to the translator.

"He wants protection for him and his family".

"Tell him he has got it and I will even get him a residency permit if he tells me who owns the car."

Once again, the translator and the man had words with some head shaking and then finally a nod and the man said.

"Pagmamay-ari ito ng doktor"

Jack did not need the interpreter to translate this answer Doktor sounded the same as Doctor.

"Ask him if he knows what the Doctor looks like?"

Once again there was a to-and-fro conversation between the two in what seemed like hurried Filipino. This was followed by a strong shake of the man's head.

"Does he know where this Doctor lives?"

Again, more conversation with head shaking and then the last sentence came with some nodding of the head.

"He said that he does not know for sure, but he has heard people say that he lives in the underground railways".

"In the tube system?"

"Oo sa tubo ng tren" The man said.

"Right take this lot into protective custody and then let's go and pay a visit to Cleanworld," Jack said

As it turned out Cleanworld was just 500 yards from the house they had just been in. Jack went in the front door while two of his men went around the back, just in case someone tried to make a run for it. There was a countertop with a man sat at a desk behind.

"Can I help you?"

Jack flashed his badge.

"Who owns this business?"

"Alejandro Del Rosario" The man replied without delay.

"Is he available?"

"This is his business, but he does not work here."

"Do you have an address for him?"

"No sorry I don't."

"In that case I am going to have to arrest for obstruction of justice." Jack said and placed his 9mm pistol on the counter next to his badge.

"I have a telephone number for him" the man said and passed over a card with the name Alejandro Del Rosario in gold script writing, under which was a telephone number. Which as Jack knew 020 was a London number. Jack opened his own telephone and called WPC Short. He gave her the entire telephone number and told her to ring back in two minutes with the address or think about working as a traffic officer for the rest of her police career. Less than a minute later she called back with the Knightsbridge address.

Making sure that the office manager for Cleanworld was in custody and unable to warn his boss that the police were coming. Jack set off for Ale's house. Jack and the two vans loaded with MI5 officers arrived at the gated entrance to the home of Alejandro Del Rosario. Jack noticed the twin CCTV Cameras on either side of the gates. There was an intercom box. Jack pressed the button and it buzzed.

Act 48

"Kanusta?"

"Hello this is the police; I would like you to open the gate" Jack said into the box and showed his card to the video camera.

"Sino?"

Jack got the translator out of the police car that was parked behind the van.

"Tell them to open the door before I break it down, make sure that they know we are here on official police business."

"Ito ang Pulis at nangangailangan kami ng pagpasok sa pag-aari. Kung hindi mo buksan ang gate kailangan naming gumamit ng puwersa"

"Please excuse my staff they are not as well educated as I am. They do not understand English. I am opening the gates please drive up to the front of the house and park at the left-hand side" Ale said. He had been watching the security monitors since the small convoy had rolled up. He pressed a button on the wall by the front door next to the intercom. Then waited for the knock on the door. It came in the from the hand of Jack. Ale opened the door and let the team in. Knowing the things that The Doctor had been involved in and matters that he himself had been complicit in, he had expected that at some point the police would arrive at his door. One of the tenants at the house had been out shopping when they saw the police break in the front door and they had called Ale on his burner phone. So, Ale had contacted his Lawyer who arrived before the police and was sat in Ale's office smoking a Cuban Cigar and drinking a cup of fine roast coffee.

Jack showed his I.D. and introduced himself. He was just about to ask the men from MI5 to tear the house to pieces looking for clues, when Ale's Lawyer came out from the Office and asked Ale if there was a problem. Ale introduced Jack and then the Lawyer introduced himself.

"Hello Inspector, I am the Right Honourable George Maitland Member of Parliament and Queens Councillor. I also happen to be the personal lawyer for Mr Alejandro Del Rosario. Is my client in some form of trouble I assume that it must be something very big to have so many armed officers with you inspector?"

Jack wanted to go and tell the toffee-nosed legal eagle to shove it up his ass, instead he knew he had to be politically savvy.

"No, we just need to ask a few questions, some people we needed to talk to have since been kidnapped, so we have to assume that your client may have been in some danger as well."

"If you have some questions Inspector, why don't you come into my office the rest of your men can follow the maid and have some coffee in the kitchen" Ale said and indicated that Jack should go first to into the office followed by the lawyer and then Ale himself.

"Please inspector have a seat and ask your questions, I have nothing to hid from the law."

"You employ illegal immigrants in your cleaning business?"

"I don't employ anyone in my cleaning business, it is a co-operative that I set up years ago, to stop the exploitation of poor refugees. The workers themselves set the wages and I am happy for my lawyer to show you the books you could say that it is a charitable institution."

"And the multi occupancy boarding house that you own?" Jack asked.

"Again, inspector I no longer own that property I gave that the Cleanworld as a gift so that those without a home could have somewhere to live until they got themselves sorted."

"One more thing Mr Del Rosario. Your Green VW Passat? It was used in the commission of a crime in the early hours of this morning."

"You found it then inspector?"

Jack was confused by the answer. Over a year ago, when Ale had given the car to The Doctor he had cloned the number plate from another green VW Passat of the same age. Then he had reported his car stolen. That way it could not really be tracked back to him if The Doctor got mixed up in anything illegal.

"Yes, we found it at the scene of a crime. Two men wearing balaclavas used it when they stole a works van from the driveway of a plumber not too far from here."

"Inspector if you checked your records that car which I bought so that my chef could do the shopping, was stolen from outside a butcher shop in Camden just over a year ago. I thought perhaps you were going to say you found it and were bringing it back. Is there anything else I can help you with inspector?" Ale asked.

"Just one thing. Do you know of or are you aware of a person who refers to himself as The Doctor? I am told he lives in the underground tube system. I am told he works for free for people that can't afford to go to regular doctors or perhaps for legal reasons can't go to hospitals for treatment."

"Inspector are you insinuating that my client is involved in some kind of illegal activity. Mr Del Rosario is a well-respected, philanthropist who heads up many charitable causes."

"I was not insinuating anything I was just asking a question."

"Well if there is nothing else Inspector you should take your men and catch the men who stole Mr Del Rosario's car, and then return it to him."

Jack left with his team but was furious. One of the MI5 men had overheard part of the conversation and decided to act on his own. He stuck a miniature camera on the edge of a hallway plant pot and another outside near the main doors. He had worked cover for MI5 for several years and rarely requested a cover surveillance order. It took too much time and was often difficult to convince a judge that they had reasonable cause.

Act 49

DS Burns went with his team to The Cossack Club they would not need to use the big door knocker. The front door to the club was already open, to be precise it was no longer there, parts of it lay on the floor. Obviously, someone else had decided the required entry to the Russians Nightclub and they had blown the doors open. There was still a smell of explosives in the air, the glass inner doors were just small cubs of glass covering the carpet on the floor. There were noises coming from upstairs, indicating also that this was a fresh crime scene. Police protocol dictated that he should call it in and call for the armed response unit, well he had his own with him. Burns indicated that part of his team should go to the side entrance and the rest of them would go in what was left of the front vestibule. He made sure his tactical vest was properly attached with its Velcro fastenings, then he drew his Glock 17m 9mm firearm and pulled the slide back to cock the weapon and released the safety. One of the men behind him tapped Burns on the shoulder and asked if he wished him to go first. Burns thanked him but as he was in charge he elected to go first.

As quietly as possible the five men made their way through the hallway and then up the carpeted stairway. All the time Burns was making sure he kept the top of the stairs and the door beyond in his view 100% of the time. When he reached the landing, they say shell casing on the floor and several bullet holes in the door. Rather than looking through the small window in the door Burns used one of the bullet holes to look into the room beyond.

There was a man who looked like he had been crucified to a central pillar. Another two men were laughing and burning him with cigar butts. DS Burns indicated that the man behind him should move to the left-hand side of the door. That man then removed a Flash Bang grenade from his tactical vest and bulled the pin but held the clip in place ready to throw. Burns looked through the bullet hole once more and just in time to see one of the men pour a bottle of spirits over the man they had crucified. DS Burns knew what they had in mind they were going to burn their victim alive. He looked at the four men with him and counted down on his fingers.

As soon as he reached one Burns pulled the door open and the man at the left threw his Flash Bang in. A second or so later there was the tremendous thud as the grenade exploded in a blaze of pure white light. The result intended to blind and disorientate, which is it did to a degree. The man who was going to light his Zippo lighter was so shocked he dropped the lighter but brought his Uzi Machine Pistol up and squeezed the trigger as he moved backwards from the grenade blast. He could not have known that his bullets would have struck anyone two rounds hit DS Burns full in the chest and he fell backwards down the stairs. Burns did not see what followed but only learned later what had happened. Two of the MI5 officers had returned fire with their HKMP5's and had instantly killed the two assailants in the room. Just at that moment the other team burst in through the side entrance doorway. It was only 30 seconds later, when two of the MI5 officers raced down the stair to where burns lay on the floor. He had struck his head on his fall down the stairs and sustained a substantial wound when his forehead had struck the edge of an ornamental shelf. Initially the MI5 officers had assumed that DS Burns had been shot in the head. Especially as the blow to his head had rendered him unconscious. DS Burns came around just as they were calling for an emergency medical evacuation, on their radio. Burns tried to sit up but immediately felt dizzy, God his chest hurt, and he was having trouble breathing. Through the fog in his mind he heard the man say his name and thought that he was being spoken too. But what was happening was they were talking to the Control Office and stating that DS Burns had been shot in the head. When he did manage to sit up there was a blast bandage to his head and it covered one eye as well. Still he found trouble breathing and pulled at the Velcro tab of his vest. The man who had applied the blast bandage helped him remove the vest and then opened Burns's shirt. There were two dark read blotches forming, one was almost dead centre of the sternum and the other was three inches to the right and about five inches below.

"You need to sit still Sir as you have a bullet wound to your head." The MI5 officer said.

Strange DS Burns thought, sure his head hurt but he was still able to think rationally, although it was entirely possible. About 3 minutes later an ambulance pulled in next to the black van belonging to the MI5 team. Then another pulled in behind that. DS Burns was loaded into the first ambulance and that sped off to hospital the second one collected the man who had been crucified in The Cossack Club. The news of the shootings at the club soon made its way to WPC Short, she then forwarded that to DI Jack Hamilton who made his way to St James Hospital arriving some 20 minutes after DS Burns. Showing his credential at the front desk he was directed to a cubical in the Accident and Emergency Department. Jack was surprised to find Burns sat on the edge of a bed, his shirt was covered in blood that had come from the head wound, which now had 8 stitches in, and a nurse was applying a dressing to cover it.

"Jesus son you have no idea how happy I am to see you are still in the land of the living. I was told you had been shot in the head?" Jack said.

"Thankfully, they think I cracked my head falling down the stairs." Burns replied.

"Why the hell did you do that?"

"Because I had been shot not once but twice." Burns said with a wince as he opened his shirt to show the two almost black marks where the bullets had struck his tactical vest with wadding and a Kevlar plate.

"What the hell did you do? Stand in front of their guns Well I am glad you are alive, so what did you learn?"

"That I should not stand in front of a gun! But apart from that there was a man inside the club that some folks were planning to Bar-B-Q and that they had blown the doors off to get in the club. Apart from that nothing sir. If the man they were torturing is still alive I think I should have some answers for you. One thing I do know is it was not Sergi in the club. So, I guess my next move is to go and ask him to help us with our enquiries."

"How long before he is fit to leave?" Jack asked the nurse.

"He should stay in overnight for observation like the Doctor has said. I am guessing that not going to happen though." the nurse replied.

"Good as I am parked in an ambulance bay." Jack said as he helped Burns get down from the bed and led him out of the hospital. They drove back to the offices of MI5 where both teams were milling around the open office space. WPC Rushed to check on DS Burns and helped him into a small side office with a sofa.

"Would you like a coffee?" She asked him.

"I could do with something a bit stronger" Burns replied.

"Bottom drawer of the desk." Said Brigadier General Peterson who had just entered the room. Then he continued.

"Still hurts with the bullet proof vest son and it's a life lesson you never forget. I am speaking from experience".

Then he walked to the desk and took out a bottle of Jura 16-year-old and a couple of glasses, which he poured a good measure into both before passing one to Burns and the other he kept for himself.

"Apart from getting shot what did you learn?" He asked.

"As I did not see much of the Club after the shooting started all I can tell you is that someone blew the front doors off rather than using a key. There were at least two attackers and one victim. The attackers were not afraid of being seen and were not afraid to use lethal force before being captured. They were armed with fully automatic weapons. The victim had been brutalised and crucified. They were about to set him on fire when we entered the room. I could see no sign of the Club owner or of his car. If I had to guess I would say that the two men either required information or possible it was a revenge attack for something." Burns said.

"You got all that within the two seconds of opening the door and getting shot? You should come and work for us on a permanent basis." The Brigadier General said

"What about the man they were torturing? Where is he now? Also, do we have his identity?".

"The man is in hospital, but he will live. I believe he is one of the employees at the club. The two man that were killed were Ukrainian Mobsters. They seem to have a links to a billionaire also from the Ukraine, who went missing on a recent trip to the UK. I have sent a team to collect the owner of The Cossack Club assuming he is still at his home."

"That's great can we interview him first." Burns responded.

Jack called Burns and Short to his office as he wished to speak to them alone. He really did want to catch the people behind the kidnappings, more importantly though, he wanted to catch Doctor Pearson.

"Are you sure you are fit to return to duty" Jack asked Burns.

"Yes, sir like you I want to get to the bottom of all this." He replied.

"So, what is your take on the kidnappings?"

"I believe that they have been orchestrated by this Doctor who is the one helping the criminals. I think that he has called in a few favours. Because there is no way one man could have done all this. I do not think we will get any help from Mr Del Rosario. However, I think if we squeeze the Russians then we may cut a break." DS Burns replied

"What about you Sort?" Jack asked.

"I think the injured man from the club would be the best place to start. He should be grateful that we saved his bacon. Let us find out where his loyalties lie." She said.

"OK how are we doing with the facial recognition software and what about this car that belonged to the Filipino, how far back have you tracked the car?"

"We have a couple of possible hits on the facial program but nothing that show a full face. The car came from a long-term car park in Chelsea. It seems to have been there for some time."

"OK Short keep at it and work backwards from the Long stay who knows we might find where these men came from." Jack said.

"There is one strange thing. When we find the possible hits on Doctor Pearson there always seems to be corrupted video for about 10 minutes either side of it. So, we cannot track the video forwards or back, as there are too many ways he could have gone in that time. Sir"

"So just like when the lab assistant was murdered on the train?"

"Yes Sir."

"Right talk to the technical boys here at MI5 and find out what sort of gadget could do that. Then find out where he could have got one and from whom." Jack said and the pair of them went off to complete their tasks.

Act 50

The Doctor had gone back to his subterranean dwellings to await the arrival of Mike Jons and Klaus Tribourne. The first man to be delivered was the German. He had a black bag over his head and had his hands zip-tied behind his back. Sergi was with one other man.

"Here you go my friend, I have brought him to you what would you like me to do with him?"

"It is OK Sergi you can use my name as he will not be telling anyone. You can remove his blindfold as well." The Doctor said.

Sergi gave a nod to the man with him and the bag was snatched away from the Germans head. Klaus squinted his eyes until they became accustomed to the bright lights at the bottom of the Brompton road underground chamber.

"Who are you and what do you want with me?" He asked.

"Herr Tribourne, you do not recognise me?" The Doctor asked him.

"Why would I recognise you? I am not the sort of man who associates with gangsters like yourself!"

"Really Klaus? You do it every day of your life. Mr Mike Jones is a Criminal he has stolen many things. He has even ordered the murder of others. Would you not say that made him a criminal?"

"I know nothing of this" Klaus replied.

"You yourself Herr Tribourne you have taken something that does not belong to you and you did so out of pure greed. You think that because you steal in millions and in billions it makes you better than the drug addict that robs a 90-year-old lady of her pension? You are worse. You rob people at the chance of life, and you do it for a profit. When is enough money enough? You cannot spend all the money you have because the interest on it makes you millions every day."

"I don't know who you are but if you let me go, I can make you all very rich men. I can make you rich beyond your wildest dreams."

"See there you go again; you think of nothing but money. Fortunately for me these men here hold loyalty and friendship above mere financial gratification."

"Tell me what you want, and I can give it to you."

"Can you give me my life back? Can you recover the respect that others had for me?" The Doctor said

"How can I don't even know who you are".

"First you are going to make a bank transfer of £500,000." the Doctor said Producing a laptop which had one of Tribourne's banks ready to put in transfer details.

"That's is you want £500,000. Then you are no better than me."

"Possibly by make the transfer to this account." The Doctor said as he passed him a strip of paper with some numbers on it.

Remarkably he did as he was told. The Doctor passed the laptop over to Sergi. He logged into his online account.

"Is it there?" The Doctor asked Sergi.

"A smart move to pay me with his money." Sergi said.

"We are square now?"

"Yes, my friend all debts are cancelled".

"Strip him please" The Doctor said to Sergi, who gave a nod to the big man who was still holding onto Tribourne's bicep.

"But I have paid you now you can let me go." Klaus almost screamed.

The big man produced a large sharp bladed stiletto flick knife. Tribourne must have thought that he was about to be stabbed and started to struggle. The big man reached behind Klaus and expertly slipped the blade inside the cable tie, which was securing Tribourne's hands cutting cleanly through the plastic tie without marking the soft wrists below.

"I asked you to strip. Now you can either do it yourself of I can have, this gentleman knock you out and he can cut your clothes off" The Doctor said

Klaus Tribourne started to remove his clothes and fold them neatly. While this was happening Sergi got a call on his mobile. He listened and said nothing before closing his phone. Then he took The Doctor to one side and started to whisper to him.

"Doctor, there are friends of the man who owned this building in the country. One of them was foolish enough to start asking questions in my club. They have a list of all the properties that he owned, and they will at some point come here. That will not be good for anyone they find here. I think they will shoot first and ask questions later. He was a very wealthy man. Some say that he was the richest criminal from all the ex-Soviet Bloc countries. He has a son and for him it will be a matter of honour to find out what happened to his father and to punish all those who had anything at all to do with his disappearance. The fact that someone came to my club makes me believe that he is on to me. It will not take him long to find out about The Doctor that heals criminals. My men will not talk but I cannot say the same for other criminals in London. If he learns that The Doctor works underground and that his father owned a tube station they will come here."

"How long do you think I have Sergi?"

"For what?"

"How long before they come here?"

"If I am honest I think 12 hours perhaps a little more."

"That is all the time I require."

The Doctor and Sergi walked back to the now naked Klaus Tribourne. He was a man who had kept his body well-toned. He was tall and athletic, none of that would help him now.

"Please put him in the empty chamber over there" The Doctor said as he pointed to one of the glass rooms that previously had help some of his wasps.

The temperature inside the chamber was a good five degrees lower than the rest of the laboratory. When he was locked in there The Doctor Thanked his friend.

"Sergi did you bring the other items I asked you to get?"

"Yes of course doctor but I hope you know what you are doing, these are dangerous things to work with." With that he passed over a heavy sports bag that had been on the floor. The doctor laid the bag back down on the floor, then he squatted down and pulled the Zip open. He looked inside, before closing it and standing up.

"Thank you for everything you have done for me Sergi. Perhaps we will meet again and perhaps not. Sergi try to stay out of trouble."

The Russian laughed and walked toward the lift with his companion and then they were gone. It was about an hour later when Ale appeared with two of his men holding on to a third who had a Balaclava on his head except it was on back to front.

Ale walked up to the Doctor and shook his hand.

"Your journey is almost over my friend. What will you do after its concluded? Where will you go?"

"You are right this part of my life is at an end. If I am fortunate then I will start afresh. But first let us finish this business. Tale the covering off his head." The Doctor asked

One of the men holding on to Mike Jons pulled the makeshift hood off. Like the man before him Mike Jons had to blink his eyes a few times to get them adjusted to the light and focus them on the man standing in front of him.

"Do you have the bank account details with you like I asked?" The Doctor Asked Ale.

"Yes, but I don't need your r money for this my friend."

"Do not worry it will not be my money. Mr Jons you are going to transfer all the money that you have in your offshore account and every minute you delay in doing it I will remove one of your toes and when I run out of toes I will start on your fingers. But first you are going to strip naked." The Doctor said

One of Ale's men removed the steel handcuffs that held their prisoner's hands behind his back.

"Strip" The Doctor said

"Wait a minute I know you. You were at the function, but I have seen you before that?"

"You are correct, and all of this is happening to you because you stole something very precious from me."

"Pearson?" Jons said.

"Give that man a coconut. Finally, you recognised me. You owe me for the work you stole so first you will strip and then you will transfer my money from your bank, to the account I give you" The Doctor said.

One of the men standing next to Jons, slapped Jons on the back of the head and said.

"Strip, he told you to strip so do it".

Jons started to take his clothes off, strangely like Tribourne, he folded them neatly before putting them on the floor. When he was completely naked The Doctor opened the laptop on the table and logged into the computer. Then he turned it around to fact Jons.

"Go you your account and then transfer to this account, all of your funds" The Doctor said as he once again passed over the details to another offshore account.

"I am not giving you all my money; you must think I am crazy." Jon said.

That was as far as he got before the two large men with Ale forced him to the floor. One of the men reached into his coat pocket and came out with a pair of electrical wire cutters. The other man put his full weight on top of Mike Jons, while the first man removed the big toe from Mike Jons left foot. He had to work hard at it and the was the crunching sound as he cut through bone. Then he snipped away at the remaining flesh until the toe lay on the floor of the laboratory. The men helped the screaming Jons up onto a chair by the table. The Doctor waited until the screaming and wailing from Jons had subsided to a whimper.

"Make the transfer and I mean every single penny that is in your account. Or do they have to remove another of your toes." The Doctor said

The one thing Mike Jons was not, was a hero. He had quite a low pain threshold. He knew that in his bank account in the Bahamas, there was a little over £750,000 but he had much more in his Chinese bank account, so he decided to give the money from the Caribbean bank. He logged in there and transferred the entire contents over to the one he had been given.

"Is it there?" he asked Ale.

"Yes, thank you."

"Can you put him in the glass chamber with the other man?" The Doctor asked the men with Ale and then happily complied. Now the glass chamber that did not have a handle on the inside held the last two men that had wronged The Doctor.

"Ale I was told some news about an hour ago, that a group of Ukrainians have recently come into the country. They have come looking for their boss. He was the billionaire who previously owned this building."

"Then we must make haste my friend." Ale said.

"No Ale. They will come to you for information about the building that he owned. I want you to tell them about this station. I want you to tell them that you think a group of black Jamaican gangsters, let them think that they moved in on the Ukrainian during a drug deal."

"If I tell them that then they will come here mob handed, in fact the whole gang is likely to come."

"You are right which is why your tobacconist should leave with you when you go. Let the Ukrainians know about the entrance through the back of the shop. You are to be a most helpful friend to them. Whatever happens though you must not come here yourself do you understand that?"

"Yes, my friend James, I understand but what about you?" Ale asked.

"I will be fine; did you bring what I asked?"

"Yes, James but why just a bag of ammunition and not the guns as well." Ale asked.

"Because I do not need guns. Now you should go, I am sure that you will have some people contact you soon. Remember tell them that it's a drug gang in here."

"Will I see you again James?"

"Perhaps, now go and take the shopkeeper with you."

Ale started to walk to the life and turned one last time to look at his friend, then he left.

Act 51

"Sir I have a hit on the VW Passat, it was put there over a week ago. I tracked it back and managed to get a shot of the driver from a traffic light camera. It is not perfect, but it does look like the E-fit picture of Doctor James Pearson. It looks like he drove to Swindon. And we also have him 12 hours later sat outside MRC Porton. Then we have the car driving through

Chelsea where we lose it again. However, I tracked it to Brampton road tobacconist shop then I lose it again." WPC Short said to her boss.

Jack looked at the map of London that was behind the desk where he was sat. He opened a drawer and took out a Sharpé marker pen. Then he drew a line from the car park to the M25 ring road then another line from the car park to Brompton Road.

"Buns!" Jack shouted.

DS Burns entered the office.

"Sir?"

"If you were friends with the Filipino and you lived near Brompton road which way would you travel to get there?" Jack asked.

"It would be pretty much a straight line and would only be about five minutes away" Burns answered.

"And how far from The Cossack Club?"

"About the same Sir"

"I think Doctor Pearson has a house somewhere on Brampton Road. I want The Filipino's house staked out and I want the same thing for the bloody Russian, I want a team outside his club and his house. And I want it now." Jack said.

Burns left and instructed men from both the teams that had been allocated to Jack.

"Don't worry about being seen just get teams there, in fact it's probably better that they know they are being watched, that way they will not be out there committing murders."

"Short get your team to look at any cameras on Brampton road and see if you can find the elusive Doctor. Also, have you got any information on the trucks that were used to snatch Tribourne."

"There are no companies that have that logo on their trucks, at least not in the UK. However, I found a company that rented out three articulated tucks of the same make and models as the ones used to snatch the German, although the number plates don't match."

"Get on to them and get me a name and address of the person or persons they hired them out too. They would have wanted to see a lot of details for their insurance." Jack said.

He could feel his net was closing in on not just Doctor James Pearson, but he was going to be able to nab two of London's organised crime gangs. The Russians and of course the polite and wealthy man from the Philippines. Jack was reading the file that Short had given him on Alejandro Del Rosario. He had entered the country Legally with his wife and son. He had made his money honestly in a deal for his farmland. The he had invested in several London Properties which he rented out. There had been a mini boom and he had sold some of his property making him a multi-millionaire. He had bought the large property in Chelsea and made this his family home. He became a Property Agent, finding properties for many of the world's richest people who wished to own Commercial buildings in and around the London area. He brokered a deal with the Ministry of defence for one of their war offices. He currently let over 100 building of various uses and had an annual declared income of around £12,000,000. Hence, he could afford the fancy MP and Barrister. Jacks head was hurting from reading the files in front of him. He changed tact and opened the file on the Russian.

Sergi Shevchenko. Had come to this country as a theoretical political refugee, claiming that he and his family were under threat of death by Putin and his former KGB cronies. He had come to this country before opening a nightclub and then his wealth had grown, and he had expanded his interests. Whilst nothing was ever proved, it was believed he was involved in prostitution, people trafficking, extortion and even some legal operations such as horse racing at which he was beginning to excel. The money he got from his stud farm gave him over £10,000,000 a year. And with that kind of wealth comes a great deal of corruption. Jack was sure there were people in the metropolitan police force who were probably in the pockets of these men.

The only thing that these men seemed to have in common was Doctor Pearson. Jack correctly assumed that Pearson was the mysterious physician to those criminals of London who could or would not go to a normal hospital or Doctor, where questions would be asked, and reports made. What made an honest hard working and caring Doctor change to become a violent and murderous criminal? It probably did not help when someone tried to murder him by dropping his house on him. But why had he not gone to the police at that point and had them arrested, that would be the 'normal' thing to do.

Jack opened the file on Doctor Pearson. It started with his qualification and then went on to tell of his work across third world countries, working for Doctors Without Borders. He had then gone back to the UK and qualified as a Toxicologist before returning to his voluntary work. Jack almost missed it he had worked in the Philippines during the time that Del Rosario had been running a medium sized farm. Whilst the notes on file did not say that they had met or even that they knew each other, it was a good enough link for Jack to put in a call to UK office for Médecins Sans Frontière. After about 30 minutes of chatting he managed to find out that Doctor Pearson had worked about 10 kilometres from where Del Rosario lived and worked. He had treated people from the local farming community. There it was. Time to go and see Del Rosario.

Act 52

The Doctor barely looked at the two men who were banging on the glass room that they were locked in. Previously the Doctor had used it to store the wasps in because he could lower the temperature to sedate the large quantity of wasps that he required for his works. Opening the large heavy bag that Ale had brought him he emptied its contents into a large steel drum that he had set above an equally large cooking ring, although for the moment it was not lit. The bag had contained about 2,000 rounds of assorted ammunition from point 22 all the way up to 50cal and everything in between, probably a dozen different calibres. Then the Doctor took the bag that the Russian had brought him, it contained plastic explosive and detonators along with six forward facing Anti-personnel Claymore mines with extending trip wires. The plastic explosive he split into two lots. One lot he put around the platform entrance tunnel to this room and then the rest he put in place around all his equipment. Then he poured gallons of Catonic Bitumen Emulsion, a tar like liquid with the consistency of treacle. It would burn well, and it would stick to anything it touched or anyone who touched it. It was also great at covering any DNA although the fire he had in mind would do that. The explosives would destroy anything that was left standing and the ammunition would confuse anyone who was investigating the deaths of whoever was in the station, when it went up in smoke.

The Doctor was going to wait until the Ukrainians arrived to take back the property. They would trip the alarm as soon as they entered the Tobacconist shop. At that point, all hell would break loose. He had planned everything including how he would escape. With luck and good fortune only the guilty would be hurt. There were twenty black polythene bags hanging from ropes of the gallery walkway above the laboratory then could all be dropped and released by pulling ion a single rope any fire or explosion and twenty different colonies would be released into the room. The noise and explosions would anger them, and they would attack anything that was a perceived threat. This meant anyone who was live in the room.

"Burns! Are you fit to travel?"

"Yes sir, where are we going?"

"We are going to join the team watching Del Rosario. That slippery bastard is the link to all this. He was living and working in the Philippine at the same time as Doctor Pearson. There is a better than average chance that they not only met but knew each other socially. So, first I want to watch him and then I want to question him, even if I have to arrest his ass to do it."

"What are we going to charge him with Sir?"

"With pissing off Mrs Hamilton, I don't bloody care. One thing I am sure of he is helping Pearson. Come on lad I don't have all night" Jack said leading the way to the underground car park, they found a driver having a smoke at the garage entrance and seconded him into driving them to the Chelsea stake out van. When they arrived Jack and burns knocked on the side door of the panel van and it slid open to allow them entry.

"Tell me what you have seen?" Jack asked the two men conducting the surveillance.

"Mr Del Rosario arrived back in his yellow Hummer about an hour ago. Then a black Jaguar arrived about 10 minutes after. The registration is one use by the Member of Parliament George Maitland QC. Then another car came to the gates and one man got out entered the property and left about 5 minutes ago, that car is from a high-end lease company at Heathrow Airport. It was leased to a Ukrainian Businessman, actually they leased four of them, this morning."

"Get on to the company and ask them if they have trackers fitted to their cars" Jack said as he looked at the screen that showed the front gate to the house.

"Sir we do have some other cameras and I can activate them."

"I took it upon myself to place a few miniature cameras around the house when we were there earlier today."

"Without a warrant?"

"Glad to see someone using their initiative, well what are you waiting for switch them on."

Earlier that day Ale, after the visit by the police and MI5 had one of his men sweep the property for listening devices and they and found four miniature cameras with wire aerials. Ale had then all moved to the top room of his house where he had a television switched on, which was connected to a DVD player that was playing vintage Mickey Mouse movies on a loop. Ale would love to have seen the faces of those who had tried to spy on him. It was one of the reasons he had called his lawyer. The other man who had visited him claimed to be a silent partner of the Oligarch that The Doctor had shot. As per the Doctors instructions he admitted that the Ukrainian had owned the Brompton station but that there had been turf war between the owner and the Jamaican gang who now used the property for their drug business. Ale state that he had not seen the Oligarch in some time and feared for his safety. The Ukrainian bought the story and returned to the Heathrow International Hotel where his cohorts were waiting the arrival of two bags loaded up with firearms. They had paid one of the smaller gangs in London a king's ransom to supply them with the firearms and ammunition. The deal was done in an almost matter of fact way. It went this way.

"My contact tells me you can supply us with guns?"

"Who is your contact?"

The Ukrainian had simply given the name of his missing Oligarch boss.

"How many?"

"I want 8 machine guns, 4 pump action shotguns and 8 automatic pistols and we want 1,000 rounds for each".

"Wow man that's a lot of firepower it could take some time and will be expensive."

"How Expensive?"

"I would think about £25,000".

"I will give you £100,000 if you can do it in two hours. Half now and the rest when you deliver. If you think about running off with my money, just remember I have killed men for smoking near me. Do we have a deal?"

"I will see you in less than two hours".

The London gang member had contacted all his friends and bought the firearms and ammunition at well above market prices, yet it still allowed him a £50,000 profit on the whole deal. True to his word one hour later he had supplied the Ukrainians with their firepower.

Act 53

Sergi went to his club with a genuine cleaning team after the police said that they no longer needed it. He sat at the bar examining the scabs to both of his hands where he previously had wounds caused by being nailed to his own bar top. He no longer need the money that he had from prostitution or people trafficking. He made enough money from his legitimate line like the Club and letting rooms in run down properties. There is aware always people desperate for a roof over their heads in London and many did not care so long as they had an address. He had expected a visit from the Ukrainian mob and was surprised when only one man came.

"You know who I am?"

"Yes, I know" Sergi replied.

"I am looking for a man and perhaps you might know of him?"

"Who is it that you wish to find?"

"An Oligarch who owns hundreds of houses and properties in London."

"Yes, I have heard of such a man, although I am not sure where to find him............ But I know of a man who rents and sells his property here in London. Your man used him as a personal estate agent. You can find him in Chelsea. His name is Alejandro Del Rosario. He is an honest man and I think he will be willing to help you."

"And you know nothing more? My friend did not come to drink in your club. It seems to me that he would drink with a fellow Cossack?"

"Alas our business interests are quite different, and he probably would not want his affairs tainted by my product. He is mostly legal, me not so much."

"Thank you Perhaps I will be seeing you again if I cannot find my boss."

"A fellow Ukrainian is always welcome to drink good Vodka with me. Stay safe my friend." Sergi said as he downed a large glass of vodka. The man left the club and Sergi breathed a sigh of relief and brought the shotgun out from under the table where he had it pointed continually at the mobster.

As soon as it was safe to do so Sergi made a call to the Filipino and told him to expect company.

When he arrived at Ale's home, he was welcomed in even if he could not see the 12 guns point at him every second that he was there. Ale had his family in the safe room just in case something should happen inside his walls.

Jack and Burns exited the van and walked over the road to Ale's home. He pressed the chrome button housed within the brushed stainless-steel plate of the call box.

"Hello"

"Mr Alejandro Del Rosario its Detective Inspector Hamilton and Detective Sergeant Burns, we would very much like to have a word with you to clarify some points".

"Inspector its late, can this not wait until morning."

"It is a matter of some importance sir."

"Very well I will meet you at my front door."

There was an audible click and a whirring sound as a screw thread wound and opened the gates. No sooner were they through the gates when they closed again. Jack thought to himself this is a man who is worried that someone could cause him harm. They walked down the well-lit driveway to the covered porch-way and pressed an elaborate bell with the face of an angel embossed on it. The bell chimed out the those of Big Ben. Then the heavy oak door swung open on silent hinges.

"Inspector, Sergeant, please come in".

"Thank you, Mr, Del Rosario, we will try not to keep you too long."

"This way please" Ale said and guided them to his office.

Inside sat in one of the chairs by the fireplace was the Queens Councillor, who stood up when the three men entered the room.

"Inspector, twice in one day I do hope you are not harassing my client."

"Mr Maitland odd that your client requires his legal eagle present for a casual chat."

"Inspector it is in my experience, that late night calls from the police are rarely routine or casual."

"You said you wanted to clarify something Inspector" Ale said

"Yes, we are interested in a man who came into the country today. I believe that you know him?" Jack said in a fishing exercise.

"I am sure in my line of work that there are many people I know that fly in and out of this country on a daily basis."

"Just what is your business Mr Del Rosario?" Jack asked.

The Lawyer raised his hand to stop Ale from answering.

"That is alright George, I don't mind answering an honest question with an honest answer. I am a philanthropist, but I am also in the property market. I buy and sell houses and businesses for my private clients, why do you ask inspector.

"I will get to the point a Ukrainian individual came to your property tonight can you tell me what that meeting was about." Jack asked.

"I see that the van over the road is not just for show Inspector. OK He was here because his boss has gone missing in the last week. I handle several properties for his boss."

"Would you be willing to give me a list of these properties, I can just make a telephone call and have warrant to search your home, I just would prefer we do this in a nice way".

"Are you making a direct threat to my client. Ale my advice to you is to say no comment to any further questions."

"It's OK I have a list of them on my computer from when the man was here I will do you a printout Inspector" Ale said and did so.

"If there is nothing else inspector I invite you to leave my home".

Jack and burns left the same way they had come.

"What do you think Burns?" Jack asked.

"I think basically he is an honest entrepreneur who had done well for himself." Burns replied.

"Did you not notice anything strange there tonight?"

"No I don't think so."

"Family, Burns. There were no other members of his family around, and the same applies to the domestic staff. A man with a home like that in Chelsea has staff. Cooks Cleaners and possibly a driver on hand. Yet there was no one there except for the lawyer. That screams fear to me. He is not frightened for himself, but he is worried about the people he loves. I think that Russian scared the shit out of him."

"Ukrainian" Burns corrected. Which got him an evil stare from his boss?

Act 54

Back in the van Jack looked at the three sheets of printed paper that he had been given by Mr Del Rosario.

"Burns get back on to the car hire company and tell them we need to know if they have trackers in their cars and if they do they need to share the codes with us. I want to know where all four of those cars have been since the moment they got them. If they give you any grief then use the power of MI5, 6 and 7."

Burns was going to point out that he did not think there was a seven, but he thought better of it, and went about his task,

Jacks phone rang it was WPC Short, Jack answered.

"What have you go for me Short."

"The Trucks were hired out to 'Eddie Stobart' Haulage. So, I checked with their head office in Warrington and whilst they do occasionally hire trucks when they have an overflow of goods. They state categorically that they have hired nothing this week. It looks like someone somewhere cloned some of their documents. I am afraid that part is a bit of a dead end now Sir. But on a positive note we have found the Germans sports car it was in a container headed for Romania. There were a lot of other high-end cars in the shipment as well. It turns out that Tesla not only put a standard tracker on their cars they also stick several others in things like the wheels. They operate on a completely different frequency to most other manufacturers as Elon Musk owns his own satellites."

"Short, find out who they were being shipped to and who the shipping client is. It might not help us today, but we should be able to help serious crime boys close some cases later." Jack replied. Then he ended the call.

Jack passed half of the list of properties to Burns while he looked at the rest most were residential although some were large commercial properties. I was certainly a good portfolio and would no doubt bring the owner a great deal of money.

"Burns this Oligarch seems to spend a great deal of time in this country give immigration a call and find out if he is in that country at present. Then get hold of the Ukrainian Embassy and get them to have the Ukrainian police send whatever files they have on him over to us." Jack said.

Burns put down the list he was reading and first called Immigration. Whilst he did not have a date of birth he did have a name and the man was incredibly rich so he probably came in on a private plane, that should slim things down a bit. He made the call. Things went a lot better than he had imagined they would. He had indeed come in on a private Leer jet which was still parked on the spaces reserved for foreign dignitaries. He had entered the country with two other men just a few days ago. According to immigration he was due to have left last night. As a flight plan, had been logged, however the plan had not left the park area. He immediately passed this information over to Jack and then he called the Embassy and spoke directly with the Ukrainian Ambassador who knew of Mr Bodashka Kravchenko as he was not only well known in this country bay even more so in his homeland. The Ambassador stated that he had dinner with Mr Kravchenko just four days ago, and had expected him for dinner last night before he was due to fly back the Ukraine. Burns thanked the Ambassador for his assistance and relayed the details to Jack.

"This is starting to sound like a Sherlock Holmes plot Burns, and as Holmes would have said 'The Plot Thickens'."

"That would work Sir if we had a Moriarty." Burns replied.

"Just read your list of properties and tell me if you find anything interesting." Jack said.

Burns sat down and kept typing addresses from the paper into Google. One of them was a disused power station on the edge of Chelsea in an industrial complex by the Thames. He brought up Google Earth and showed it to Jack. It says that he has applied for a development of affordable housing, which has been passed but that he has done nothing with it. Just then a note was passed to DS Burns from one of the MI5 officers.

Burns looked at it and immediately passed it over to his boss. The car rental company had given over the tracking codes and it put two of the hired BMW's at the power plant. The other two were mobile at the moment.

Jack and burns went back to their car and headed for the industrial site near the Thames. On the way, Burns called for a full Armed Response Unit. Jack was driving like a man possessed. The gates to the site were wide open and they could see the pair of BMW cars parked outside what would have previously been the administration section of the power plant. Jack pulled up next to the two black cars and killed his lights. To go in with just the two of them when they had no idea as to how many they were going up against would have been not only stupid but irresponsible. Jack was not a cowboy, so he waited until the armed unit came through the gates. Jack went and spoke with their senior officer and gave him command of the scene. The firearms Inspector went through all the buildings without success, there was no one there, just the two cars. Jack opened the unlocked door and hit the boot release but there was nothing there either.

"Wild goose chase" he said more to himself but Burns overheard it.

"Do you think they are one step ahead of us and have deliberately set this to deliberately take us away from where they really are. They would probably guess that there are trackers in these hired cars" Burns said.

"What other large commercial properties do you have on your list, even ones that are undeveloped ones" Jack said.

"Why undeveloped ones Sir?"

"Good place to dump bodies".

"What about this one Sir, and it's not too far from here It used to belong to the ministry of defence, for an anti-aircraft battery and then it was used by the Royal Observer Core and finally it was London University Air Squadron?"

"Where is it?"

"Brompton Road Sir"

"Jesus Burns you waited until now to tell me about this. We have Doctor Pearson at a car park near there and there was an attack just down the road from there. Call everybody that is where we will find Doctor Pearson also you will probably find Jons and Tribourne there as well."

Jack raced over to the commander of the firearms team and requested that he redeploy his team to Brompton Road.

"Get me a floor plan of the address I don't want to be going in anywhere blind. I do not care who you have to wake up at the ministry of defence to get it, better yet, call through to the Brigadier General and have him send it to your laptop. Go on Burns do it now!"

"Yes Sir" Burns said and went about his tasks as Jack drove them back towards Knightsbridge area of Chelsea.

Act 55

It worked just like clockwork. The Oligarch's men came in mob handed. Having burst through the door at the tobacconists they found themselves in the main entrance way to the tube station below. Having jammed the lift doors open with a screwdriver. The Doctor knew there was only one other way that the men could come down, that was down the stairs and then the tunnels until they came to the upper landing area above the wasps. There was a total of eight men, and they were heavily armed. Looking at the CCTV The Doctor waited until they were in the final tunnel to his lair. Then he blew the front entrance to it. Meaning as far as the men were concerned there was no way out. They made it as far as the top landing when The Doctor let loose the wasps then when the men ran they tripped the first set of Claymores, killing three of them instantly and wounding another. The five men made it down the stairs and the doctor remotely opened the glass chamber and at the same time set off a smoke bomb making it almost impossible for the attackers to clearly see their target and as such the fired blindly into the fog. Mike Jones took a bullet to the head and died instantly. The Doctor light the gas ring below the barrel of assorted bullets the smoke started to clear, and the Ukrainian gangsters looked and saw a naked man standing in front of them with his hands in the air. Unsure what to do they forced him face down on the floor from behind them the bullets started to go off in the barrel some of them made it out and there were ricochets from all around the lab. Two more men died in the hail of led, surprisingly Tribourne was still unscathed. The wasps were all over the inside of the laboratory now the three surviving members of the gang were now being stung but this time it was Tribourne who was running around screaming and the more he panicked the more he was stung. In this Doctor took some modicum of joy. The three men would also die in some of the resulting explosions that The Doctor had set up. When the last man died, The Doctor came out from his hiding place in the tunnel that went from Brompton to Knightsbridge Underground Station. There was one more thing he had to do before bringing down the entire Command Centre of Brompton Road Station. He himself had to die. And there had to be proof of it, not just blood this time. The Doctor took a small razor-sharp hand axe and brought it down on the little finger of his left hand, severing it at the midway point. He screamed out in pan as he did it. The he moved back to the safety of the tunnel to Knightsbridge before setting of the final load of explosives. It had the desired effect the entire upper floor came down into the laboratory. The Doctor took his severed finger and laid it on a chunk of concrete and hit it with another chunk of concrete at the point where he had cleanly removed the digit. The result now, was that it was no longer a clean cut. He placed it so that it was partially hidden then allowed his blood to be splashed around. Quickly he dressed the stump of his little finger and hefted his backpack with all the data he had been working on for years. He would go to a country without an extradition treaty to the UK. But immediately he would go to the Knightsbridge station and out into the fresh air.

Even before Jack and his team made it to the Brompton Road Station there were reports of heavy gunfire and explosions coming in. As Jack rounded the corner and pulled into the small car park outside the station the final explosion ripped through the building causing part of it to fall inwards. Outside in the car park were the other two BMW's that had been on lease. Jack and DS Burns got out of their cars and like everyone else they could only look on from outside, the building was destroyed. It was obvious, that it was too unsafe now for anyone to enter. Jack had his team claim the scene and clear the area. It was almost two days before the Fire Brigade and the City engineers declared it safe enough for Jack and his forensic team to enter the building. It really did look like a bomb had gone off in it. The dust had settled but in places there were some body parts and blood splatters. When the portion of finger was found, it was immediately sent off for detailed forensic examination with a full blood work and DNA along with fingerprint checks. There were of course a lot of body part some that had mingled with others making it difficult to tell which part belonged to which body. They also would go for DNA to check how many bodies there were in total and some would be identified others perhaps not. Three definite people were identified early in the investigation. Herr Klaus Tribourne, Mike Jons and Doctor James Pearson. The government already had DNA samples of Mike Jons and Doctor Pearson on record at CDE/MRC Porton Down They also had blood groups and fingerprint I.D. Tribourne was more difficult, but they were able to get a DNA sample from his home and from his car and matched that to some body parts. The final count was 11 bodies. The official line was that it had been a gas leak that had set of a series of explosions that sounded like gunfire. They also said that the 11 sets of human remains were some homeless squatters. Jack, Burns and Short, returned to Swindon. The Commissioner privately agreed that several the deaths had been carried out by one man and that man was Doctor James Pearson. Jack concluded he serial killer had died in the gas explosion in Chelsea. For his part in the investigation Jack was promoted to Chief Inspector, which really meant that he would sit behind a desk and count the beans. Mrs Hamilton was happy about it, because her husband would be home at 5:30pm every night and he would be safe. Burns was given a full promotion to Detective Sergeant. WPC Short was offered the chance to become a detective which she took.

Act 56

James Pearson had exited the Knightsbridge Tube station and kept his head down as he walked to Ale's home. The Van had gone from outside and Ale was standing at his gate smoking a fine Cuban cigar.

"Welcome back to my home James. You will stay here until the dust has settled and no one even remembers you then I will get you passage to the Dominican Republic and then from there you can travel to Cuba. I know someone there, who is a Professor at the School of Medicine in Havana. You could continue your work there and use your work for the good of mankind. But for now, let us share a Harewood and relax. If anyone comes to my home looking for you, you can use my panic room, it is not on the plans and it is impossible to see from the outside. You are 100% safe my friend."

James entered the driveway and the gates closed behind him. True to his word, ale arranged a boat for James to The Dominican Republic. Along with the passage was a completely new Identity. Officially he was now Doctor Mark O'Connor, consultant toxicologist. He worked for 12 months in the public health care system. Then he was invited to go and teach in Havana. He accepted the invitation and flew over to Cuba. For his reward, he was given a full Cuban Passport. His cares for Prostate Cancer radically changed things for a large percentage of Cubans who would otherwise die from this common form of cancer. There were now vast sums of money pouring into the Cuban healthcare System from Rich Americans who could not get this treatment elsewhere. Obviously, it was free for all Cubans for other nationals though it was on a sliding scale against their wealth. The richer you were the more you paid. As such it was medicine for everyone who wanted it or needed it.

A few years later the now Professor Mark O'Connor previously of Canada and now a naturalised Cuban Citizen, took a short holiday to see some true and trusted friends. Sergi met him at the Airport and drove him first to the Cossack Club which was now a Coffee House and a place for folks to use as a drop-in centre. Then they went to his home in the Chiltern hundreds, which was now a full-blown horse farm and stud centre. After spending two nights with Sergi's family, the doctor had Sergi take him to Ale's home. Sergi dropped him off at the gates and left with a wave over his shoulder. The Doctor pressed the intercom. Around the same time as The Doctor was staying in Chelsea, Jack and Mrs Hamilton were in Chelsea to take in a show at Chelsea's famous World's End Place Theatre, Jack could have sworn that a man he saw walking the street in a fine Italian suit and business haircut looked remarkably like Doctor Pearson, although this man wore gloves and appeared to have all his fingers. Jack dismissed it he would retire tomorrow knowing that he had cracked the serial killer case and brought it to a conclusive end. Still that man could have been Pearson's twin had he not been so fit and tanned. Jack loved warm summer nights out on the town but so did the bloody wasps as he swatted one away from the back of his wife's shawl.